# BASEBALL'S *Best*

## SHORT STORIES

### Edited by Paul D. Staudohar

CHICAGO
REVIEW
PRESS

**Library of Congress Cataloging-in-Publication Data**
Baseball's best stories / [edited] by Paul D. Staudohar.
    p. cm.
    Includes bibliographical references.
    Hardcover ISBN 1-55652-247-9  Paperback ISBN 1-55652-319-X
    1. Baseball stories, American.  I. Staudohar, Paul D.
[PS648.B37B4  1995]
813'.0108355—dc20                                     95-37937
                                                      CIP

*The stories in this collection originally appeared in a variety of publications. A complete listing of sources is given on page 389.*

© 1995 by Paul D. Staudohar
Illustrations © 1995 by Sean O'Neill
All rights reserved
Published by Chicago Review Press, Incorporated
814 North Franklin Street
Chicago, Illinois 60610
ISBN 978-1-55652-319-9
Printed in the United States of America
10  9  8  7  6

# CONTENTS

# ACKNOWLEDGMENTS

Several people gave generously of their time and expertise to make this collection of stories possible. Research help was provided by Roger Siebert of the library at California State University, Hayward. Florence Bongard of Cal State served as secretary for the project. Thanks also to the Paul Ziffren Sports Resource Center in Los Angeles, especially librarian Shirley Ito. Leonard Koppett, former sportswriter for the *New York Times,* gave early direction and inspiration. So did baseball fiction writers Mark Harris and Ron Carlson from Arizona State University. Peter C. Bjarkman, author and editor of baseball books, was a valuable consultant. Also deserving of credit for their inputs on the literature were Stephen Jay Gould of Harvard University, Frederick T. Courtright of Macmillan Publishing Company, Richard L. Wentworth of the University of Illinois, Daniel J. J. Ross of the University of Nebraska, Lawrence J. Malley of Duke University, and Frank Koughan of Harper's. Kudos to my baseball pals, who offered useful thoughts at games of the Oakland Athletics and San Francisco Giants: E. D. Conklin, Ron Friis, Harry Koplan, Nick McIntosh, and fellow professors Robert E. Kelly, Donald Wort, and Richard Zock. The publishing staff deserves credit, particularly Brian Feltes, whose editorial knowhow was indespensible, and Terry Duffin, who did a superb job in typing up the manuscript. And, most of all, special appreciation to Amy Teschner, Editorial Director of Chicago Review Press, who held everything together with such style, enthusiasm, and intelligence.

This book is dedicated to the memory of my father, Matt, who taught me to love baseball.

Paul D. Staudohar

# INTRODUCTION

The short story has universal appeal as a staple of American fiction. Its brevity allows for consumption in a single sitting. Authors of this literary form must catch the reader's attention, hold it fast, and provide a smart conclusion. It takes a skilled writer to do this well.

Some of the best short stories are about baseball, either the game itself or as a backdrop to morality, greed, love, envy, aging, and other literary themes. Several of the best American writers have authored short stories on baseball, and this has been the case for a long time. Among the first stories were those in pulp magazines around the turn of the century. Shortly thereafter, writer Ring Lardner popularized the genre. The flow of good baseball stories accelerated in the 1940s and 1950s, with frequent appearances in magazines like *Collier's, Esquire,* and the *Saturday Evening Post.* In recent years there has been a resurgence of interest, with stories in the *New Yorker, Harper's,* and *Sports Illustrated.*

The revival of the baseball short story has accompanied a wave of nostalgia for the game. Many fans deplore that the business side of baseball, with its owner and player cupidity, has overshadowed the game. Yet, overall fan interest remains high at the major-league level. The minor leagues have come back nicely with a surge in franchises and attendance. Hollywood's infatuation with baseball is evident from a host of recent movies. One of the top television shows in 1994 was Ken Burns' documentary "Baseball." People are attracted, sometimes wildly, to baseball memorabilia, cards, apparel, autographs, and art.

INTRODUCTION

The goal in editing this book was to collect the very best baseball short stories ever written. Excerpts from novels are not included, because they don't have compact beginnings and endings. Nonfiction was ruled out too, because it has a way of becoming dated, sooner or later. While there are some outstanding short stories from other sports, this collection is confined to baseball because of its long history and tradition and the abundance of quality material to choose from. The date of a particular story is not important. Human nature doesn't change much and a good story can live forever.

Finding the best baseball stories is a little like playing detective. You round up the usual suspects, old tales that you've read and remembered. You talk to writers on the subject. There are some meticulously prepared bibliographies on baseball literature, as well as electronic search facilities from data bases available in good libraries. So, with the exception of relatively obscure sources from the distant past, it is possible to lay hands on virtually all the significant literature. It turned out to be a far larger body of material than I imagined.

A pleasant finding from the research is that many of the truly great American authors have written short stories on baseball. Perhaps this is not surprising, since most kids grow up playing the game and it is deeply rooted in our culture. Just because a well-known writer has a baseball story, though, doesn't mean that it's one of the best. But cream has a way of rising to the top. Also, some excellent stories have been written by lesser known authors, usually sports columnists who tried their hand at fiction.

What it came down to, once all the gathered stories were carefully considered, was making the cuts, picking the team of the very best. This is admittedly a subjective process, reminiscent of Ogden Nash's limerick:

There once was an umpire whose vision
Was cause for abuse and derision.
He remarked in surprise,
"Why pick on my eyes?
It's my heart that dictates my decision."

Eventually picked were twenty-eight stories, many written by authors familiar to literature buffs, like Zane Grey, Robert Penn Warren, Damon Runyon, James Thurber, P. G. Wodehouse, Ring Lardner, Garrison Keillor, Frank Deford, and T. Coraghessan Boyle. While perhaps not as famous, a number of other very successful writers grace this collection, including Eliot Asinof, W. C. Heinz, Herbert Warren Wind, J. F. Powers, Lloyd Biggle, Jr., Arnold Hano, Stuart Dybeck, Chet Williamson, and Michael Chabon.

These stories were originally published during the years 1910–1990. Like fine wine, the older stories have aged well. Beginning with "Casey at the Bat," we find unforgettable characters, abundant humor, a touch of melancholy, and lots of great baseball talk, action, and drama. The authors aren't concerned much with transmitting facts. They try to make us think and feel, to involve the heart as well as the mind. Good thoughts, good feelings. Batter up.

Paul D. Staudohar

*Baseball's most famous poem is "Casey at the Bat." As much a story as a poem, it was written in 1888 by Ernest L. Thayer, a young newspaper reporter for the San Francisco Examiner. Whether one is reading "Casey" for the first time or the tenth, it is always fresh and loaded with imagery. Will the big slugger save the day for the Mudville team? High drama on the diamond, a tasty slice of Americana served up with sparkling verse, "Casey" has spawned dozens of imitative poems and stories. For instance, sportswriter Grantland Rice's poem "Casey's Revenge," artfully changed the original outcome. Columnist Art Buchwald wrote a delightful sequel, using the structure of the poem to parody baseball's allowing women reporters in the locker room. Science fiction writer Rod Serling did a send-up on the Casey theme. But the original is still the best.*

*Ernest L. Thayer*

# CASEY AT THE BAT

(As it appeared in the *San Francisco Examiner* June 3, 1888)

THE OUTLOOK WASN'T BRILLIANT FOR the Mudville nine that day;
The score stood four to two with but one inning more to play.
And then when Cooney died at first, and Barrows did the same,
A sickly silence fell upon the patrons of the game.

A straggling few got up to go in deep despair. The rest
Clung to that hope which springs eternal in the human breast;

They thought if only Casey could but get a whack at that—
We'd put up even money now with Casey at the bat.

But Flynn preceded Casey, as did also Jimmy Blake,
And the former was a lulu and the latter was a cake;
So upon that stricken multitude grim melancholy sat,
For there seemed but little chance of Casey's getting to the bat.

But Flynn let drive a single, to the wonderment of all,
And Blake, the much despis-ed, tore the cover off the ball;
And when the dust had lifted, and the men saw what had occurred,
There was Jimmy safe at second and Flynn a-hugging third.

Then from 5,000 throats and more there rose a lusty yell;
It rumbled through the valley, it rattled in the dell;
It knocked upon the mountain and recoiled upon the flat,
For Casey, mighty Casey, was advancing to the bat.

There was ease in Casey's manner as he stepped into his place;
There was pride in Casey's bearing and a smile on Casey's face.
And when, responding to the cheers, he lightly doffed his hat,
No stranger in the crowd could doubt 'twas Casey at the bat.

Ten thousand eyes were on him as he rubbed has hands with dirt;
Five thousand tongues applauded when he wiped them on his shirt.
Then while the writhing pitcher ground the ball into his hip,
Defiance gleamed in Casey's eye, a sneer curled Casey's lip.

And now the leather-covered sphere came hurtling through the air,
And Casey stood a-watching it in haughty grandeur there.
Close by the sturdy batsman the ball unheeded sped—
"That ain't my style," said Casey. "Strike one," the umpire said.

From the benches, black with people, there went up a muffled roar,
Like the beating of the storm-waves on a stern and distant shore.
"Kill him! Kill the umpire!" shouted some one on the stand;
And it's likely they'd have killed him had not Casey raised his hand.

With a smile of Christian charity great Casey's visage shone;
He stilled the rising tumult; he bade the game go on;
He signaled to the pitcher, and once more the spheroid flew;
But Casey still ignored it, and the umpire said, "Strike two."

"Fraud!" cried the maddened thousands, and echo answered fraud;
But one scornful look from Casey and the audience was awed.
They saw his face grow stern and cold, they saw his muscles strain,
And they knew that Casey wouldn't let that ball go by again.

The sneer is gone from Casey's lip, his teeth are clenched in hate;
He pounds with cruel violence his bat upon the plate.
And now the pitcher holds the ball, and now he lets it go,
And now the air is shattered by the force of Casey's blow.

Oh, somewhere in this favored land the sun is shining bright;
The band is playing somewhere, and somewhere hearts are light,
And somewhere men are laughing, and somewhere children shout;
But there is no joy in Mudville—mighty Casey has struck out.

*Casey struck out. But can't there be more to the story? Frank Deford writes about the mighty swinger's colorful life before and after that fateful day at Mudville, creating a bawdy hero worthy of the "Casey at the Bat" myth. Deford's story links Casey with real-life characters like heavyweight champ John L. Sullivan and James Naismith of peach basket fame, providing fascinating glimpses of turn-of-the-century America. Deford, the nation's premier sportswriter during his many years with* Sports Illustrated, *also founded the critically acclaimed but ill-fated daily sports newspaper, the* National. *He has written popular books with tennis personalities Arthur Ashe, Billie Jean King, Jack Kramer, and Pam Shriver, and published* The World's Tallest Midget: The Best of Frank Deford *(1978). His most recent book,* Love and Infamy *(1993), is about the 1941 Japanese naval air attack on Pearl Harbor.*

*Frank Deford*

# CASEY AT THE BAT (1988)

**I**F EVER YOU LOVED BASEBALL or if ever you had a hero, you surely would like to know what happened to Casey after he struck out in the bottom of the ninth on Saturday, June 2, 1888. And so . . .

The porters scrambled to grab Richard K. Fox's bag when he arrived at New York's Grand Central that bright Thursday morning, May 31, a century ago. "Boston" was all Fox said, and the lucky fellow who had ended up with Fox's valise rushed ahead to the Pullman car. Fox was not handsome, with a mustache too bushy for his little head, a nose too big by half and cold, hooded eyes. But if he lacked the sleek looks of his animal namesake, he was every bit as clever. Like so many men who have succeeded in his profession—Fox was an editor—his strength lay in the deployment of better men's talents. On his cravat he wore a horseshoe pin of gold, studded with diamonds, open side down.

Fox settled in his seat and turned to the paper he'd brought onto the train. The Democrats, party of the incumbent president, Grover Cleveland, were about to convene in St. Louis and go through the formality of renominating their man. So the press, its priorities ever straight, was much more interested in what the President's young bride, the 23-year-old beauty, Frances Folsom, had worn the day before, Memorial Day. Quickly then, Fox skimmed through the pages until he came to the sports section. He was home now.

The sports pages in the '80s—the 1880s—had become a popular force. For the cranks (as baseball fans were so aptly known), there were the major-club box scores telegraphed from all over. There were even line scores from the burgeoning minor leagues. If Fox had looked closely, for example, he would have seen the scores from the Bay State League, which included this doubleheader result: Mudville 16, 8—Lynn 5, 2. And there were stories on boxing for the fancy (as the pugilistic world was called), horse racing, crew, tennis, cricket and many other games. No one was more responsible for this boom in sports reportage—or for the profit derived from it—than Fox, who had made his magazine, the *National Police Gazette,* a successful institution largely because of sports.

An item down near the bottom of the *Tribune's* sports page caught Fox's eye: CHAMPION RETURNS FROM EUROPE. John L. Sullivan, the report said, had arrived back in Boston last month and would be engaging in some stage exhibitions. "Champion," Fox muttered, crumpling up the paper. "Fat Mick lout." Sullivan was Fox's bête noir, for he was one man in sports Fox could not control, and everything he did to thwart the Boston Strong Boy only served to enhance Sullivan's reputation. It was Fox who had put up Paddy Ryan to fight Sullivan in '82, and Sullivan's victory established him as America's first great athletic hero.

Nonetheless, Sullivan would not do Fox's bidding, would not defend his title again. Instead, he went about making a fortune fighting in exhibitions—"My name is John L. Sullivan, and I can beat any sonuvabitch in the house!" he would bellow—plus eating everything in the house, gulping bourbon from beer steins and whoring his time away. Frustrated, Fox made up a magnificent "championship" belt for the pretender, Jake Kilrain. So the whole damn city of Boston gave Sullivan an even grander bejeweled belt, and the Great John L. grew greater still.

The train pulled out of Grand Central, billowing smoke. Fox was on his way to Boston to personally goad—somehow—Sullivan into action. "The *Great* John L.," he muttered. "My arse."

About the time Fox's Pullman was passing through Bridgeport, Chester Drinkwater was escorting a handsome young couple into the amazing Cyclorama on Tremont Street in Boston's South End. The couple quickly became bug-eyed, for there before them—all around them, really, in a circular vista 400 feet in circumference and 50 feet high—was a painted re-creation of the Battle of Gettysburg. Timothy F. X. Casey didn't have to have it explained to him, either. He hadn't been born till '67, but his father had fought in the war, and an uncle had died at Antietam. Casey knew his America.

And America was aboomin'—the West filling, the cities bursting their seams, trolleys (some electric!) carrying the middle classes out into these new things called suburbs. Industry. Commerce. Science. Inventions. Wires were everywhere: Telegraph lines, telephone lines, electric lines. Yet America in '88 was still closer to Gettysburg than to the Ardennes, closer to Jeb Stuart than to Sergeant York, closer to Abraham Lincoln than to, uh, Babe Ruth.

Flossie Cleary had heard about Gettysburg, but because she hadn't crossed the ocean from Cork until '84, she was more impressed by the scope of the Cyclorama than by the scenes it depicted. So Casey took it upon himself to fill her in. Here's Little Round Top, there Culp's Hill. . . . Pickett's Charge is over. . . . Uh, oh. His hand went out, and it grazed against Flossie. Grazed. Lingered. Then it passed on, and Casey was telling Flossie about the cavalry, but she didn't hear a word. How many times had she whispered to Father O'Reilly in the confessional that she had sinned by hoping Timothy F. X. Casey might touch her . . . and now he had . . . and now they would be alone tonight. Chaperoned, of course, by Mr. Chester Drinkwater and his sister, but alone at beautiful, alluring Nantasket Beach. Different rooms in the hotel, of course. But still . . . . There was so much about this that left Flossie uneasy.

"Ah, Timothy, but exactly who might this Mr. Drinkwater be, and why would he be doing these lovely things for you?" Flossie had asked when Casey first told her that he had this benefactor, this rich crank, who wanted to take them to Nantasket, in his own surrey, in his own sloop across Hingham Bay, put them up at the finest hotel, take them to the finest show.

"Flossie, would you be looking a gift horse in the mouth?" Casey had replied, and a bit testily. "Mr. Chester Drinkwater is not only a sporting man, but one of the most successful businessmen in Boston. He owns several trolley lines and the big amusement park in Newton."

Still, something stayed under Flossie's fair skin. On the occasion of that exchange, she and Timothy had been alone at the far end of the magnificent veranda at the house of Mr. and Mrs. Alfred L. Evans Jr., in the finest section of Mudville, where Flossie was employed as a downstairs maid. But she turned away from Casey, fretting. Things were moving too fast, and she was suspicious. Why, it had been quite enough, her falling in love with a ballist. In many quarters, ballists were dismissed as riffraff, which was fair enough, because that was what they were. Young men who played baseball, it was widely known, generally drank too much, gambled and specialized in separating young ladies from their virtue whenever the opportunity arose. Mostly, they consorted with other lowlifes, such as actors, dance hall girls, boodlers, flimflammers, second-story men, chippies, tarts and cracksmen. In fact, a great many ballists spent their off-seasons onstage or with a circus. Casey had joined the Mudville nine late in the '87 season and had met Flossie then, but he'd gone away soon enough, traveling with Barnum & Bailey. Mostly he worked as a roustabout for the side show, although he and another strong fellow would dress in leopard skins at show time and go onstage to try (unsuccessfully) to hoist the fat lady.

Casey frightened Flossie some because she loved him even though he was sort of mysterious. He didn't seem to have anyone close to him. He'd grown up in Baltimore but was orphaned, and his only sibling, his left-handed twin sister, Kate, had married into a German family. He saw her only when the circus passed through Baltimore.

"It's this baseball craze, Flossie," Casey said, moving closer to her on the veranda. "People just think it's a humdinger. Not just in Mudville. Why, did you know the Beaneaters paid $10,000 to the Chicagos just to get King Kelly to come play in Boston?"

Flossie gasped. Ten thousand dollars was more money that she expected to see in her lifetime. But something was happening in the '80s. Baseball was developing as a kind of adhesive that held together the evolving city and all its diverse types. It was said that any middling city that aspired to the big time needed three things: trolley lines, an opera house and a baseball team. "What can I do, Flossie?" Casey asked. "I found out I could hit a horsehide, and now people love me for it."

Mudville had gone bonkers over its nine that spring, and it was almost entirely because of Casey. The Evanses at first didn't want Flossie to have anything to do with a ballist, but after Mr. Evans left the bank early one day and went out to the Grounds to see Mudville whip Framingham 8–1 and Casey hit two triplets and a two-bagger, he let the young fellow come call on Flossie.

Casey had kept up the tattoo all spring. Why, not a single pitcher had yet struck him out. The baseballs didn't have much bounce in them, and the wheelman delivered from only 50 feet away, but Casey had such power that soon enough the local papers were calling him Mighty Casey. He was hitting .386, too, and grumpy old Cyrus Weatherly, the town miser who owned the team and the Mudville Grounds as well, was delighted to see that the ladies and gentlemen of the town were flocking to the East Side to watch the games. Even Mrs. Evans went to a game one afternoon.

Later that same day, Casey was on the Evans's veranda with Flossie when a rather ascetic young gentleman appeared. He explained that he had been directed to this address by someone at Casey's boardinghouse, so Mr. Evans steered him out to the veranda. "Mr. Casey," the man said, "my name is Jim Naismith, and I'm a student in Canada. I'm visiting at the training school over in Springfield, considering becoming what they call a physical education instructor there."

"How do you do, sir," Casey said.

Naismith explained that word had reached Springfield that Casey had the finest natural swing in all the world. "When the season is over," Naismith said, "if they send you a rail ticket, would you come show the students your swing?"

"Gee, I don't know," Casey said, taken aback. "The past two winters I traveled with the circus."

"Oh, I see," Naismith said, clearly disappointed.

Casey glanced over at Flossie, then lowered his head. " 'Course, I'm thinking maybe I won't be leaving Mudville this fall." Flossie's face turned crimson, and her heart bobbled.

"Well, now," Naismith said. "I think you'd be interested in what they do in Springfield. Besides baseball in the spring, they have gymnastics and swimming and football in the fall."

"What game do they play in the winter?" Casey asked.

"Nothing satisfactory, I'm afraid," Naismith said. "But I'm going to work on that."

Mr. Evans stepped up. "You know, Timothy, you're a bright lad and good at sport. Maybe you ought to think about *attending* that school in Springfield after the season."

Casey gulped. "But that's like a *college*, Mr. Evans."

"There's no law says a ballist can't go to college, is there, Mr. Naismith?" And then he turned to Flossie. "You wouldn't be bothered being married to a college man, would you, Flossie?"

Casey's jaw dropped. Flossie shrieked. "Faith and begorra, sir," and dashed away. Mr. Evans threw an arm about Casey's shoulders, more as he would with a son than with some roisterous ballplayer. "A real nice piece of dry goods," Mr. Evans said, winking at Casey, as they watched Flossie's trim ship sail away. "A very nice piece of calico."

Two weeks later, just before Memorial Day when Chester Drinkwater came by, Mr. Evans brought Casey right into the parlor. After Flossie had served tea, Drinkwater came to the point. "Mr. Evans, would it be possible for Flossie to come away with Mr. Casey and myself—and my sister Maud, who'll chaperon, of course—and go down to visit Nantasket Beach on Thursday?" he asked.

That week the Mudvilles would exploit Memorial Day on Wednesday by playing a doubleheader. But then they'd be off until Saturday, so Casey could get away to the beach. "I've taken a keen liking to this young man," Drinkwater said, patting Casey on the knee. "And the way baseball is taking hold, there may be a lot of cranks out there who'd love to deal with Timothy if he were a salesman for me."

"Good business," said Mr. Evans.

"It'd sure be better than trying to lift that fat lady three times a day," Casey allowed.

Mr. Evans curled his mustache, thinking. "Well, as long as she's chaperoned, and as long as she can make up the time, working her off-afternoons, I can't see why Flossie can't go to Nantasket."

"Oh, thank you, sir." Casey whooped, and he bolted into the kitchen to tell Flossie the good news.

Mr. Evans turned back to his visitor. "You know, Mr. Drinkwater, I can't tell you what a difference Casey has made to this town. Why he's not only changed the whole spirit of Mudville, but he's got people going over to that old East Side again. We haven't had any interest out there in years, but people go out to the Grounds, see Casey wallop one, and . . . all of a sudden I've got a mortgage application on my desk for property out there. It's amazing what a team can do for a town. Something new in our modern society, I believe. Amazing. Had you ever thought about that?"

"No, I never had," Drinkwater said, lying through his teeth.

Casey's Memorial Day performance was as fine as a hitter could have:

8 for 12, 2 homers, 11 runs batted in. And what crowds! SRO! Waving American flags! The children hung from the trees, and all the bands from the Memorial Day parade reassembled at the Grounds, so grumpy old Cyrus Weatherly let them sit inside the centerfield fence—for two bits a head—and they played music all afternoon, adding to the holiday air.

The Mudvilles had never drawn so many people, and it was only May. Word of the Mighty Casey had even reached Boston, and because the Beaneaters were away on a western swing, a few cranks took the train out from the city. Ernest Thayer, Harvard '85, a frustrated poet who was re-assigned to working in one of the family's woolen mills, came in from Worcester. Flossie snuck away from the house late in the day and was at the Grounds for the eighth inning of the second game, in time to see Casey at the bat for the last time.

Hughie Barrows was on second and Johnny Flynn on first, and Casey knocked them both in with a ground rule double that rolled into a French horn in centerfield. The crowd went berserk. The score didn't mean anything now. In fact, baseball didn't matter. It was mostly a matter of pride. Not only did the people of Mudville have a hero, but they also were made heroic, touched by him.

However, all Flossie could see was that glorious, innocent face on second base: Casey, standing there, his cap off, waving to the throng, beaming. Practically all the players wore mustaches, and many of them bushy sideburns to boot. But Casey was apart. His face was as clean as it was bright, his eyes clear blue, his hair the color of a base path, his uniform happily dirty. Not poverty dirty or grubby dirty, but boyishly dirty, good dirty, thought Flossie. God, but Casey was clean. The tears poured down Flossie's cheeks. She was so in love, and maybe even better, she knew Casey loved her, too.

In the stands back of third base Thayer turned to a friend. "You know," he said, "there's that song about King Kelly."

"You mean *Slide, Kelly, Slide?*"

"Right. And there's that barroom rhyme for John L." Thayer recited from memory:

*His colors are the Stars and Stripes.*
*He also wears the green.*
*And he's the greatest slugger that*
*The ring has ever seen.*
*No fighter in the world can beat*
*Our true American:*
*The champion of all champions,*
*John L. Sullivan!*

"Pretty good memory, Ernest."

"Yeah, well this guy Casey deserves even more. He deserves an epic poem. I think I'll come back out here Saturday."

On second base. Casey put his cap back on, and when he did, it was as if he caught a sunbeam in it and the rays wreathed his head in amber. Then he hitched up his pants and took a long lead off second.

# 2

Drinkwater escorted Flossie and Casey out of the Cyclorama. Her mind was still swimming at that marvel, the grandest thing she had ever seen. And now Drinkwater took her by the elbow and helped her into his rig, a magnificent surrey drawn by a pair of matching chestnuts. Why, Cinderella herself hadn't gone to the ball in anything finer, and Flossie only wished that Mr. Drinkwater wasn't along with them so that she could snuggle up next to Timothy—and hang that anyone would see her carrying on so brazenly.

Flossie had been in the big city before, but this was different, looking from the surrey on the humanity scrambling about her. Boston had burst into a city of 400,000 people, easily double what it had been before the Civil War, and that didn't take into account the trolley suburbs. There were 231 miles of trolley lines now, carrying 85 million passengers every year—all manner of souls: Chinese men with pigtails, Jews with long beards, Poles and Gypsies, sailors, beggars and urchins. Almost three quarters of the city was immigrant or first generation. Since '85, Boston had even had an Irish mayor. What else could hold this disjointed mass together but churches, saloons and baseball?

The surrey headed south, toward Quincy and the sloop that would take them across Hingham Bay. A trolley flashed across their path, the passengers hanging on, jaunty in the warm air. Tomorrow would be June! Flossie eyed the theaters, the shops, the department stores. In one window were fancy shawls on sale for $2.25. How Flossie wanted one, but there was no time and so much to see. Druggists on every corner, curing the ails of mankind. Signs and sandwich boards boasting of nostrums to correct OBESITY! OPIUM ADDICTION! THE ILL EFFECTS OF YOUTHFUL ERRORS! SUMMER DEBILITIES! There was Lydia Pinkham's famous vegetable compound for women, and Unrivalled Eureka Pills for Weak Men who suffered from early decay and lost manhood. The way things were going, what would doctors have left to cure in the 20th Century?

When they reached Dorchester the driver pulled off the main road, and Drinkwater explained that his sister had a touch of the vapors, it seemed, and so his niece Phoebe had graciously consented to fill in as a substitute chaperon. As soon as Drinkwater got down from the rig to go in the house and fetch her, Casey turned to Flossie and, taking her by the shoulders, looked into her face.

How smooth it was. And in a world where so many people had disfiguring smallpox marks, Flossie's countenance seemed all the more polished, the rosy cheeks blushing, the green eyes enraptured, the tendrils of hair falling gently across her forehead. She knew he was going to embrace her then, kiss her right there in the surrey, in the sunlight. She also knew she wasn't going to stop him, and, indeed, when Casey didn't disappoint, when he took her in his arms and pressed his lips against hers, Flossie fell onto him and kissed him back with every bit as much fervor.

She absolutely astonished Casey, and so it was he who, finally, pulled back, wide-eyed. "You're as beautiful as Frances Folsom herself," he gasped at last, paying her the ultimate compliment.

Flossie's mother had told her about boys like him. "Am I now?"

"Oh yes, only I'm sure she doesn't kiss the President nearly so well," he smirked, making Flossie duck her head in proud embarrassment.

When she looked up, she knew Casey was going to try to kiss her again. To stop this madness, she put a finger to his lips. "Tell me now, Timothy. What *does* Mr. Drinkwater seek from you?"

Casey glared at her. "Dammit, Florence Cleary, I told you not to ask me that," he snapped. And he was so peeved at her, he sulked intermittently the rest of the trip, or at least until they put on their bathing costumes at Nantasket Beach and Casey got to see the flesh of Flossie's ankles.

Richard Fox alighted at Boston's new Park Square Terminal that afternoon. What a ride: mile-a-minute, throttle out; a sumptuous meal; exquisite comfort and service. At the Parker House his suite was ready, but before going up, Fox asked the telephone traffic operator, the hello girl, to ring up the Third Base Saloon at 940 Columbus Avenue. After a moment a voice came on. "Hello," it said.

"I'd like to talk to Mr. McGreevey," Fox said.

"This is Nuf Ced. Who's this?"

"This is Richard Fox . . . of the *Police Gazette*."

There was a pause on the other end, and Michael T. McGreevey, known by one and all as Nuf Ced, clearly let fly into a spittoon. "I don't know if I want to talk to ya."

"Is Sullivan there?"

"Maybe he is. Maybe he isn't."

"Look, Nuf Ced, I'm trying to make a lot of money for Sullivan. Tell 'im I came to Boston, and . . ."

*Pit-too.* "He ain't in Boston."

"So, when's he get back?"

"Maybe tomorrow." *Pit-too.*

"OK, you just tell Sullivan I'll be at your place tomorrow night."

"Aye, I'll tell 'im." *Pit-too.* "But I ain't sayin' Johnny'll like it, Fox. Nough said?" said Nuf Ced.

The reason Sullivan wasn't in Boston that Thursday was that he was the featured attraction at the Nantasket Beach show. Why shoud he defend his title against Jake Kilrain when he could make a king's ransom walking through exhibitions?

Drinkwater had the choicest seats for Flossie and Casey, himself and Phoebe, his niece. Truth to tell, Phoebe didn't look much like a chaperon. While she couldn't have been much older than Flossie, an aura of maturity hung on her no less than the men did. Many of those in the dining room seemed to know Drinkwater's niece as well as they knew Drinkwater. And he was a much recognized man. The Trolley King, everyone called him.

Flossie kept her eyes on Drinkwater, though not, perhaps quite as much as Phoebe kept hers on Casey. And how raggedy Flossie felt beside Phoebe. Flossie was in her very best Sunday gingham, but it looked absolutely shabby compared with Phoebe's magnificent brown foulard gown, with white polka dots and a parasol to match. No wonder the men stared at her so. No wonder Casey did. Flossie was relieved when they could finally get over to the pavilion to see the show.

And what a performance it was! Though Flossie had believed that nothing could possibly compare to the Gettysburg Cyclorama, this surely was entertainment unrivaled. Here was the bill:

First, Gardini and Hamlet, blackface singers. Then the solemn dramatic recitations of Amos P. Lawrence, followed by John Mahoney, who performed a "laughable trapeze," adroitly mixing humor and danger. Jessie Allyne came next, a brief novelty act. She let her magnificent hair down and down and down, until the golden tresses lay in great coiled rings at her feet. "I seen something like that in a sideshow once," Casey said, "but the lady in question wasn't nearly so grand." This was followed by the Authentic Monkey Orchestra, then Fairfax and Siegfried, human statues extraordinaire, and the ever-popular Willie Arnold, New England's favorite jig dancer.

Then it was time for the fisticuffs. First, before John L. came on, Patsey Kerrigan and George LaBlanche fought under the old ring rules, which the announcer explained meant "anything but biting." Sullivan himself would have none of that. It was odd about John L. As utterly crude as he was—almost barbaric in his personal habits—he preferred gloves and the new Marquis of Queensberry rules, with scoring by timed rounds. Still, even the fashionable Nantasket crowd showed atavistic fascination as Kerrigan and LaBlanche clawed one another.

Drinkwater leaned across to Casey. "Look about," he said. "Look at your Miss Cleary and my, uh, niece. Look all around, and you'll espy that much of the applause here comes from the dainty gloved hands." Casey nodded, "You see, Timothy, if women can favor a raw free-for-all as we've just seen, think how many of the lovelies would be attracted to a fine, clean sporting event like baseball"—Drinkwater lifted a finger—"particularly if it were played in a better part of town."

Casey started to approve this wisdom, but he was stopped cold, for at that moment the Great John L. Sullivan entered the stage, a huge green robe slung loosely over his shoulders. Casey was aghast. The Boston Strong Boy was, in fact, the Boston Fat Boy. "He's fat," Flossie said, with shock. "Disgustingly fat," said Phoebe, with disgust.

The heavyweight champion of the world, 29 years old, looked closer to 39 and packed 243 pounds on his 5'10½" frame. He was grotesquely flabby. His attendant, a spidery little sort named Smiler Pippen, laced on the champ's gloves, and that motion was enough to jiggle Sullivan's jowls and belly. John L. liked having Smiler around, for he was a self-professed druggist, who dispensed rubdowns and a favored potion, a so-called physic, which was made up of zinnia, salts and licorice. That was Sullivan's only concession to training.

He sauntered out to face one Francis Rooney, and to Casey's surprise, he had to admit that Sullivan could be remarkably nimble when he had to be—for a second or two. But he was too much the walrus to maintain any pace, and though his blows obviously devastated poor Rooney, John L. was hardly a scintillating climax to the evening. Drinkwater and his guests left a bit disappointed.

Casey had hoped then for a stroll down the boardwalk, perhaps even a little trip along the beach, but Flossie was exhausted from the long day, and he had to settle for a chaste peck on her cheek. Then Phoebe conscientiously assumed her chaperon's mantle and ushered Flossie off to her room. "A little nose paint?" Drinkwater said to Casey, beckoning to the bar, where they took a table for brandy and cigars.

"Well, Timothy, my boy, have you decided to accept my little proposition?" Drinkwater asked after they'd lit up.

"I think so, but I'm not. . . . "

"I understand. You're a prudent young man," Drinkwater said, toasting him. "So, let's run over it again. Now, you tell me you make . . ."

"Eight hundred dollars for the season. . . . "

". . . playing for Mudville."

So Drinkwater took out his billfold and laid out eight $100 bills. Casey blinked.

"And if you stay with Mudville after this season, you'll be reserved," Drinkwater said. "You understand? They'll own you. Reserve is just a pretty word for own. Bad enough that provision was put in for the major-club players, now it's in the minors, too. What is this? This is 1888. We fought a war over this 25 years ago."

"Yes sir." The nerve of old Cyrus Weatherly and those other owners.

"Now, I'm prepared to pay you three thousand dollars"—to spell things out, Drinkwater laid down two more centuries and a pair of $1,000 bills—"to leave Mudville."

Casey gasped. "Take the summer off," Drinkwater went on. "Next season, I'll help you sign with anyone."

"The Beaneaters," said Casey.

"Why not, Timothy, my boy?"

Casey's eyes twinkled.

"And finally, an extra $500 to seal the bargain." Drinkwater said, and he laid out a $500 bill. "And I'll throw in a beautiful new gown for that young lady of yours. You get this right now"—he slid the $500 closer to Casey—"and the rest after five more games. Only you're not to get a single hit in any of those games. I don't want you just disappearing. That'd be too curious. But if all of a sudden you start striking out, it'll look like something went wrong with Mighty Casey. People will think he went lame, lost his ginger. Then you take the $3,000 and drop out of sight. Only, when you materialize next year, you're in the National League."

Casey's hand itched to reach out and take the $500, but, after hesitating, he took up the brandy glass instead. Casey was no dummy. "Mr. Drinkwater, I'm no dummy," he said. "There must be a reason you'd pay me all this."

"Of course there is, my boy. But there's an expression going around: What you don't know won't hurt you. You just have my word as a sporting man that it's not illegal. What do you say?"

Casey paused a moment. "Let me sleep on it."

"Very wise, my boy," Drinkwater said, chuckling. "Yes indeed, you sleep on it tonight. Heh, heh."

Casey entered his room. From out of the shadows Phoebe came toward him, letting her long sable hair tumble down to the brown foulard dress with the white polka dots. Only then did Casey realize that she didn't have the brown foulard dress with the white polka dots on anymore. "I thought you'd never come up, Timothy," Phoebe said with a sigh.

Later, when Phoebe had dressed, she pulled a $500 bill out of her purse and left it on the bedside table. "So, we're in business . . . with my uncle," she said. And Casey smiled and nodded.

He felt rotten, dirty and deceitful, and wondered when he could see her again.

# 3

Late the next afternoon, back in Boston, Casey and Flossie walked along the Charles. They'd come up from Nantasket with Phoebe and Drinkwater and had checked into the Parker House, where they planned to spend the night before heading out to Mudville the next morning for the big game. It was a glorious day—the emerald grass, the sculls and sails upon the water, the promenading swells from the Back Bay—but Casey knew that none of the ladies of Boston was as gorgeous as his Flossie.

Drinkwater had arranged for a new outfit to be waiting for Flossie at the hotel: Blue-and-white-striped silk it was, and her splendid figure filled it like one of those sails on the Charles. The dress had wide cuffs and a deep collar of white linen. And there was a leghorn straw sailor with a blue band and flowing white ribbon. Parasol to match. "You're the loveliest, Flossie," Casey said. "There's not a man on the esplanade who's not trying to catch your eye."

"Pshaw. No one would buck a gentleman so pleasing to the eye as *you*," Flossie said, giving a little flip to her parasol. She was learning quickly how much more effectively she could flirt when she was well dressed. "But, ah, I must be watching you, I must."

"Oh, how's that?"

"That Phoebe woman. I truly don't believe she's Mr. Drinkwater's niece, but I do believe she'd like to seduce you, Timothy Casey."

Casey threw his hands to his head and rolled his eyes. "Flossie, that is the most ridiculous thing I've ever heard," he said. He shook his head one more time for effect and stared out at the river.

Whew, he thought, I nipped that in the bud.

Ohhh, thought Flossie, she's seduced him already.

She turned to face him squarely. "You made your deal with Mr. Drinkwater, didn't you now?"

"Sure enough." Casey said, beaming. He pulled out the $500 bill, brandishing it and telling her all the benign details of the arrangement.

But Flossie turned away. "I love you, Timothy Casey. I surely do," she said. "But I can't be marryin' you if you're involved in . . ."

"But there's nothing illegal. I told . . ."

"Well, let me tell you," Flossie snapped, whirling around, her green eyes searing. "Mudville loves you, Mr. Casey. Why, I've heard Mr. Evans tell that you're bringin' the whole East Side back to life, you are. Can't you see what Mr. Drinkwater and that wicked lady want? They want to build a trolley line way out in the opposite direction from Mudville, practically to Devonbury, to move everything out there. Can't you understand what he'll do to Mudville?"

"Flossie, it's just good old American business know-how."

Flossie stamped her parasol on the ground as if it were a shillelagh. "Timothy Casey, would you be a dumb Mick? Can't you see? I'll bet Mr. Drinkwater's bought every bit of real estate out there. I'll wager he's going to build an amusemanet park, a . . . another baseball grounds. Can't you see that? You breathed life back into our little town, and now he's stealing you from us. That's worse than breakin' any law. Ah, that's breakin' th' spirit."

"But . . ." Casey began to protest, and made the mistake of holding up the $500 bill. When he did, Flossie slapped it away, and he had to scramble after it. By the time he had retrieved the money, his Flossie was weaving in and out among the strollers, disappearing.

When Casey got back to the Parker House, a package was waiting for him at the bell stand. He opened it, and there was Flossie's new dress. A note was pinned to it. It said. "Dear Timothy, I'm sorry, but I cannot accept this or what you are doing with yourself. Do not come calling on me again. Very truly yours, Florence M. Cleary."

Casey crumpled up the note in anger and rushed over to the front desk with the open package in his hands. A well-dressed man with a horseshoe pin on his cravat was standing there. He looked over Casey, looked over the dress. "Woman trouble?" he asked, but sympathetically.

Casey ignored him. To the clerk, he said, "What room is Miss Phoebe Alexander in, please?"

"Seven-eighteen."

Casey grabbed a pen, dashed off a note and called for a bellboy.

"I'm sorry," said the man with the horseshoe pin. "I didn't mean to bother you, but you look like a boxer."

"A fighter? Not me. I'm a ballist."

"Oh, well, I'm sorry. It's just that I'm a fancy man." He put out his hand. "Richard Fox, of the *Police Gazette*."

"No fooling," Casey said, licking the envelope. "Gee, I read the *Gazette* every month."

He handed the bellboy the note and a half a dime. "Seven-eighteen. And wait for the lady's reply."

Then he stuck out his hand to Fox. "I'm Timothy Casey, rightfielder on the Mudville nine."

"Well, well," said Fox. "I've got a bit of business in a while, but would you join me for some nose paint while I'm waiting?"

Casey looked at Fox. The *Police Gazette*. He looked at the bellboy waiting for the elevator, and he thought of Phoebe's hair cascading over her bare shoulders. He looked back at Fox. He saw Flossie's eyes. Back to the bellboy. He was just getting on the elevator. He saw all of Flossie. He saw Flossie's love and his own shame—and in the split second it takes a horsehide to travel 50 feet to the bat, Casey dashed to the elevator and yanked the little bellboy out through the closing doors. "Keep the half a dime, but gimme the note back," he said, and then, smiling, he hustled back over to Fox.

Nobody had come up with the term *sports bar* in 1888, but if they had, the Third Base Saloon, Michael T. McGreevey, Prop., would surely have been recognized as the first such institution. Athletic souvenirs—especially baseball gear—cluttered the place, barely leaving room for the cranks who jammed in, particularly after Beaneater games at the South End Grounds nearby. "I call it Third Base 'cause it's the last place you stop before you steal home," McGreevey would growl. " 'Nough said?"

McGreevey was stout and tiny, a terrier among men, with a handle-bar mustache, and while he had been baptized Michael Thomas, he was always called Nuf Ced. Fox explained this to Casey as they entered the Third Base Saloon and trod across the large mosaic on the floor that spelled out NUF CED. "He's here, Johnny," Nuf Ced roared from behind the bar.

"Who's here?" The great booming voice of John L. Sullivan answered from somewhere in the back. "Anybody important?"

"No, just Richard Fox, the chucklehead who gave a championship belt to Jake Kilrain." *Pit-too.*

Fox smiled facetiously, tipped his hat to Nuf Ced and bade Casey join him at a table. They ordered beers, and Fox explained they would just have to wait for Sullivan. Sure enough, it was an hour or more before Sullivan, with a big tankard of ale in one hand, appeared. He was accompanied by Smiler Pippen on the one side and by his floozy of the evening, Rosie, on the other. "All right, Fox, what is it you're wantin'?" John L. snarled, and Nuf Ced, taking his cue, came over to the table to stand between the two men.

"I just want you to fight Kilrain, Johnny."

"For you, Fox? I ain't no henhouse to let a fox into," he said, and everyone in the Third Base Saloon roared.

"Then don't do it for me," Fox went on. "Just fight him. That's what all the fancy wants. Or are you too fat, Johnny? Too old?"

"Why you goddamn–" said Sullivan, reaching down to grab Fox. John L. had taken the bait. Fox figured that Nuf Ced would jump in, and he did, but Fox didn't figure that, faster still, his new friend Casey would spring to his feet. Casey shoved Sullivan. The ale went flying, and the big fellow needed help from Smiler and Rosie before he could regain his balance. He glared at Casey, at this white-faced, clean-shaven bumpkin. "And who the hell are you, sonny?" Sullivan shouted.

Casey didn't back down. Indeed, he leaned forward a little, never taking his eyes off Sullivan. "My name is Timothy F. X. Casey, and I can beat any sonuvabitch in the house."

The Third Base Saloon fell into a hush. "Is he serious?" Sullivan said at last.

"Are you serious?" Nuf Ced said. *Pit-too.*

Fox pulled at Casey's sleeve. "You're not serious, are you?" he asked.

"Sure, for a price. What are the odds on me?"

"A thousand to one," Nuf Ced said. *Pit-too.*

"I'll take anything he wants at 20 to 1," Sullivan snapped.

Immediately, Casey yanked the $500 bill out of his pocket and waved it. "You're on, John L.," he said. "For this." The crowd gasped as one.

Nuf Ced closed the bar, and the entire ensemble traipsed over to the South End Grounds, where they staked out a ring between the pitcher's box and first base. There was a good moon and enough city light.

"You sure you wanna go through with this, Casey?" Fox asked, helping him off with his coat. "I had Paddy Ryan fight him in '82, and he said it was like a telegraph pole went through him the first time Sullivan hit him."

"That was '82. I seen Sullivan last night," Casey said. "He's fat as a hog, and he's drunk a lotta ale tonight. Besides, my girl left me, and I'm mean."

"Up to scratch," Nuf Ced cried out, and the two fighters stepped forward to a line Nuf Ced had drawn in the dirt. The spectators stood about in a square, already screaming.

"Four rounds," Nuf Ced said. *Pit-too.* "No biting, scratching, gouging, tripping or wrestling."

Both men nodded. Sullivan spit on his hands. Nuf Ced raised his arm. Sullivan knew what to expect. But Casey had figured it out, too. He didn't even look at Sullivan. He kept his eyes on Nuf Ced, and the instant his arm moved, Casey ducked. Good thing. The air was shattered by the force of John L.'s blow.

Casey came up, in one motion banging his right to the big belly, and then his left. By the time Casey was standing full up, Sullivan was holding his stomach. So Casey stepped in and, with all his might, pounded his right to the champion's meaty face. And with that, barely 10 seconds into the fight, Casey had hit a home run. The Great John L. buckled and fell.

The crowd fell into utter silence, shocked. Blood trickled from the corner of Sullivan's mouth, but he wouldn't dab at it, any more than Casey would grab his throbbing knuckles. Instead, the two men just glared at each other, until finally Sullivan began to rise on the count of eight. He got up like a bull elephant, slowly at first, but once he had lifted his great bulk off the ground and leaned forward, he possessed a momentum that no sleek creature could achieve. He pounded the few steps toward Casey. It would have been easy for Casey to step aside, except he was backed up against the crowd–John L.'s crowd–and the loyal spectators blocked Casey's movement. He tried to duck, but as he'd seen in Nantasket, Sullivan, for all his corpulence, still had some agility. John L. caught Casey flush with an uppercut. Casey staggered back, his face exploding, his brains rattling about.

He wanted to go down and regroup, but not only did the spectators block his fall, they also propped Casey up–and then bounced him back toward Sullivan. Casey was a helpless target, and he could see, in his daze, John L. winding up for the knockout.

Then, inexplicably, just like that, Sullivan dropped his dukes and idly watched Casey fly past him, still propelled by the push from the crowd. Sullivan put his hands on his hips and glared at the spectators.

"John L. Sullivan doesn't need any help when he's in the ring," he bellowed. The offenders shrank back.

His rebuke complete, Sullivan turned to finish off Casey. But the moment was lost; Casey had shaken his head clear. When John L. swung, Casey hopped aside, as if he were getting away from a high inside pitch, and with everything left in him, he ducked and came up throwing, like a shortstop pegging to first. Whoosh. Into the champion's soft underbelly. Sullivan gasped. His chin was wide open, but Casey went for the tummy again. And again. The champion doubled over, and only then did Casey aim his left hand—the one that still had its knuckles intact—for Sullivan's chin. Bam! John L. crumpled to his knees and then pitched forward, spitting out blood and ale, spilling his beans.

"Start the goddam count, Nuf Ced!" Fox screamed.

Sullivan peeked up. He didn't know how Casey's hands ached. So he just waved Nuf Ced away and sank back onto the infield grass, into his own blood and guts. The Great John L. was beaten. "Congratulations, sonny," he said. "Now you can tell the whole world you was the first sonuvab. . . . You was the first man ever to beat the Great John L."

"Gimme my $10,000, and I'll never tell a soul on God's green earth," Casey said.

"Don't matter none. That viper Fox'll put it in the *Gazette*."

Fox stepped forward to Sullivan. "Not if you fight Kilrain, I won't, Johnny," he said.

"Yeah now?" said Sullivan, the possibilities dawning on him, and he looked all around at the crowd. "Any sonuvabitch here see John L. Sullivan get beat tonight?"

There was silence for another moment as the crowd looked at one another. Finally, Nuf Ced spit and spoke up: "No, indeed, not me." And then the others cried out, "Not these eyes!" "No, no, no." "I didn't see nuthin'."

Sullivan nodded. "All right, Fox. I'll fight your boy."

"Bare-knuckle."

"Yeah, bare-knuckle. One last time."

Casey started to walk away. "Get me my money, Fox," he called out, and the onlookers stepped aside for him, standing back in awe, afraid even to whisper in the presence of, let alone get in the way of, the man who beat John L.

Suddenly, Fox ran after Casey and caught him near home plate. He took his diamond-studded gold horseshoe off and pinned it on Casey's shirt. "Thanks" was all Fox said.

Casey took the pin off. "You never worked a circus, did you, Fox?" he asked.

"No."

Casey put the pin back on his shirt, but he fixed it with the open end of the horseshoe up. "You never hang a horseshoe down," said Casey. "Anybody on a circus knows that. Hang it down, all the good luck will run out."

Fox nodded and smiled.

"No wonder you never beat John L. before," Casey said.

**4**

Flossie was hanging the washing on the clothesline the next afternoon when Casey came tearing up to her, his face all bruised. "Timothy, what in heaven's name. . . . "

"I haven't got time," he said. "I'm already late for the game, and I gotta see Drinkwater, too."

She gritted her teeth at the mere mention of that name, but Casey only reached out and pinned the horseshoe pin above her breast. "We can pluck the diamonds out and make a proper engagement ring," he said, and with that he dashed off to the ball yard. Flossie unfastened the pin to look it over. Why, it obviously cost even more than the silk dress. How much more money was Drinkwater paying him now? And for what? Furious, Flossie pinned the horseshoe back on, and even though only half the washing had gone up on the line, she rushed off.

There had never been a larger crowd for a baseball game in Mudville. Had everybody in town skipped work? Had every kid robbed his piggy bank? Grumpy old Cyrus Weatherly had stuck the overflow behind ropes in center field. Ernest Thayer had arrived in time to get a ticket, but the crowd spilled over into the aisles, and he had a hard time seeing some of the action.

But where was Casey? Mighty Casey? Nobody knew. Only Drinkwater, sitting in his box by the Mudville bench, beamed.

Willie Flaherty, the Mudville manager, put McGillicuddy in for Casey, but the Mudvilles were at sea without their star, and the Lynns built a 4–2 lead. Then, just as Lynn made out in the seventh, here came Casey sauntering onto the diamond. The people roared and screamed his name, everyone standing and stretching for just a glance. Weatherly glowered at his tardy slugger. Drinkwater nodded his head and winked at Casey as he jogged to the bench. The kid has a real sense of theater, Drinkwater mused. To show up like this and *then* strike out—an even greater disappointment for the gullible locals. Casey went right to the manager. "I'm ready, Willie," he said.

Jimmy Blake was leading off in the seventh, so McGillicuddy was on deck—Casey's spot. But Flaherty waved the Mudville star away. "Sit down, Mr. Casey," he said. "I play the guys who are here when the game starts."

While the crowd booed, poor McGillicuddy batted—bumping a little dribbler back to the wheelman. Three up and three down. And the same in the Mudville eighth. However, when Barry O'Connor, the Mudville pitcher, retired the Lynns in order in the ninth inning, he came out of the pitcher's box and headed straight for Flaherty, to beseech him to let Casey have his licks. Flaherty spit and then said, "OK, Barry, if we get to McGillicuddy's spot, I'll give him a swing."

But the elation on the Mudville bench was short-lived because Cooney grounded out and Barrows topped a ball to first. "I've never seen such a sickly silence," Thayer said to the fellow next to him.

"Still," the other gentleman said, "I'd put up even money if Casey could get at the bat."

The pitcher for the Lynns was a wiry little guy named Kenny Landis, who was a law student pitching under the nom de baseball of Walt Mueller. In his heavy flannel, he was sweating copiously as he peered in for the final out against Johnny Flynn. Landis tried to dry his pitching hand on his trousers, but they were almost soaked through with sweat. With his wet fingers, and his being tired, too, he hung an in-shoot, and Flynn knocked it cleanly up the middle. That brought Blake to the plate, and the Mudville Grounds exploded, but even Blake knew it wasn't for him. No, the roar was for who would come after Blake: Casey, the Mighty Casey, was moving up on deck.

Casey detoured on the way, going over to speak to Drinkwater. Flossie had found her way into the Grounds by now and had worked her way to the first row in the centerfield overflow. When she saw Casey consorting with Drinkwater again—and right out in the open!—she slammed her arms folded across her chest and cursed the best way she knew how.

Blake was an old-timer, cagey when he was sober, and he decided to rip into the kid pitcher's first pitch. He rifled it down the leftfield line, and when the dust was settled, he was standing on second base and Flynn on third.

Here came Casey. Poor Landis could hardly see through his sweat. But, he thought, Casey probably wants to see what kind of stuff I have, so he'll be taking. Good thinking: Casey let a waist-high fastball go by. "Strike one," said the umpire. Flossie wrung her hands and prayed that Casey would find his conscience and hit the ball.

Landis came back with an outdrop, but Casey thought it was off the plate. The umpire, standing behind the pitcher, saw it nick the corner. "Strike two," he said.

But the Mudvilles weren't worried. Casey had seen the kid's repertoire, and he was a celebrated two-strike hitter. The cranks were all on their feet, hollering, and Thayer, even on tiptoes, had to hop this way and that to follow the action. In fact, he missed it when Casey, staring out at the pitcher, spotted Flossie directly behind him, watching from straight-away center, standing out against the crowd in her maid's uniform. For just a moment Casey smiled at her, and then something came over him. Before he knew it, he had raised his bat, pointing it toward center, calling a home run right over his dear Flossie's head. The crowd roared.

"What was that? What was that?" Thayer cried.

"I couldn't see, either," the guy next to him said.

Then the crowd parted a little, and Thayer was able to watch as Casey clenched his teeth and pounded his bat. Landis sweated even more. He would have gone to the resin bag, only there weren't any resin bags yet, so he rubbed his hand on his clothes, on his cap, his socks, his hair, his mustache. Then he reared back and let the ball go. Casey saw it all the way. The pitch didn't have a thing on it. He began his swing, poised, evenly, perfectly. . . .

Casey missed it by a country mile.

Mudville blinked. Mudville couldn't believe it. Flossie could. Flossie cried. Casey had gone on the take. There was no joy in Mudville.

Only . . . wait. The pitch had darted down, and it went under the catcher's glove. It began to roll to the backstop, and here came Flynn, already bearing down on the plate. Casey began to run for first. The catcher got to the ball, picked it up, dropped it, picked it up again, and there went the throw, soaring over the first baseman's head by five feet. Flynn scored. It was 4–3. And here came old Blake right behind. Tie score. Four-up. And Casey was on his way to second. He rounded the bag, and the rightfielder picked up the horsehide down the line and threw behind Casey, to nail him as he tried to scramble back to second. Only Casey saw where the throw was going, and he put his head down and kept on for third. The second-sacker took the throw, a good one, whirled and whipped it to third. It bounced in the dirt as Casey slid, and ricocheted off the third baseman's shoulder and down the leftfield line. Casey scrambled to his feet and was on his way home. The third baseman tore back, picked up the ball and fired it to the plate. Casey slid. The catcher took the ball and slapped it on him. "Safe," the umpire said.

"Curses," Chester Drinkwater muttered.

There was joy in Mudville. The crowd poured onto the field and lifted Casey to its shoulders. He had struck out, but they hoisted him up and began to parade him around.

Casey saw Flossie out in center. The rest of the crowd had run in, and she was just standing there, all alone, the tears flowing down her cheeks. "Let me down, let me down!" Casey cried, and he fought his way off the shoulders to the ground and ran to her, ran as fast as he could, ran even faster than he had when he'd circled the bases.

Only, when he grabbed her, Flossie said, "I hate you, Timothy Casey."

"Listen to me, Flossie. Dammit, listen to me! I tried. I tried! *I tried!* He just struck me out."

"I don't believe you," she said, and she twisted away from him.

"But you must," Casey screamed. "It happens. Somewhere, someday, somebody's even gonna beat John L. Sullivan. It happens."

"You cheated us all!" Flossie cried.

Before he could go on, Casey felt a tap on his shoulder. All the Lynn players were filing past, leaving the Grounds, and there was Landis, the pitcher. "Mr. Casey, no matter what happened, I just want you to know it was an honor facing you," he said. "And I want you to know that that last pitch was the best one I ever hurled in all my life. I don't even know how I did it."

"It was sure some pitch," Casey said. "If you can throw that pitch again, you can strike out King Kelly hisself."

Only Landis never did throw that pitch again. He tried. He tried holding the ball this way and that, releasing it here and there, firing it fast and slow. But all he did was give himself a sore arm and hurry himself into the judiciary. Landis didn't realize he'd mixed his sweat with his mustache wax and thrown the first spitball. Because he didn't know that, he would never do it again, and it was 14 more years before somebody invented the spitball.

Casey yanked Landis over to Flossie. "Tell her, tell her," he screamed at Landis.

"Well, ma'am" said Landis, "like I just said, that was the best pitch I ever threw."

"You hear that Flossie?" said Casey. "He just struck me out. He was just better'n me."

He chased after her some more, but she wasn't convinced. "I don't believe you," she said. "I even saw you talking to Drinkwater just before you went to the bat." "That was because I told him I left his $500 and the silk dress with Phoebe at the Parker House, because you were right and I don't want nothing to do with his deal." He grabbed Flossie by her cheeks and held her face before his. "You hear me, Flossie? I love you! I love you!"

She appeared to be considering this, so Casey pulled out all the stops. He sank to one knee, took her hands and said, "Florence Cleary, will you do me the honor of being my wife?"

Flossie believed him. "Yes, I will," she said.

Casey jumped to his feet and kissed her, and all the cranks who were standing around watching began to cheer. Then Casey said, "It's a good thing for you that you said that, because I'm also a rich man now. I got ten $1,000 bills in my shoes."

"What?"

"I'll tell you all about it sometime, but right now. . . . " He reached over and took off the horseshoe pin, because he'd just noticed that Flossie had put it back on upside down. "Don't ever wear a horseshoe pointing down, because then all the luck will run out of it," he said, and he pinned it back on her, the right way.

Then he put his arm around her, and they walked off together, toward the sunset, as a matter of fact. "You mean if I'd worn the pin right you'd have hit a home run over my head, the way you pointed?" Flossie said.

"Nah, nobody could've hit that pitch," said Casey. "You gotta understand, darling—in baseball, even the best ballists only get a hit one out of every three times up."

# Epilogue

Here is what happened to the principals after June 2, 1888.

John L. Sullivan kept his word to Richard Fox and, on July 8, 1889, fought Jake Kilrain, successfully defending his championship in 75 rounds. It was the last bare-knuckle title bout ever fought.

Richard Fox remained a pillar of popular journalism, and the *National Police Gazette* prospered until 1977. Fox's mix of sex, sport and crime serves many well even today, especially if you add weather.

Nuf Ced McGreevey continued to preside over his sports saloon until Prohibition. To this day, no Boston baseball team has won the championship of the world without Nuf Ced being present at all home games.

Jim Naismith invented basketball in 1891.

Chester Drinkwater became one of the richest men in America, gaining his fortune building ball yards and amusement parks outside the city, running streetcar lines to them and selling real estate all along the way. The only locale where this scheme did not work was Mudville, where, at considerable loss, Drinkwater let many land options lapse. Returning on the *Titanic* from his honeymoon with his fourth wife, the Countess Nina von Munschauer, 23, Drinkwater went to a watery grave.

Grumpy old Cyrus Weatherly, the town miser, refurbished Mudville Grounds after the exciting '88 season, and for decades it was known as the Jewel of the Bushes. Taking this cue, Alfred L. Evans Jr. urged his bank to support the redevelopment of the entire East Side, and the area became a national model for downtown revival. Only after World War I, when the East Side population had become largely Italian, Lithuanian and Pole, were the old Mudville Grounds razed. In 1976 a real estate developer put up middle-class housing. The area is now known as Covent Gardens Estates, and on the actual site of the diamond where Casey struck out is a 24-hour convenience store.

Timothy F. X. Casey finished the '88 season with Mudville, but though he continued to have a fine year, the events of those days in late May and early June seemed to have extracted some spirit from him that he never regained. He and Flossie became engaged, and on the day after the season ended in September, they eloped.

The Caseys spent the next couple of years traveling in America, investing their fortune in prime real estate, buying downtown tracts in such promising minor-league towns as Dallas, Seattle and Los Angeles.

However, Casey had never stopped thinking about what Mr. Evans had once said to him in Mudville. So when Flossie became pregnant, he went back to school, enrolling, in the autumn of 1891, in the very first freshman class at a small new institution that was known as Leland Stanford Jr. University. He graduated with high honors in 1895.

The Caseys settled in Stockton, Calif., where he quickly made his mark in trolleys. Flossie bore him four daughters, and Casey became a pillar of the community—daily communicant, councilman and, finally, philanthropist.

Thayer's poem became more and more famous, spawning vaudeville skits, books, paintings, songs, movies, even a whole opera. The supposedly fictional Casey became something of an American Dauphin, because for years all sorts of washed-up ballplayers maintained that they had been the model for the Mighty One. But after that famous day in Mudville, the real Casey only told one person who he actually was.

That was his nephew George, son of Casey's left-handed twin sister, Kate. Once in 1909, when he had to travel East on trolley business, Casey visited Kate in Baltimore, and the young lad seemed so keen on baseball that Casey took him over to a corner table in the family saloon on Conway Street and told him the tale of '88. "But Uncle Timothy, why did Mr. Thayer end his poem the way he did?" young George asked.

"Aw, you know sportswriters. They only write what makes a good story," Casey said.

Young George especially liked the part about Casey pointing to centerfield, daring to foretell a home run. "Imagine a player doin' a thing like that." George said.

Over the years Casey played a lot of golf. He was long off the tee but dicey around the greens. He and Flossie traveled a lot—to Europe, to Lake Louise and to the 1932 Los Angeles Olympics. They had an even dozen grandchildren, but, of course, the name Casey had run out.

Then, in the spring of 1941, Casey's health began to fail, and he took to his bed in June. He knew by then that the jig was up. He got weaker and weaker. It was the 75th summer of his life.

Three of his daughters still lived around Stockton, but Mary Louise had moved to San Francisco, so Flossie called her on July 17 and said she had better come. She brought her youngest son, Casey's favorite grandchild, John Lawrence Sullivan Gambardella. They just made it to Stockton, to the old family house, in time and went directly to the master bedroom, where the old man lay.

"Well, Johnny, how's tricks?" Casey said, just barely getting the words out. He was going fast. Peacefully, but fast, the sands of his time, 1867–1941.

"Oh, I'm OK Grandpop," the boy said, "but I heard on the radio the Indians got DiMaggio out tonight. So it ends at 56 in a row."

Casey shook his head a bit, and he said, "Well, if he's any good, he'll get over it."

"Yes, sir."

Mary Louise kissed her father, and then she stepped back next to her sisters so her mother could stand closest to the old man. Flossie leaned down and kissed Casey gently on the forehead and squeezed his hand. He sighed, and his eyes began to close. He could all but see the angels now. But then, somehow, Casey forced one more breath of life into his body, and he opened his eyes, even smiled a tiny little bit. Looking up at his beloved Flossie, he said. "Oh, somewhere in this favored land, the sun is shining bright."

Then Casey closed off his smile, turned down his eyes and died. Flossie kept hold of his hand and said. "The band is playing somewhere, and somewhere hearts are light."

The four daughters turned to look at one another, tears in their eyes, but wondering what in the world had come over their mother. "And somewhere men are laughing." Flossie went on. "And somewhere children shout." She smiled broadly and didn't say another word.

As for the one other principal in this story, as for baseball, it grew to become the national pastime and lived happily ever after.

*This story first appeared in Zane Grey's book* The Redheaded Outfield, *which was inspired by Grey's younger brother, Romer or "Reddy," who played two games for the Pittsburgh Pirates in 1903. Zane himself was quite a ballplayer. Born Pearl Zane Grey in Zanesville, Ohio, he graduated from the University of Pennsylvania where he was the captain of the baseball team. While a student at Penn he also played minor-league ball, under the name Pearl Zane. He continued with professional baseball after college and also tried to establish a dental practice. Grey left these pursuits to become an author, even though he was close to making the big leagues. Altogether he wrote 89 books, mostly Western novels. Two special favorites are* Riders of the Purple Sage *(1912) and* The Thundering Herd *(1925).*

## Zane Grey

# THE RUBE'S WATERLOO (1920)

IT WAS ABOUT THE SIXTH inning that I suspected the Rube of weakening. For that matter he had not pitched anything resembling his usual brand of baseball. But the Rube had developed into such a wonder in the box that it took time for his letdown to dawn upon me. Also it took a tip from Raddy, who sat with me on the bench.

"Con, the Rube isn't himself today," said Radbourne. "His mind's not on the game. He seems hurried and flustered, too. If he doesn't explode presently, I'm a dub at callin' the turn."

Raddy was the best judge of a pitcher's condition, physical or mental, in the Eastern League. It was a Saturday and we were on the road and finishing up a series with the Rochesters. Each team had won and lost a game, and, as I was climbing close to the leaders in the pennant race, I wanted the third and deciding game of that Rochester series. The usual big Saturday crowd was in attendance, noisy, demonstrative and exacting.

In this sixth inning the first man up for Rochester had flied to Mc-Call. Then had come the two plays significant of the Rube's weakening. He had hit one batter and walked another. This was sufficient, considering the score was three to one in our favor, to bring the audience to its feet with a howling, stamping demand for runs.

"Spears is wise all right," said Raddy.

I watched the foxy old captain walk over to the Rube and talk to him while he rested, a reassuring hand on the pitcher's shoulder. The crowd yelled its disapproval and umpire Bates called out sharply, "Spears, get back to the bag!"

"Now, Mr. Umpire, ain't I hurrin' all I can?" queried Spears as he leisurely ambled back to first.

The Rube tossed a long, damp welt of hair back from his big brow and nervously toed the rubber. I noted that he seemed to forget the runners on bases and delivered the ball without glancing at either bag. Of course this resulted in a double steal. The ball went wild—almost a wild pitch.

"Steady up, old man," called Gregg between the yells of the bleachers. He held his mitt square over the plate for the Rube to pitch to. Again the long twirler took his swing, and again the ball went wild. Clancy had the Rube in the hole now and the situation began to grow serious. The Rube did not take half his usual deliberation, and of the next two pitches one of them was a ball and the other a strike by grace of the umpire's generosity. Clancy rapped the next one, an absurdly slow pitch for the Rube to use, and both runners scored to the shrill tune of the happy bleachers.

I saw Spears shake his head and look toward the bench. It was plain what that meant.

"Raddy, I ought to take the Rube out," I said, "but whom can I put in? You worked yesterday—Cairns' arm is sore. It's got to be nursed. And Henderson, that ladies' man I just signed, is not in uniform."

"I'll go in," replied Raddy, instantly.

"Not on your life." I had as hard a time keeping Radbourne from over-working as I had in getting enough work out of some other players. "I guess I'll let the Rube take his medicine. I hate to lose this game, but if we have to, we can stand it. I'm curious, anyway, to see what's the matter with the Rube. Maybe he'll settle down presently."

I made no sign that I had noticed Spears's appeal to the bench. And my aggressive players, no doubt seeing the situation as I saw it, sang out their various calls of cheer to the Rube and of defiance to their antagonists. Clancy stole off first base so far that the Rube, catching somebody's warning too late, made a balk and the umpire sent the runner on to second. The Rube now plainly showed painful evidences of being rattled.

He could not locate the plate without slowing up and when he did that a Rochester player walloped the ball. Pretty soon he pitched as if he did not care, and but for the fast fielding of the team behind him the Rochesters would have scored more than the eight runs it got. When the Rube came in to the bench I asked him if he was sick and at first he said he was and then that he was not. So I let him pitch the remaining innings, as the game was lost anyhow, and we walked off the field a badly beaten team.

That night we had to hurry from the hotel to catch a train for Worcester and we had dinner in the dining car. Several of my players' wives had come over from Worcester to meet us, and were in the dining car when I entered. I observed a pretty girl sitting at one of the tables with my new pitcher, Henderson.

"Say, Mac," I said to McCall, who was with me, "is Henderson married?"

"Naw, but he looks like he wanted to be. He was in the grandstand to-day with that girl."

"Who is she? Oh! a little peach!"

A second glance at Henderson's companion brought this compliment from me involuntarily.

"Con, you'll get it as bad as the rest of this mushy bunch of ballplayers. We're all stuck on that kid. But since Henderson came she's been a frost to all of us. An' it's put the Rube in the dumps."

"Who's the girl?"

"That's Nan Brown. She lives in Worcester an' is the craziest girl fan I ever seen. Flirt! Well, she's got them all beat. Somebody introduced the Rube to her. He has been moony ever since."

That was enough to whet my curiosity, and I favored Miss Brown with more than one glance during dinner. When we returned to the parlor car I took advantage of the opportunity and remarked to Henderson that he might introduce his manager. He complied, but not with amiable grace.

So I chatted with Nan Brown, and studied her. She was a pretty, laughing coquettish little minx and quite baseball-mad. I had met many girl fans, but none so enthusiastic as Nan. But she was wholesome and sincere, and I liked her.

Before turning in I sat down beside the Rube. He was very quiet and his face did not encourage company. But that did not stop me.

"Hello, Whit; have a smoke before you go to bed?" I asked cheerfully.

He scarcely heard me and made no move to take the proffered cigar. All at once it struck me that the rustic simplicity which had characterized him had vanished.

"Whit, old fellow, what was wrong today?" I asked, quietly, with my hand on his arm.

"Mr. Connelly, I want my release, I want to go back to Rickettsville," he replied hurriedly.

For the space of a few seconds I did some tall thinking. The situation suddenly became grave. I saw the pennant for the Worcesters fading, dimming.

"You want to go home?" I began slowly. "Why, Whit, I can't keep you. I wouldn't try if you didn't want to stay. But I'll tell you confidentially, if you leave me at this stage I'm ruined."

"How's that?" he inquired, keenly looking at me.

"Well, I can't win the pennant without you. If I do win it there's a big bonus for me. I can buy the house I want and get married this fall if I capture the flag. You've met Milly. You can imagine what your pitching means to me this year. That's all."

He averted his face and looked out of the window. His big jaw quivered.

"If it's that—why, I'll stay, I reckon," he said huskily.

That moment bound Whit Hurtle and Frank Connelly into a far closer relation than the one between player and manager. I sat silent for a while, listening to the drowsy talk of the other players and the rush and roar of the train as it sped on into the night.

"Thank you, old chap," I replied. "It wouldn't have been like you to throw me down at this stage. Whit, you're in trouble?"

"Yes."

"Can I help you—in any way?"

"I reckon not."

"Don't be too sure of that. I'm a pretty wise guy, if I do say it myself. I might be able to do as much for you as you're going to do for me."

The sight of his face convinced me that I had taken a wrong tack. It also showed me how deep Whit's trouble really was. I bade him good night and went to my berth, where sleep did not soon visit me. A saucy, sparkling-eyed woman barred Whit Hurtle's baseball career at its threshold.

Women are just as fatal to ballplayers as to men in any other walk of life. I had seen a strong athlete grow palsied just at a scornful slight. It's a great world, and the women run it. So I lay awake racking my brains to outwit a pretty disorganizer; and I plotted for her sake. Married, she would be out of mischief. For Whit's sake, for Milly's sake, for mine, all of which collectively meant for the sake of the pennant, this would be the solution of the problem.

I decided to take Milly into my confidence, and finally on the strength of that I got to sleep. In the morning I went to my hotel, had breakfast, attended to my mail, and then boarded a car to go out to Milly's house.

She was waiting for me on the porch, dressed as I liked to see her, in blue and white, and she wore violets that matched the color of her eyes.

"Hello, Connie. I haven't seen a morning paper, but I know from your face that you lost the Rochester series," said Milly, with a gay laugh.

"I guess yes. The Rube blew up, and if we don't play a pretty smooth game, young lady, he'll never come down."

Then I told her.

"Why, Connie, I knew long ago. Haven't you seen the change in him before this?"

"What change?" I asked blankly.

"You are a man. Well, he was a gawky, slouchy, shy farmer boy when he came to us. Of course the city life and popularity began to influence him. Then he met Nan. She made the Rube a worshiper. I first noticed a change in his clothes. He blossomed out in a new suit, white negligee, neat tie and a stylish straw hat. Then it was evident he was making heroic struggles to overcome his awkwardness. It was plain he was studying and copying the other boys. He's wonderfully improved, but still shy. He'll always be shy. Connie, Whit's a fine fellow, too good for Nan Brown."

"But, Milly," I interrupted, "the Rube's hard hit. Why is he too good for her?"

"Nan is a natural-born flirt," Milly replied. "She can't help it. I'm afraid Whit has a slim chance. Nan may not see deep enough to learn his fine qualities. I fancy Nan tired quickly of him, though the one time I saw them together she appeared to like him very well. This new pitcher of yours, Henderson, is a handsome fellow and smooth. Whit is losing to him. Nan likes flash, flattery, excitement."

"McCall told me the Rube had been down in the mouth ever since Henderson joined the team. Milly, I don't like Henderson a whole lot. He's not in the Rube's class as pitcher. What am I going to do? Lose the pennant and a big slice of purse money just for a pretty little flirt?"

"Oh, Connie, it's not so bad as that. Whit will come around all right."

"He won't unless we can pull some wires. I've got to help him win Nan Brown. What do you think of that for a manager's job? I guess maybe winning pennants doesn't call for diplomatic genius and cun-

THE RUBE'S WATERLOO

ning! But I'll hand them a few tricks before I lose. My first move will be
to give Henderson his release."

I left Milly, as always, once more able to make light of discouragements and difficulties.

Monday I gave Henderson his unconditional release. He celebrated
the occasion by verifying certain rumors I had heard from other managers. He got drunk. But he did not leave town, and I heard that he was
negotiating with Providence for a place on that team.

Radbourne pitched one of his gilt-edged games that afternoon against
Hartford and we won. And Milly sat in the grandstand, having contrived
by cleverness to get a seat next to Nan Brown. Milly and I were playing
a vastly deeper game than baseball—a game with hearts. But we were
playing it with honest motive, for the good of all concerned, we believed, and on the square. I sneaked a look now and then up into the
grandstand. Milly and Nan appeared to be getting on famously. It was
certain that Nan was flushed and excited, no doubt consciously proud
of being seen with my affianced. After the game I chanced to meet them
on their way out. Milly winked at me, which was her sign that all was
working beautifully.

I hunted up the Rube and bundled him off to the hotel to take dinner with me. At first he was glum, but after a while he brightened up
somewhat to my persistent cheer and friendliness. Then we went out on
the hotel balcony to smoke, and there I made my play.

"Whit, I'm pulling a stroke for you. Now listen and don't be offended.
I know what's put you off your feed, because I was the same way when
Milly had me guessing. You've lost your head over Nan Brown. That's
not so terrible, though I daresay you think it's a catastrophe. Because
you've quit. You've shown a yellow streak. You've lain down.

"My boy, that isn't the way to win a girl. You've got to scrap. Milly
told me yesterday how she had watched your love affair with Nan, and
how she thought you had given up just when things might have come
your way. Nan is a little flirt, but she's all right. What's more, she was
getting fond of you. Nan is meanest to the man she likes best. The
way to handle her, Whit, is to master her. Play high and mighty. Get

tragical. Then grab her up in your arms. I tell you, Whit, it'll all come your way if you only keep your nerve. I'm your friend and so is Milly. We're going out to her house presently—and Nan will be there."

The Rube drew a long, deep breath and held out his hand. I sensed another stage in the evolution of Whit Hurtle.

"I reckon I've taken baseball coachin'," he said presently, "an' I don't see why I can't take some other kind. I'm only a Rube, an' things come hard for me, but I'm a-learnin'."

It was about dark when we arrived at the house.

"Hello, Connie. You're late. Good evening, Mr. Hurtle. Come right in. You've met Miss Nan Brown? Oh, of course; how stupid of me!"

It was a trying moment for Milly and me. A little pallor showed under the Rube's tan, but he was more composed than I had expected. Nan got up from the piano. She was all in white and deliciously pretty. She gave a quick, glad start of surprise. What a relief that was to my troubled mind! Everything had depended upon a real honest liking for Whit, and she had it.

More than once I had been proud of Milly's cleverness, but this night as hostess and an accomplice she won my everlasting admiration. She contrived to give the impression that Whit was a frequent visitor at her home and very welcome. She brought out his best points, and in her skillful hands he lost embarrassment and awkwardness. Before the evening was over Nan regarded Whit with different eyes, and she never dreamed that everything had not come about naturally. Then Milly somehow got me out on the porch, leaving Nan and Whit together.

"Milly, you're a marvel, the best and sweetest ever," I whispered. "We're going to win. It's a cinch."

"Well, Connie, not that—exactly," she whispered back demurely. "But it looks hopeful."

I could not help hearing what was said in the parlor.

"Now I can roast you," Nan was saying, archly. She had switched back to her favorite baseball vernacular. "You pitched a swell game last Saturday in Rochester, didn't you? Not! You had no steam, no control, and you couldn't have curved a saucer."

"Nan, what could you expect?" was the cool reply. "You sat up in the stand with your handsome friend. I reckon I couldn't pitch. I just gave the game away."

"Whit!–Whit!–"

Then I whispered to Milly that it might be discreet for us to move a little way from the vicinity.

It was on the second day afterward that I got a chance to talk to Nan. She reached the grounds early, before Milly arrived, and I found her in the grandstand. The Rube was down on the card to pitch and when he started to warm up Nan said confidently that he would shut out Hartford that afternoon.

"I'm sorry, Nan, but you're way off. We'd do well to win at all, let alone get a shutout."

"You're a fine manager!" she retorted, hotly. "Why won't we win?"

"Well, the Rube's not in good form. The Rube–"

"Stop calling him that horrid name."

"Whit's not in shape. He's not right. He's ill or something is wrong. I'm worried sick about him."

Why–Mr. Connelly!" exclaimed Nan. She turned quickly toward me.

I crowded on a full canvas of gloom to my already long face.

"I'm serious, Nan. The lad's off, somehow. He's in magnificent physical trim, but he can't keep his mind on the game. He has lost his head. I've talked with him, reasoned with him, all to no good. He only goes down deeper in the dumps. Something is terribly wrong with him, and if he doesn't brace, I'll have to release–"

Miss Nan Brown suddenly lost a little of her rich bloom. "Oh! you wouldn't–you couldn't release him!"

"I'll have to if he doesn't brace. It means a lot to me, Nan, for of course I can't win the pennant this year without Whit being in shape. But I believe I wouldn't mind the loss of that any more than to see him fall down. The boy is a magnificent pitcher. If he can only be brought around he'll go to the big league next year and develop into one of the greatest pitchers the game has ever produced. But somehow or other he has lost heart. He's quit. And I've done my best for him. He's beyond me now. What a shame it is! For he's the making of such a splendid man

43

outside of baseball. Milly thinks the world of him. Well, well; there are disappointments—we can't help them. There goes the gong. I must leave you. Nan, I'll bet you a box of candy Whit loses today. Is it a go?"

"It is," replied Nan, with fire in her eyes. "You go to Whit Hurtle and tell him I said if he wins today's game I'll kiss him!"

I nearly broke my neck over benches and bats getting to Whit with that message. He gulped once.

Then he tightened his belt and shut out Hartford with two scratch singles. It was a great exhibition of pitching. I had no means to tell whether or not the Rube got his reward that night, but I was so happy that I hugged Milly within an inch of her life.

But it turned out that I had been a little premature in my elation. In two days the Rube went down into the depths again, this time clear to China, and Nan was sitting in the grandstand with Henderson. The Rube lost his next game, pitching like a schoolboy scared out of his wits. Henderson followed Nan like a shadow, so that I had no chance to talk to her. The Rube lost his next game and then another. We were pushed out of second place.

If we kept up that losing streak a little longer, our hopes for the pennant were gone. I had begun to despair of the Rube. For some occult reason he scarcely spoke to me. Nan flirted worse than ever. It seemed to me she flaunted her conquest of Henderson in poor Whit's face.

The Providence ball team came to town and promptly signed Henderson and announced him for Saturday's game. Cairns won the first of the series and Radbourne lost the second. It was Rube's turn to pitch the Saturday game and I resolved to make one more effort to put the lovesick swain in something like his old fettle. So I called upon Nan.

She was surprised to see me, but received me graciously. I fancied her face was not quite so glowing as usual. I came bluntly out with my mission. She tried to freeze me but I would not freeze. I was out to win or lose and not to be lightly laughed aside or coldly denied. I played to make her angry, knowing the real truth of her feelings would show under stress.

For once in my life I became a knocker and said some unpleasant things—albeit they were true—about Henderson. She championed Henderson royally, and when, as a last card, I compared Whit's fine record with Henderson's, not only as a ballplayer, but as a man, particularly in his reverence for women, she flashed at me:

"What do you know about it? Mr. Henderson asked me to marry him. Can a man do more to show his respect? Your friend never so much as hinted such honorable intentions. What's more—he insulted me!" The blaze in Nan's black eyes softened with a film of tears. She looked hurt. Her pride had encountered a fall.

"Oh, no, Nan, Whit couldn't insult a lady." I protested.

"Couldn't he? That's all you know about him. You know I—I promised to kiss him if he beat Hartford that day. So when he came I—I did. Then the big savage began to rave and he grabbed me up in his arms. He smothered me; almost crushed the life out of me. He frightened me terribly. When I got away from him—the monster stood there and coolly said I belonged to him. I ran out of the room and wouldn't see him anymore. At first I might have forgiven him if he had apologized—said he was sorry, but never a word. Now I never will forgive him."

I had to make a strenuous effort to conceal my agitation. The Rube had most carefully taken my fool advice in the matter of wooing a woman.

When I had got a hold upon myself, I turned to Nan white-hot with eloquence. Now I was talking not wholly for myself or the pennant, but for this boy and girl who were at odds in the strangest game of life—love.

What I said I never knew, but Nan lost her resentment, and then her scorn and indifference. Slowly she thawed and warmed to my reason, praise, whatever it was, and when I stopped she was again the radiant bewildering Nan of old. "Take another message to Whit for me," she said, audaciously. "Tell him I adore ballplayers, especially pitchers. Tell him I'm going to the game today to choose the best one. If he loses the game—"

She left the sentence unfinished. In my state of mind I doubted not in the least that she meant to marry the pitcher who won the game, and so I told the Rube. He made one wild upheaval of his arms and shoulders, like an erupting volcano, which proved to me that he believed it, too.

When I got to the bench that afternoon I was tired. There was a big crowd to see the game; the weather was perfect; Milly sat up in the box and waved her scorecard at me; Raddy and Spears declared we had the game; the Rube stalked to and fro like an implacable Indian chief—but I was not happy in mind. Calamity breathed in the very air.

The game began. McCall beat out a bunt; Ashwell sacrificed and Stringer laced one of his beautiful triples against the fence. Then he scored on a high fly. Two runs! Worcester trotted out into the field. The Rube was white with determination; he had the speed of a bullet and perfect control of his jumpball and drop. But Providence hit and had the luck. Ashwell fumbled, Gregg threw wild. Providence tied the score.

The game progressed, growing more and more of a nightmare to me. It was not Worcester's day. The umpire could not see straight; the boys grumbled and fought among themselves; Spears roasted the umpire and was sent to the bench; Bogart tripped, hurting his sore ankle, and had to be taken out. Henderson's slow, easy ball baffled my players, and when he used speed they lined it straight at a Providence fielder.

In the sixth, after a desperate rally, we crowded the bases with only one out. Then Mullaney's hard rap to left, seemingly good for three bases, was pulled down by Stone with one hand. It was a wonderful catch and he doubled up a runner at second. Again in the seventh we had a chance to score, only to fail on another double play, this time by the infield.

When the Providence players were at bat their luck not only held good but trebled and quadrupled. The little Texas-league hits dropped safely just out of reach of the infielders. My boys had an off day in fielding. What horror that of all days in a season this should be the one for them to make errors!

But they were game, and the Rube was the gamest of all. He did not seem to know what hard luck was, or discouragement, or poor support. He kept everlastingly hammering the ball at those lucky Providence hitters. What speed he had! The ball streaked in, and somebody would shut his eyes and make a safety. But the Rube pitched on, tireless, irresistibly, hopeful, not forgetting to call a word of cheer to his fielders.

It was one of those strange games that could not be bettered by any labor or daring or skill. I saw it was lost from the second inning, yet so deeply was I concerned, so tantalizingly did the plays reel themselves off, that I groveled there on the bench unable to abide by my baseball sense.

The ninth inning proved beyond a shadow of doubt how baseball fate, in common with other fates, loved to balance the chances, to lift up one, then the other, to lend a deceitful hope only to dash it away.

Providence had almost three times enough to win. The team let up in that inning or grew overconfident or careless, and before we knew what had happened some scratch hits, and bases on balls, and errors, gave us three runs and left two runners on bases. The disgusted bleachers came out of their gloom and began to whistle and thump. The Rube hit safely, sending another run over the plate. McCall worked his old trick, beating out a slow bunt.

Bases full, three runs to tie! With Ashwell up and one out, the noise in the bleachers mounted to a high-pitched, shrill, continuous sound. I got up and yelled with all my might and could not hear my voice. Ashwell was a dangerous man in a pinch. The game was not lost yet. A hit, anything to get Ash to first—and then Stringer!

Ash laughed at Henderson, taunted him, shook his bat at him and dared him to put one over. Henderson did not stand under fire. The ball he pitched had no steam. Ash cracked it—square on the line into the shortstop's hands. The bleachers ceased yelling.

Then Stringer strode grimly to the plate. It was a hundred to one, in that instance, that he would lose the ball. The bleachers let out one deafening roar, then hushed. I would rather have had Stringer at the bat than any other player in the world, and I thought of the Rube and Nan and Milly—and hope would not die.

Stringer swung mightily on the first pitch and struck the ball with a sharp, solid bing! It shot toward center, low, level, exceedingly swift, and like a dark streak went straight into the fielder's hands. A rod to right or left would have made it a home run. The crowd strangled a victorious yell. I came out of my trance, for the game was over and lost. It was the Rube's Waterloo.

I hurried him into the dressing room and kept close to him. He looked like a man who had lost the one thing worthwhile in his life. I turned a deaf ear to my players, to everybody, and hustled the Rube out and to the hotel. I wanted to be near him that night.

To my amazement we met Milly and Nan as we entered the lobby. Milly wore a sweet, sympathetic smile. Nan shone more radiant than ever. I simply stared. It was Milly who got us all through the corridor into the parlor. I heard Nan talking.

"Whit, you pitched a bad game but"—there was the old teasing, arch, coquettishness—"but you are the best pitcher!"

"Nan!"

"Yes!"

*Ringold W. Lardner (1885–1933) is widely praised as one of America's best short-story writers. The great critic Edmund Wilson and others likened Lardner to Mark Twain. Britain's queen of literature, Virginia Woolf, said that "he writes the best prose to come our way." The story below, one of three by Lardner in this book, is about a ballplayer who has an excuse for everything, even what he does very well. A fine satirist, Lardner pokes fun at the delightfully goofy Alibi Ike, while more broadly lampooning the apologists, complainers, and prevaricators among us. Born in Niles, Michigan, Lardner left engineering school after two years to become a reporter for the* South Bend Tribune. *He made his early mark as a sportswriter with the* Chicago Tribune. *It was there that he wrote the first of his "You Know Me, Al" stories, which caused a national sensation when published in the* Saturday Evening Post.

# Ring Lardner

# ALIBI IKE (1915)

## 1

**H**IS RIGHT NAME WAS FRANK X. Farrell, and I guess the X stood for "Excuse me." Because he never pulled a play, good or bad, on or off the field, without apologizin' for it.

"Alibi Ike" was the name Carey wished on him the first day he reported down south. O' course we all cut out the "Alibi" part of it right away for the fear he would overhear it and bust somebody. But we called him "Ike" right to his face and the rest of it was understood by everybody on the club except Ike himself.

He ast me one time, he says:

"What do you all call me Ike for? I ain't no Yid."

"Carey give you the name," I says. "It's his nickname for everybody he takes a likin' to."

"He mustn't have only a few friends then," says Ike. "I never heard him say 'Ike' to nobody else."

But I was goin' to tell you about Carey namin' him. We'd been workin' out two weeks and the pitchers was showin' somethin' when this bird joined us. His first day out he stood up there so good and took such a reef at the old pill that he had everyone lookin'. Then him and Carey was together in left field, catchin' fungoes, and it was after we was through for the day that Carey told me about him.

"What do you think of Alibi Ike?" ast Carey.

"Who's that?" I says.

"This here Farrell in the outfield," says Carey.

"He looks like he could hit," I says.

"Yes," says Carey, "but he can't hit near as good as he can apologize."

Then Carey went on to tell me what Ike had been pullin' out there. He'd dropped the first fly ball that was hit to him and told Carey his glove wasn't broke in good yet, and Carey says the glove could easy of been Kid Gleason's gran'father. He made a whale of a catch out o' the next one and Carey says "Nice work!" or somethin' like that, but Ike says he could of caught the ball with his back turned only he slipped when he started after it and, besides that, the air currents fooled him.

"I thought you done well to get to the ball," says Carey.

"I ought to been settin' under it," says Ike.

"What did you hit last year?" Carey ast him.

"I had malaria most o' the season," says Ike. "I wound up with .356."

"Where would I have to go to get malaria?" says Carey, but Ike didn't wise up.

I and Carey and him set at the same table together for supper. It took him half an hour longer'n us to eat because he had to excuse himself every time he lifted his fork.

"Doctor told me I needed starch," he'd say, and then toss a shovelful o' potatoes into him. Or, "They ain't much meat on one o' these chops," he'd tell us, and grab another one. Or he'd say: "Nothin' like onions for a cold," and then he'd dip into the perfumery.

"Better try that apple sauce," says Carey. "It'll help your malaria."

"Whose malaria?" says Ike. He'd forgot already why he didn't only hit .356 last year.

I and Carey begin to lead him on.

"Whereabouts did you say your home was?" I ast him.

"I live with my folks," he says. "We live in Kansas City—not right down in the business part—outside a ways."

"How's that come?" says Carey. "I should think you'd get rooms in the post office."

But Ike was too busy curin' his cold to get that one.

"Are you married?" I ast him.

"No," he says. "I never run round much with girls, except to shows onct in a wile and parties and dances and roller skatin'."

"Never take 'em to the prize fights, eh?" says Carey.

"We don't have no real good bouts," says Ike. "Just bush stuff. And I never figured a boxin' match was a place for the ladies."

Well, after supper he pulled a cigar out and lit it. I was just goin' to ask him what he done it for, but he beat me to it.

"Kind o' rests a man to smoke after a good work-out," he says. "Kind o' settles a man's supper, too."

"Looks like a pretty good cigar," says Carey.

"Yes," says Ike. "A friend o' mine give it to me—a fella in Kansas City that runs a billiard room."

"Do you play billiards?" I ast him.

"I used to play a fair game," he says. "I'm all out o' practice now—can't hardly make a shot."

We coaxed him into a four-handed battle, him and Carey against Jack Mack and I. Say, he couldn't play billiards as good as Willie Hoppe; not quite. But to hear him tell it, he didn't make a good shot all evenin'. I'd leave him an awful-lookin' layout and he'd gather 'em up in one try and then run a couple o' hundred, and between every carom he'd say he'd put too much stuff on the ball, or the English didn't take, or the table wasn't true, or his stick was crooked, or somethin'. And all the time he had the balls actin' like they was Dutch soldiers and him Kaiser William. We started out to play fifty points, but we had to make it a thousand so as I and Jack and Carey could try the table.

The four of us set round the lobby a wile after we was through playin', and when it got along toward bedtime Carey whispered to me and says:

"Ike'd like to go to bed, but he can't think up no excuse."

Carey hadn't hardly finished whisperin' when Ike got up and pulled it:

"Well, good night, boys," he says. "I ain't sleepy, but I got some gravel in my shoes and it's killin' my feet."

We knowed he hadn't never left the hotel since we'd came in from the grounds and changed our clo'es. So Carey says:

"I should think they'd take them gravel pits out o' the billiard room."

But Ike was already on his way to the elevator, limpin'.

"He's got the world beat," says Carey to Jack and I. "I've knew lots o' guys that had an alibi for every mistake they made; I've heard pitchers say that the ball slipped when somebody cracked one off'n 'em; I've heard infielders complain of a sore arm after heavin' one into the stand, and I've saw outfielders tooken sick with a dizzy spell when they've misjudged a fly ball. But this baby can't even go to bed without apologizin', and I bet he excuses himself to the razor when he gets ready to shave."

"And at that," says Jack, "he's goin' to make us a good man."

"Yes," says Carey, "unless rheumatism keeps his battin' average down to .400."

Well, sir, Ike kept whalin' away at the ball all through the trip till everybody knowed he'd won a job. Cap had him in there regular the last few exhibition games and told the newspaper boys a week before the season opened that he was goin' to start him in Kane's place.

"You're there, kid," says Carey to Ike, the night Cap made the 'nnouncement. "They ain't many boys that wins a big league berth their third year out."

"I'd of been up here a year ago," says Ike, "only I was bent over all season with lumbago."

# 2

It rained down in Cincinnati one day and somebody organized a little game o' cards. They was shy two men to make six and ast I and Carey to play.

"I'm with you if you get Ike and make it seven-handed," says Carey.

So they got a hold of Ike and we went up to Smitty's room.

"I pretty near forgot how many you deal," says Ike. "It's been a long wile since I played."

I and Carey give each other the wink, and sure enough, he was just as ig'orant about poker as billiards. About the second hand, the pot was opened two or three ahead of him, and they was three in when it come his turn. It cost a buck, and he throwed in two.

"It's raised, boys," somebody says.

"Gosh, that's right, I did raise it," says Ike.

"Take out a buck if you didn't mean to tilt her," says Carey.

"No," says Ike, "I'll leave it go."

Well, it was raised back at him and then he made another mistake and raised again. They was only three left in when the draw come. Smitty'd opened with a pair o' kings and he didn't help 'em. Ike stood pat. The guy that'd raised him back was flushin' and he didn't fill. So Smitty checked and Ike bet and didn't get no call. He tossed his hand away, but I grabbed it and give it a look. He had king, queen, jack and two tens. Alibi Ike he must have seen me peekin', for he leaned over and whispered to me.

"I overlooked my hand," he says. "I thought all the wile it was a straight."

"Yes," I says, "that's why you raised twice by mistake."

They was another pot that he come into with tens and fours. It was tilted a couple o' times and two o' the strong fellas drawed ahead of Ike. They each drawed one. So Ike threw away his little pair and come out with four tens. And they was four treys against him. Carey'd looked at Ike's discards and then he says:

"This lucky bum busted two pair."

"No, no, I didn't," says Ike.

"Yes, yes, you did," says Carey, and showed us the two fours.

"What do you know about that?" says Ike. "I'd of swore one was a five spot."

Well, we hadn't had no pay day yet, and after a wile everybody except Ike was goin' shy. I could see him gettin' restless and I was wonderin' how he'd make the get-away. He tried two or three times. "I got to buy some collars before supper," he says.

"No hurry," says Smitty. "The stores here keeps open all night in April."

After a minute he opened up again.

"My uncle out in Nebraska ain't expected to live," he says. "I ought to send a telegram."

"Would that save him?" says Carey.

"No, it sure wouldn't," says Ike, "but I ought to leave my old man know where I'm at."

"When did you hear about your uncle?" says Carey.

"Just this mornin'," says Ike.

"Who told you?" ast Carey.

"I got a wire from my old man," says Ike.

"Well," says Carey, "your old man knows you're still here yet this afternoon if you was here this mornin'. Trains leavin' Cincinnati in the middle o' the day don't carry no ball clubs."

"Yes," says Ike, "that's true. But he don't know where I'm goin' to be next week."

"Ain't he got no schedule?" ast Carey.

"I sent him one openin' day," says Ike, "But it takes mail a long time to get to Idaho."

"I thought your old man lived in Kansas City," says Carey.

"He does when he's home," says Ike.

"But now," says Carey, "I s'pose he's went to Idaho so as he can be near your sick uncle in Nebraska."

"He's visitin' my other uncle in Idaho."

"Then how does he keep posted about your sick uncle?" ast Carey.

"He don't," says Ike. "He don't even know my other uncle's sick. That's why I ought to wire and tell him."

"Good night!" says Carey.

"What town in Idaho is your old man at?" I says.

Ike thought it over.

"No town at all," he says. "But he's near a town."

"Near what town?" I says.

"Yuma," says Ike.

Well, by this time he'd lost two or three pots and he was desperate. We was playin' just as fast as we could, because we seen we couldn't hold him much longer. But he was tryin' so hard to frame an escape that he couldn't pay no attention to the cards, and it looked like we'd get his whole pile away from him if we could make him stick.

The telephone saved him. The minute it begun to ring, five of us jumped for it. But Ike was there first.

"Yes," he says, answerin' it. "This is him. I'll come right down."

And he slammed up the receiver and beat it out o' the door without even sayin' good-bye.

"Smitty'd ought to locked the door," says Carey.

"What did he win? ast Carey.

We figured it up—sixty-odd bucks.

"And the next time we ask him to play," says Carey, "his fingers will be so stiff he can't hold the cards."

Well, we set round a wile talkin' it over, and pretty soon the telephone rung again. Smitty answered it. It was a friend of his'n from Hamilton and he wanted to know why Smitty didn't hurry down. He was the one that had called before and Ike had told him he was Smitty.

"Ike'd ought to split with Smitty's friend," says Carey.

"No," I says, "he'll need all he won. It costs money to buy collars and to send telegrams from Cincinnati to your old man in Texas and keep him posted on the health o' your uncle in Cedar Rapids, D.C."

## 3

And you ought to heard him out there on that field! They wasn't a day when he didn't pull six or seven, and it didn't make no difference whether he was goin' good or bad. If he popped up in the pinch he should of made a base hit and the reason he didn't was so-and-so. And if he cracked one for three bases he ought to had a home run, only the ball wasn't lively, or the wind brought it back, or he tripped on a lump o' dirt, roundin' first base.

They was one afternoon in New York when he beat all records. Big Marquard was workin' against us and he was good.

In the first innin' Ike hit one clear over that right field stand, but it was a few feet foul. Then he got another foul and then the count come to two and two. Then Rube slipped one acrost on him and he was called out.

"What do you know about that!" he says afterward on the bench. "I lost count. I thought it was three and one, and I took a strike."

"You took a strike all right," says Carey. "Even the umps knowed it was a strike."

"Yes," says Ike, "but you can bet I wouldn't of took it if I'd knew it was the third one. The score board had it wrong."

"That score board ain't for you to look at," says Cap. "It's for you to hit that old pill against."

"Well," says Ike, "I could of hit that one over the score board if I'd knew it was the third."

"Was it a good ball?" I says.

"Well, no, it wasn't," says Ike. "It was inside."

"How far inside?" says Carey.

"Oh, two or three inches or half a foot," says Ike.

"I guess you wouldn't of threatened the score board with it then," says Cap.

"I'd of pulled it down the right foul line if I hadn't thought he'd call it a ball," says Ike.

Well, in New York's part o' the innin' Doyle cracked one and Ike run back a mile and a half and caught it with one hand. We was all sayin' what a whale of a play it was, but he had to apologize just the same as for gettin' struck out.

"That stand's so high," he says, "that a man don't never see a ball till it's right on top o' you."

"Didn't you see that one?" ast Cap.

"Not at first," says Ike; "not till it raised up above the roof o' the stand."

"Then why did you start back as soon as the ball was hit?" says Cap.

"I knowed by the sound that he'd got a good hold of it," says Ike.

"Yes," says Cap, "but how'd you know what direction to run in?"

"Doyle usually hits 'em that way, the way I run," says Ike.

"Why don't you play blindfolded?" says Carey.

"Might as well, with that big high stand to bother a man," says Ike. "If I could of saw the ball all the time I'd of got it in my hip pocket."

Along in the fifth we was one run to the bad and Ike got on with one out. On the first ball throwed to Smitty, Ike went down. The ball was outside and Meyers throwed Ike out by ten feet.

You could see Ike's lips movin' all the way to the bench and when he got there he had his piece learned.

"Why didn't he swing?" he says.

"Why didn't you wait for his sign?" says Cap.

"He give me his sign," says Ike.

"What is his sign with you?" says Cap.

"Pickin' up some dirt with his right hand," says Ike.

"Well, I didn't see him do it," Cap says.

"He done it all right," says Ike.

Well, Smitty went out and they wasn't no more argument till they come in for the next innin'. Then Cap opened it up.

"You fellas better get your signs straight," he says.

"Do you mean me?" says Smitty.

"Yes," Cap says. "What's your sign with Ike?"

"Slidin' my left hand up to the end o' the bat and back," says Smitty.

"Do you hear that, Ike?" ast Cap.

"What of it?" says Ike.

"You says his sign was pickin' up dirt and he says it's slidin' his hand. Which is right?"

"I'm right," says Smitty. "But if you're arguin' about him goin' last innin', I didn't give him no sign."

"You pulled your cap down with your right hand, didn't you?" ast Ike.

"Well, s'pose I did," says Smitty. "That don't mean nothin'. I never told you to take that for a sign, did I?"

"I thought maybe you meant to tell me and forgot," says Ike.

They couldn't none of us answer that and they wouldn't of been no more said if Ike had of shut up. But wile we was settin' there Carey got on with two out and stole second clean.

"There!" says Ike. "That's what I was tryin' to do and I'd of got away with it if Smitty'd swang and bothered the Indian."

"Oh!" says Smitty. "You was tryin' to steal then, was you? I thought you claimed I give you the hit and run."

"I didn't claim no such a thing," says Ike. "I thought maybe you might of gave me a sign, but I was goin' anyway because I thought I had a good start."

Cap prob'ly would of hit him with a bat, only just about that time Doyle booted one on Hayes and Carey come acrost with the run that tied.

Well, we go into the ninth finally, one and one, and Marquard walks McDonald with nobody out.

"Lay it down," says Cap to Ike.

And Ike goes up there with orders to bunt and cracks the first ball into that right-field stand! It was fair this time, and we're two ahead, but I didn't think about that at the time. I was too busy watchin' Cap's face. First he turned pale and then he got red as fire and then he got blue and purple, and finally he just laid back and busted out laughin'. So we wasn't afraid to laugh ourself when we seen him doin' it, and when Ike come in everybody on the bench was in hysterics.

But instead o' takin' advantage, Ike had to try and excuse himself. His play was to shut up and he didn't know how to make it.

"Well," he says, "if I hadn't hit quite so quick at that one I bet it'd of cleared the center-field fence."

Cap stopped laughin'.

"It'll cost you plain fifty," he says.

"What for?" says Ike.

"When I say 'bunt' I mean 'bunt,' " says Cap.

"You didn't say 'bunt,' " says Ike.

"I says 'Lay it down,' " says Cap. "If that don't mean 'bunt,' what does it mean?"

" 'Lay it down' means 'bunt' all right," says Ike, "but I understood you to say 'Lay on it.' "

"All right," says Cap, "and the little misunderstandin' will cost you fifty."

Ike didn't say nothin' for a few minutes. Then he had another bright idear.

"I was just kiddin' about misunderstandin' you," he says. "I knowed you wanted me to bunt."

"Well, then, why didn't you bunt?" ast Cap.

"I was goin' to on the next ball," says Ike. "But I thought if I took a good wallop I'd have 'em all fooled. So I walloped at the first one to fool 'em, and I didn't have no intention o' hittin' it."

"You tried to miss it, did you?" says Cap.

"Yes," says Ike.

"How'd you happen to hit it?" ast Cap.

"Well," Ike says, "I was lookin' for him to throw me a fast one and I was goin' to swing under it. But he come with a hook and I met it right square where I was swingin' to go under the fast one."

"Great!" says Cap. "Boys," he says, "Ike's learned how to hit Marquard's curve. Pretend a fast one's comin' and then try to miss it. It's a good thing to know and Ike'd ought to be willin' to pay for the lesson. So I'm goin' to make it a hundred instead o' fifty."

The game wound up 3 to 1. The fine didn't go, because Ike hit like a wild man all through that trip and we made pretty near a clean-up. The night we went to Philly I got him cornered in the car and I says to him:

"Forget them alibis for a wile and tell me somethin'. What'd you do that for, swing that time against Marquard when you was told to bunt?"

"I'll tell you," he says. "That ball he throwed me looked just like the one I struck out on in the first innin' and I wanted to show Cap what I could of done to that other one if I'd knew it was the third strike."

"But," I says, "the one you struck out on in the first innin' was a fast ball."

"So was the one I cracked in the ninth," says Ike.

# 4

You've saw Cap's wife, o' course. Well, her sister's about twict as good-lookin' as her, and that's goin' some.

Cap took his missus down to St. Louis the second trip and the other one come down from St. Joe to visit her. Her name is Dolly, and some doll is right.

Well, Cap was goin' to take the two sisters to a show and he wanted a beau for Dolly. He left it to her and she picked Ike. He'd hit three on the nose that afternoon—off 'n Sallee, too.

They fell for each other that first evenin'. Cap told us how it come off. She begin flatterin' Ike for the star game he'd played and o' course he begin excusin' himself for not doin' better. So she thought he was modest and it went strong with her. And she believed everything he said and that made her solid with him—that and her make-up. They was together every mornin' and evenin' for the five days we was there. In the afternoons Ike played the grandest ball you ever see, hittin' and runnin' the bases like a fool and catchin' everything that stayed in the park.

I told Cap, I says: "You'd ought to keep the doll with us and he'd make Cobb's figures look sick."

But Dolly had to go back to St. Joe and we come home for a long serious.

Well, for the next three weeks Ike had a letter to read every day and he'd set in the clubhouse readin' it till mornin' practice was half over. Cap didn't say nothin' to him, because he was goin' so good. But I and Carey wasted a lot of our time tryin' to get him to own up who the letters was from. Fine chanct!

"What are you readin'?" Carey'd say. "A bill?"

"No," Ike'd say, "not exactly a bill. It's a letter from a fella I used to go to school with."

"High school or college?" I'd ask him.

"College," he'd say.

Then he'd stall a wile and then he'd say:

"I didn't go to the college myself, but my friend went there."

"How did it happen you didn't go?" Carey'd ask him.

"Well," he'd say, "they wasn't no colleges near where I lived."

"Didn't you live in Kansas City?" I'd say to him.

One time he'd say he did and another time he didn't. One time he says he lived in Michigan.

"Where at?" says Carey.

"Near Detroit," he says.

"Well," I says, "Detroit's near Ann Arbor and that's where they got the university."

"Yes," says Ike, "they got it there now, but they didn't have it there then."

"I come pretty near goin' to Syracuse," I says, "only they wasn't no railroads runnin' through there in them days."

"Where'd this friend o' yours go to college?" says Carey.

"I forget now," says Ike.

"Was it Carlisle?" ast Carey.

"No," says Ike, "His folks wasn't very well off."

"That's what barred me from Smith," I says.

"I was goin' to tackle Cornell's," says Carey, "But the doctor told me I'd have hay fever if I didn't stay up North."

"Your friend writes long letters," I says.

"Yes," says Ike; "he's tellin' me about a ballplayer."

"Where does he play?" ast Carey.

"Down in the Texas League—Fort Wayne," says Ike.

"It looks like a girl's writin'," Carey says.

"A girl wrote it," says Ike. "That's my friend's sister, writin' for him."

"Didn't they teach writin' at this here college where he went?" says Carey.

"Sure," Ike says, "they taught writin', but he got his hand cut off in a railroad wreck."

"How long ago?" I says.

"Right after he got out o' college," says Ike.

"Well," I says, "I should think he'd of learned to write with his left hand by this time."

"It's his left hand that was cut off," says Ike; "and he was left-handed."

"You get a letter every day," says Carey. "They're all the same writin'. Is he tellin' you about a different ball player every time he writes?"

"No," Ike says. "It's the same ball player. He just tells me what he does every day."

"From the size o' the letters, they don't play nothin' but double-headers down there," says Carey.

We figured that Ike spent most of his evenin's answerin' the letters from his "friend's sister," so we kept tryin' to date him up for shows and parties to see how he'd duck out of 'em. He was bugs over spaghetti, so we told him one day that they was goin' to be a big feed of it over to Joe's that night and he was invited.

"How long'll it last?" he says.

"Well," we says, "we're goin' right over there after the game and stay till they close up."

"I can't go," he says, "Unless they leave me come home at eight bells."

"Nothin' doin'," says Carey. "Joe'd get sore."

"I can't go then," says Ike.

"Why not?" I ast him.

"Well," he says, "my landlady locks up the house at eight and I left my key home."

"You can come and stay with me," says Carey.

"No," he says, "I can't sleep in a strange bed."

"How do you get along when we're on the road?" says I.

"I don't never sleep the first night anywheres," he says. "After that I'm all right."

"You'll have time to chase home and get your key right after the game," I told him.

"The key ain't home," says Ike. "I lent it to one o' the other fellas and he's went out o' town and took it with him."

"Couldn't you borry another key off 'n the landlady?" Carey ast him.

"No," he says, "that's the only one they is."

Well, the day before we started East again, Ike come into the club-house all smiles.

"Your birthday?" I ast him.

"No," he says.

"What do you feel so good about?" I says.

"Got a letter from my old man," he says. "My uncle's goin' to get well."

"Is that the one in Nebraska?" says I.

"Not right in Nebraska," says Ike. "Near there."

But afterwards we got the right dope from Cap. Dolly'd blew in from Missouri and was goin' to make the trip with her sister.

# 5

Well, I want to alibi Carey and I for what come off in Boston. If we'd of had any idear what we was doin', we'd never did it. They wasn't nobody outside o' maybe Ike and the dame that felt worse over it than I and Carey.

The first two days we didn't see nothin' of Ike and her except out to the park. The rest o' the time they was sight-seein' over to Cambridge and down to Revere and out to Brook-a-line and all the other places where the rubes go.

But when we come into the beanery after the third game Cap's wife called us over.

"If you want to see somethin' pretty," she says, "look at the third finger on Sis's left hand."

Well, o' course we knowed before we looked that it wasn't goin' to be no hangnail. Nobody was su'prised when Dolly blew into the dinin' room with it—a rock that Ike'd bought off 'n Diamond Joe the first trip to New York. Only o' course it'd been set into a lady's-size ring instead o' the automobile tire he'd been wearin'.

Cap and his missus and Ike and Dolly ett supper together, only Ike didn't eat nothin', but just set there blushin' and spillin' things on the table-cloth. I heard him excusin' himself for not havin' no appetite. He says he couldn't never eat when he was clost to the ocean. He'd forgot about them sixty-five oysters he destroyed the first night o' the trip before.

He was goin' to take her to a show, so after supper he went upstairs to change his collar. She had to doll up, too, and o' course Ike was through long before her.

If you remember the hotel in Boston, they's a little parlor where the piano's at and then they's another little parlor openin' off o' that. Well, when Ike come down Smitty was playin' a few chords and I and Carey was harmonizin'. We seen Ike go up to the desk to leave his key and we called him in. He tried to duck away, but we wouldn't stand for it.

We ast him what he was all duded up for and he says he was goin' to the theayter.

"Goin' alone?" says Carey.

"No," he says, "a friend o' mine's goin' with me."

"What do you say if we go along?" says Carey.

"I ain't only got two tickets," he says.

"Well," says Carey, "we can go down there with you and buy our own seats; maybe we can all go together."

"No," says Ike. "They ain't no more seats. They're all sold out."

"We can buy some off 'n the scalpers," says Carey.

"I wouldn't if I was you," says Ike. "They say the show's rotten."

"What are you goin' for, then?" I ast.

"I didn't hear about it bein' rotten till I got the tickets," he says.

"Well," I says, "if you don't want to go I'll buy the tickets from you."

"No," says Ike, "I wouldn't want to cheat you. I'm stung and I'll just have to stand for it."

"What are you goin' to do with the girl, leave her here at the hotel?"

"What girl?" says Ike.

"The girl you ett supper with." I says.

"Oh," he says, "we just happened to go into the dinin' room together, that's all. Cap wanted I should set down with 'em."

"I noticed," says Carey, "that she happened to be wearin' that rock you bought off 'n Diamond Joe."

"Yes," says Ike. "I lent it to her for a wile."

"Did you lend her the new ring that goes with it?" I says.

"She had that already," says Ike. "She lost the set out of it."

"I wouldn't trust no strange girl with a rock o' mine," says Carey.

"Oh, I guess she's all right," Ike says. "Besides, I was tired o' the stone. When a girl asks you for somethin', what are you goin' to do?"

He started out toward the desk, but we flagged him.

"Wait a minute!" Carey says. "I got a bet with Sam here, and it's up to you to settle it."

"Well," says Ike, "make it snappy. My friend'll be here any minute."

"I bet," says Carey, "that you and that girl was engaged to be married."

"Nothin to it," says Ike.

"Now look here," says Carey, "this is goin' to cost me real money if I lose. Cut out the alibi stuff and give it to us straight. Cap's wife just as good as told us you was roped."

Ike blushed like a kid.

"Well, boys," he says, "I may as well own up. You win, Carey."

"Yatta boy!" says Carey. "Congratulations!"

"You got a swell girl, Ike," I says.

"She's a peach," says Smitty.

"Well, I guess she's OK ," says Ike. "I don't know much about girls."

"Didn't you never run round with 'em?" I says.

"Oh, yes, plenty of 'em," says Ike. "But I never seen none I'd fall for."

"That is, till you seen this one," says Carey.

"Well," says Ike, "this one's OK , but I wasn't thinkin' about gettin' married yet a wile."

"Who done the askin'—her?" says Carey.

"O, no," says Ike, "but sometimes a man don't know what he's gettin' into. Take a good-lookin' girl, and a man gen'ally almost always does about what she wants him to."

"They couldn't no girl lasso me unless I wanted to be lassoed," says Smitty.

"Oh, I don't know," says Ike. "When a fella gets to feelin' sorry for one of 'em it's all off."

Well, we left him go after shakin' hands all round. But he didn't take Dolly to no show that night. Some time wile we was talkin' she'd came into that other parlor and she'd stood there and heard us. I don't know how much she heard. But it was enough. Dolly and Cap's missus took the midnight train for New York. And from there Cap's wife sent her on her way back to Missouri.

She'd left the ring and a note for Ike with the clerk. But we didn't ask Ike if the note was from his friend in Fort Wayne, Texas.

# 6

When we'd came to Boston Ike was hittin' plain .397. When we got back home he'd fell off to pretty near nothin'. He hadn't drove one out o' the infield in any o' them other Eastern parks, and he didn't even give no excuse for it.

To show you how bad he was, he struck out three times in Brooklyn one day and never opened his trap when Cap ast him what was the matter. Before, if he'd whiffed oncet in a game he'd of wrote a book tellin' why.

Well, we dropped from first place to fifth in four weeks and we was still goin' down. I and Carey was about the only ones in the club that spoke to each other, and all as we did was remind ourself o' what a boner we'd pulled.

"It's goin' to beat us out o' the big money," says Carey.

"Yes," I says. "I don't want to knock my own ball club, but it looks like a one-man team, and when that one man's dauber's down we couldn't trim our whiskers."

"We ought to knew better," says Carey.

"Yes," I says, "but why should a man pull an alibi for bein' engaged to such a bearcat as she was?"

"He shouldn't," says Carey. "But I and you knowed he would or we'd never started talkin' to him about it. He wasn't no more ashamed o' the girl than I am of a regular base hit. But he just can't come clean on no subjec'."

Cap had the whole story, and I and Carey was as pop'lar with him as an umpire.

"What do you want me to do, Cap?" Carey'd say to him before goin' up to hit.

"Use your own judgment," Cap'd tell him. "We want to lose another game."

But finally, one night in Pittsburgh, Cap had a letter from his missus and he come to us with it.

"You fellas," he says, "is the ones that put us on the bum, and if you're sorry I think theys a chancet for you to make good. The old lady's out to St. Joe and she's been tryin' her hardest to fix things up. She's explained that Ike don't mean nothin' with his talk; I've wrote and explained that to Dolly, too. But the old lady says that Dolly says that she can't believe it. But Dolly's still stuck on this baby, and she's pinin' away just the same as Ike. And the old lady says she thinks if you two fellas would write to the girl and explain how you was always kiddin' with Ike and leadin' him on, and how the ball club was all shot to pieces since Ike quit hittin', and how he acted like he was goin' to kill himself, and this and that, she'd fall for it and maybe soften down. Dolly, the old lady says, would believe you before she'd believe I and the old lady, because she thinks it's her we're sorry for, and not him."

Well, I and Carey was only too glad to try and see what we could do. But it wasn't no snap. We wrote about eight letters before we got one that looked good. Then we give it to the stenographer and had it wrote out on a typewriter and both of us signed it.

It was Carey's idear that made the letter good. He stuck in somethin' about the world's serious money that our wives wasn't goin' to spend unless she took pity on a "boy who was so shy and modest that he was afraid to come right out and say that he had asked such a beautiful and handsome girl to become his bride."

That's prob'ly what got her, or maybe she couldn't of held out much longer anyway. It was four days after we sent the letter that Cap heard from his missus again. We was in Cincinnati.

"We've won," he says to us. "The old lady says that Dolly says she'll give him another chance. But the old lady says it won't do no good for Ike to write a letter. He'll have to go out there."

"Send him tonight," says Carey.

"I'll pay half his fare," I says.

"I'll pay the other half," says Carey.

"No," says Cap, "the club'll pay his expenses. I'll send him scoutin'."

"Are you goin' to send him tonight?"

"Sure," says Cap. "But I'm goin' to break the news to him right now. It's time we win a ball game."

So in the clubhouse, just before the game, Cap told him. And I certainly felt sorry for Rube Benton and Red Ames that afternoon! I and Carey was standin' in front o' the hotel that night when Ike come out with his suitcase.

"Sent home?" I says to him.

"No," he says, "I'm goin' scoutin'."

"Where to?" I says. "Fort Wayne?"

"No, not exactly," he says.

"Well," says Carey, "have a good time."

"I ain't lookin' for no good time," says Ike. "I says I was goin' scoutin'."

"Well, then," says Carey, "I hope you see somebody you like."

"And you better have a drink before you go," I says.

"Well," says Ike, "they claim it helps a cold."

*Garrison Keillor was born in 1942 in Anoka, Minnesota. He received his bach-
elor's degree in English from the University of Minnesota. Keillor is well-known
for his novels, short stories, and a radio program called* A Prairie Home Companion, *featuring live music, humor, and variety. In 1980 this program, a staple of American Public Radio, won a George Foster Peabody Award for
distinguished broadcasting. "Three New Twins Join Club in Spring," the first
of two Keillor stories in the book, originally appeared in the* New Yorker. *It
contains the kind of folksy Midwest humor that typifies his work.*

*Garrison Keillor*

# THREE NEW TWINS JOIN CLUB IN SPRING (1988)

**M**Y TEAM WON THE WORLD Series. You thought we couldn't but
we knew we would and we did, and what did your team do? Not much.
Now we're heading down to spring training looking even better than before, and your team that looked pitiful then looks even less hot now.
Your hometown paper doesn't say so, but your leadoff guy had a bad
ear infection in January and now he gets dizzy at the first sign of stress
and falls down in a heap. Sad. Your cleanup guy spent the winter clean-
ing his plate. He had to buy new clothes in a size they don't sell at regular stores. Your great relief guy, his life has been changed by the Rama

Lama Ding Dong, and he is now serenely throwing the ball from a place deep within himself, near his gallbladder. What a shame. Your rookie outfielder set a world record for throwing a frozen chicken, at a promotional appearance for Grandma Fanny's Farm Foods. Something snapped in his armpit and now he can't even throw a pair of dice. Tough beans. Your big left-hander tried hypnosis to stop smoking and while in a trancelike state discovered he hated his mother for tying his tiny right hand behind his back and making him eat and draw and tinkle with his left. So he's right-handed now, a little awkward but gradually learning to point with it and wave goodbye. That's what your whole team'll be doing by early May.

Meanwhile, my team, the world-champion Minnesota Twins, are top dogs who look like a lead-pipe cinch to take all the marbles in a slow walk. My guys had a good winter doing youth work. Last October they pooled their Series pay to purchase a farm, Twin Acres, north of Willmar, where they could stay in shape doing chores in the off-season, and they loved it so much they stayed through Thanksgiving and Christmas (celebrating them the good old-fashioned Midwestern way), and raised a new barn, bought a powerful new seed drill to plant winter wheat with, built up the flock of purebred Leghorns, chopped wood, carried water, etc., along with their guests—delinquent boys and girls from St. Louis and Detroit who needed to get out of those sick and destructive environments and learn personal values such as hard work and personal cleanliness. Meanwhile, back in Minneapolis, the Twins front office wasn't asleep on its laurels but through shrewd deals made mostly before 8:15 A.M. added to what they had while giving up nothing in return. It seems unfair.

## Other Teams Gnash Teeth or Sulk

It's considered impossible to obtain *three top premium players* without paying a red cent, but the Twins:

Traded away some useless air rights for Chuck Johnson (23, 187 lbs., 6'1", bats left, throws left), a native of Little Falls, Minnesota. Maybe that's why the scouts who work the Finger Lakes League ignored his phenomenal season with the Seneca Falls Susans. They figured, "Minnesota? Forget it!" But how can you forget thirty-eight doubles, twenty-two triples, and twenty-nine round-trippers—and in spacious Elizabeth Cady Stanton Stadium! That's a lot of power for a lifelong liberal like Chuck. And what's more, he *never struck out*. Not once. Plays all positions cheerfully.

Sent a couple in their mid-forties to the San Diego Padres in exchange for Duane (Madman) Mueller (29, 280 lbs., 6'2", right/right, a.k.a. Mule, Hired Hand, The Barber). Duane is a big secret because after he was suspended by the Texas League for throwing too hard he played Nicaraguan winter ball for three years and then spent two more doing humanitarian stuff, so scouts forgot how, back when he was with the Amarillo Compadres, nobody wanted to be behind the plate, Duane threw so hard. His own team kept yelling, "Not so *hard*, Man!" If that sounds dumb, then you never saw him throw: he threw *hard*. A devoted Lutheran, he never ever hit a batter, but in one game a pitch of his nicked the bill of a batting helmet and spun it so hard it burned off the man's eyebrows. No serious injury, but big Duane took himself out of organized ball until he could learn an offspeed pitch. He's from Brainerd, Minnesota, where he lives across the street from his folks. His mom played kittenball in the fifties and had a good arm but not like her son's. She thinks he got it from delivering papers and whipping cake mix. "I'd sure hate to have to bat against him," she says.

Gave up a dingy two-bedroom house in St. Paul (it needs more than just a paint job and a new roof, and it's near a rendering plant) to acquire and activate Bob Berg (24, 112 lbs., 5'3", right/left), the fastest man on the base paths today (we *think*), but he sat out last year and the year before last and the year before *that* because he didn't have shoes. Reason: he's so fast he runs the shoes right off his own feet. Now athletic foot specialists have studied his film clips (sad to see: three lightning strides, a look of dismay on Bob's face, and down he goes with his loose laces like a lasso round his ankles) and come up with a new pair of pigskin shoes with barbed cleats that stick in the turf and slow him down. Born and raised in Eveleth, Minnesota, he is probably the nicest fast man in baseball. Nicknamed The Hulk ("berg" means "mountain" in

Norwegian). He used those three years on the bench to earn a B.A. in history, by the way.

## That's Not All

Joining the team later will be Wally Gunderson (17, 191 lbs., 6'4", left/right), who dons a Twins uniform June 8th, the day after he graduates from West High in Minneapolis. The Twins have saved him a number, 18, and assigned him a locker and paid him a bonus, twelve hundred dollars, which was all he would accept. He's thrilled just to be on the team. A big lanky loose-jointed kid with long wavy blond hair and a goofy grin, he throws a screwball that comes in and up, a slider that suddenly jumps, a curve that drops off the table, and a stinkball that hangs in the air so long some batters swing twice. You don't expect so much junk from an Eagle Scout, but Wally's got one more: a fastball that decelerates rapidly halfway to the plate—a braking pitch. Some he learned from his dad and the rest he invented for a Science Fair project. "Pitching is physics, that's all," he says, looking down at his size-13 shoes, uneasy at all the acclaim.

Detroit and St. Louis offered the lad millions in cash, land, jewelry, servants, tax abatements, but he wasn't listening. "I want to play my ball where my roots are," he says quietly.

Twinsville wasn't one bit surprised. Personal character and loyalty and dedication are what got us where we are right now, and that's on top. We're No. 1. We knew it first and now you know it, too. You thought we were quiet and modest in the Midwest but that's because you're dumb, as dumb as a stump, dumber than dirt.

You're so dumb you don't know that we're on top and you're below. Our team wins and your team loses; we need your team to amuse us. Minnesota soybeans, corn, and barley; we're the best, so beat it, Charley, or we'll shell ya like a pea pod, dunk ya like a doughnut—sure be nice when the game's over, won't it—take ya to the cleaners for a brand-new hairdo. We can beat ya anytime we care to. Shave and a haircut, two bits.

*Robert Penn Warren*

# GOODWOOD COMES BACK (1948)

**L**UKE GOODWOOD ALWAYS COULD PLAY baseball, but I never could, to speak of. I was little for my age then, but well along in my studies and didn't want to play with the boys my size; I wanted to play with the boys in my class, and if it hadn't been for Luke, I never would have been able to. He was a pitcher then, like he has always been, and so he would say, "Aw, let him field." When he was pitching, it didn't matter much who was fielding, anyway, because there weren't going to be any hits to amount to anything in the first place. I used to play catcher some, too, because I had the best mitt, but he pitched a mighty hard ball and it used to fool the batter all right, but it fooled me too a good part of the time so I didn't hold them so good. Also, I was a little shy about standing close up to the plate on account of the boys flinging the bat the way they did when they started off for first base. Joe Lancaster was the worst for that, and since he almost always played on the other side, being a good hitter to balance off Luke's pitching, I had to come close, nearly getting scared to death of him braining me when he did get a hit. Luke used to yell, "For Christ sake get up to that plate or let somebody else catch for Christ sake that can!"

Joe Lancaster wasn't much bigger than I was, but he was knotty and old-looking, with a white face and hair that was almost white like an old man's, but he wasn't exactly an albino. He was a silent and solemn kind of boy, but he could sure hit; I can remember how he used to give that ball a good solid crack, and start off running the bases with his short legs working fast like a fox terrier's trying to catch up with something, but his face not having any expression and looking like it was dead or was thinking about something else. I've been back home since and seen him in the restaurant where he works behind the counter. I'm bigger than he is now, for he never did grow much. He says hello exactly like a stranger that never saw you before and asks what you want. When he has his sleeves rolled up in the summertime, and puts an order on the counter for you, his arms are small like a boy's, still, with very white skin you can see the veins through.

It was Joe hit me in the head with a bat when I was catching. Luke ran up toward the plate, yelling, "You've killed him!"—for the bat knocked me clean over. It was the last time I played catcher; the next time I came out bringing my mitt, which was a good one, Luke said, "Gimme that mitt." He took it and gave it to another boy, and told me to go play field. That was the only thing I didn't like about Luke, his taking my mitt.

I stayed at the Goodwood house a lot, and liked it, even if it was so different from my own. It was like a farmhouse, outside and inside, but the town was growing out toward it, making it look peculiar set so far back off the street with barns and chicken yards behind it. There was Mr. Goodwood, who had been a sheriff once and who had a bullet in his game leg, they said, a big man one time, but now with his skin too big for him and hanging in folds. His mustache was yellow from the chewing tobacco he used and his eyes were bloodshot; some people said he was drinking himself to death, but I'll say this for him, he drank himself to death upstairs without making any fuss. He had four boys, and drink was their ruination. They say it was likker got Luke out of the big league, and none of the Goodwoods could ever leave the poison alone. Anyway, the Goodwood house was a man's house with six men sitting down to the table, counting the grandfather, and Mrs. Goodwood and her daughter going back and forth to the kitchen with sweat on their faces and their hair damp from the stove. There would be men's coats on the chairs in the living room, sometimes hunting coats with the old blood caked on the khaki, balls of twine and a revolver on the mantel-piece, and shotguns and flyrods lying around, even on the spare bed that was in the living room. And the bird dogs came in the house whenever they got good and ready. At my house everything was different, for men there always seemed to be just visiting.

Luke took me hunting with him, or sometimes one of his big brothers took us both, but my mother didn't like for me to go with the grown boys along, because she believed that their morals were not very good. I don't suppose their morals were much worse than ordinary for boys getting their sap up, but hearing them talk was certainly an education for a kid. Luke was as good a shot as you ever hope to see. He hunted a lot by himself, too, for my folks wouldn't let me go just all the time. He would get up before day and eat some cold bread and coffee in the kitchen and then be gone till after dark with his rifle or his shotgun. He never took anything to eat with him, either, for when he was hunting he was like they say the Indians were in that respect. Luke reminded you of an Indian, too, even when he was a boy and even if he was inclined to be a blond and not a brunette; he was long and rangy, had a big fine-cut nose, and looked to be setting his big feet always carefully on the ground, and came up on his toes a little, like a man testing his footing. He walked that way even on a concrete walk, probably from being in the woods so much. It was no wonder with all his hunting he never did study or make any good use and profit of his mind, which was better than most people's, however. The only good grades he made were in penmanship, copybooks still being used then in the grammar school part of school. He could make his writing look exactly like the writing at the top of the page, a Spencerian hand tilted forward, but not too much like a woman's. He could draw a bird with one line without taking the pencil off the paper once, and he'd draw them all afternoon in school sometimes. The birds all looked alike, all fine and rounded off like his Spencerian writing, their beaks always open, but not looking like any birds God ever made in this world. Sometimes he would put words coming out of a bird's bill, like "You bastard," or worse; then he would scratch it out, for he might just as well have signed his name to it, because the teachers and everybody knew how well he could draw a bird in that way he had.

Luke didn't finish high school. He didn't stop all at once, but just came less and less, coming only on bad days most of the time, for on good days he would be off hunting or fishing. It was so gradual, him not coming, that nobody, maybe not even the teachers, knew when he really stopped for good. In the summer he would lie around the house, sleeping out in the yard on the grass where it was shady, stretched out like a cat, with just a pair of old pants on. Or he would fish or play baseball. It got so he was playing baseball for little town teams around that section, and he picked up some change to buy shells and tackle.

That was the kind of life he was living when I finished school and left town. We had drifted apart, you might say, by that time, for he didn't fool around with the school kids any more. I never found out exactly how he broke into real baseball and got out of what you call the sand lot. My sister wrote me some big man in the business saw Luke pitch some little game somewhere and Luke was gone to pitch for a team up in Indiana somewhere. Then the next year he got on the sport page in the papers. My sister, knowing I would be interested in the boy that was my friend, you might say, used to find out about the write-ups and send me clippings when the home paper would copy stories about Luke from the big papers. She said Luke was making nine thousand dollars playing for the Athletics, which was in Philadelphia. The papers called him the

Boy Wizard from Alabama. He must have been making a lot of money that year to judge from the presents he sent home. He sent his mother a five-hundred-dollar radio set and a piano, and I admired him for the way he remembered his mother, who had had a hard time and no doubt about it. I don't know why he sent the piano, because nobody at his house could play one. He also fixed up the house, which was in a bad shape by that time. Mr. Goodwood was still alive, but according to all reports he was spending more time upstairs than ever, and his other three boys never were worth a damn, not even for working in the garden, and didn't have enough git-up-and-git to even go fishing.

The next year Luke pitched in the World Series, for the team that bought him from the Athletics, in Philadelphia, and he got a bonus of three thousand dollars, plus his salary. But he must have hit the skids after that, drink being the reason that was reported to me. When he was home on vacation, my sister said he did some fishing and hunting, but pretty soon he was drunk all the time, and carousing around. The next year he didn't finish the season. My sister sent me a clipping about it, and wrote on the margin, "I'm sure you will be sorry to know this because I know you always liked Luke. I like Luke too." For a matter of fact, I never saw a woman who didn't like Luke, he was so good-looking and he had such a mixture of wildness and a sort of embarrassment around women. You never saw a finer-looking fellow in your life than he was going down the street in summer with nothing on except old khaki pants and underwear tops and his long arms and shoulders near the color of coffee and his blondish hair streaked golden color with sunburn. But he didn't have anything to do with girls, that is, decent girls, probably because he was too impatient. I don't suppose he ever had a regular date in his life.

But the next year he was back in baseball, but not in such a good team, for he had done some training and lived clean for a while before the season opened. He came back with great success, it looked like at first. I was mighty glad when I got a clipping from my sister with the headlines, *Goodwood Comes Back*. He was shutting them out right and left. But it didn't last. The drink got him, and he was out of the big-time game for good and all, clean as a whistle. Then he came back home.

It was on a visit home I saw him after all that time. I was visiting my sister, who was married and lived there, and I had taken a lawn mower down to the blacksmith shop to get it fixed for her. I was waiting out in front of the shop, leaning against one side of the door and looking out in the gravel street, which was sending up heat-dazzles. Two or three old men were sitting there, not even talking; they were the kind of old men you find sitting around town like that, who never did amount to a damn and whose names even people in town can't remember half the time. I saw Luke coming up the road with another boy, who didn't strike me as familiar right off because he was one of those who had grown up in the meantime. I could see they were both nearly drunk, when they got under the shade of the shed; and I noticed Luke's arms had got pretty stringy. I said hello to Luke, and he said, "Well, I'll be damned, how you making it?" I said, "Fine, how's it going?" Then he said, "Fine."

After they stood there a while I could see the other boy wasn't feeling any too good with the combination of whiskey and the heat of the day. But Luke kept kidding him and trying to make him go up to the Goodwood house, where he said he had some more whiskey. He said he had kept it under a setting hen's nest for two weeks to age, and the other boy said Luke never kept any whiskey in his life two days, let alone two weeks, without drinking it up. It was bootleg whiskey they were drinking, because Alabama was a dry state then, according to the law, even after repeal; Luke must have been kidding too, because he ought to know if anybody does, whiskey don't age in glass whether it's under a setting hen or not. Then he tried to make the boy go up to Tangtown, which is what they call nigger town because of the immoral goings-on up there, where they could get some more whiskey, he said, and maybe something else. The other boy said it wasn't decent in the middle of the afternoon. Then he asked me to go, but I said no thanks to the invitation, not ever having approved of that, and Tangtown especially, for it looks like to me a man ought to have more self-respect. The old men sitting there were taking in every word, probably jealous because they weren't good for drinking or anything any more.

Finally Luke and the other boy started up the road in the hot sun, going I don't know where, whether to his house or off to Tangtown in the middle of the afternoon. One of the old men said, "Now, ain't it a shame the way he's throwed away his chances." One of the others said likker always was hard on the Goodwoods. Luke, not being any piece off and having good ears even if he was drinking, must have heard them, for he stooped down and scooped up a rock from the road like a baseball player scooping up an easy grounder, and yelled, "Hey, see that telephone pole?" Then he threw the rock like a bullet and slammed the pole, which was a good way off. He turned around, grinning pretty sour, and yelled, "Still got control, boys!" Then the two of them went off.

It was more than a year before I saw him again, but he had been mentioned in letters from my sister, Mrs. Hargreave, who said that Luke was doing better and that his conduct was not so outrageous, as she put it. His mother's dying that year of cancer may have quieted him down some. And then he didn't have any money to buy whiskey with. My sister said he was hunting again and in the summer pitching a little ball for the town team that played on Saturday and Sunday afternoons with the other teams from the towns around there. His pitching probably was still good enough to make the opposition look silly. But maybe not, either, as might be judged from what I heard the next time I saw him. I was sitting on the front porch of my sister's house, which is between the Goodwood house and what might be called the heart of town. It stands close up to the street without much yard like all the houses built since the street got to be a real street and not just a sort of road with a few houses scattered along it. Some men were putting in a concrete culvert just in front of the house, and since it was the middle of the day, they were sitting on the edge of the concrete walk eating their lunch and smoking. When Luke came along, he stopped to see what they were doing and got down in the ditch to inspect it. Although it was getting along in the season, there were still enough leaves on the vine on my sister's porch to hide me from the street, but I could hear every word they said. One of the workmen asked Luke when the next game would be. He said Sunday with Millville. When they asked him if he was going to win, he said he didn't know because Millville had a tough club to beat all right. I noticed on that trip home that the boys talked about their ball club, and not their ball team. It must have been Luke's influence. Then one of the men sitting on the curb said in a tone of voice that sounded righteous and false somehow in its encouragement, "We know you can beat 'em, boy!" For a minute Luke didn't say anything; then he said, "Thanks," pretty short, and turned off down the street, moving in that easy yet fast walk of his that always seemed not to be taking any effort.

It was a couple of days later when I was sitting in my sister's yard trying to cool off, that he came by and saw me there and just turned in at the gate. We said hello, just like we had been seeing each other every day for years, and he sat down in the other chair without waiting to be asked, just like an old friend, which he was. It wasn't long before he got out of the chair, though, and lay on the grass, just like he always used to do, lying relaxed all over just like an animal. I was a little bit embarrassed at first, I reckon, and maybe he was, too, for we hadn't sort of sat down together like that for near fifteen years, and he had been away and been a big league pitcher, at the top of his profession almost, and here he was back. He must have been thinking along the same lines, for after he had been there on the grass a while he gave a sort of laugh and said, "Well, we sure did have some pretty good times when we were kids going round this country with our guns, didn't we?" I said we sure did. I don't know whether Luke really liked to remember the times we had or whether he was just being polite and trying to get in touch with me again, so to speak.

Then he got to talking about the places he had been and the things he had seen. He said a man took him to a place in some city, Pittsburgh I believe it was, and showed him the biggest amount of radium there is in the world in one place. His mother having died of cancer not much more than a year before that day we were talking must have made him remember that. He told me how he shot alligators in Florida and went deep-sea fishing. That was the only good time he had away from home, he said, except the first year when the Athletics farmed him out to a smaller team. I was getting embarrassed when he started to talk about baseball, like you will when somebody who has just had a death in the family starts talking natural, like nothing had happened, about the departed one. He said his first year in Pennsylvania he got six hundred dollars a month from the club he was pitching for, plus a little extra. "Being raised in a town like this," he said, "a fellow don't know what to do with real money." So he wrote home for them to crate up his bird dogs and express them to him, which they did. He leased a farm to put his dogs on and hired somebody to take care of them for him, because he couldn't be out there all the time, having his job to attend to. Then he bought some more dogs, for he always was crazy about dogs, and bought some Chinese ring-neck pheasants to put on his farm. He said that was a good time, but it didn't last.

He told me about some other pitchers too. There was one who used to room with him when the club went on the road. Every time they got to a new city, that pitcher made the rounds of all the stores, then the boxes would begin coming to the hotel room, full of electric trains and mechanical automobiles and boats, and that grown man would sit down and play with them and after the game would hurry back so he could play some more. Luke said his friend liked trains pretty well, but boats best, and used to keep him awake half the night splashing in the bathtub. There was another pitcher up in Indiana who went to a roadhouse with Luke, where they got drunk. They got thrown out of the place because that other pitcher, who was a Polak, kept trying to dance with other people's women. The Polak landed on a rock pile and put his hand down and found all the rocks were just the size of baseballs, and him a pitcher. He started breaking windows, and stood everybody off till the cops came. But Luke was gone by that time; so the police called up the hotel to tell Luke there was a guy needed two thousand dollars to get out of jail. So he and three other players went down and put up five hundred apiece to get the fellow out, who was sobered up by that time and wanted to go to bed and get some rest. Luke didn't know that fellow very well and when the Polak went off with the team to play some little game and Luke didn't go, he figured his five hundred was gone too. The fellow didn't come back with the team, either, for he had slipped off, so he figured he had really kissed his five hundred good-bye. But the night before the trial, about three o'clock in the morning, there was a hammering on the hotel-room door and before Luke could open it, somebody stuck a fist through the panel and opened it. And there was the Polak, wearing a four-bit tuxedo and patent-leather shoes and a derby hat, and his tie under one ear, drunk. He fell flat on the floor clutching twenty-three hundred dollars' worth of bills in his hands. That Polak had gone back to the mines, having been a miner before he got in baseball, and had gambled for three days, and there he was to pay back the money as soon as he could. Luke said he wouldn't take money from a man who was drunk because the man might not remember and might want to pay him again when he got sober; so he got his the next morning. The fine and expense of fixing up the roadhouse wasn't as much as you'd expect, and the Polak had a good profit, unless a woman who got hit in the head with a rock and sued him got the rest. Luke didn't know how much she got. He said all pitchers are crazy as hell one way or another.

He told me about things that he saw or got mixed up with, but he said he never had a good time after he had to give up the farm where he had the dogs and the Chinese ring-neck pheasants. He said after that it wasn't so good any more, except for a little time in Florida, shooting alligators and fishing. He had been raised in the country, you see, and had the habit of getting up mighty early, with all that time on his hands till the game started or practice. For a while he used to go to the gymnasium in the mornings and take a work-out, but the manager caught on and stopped that because he wouldn't be fresh for the game. There wasn't anything to do in the mornings after that, he said, except pound the pavements by himself, everybody else still being asleep, or ride the lobbies, and he didn't have a taste for reading, not ever having cultivated his mind like he should. Most of the boys could sleep late, but he couldn't, being used to getting up before sun to go fishing or hunting or something. He said he could have stood the night drinking all right, it was the morning drinking got him down. Lying there on the grass, all relaxed, it didn't look like he gave a damn either.

He had his plans all worked out. If he could get hold of a few hundred dollars he was going to buy him a little patch of ground back in the country where it was cheap, and just farm a little and hunt and fish. I thought of old Mr. Bullard, an old bachelor who lived off in a cabin on the river and didn't even bother to do any farming any more, they said, or much fishing, either. I used to see him come in town on a Saturday afternoon, walking nine miles in just to sit around in the stores looking at people, but not talking to them, or, if the weather was good, just standing on the street. But Luke probably liked to hunt and fish better than Mr. Bullard ever did in his life, and that was something for a man to hold on to. I told Luke I hoped he got his farm, and that now was the time to buy while the depression was on and land was cheap as dirt. He laughed at that, thinking I was trying to make a joke, which I wasn't, and said, "Hell, a farm ain't nothing but dirt, anyway."

After lying there some more, having about talked himself out, he got up and remarked how he had to be shoving on. We shook hands in a formal way, this time, not like when he came in the yard. I wished him luck, and he said, "The same to you," and when he got outside the gate, he said, "So long, buddy."

About six months later he got married, much to my surprise. My sister wrote me about it and sent a clipping about it. His bride was a girl named Martha Sheppard, who is related to my family in a distant way, though Lord knows my sister wouldn't claim any kin with them. And I reckon they aren't much to brag on. The girl had a half-interest in a piece of land out in the country, in the real hoot-owl sticks, you might say, where she lived with her brother, who had the other half-share. I guessed at the time when I read the letter that Luke just married that girl because it was the only way he could see to get the little piece of ground he spoke of. I never saw the girl to my recollection, and don't know whether she was pretty or not.

I have noticed that people living way back in the country like that are apt to be different from ordinary people who see more varieties and kinds of people every day. That maybe accounts for the stories you read in papers about some farmer way back off the road getting up some morning and murdering his whole family before breakfast. They see the same faces every day till some little something gets to preying on their mind and they can't stand it. And it accounts for the way farmers get to brooding over some little falling-out with a neighbor and start bush-whacking each other with shotguns. After about a year Martha Shep-pard's brother shot Luke. My sister wrote me the bad blood developed between them because Luke and his wife didn't get along so well to-gether. I reckon she got to riding him about the way he spent his time, off hunting and all. Whatever it was, her brother shot Luke with Luke's own shotgun, in the kitchen one morning. He shot him three times. The gun was a .12-gauge pump gun, and you know what even one charge of a .12-gauge will do at close range like a kitchen.

*Eliot Asinof is well-known for his screen and television writing. He has authored several fiction and nonfiction books. Among them are* Eight Men Out: The Black Sox and the 1919 World Series *(1963), a mystery titled* The Name of the Game is Murder *(1968), and a book about the Wilson Administration and the post-World War I era called* 1919: America's Loss of Innocence *(1990). Asinof's story "The Rookie" captures the stark realism and sacrifice that many players face in struggling to make the major leagues. It's about fate and fading youth, guts and dreams, as a thirty-five-year-old rookie finally gets his big chance for glory after sixteen frustrating years in the minors.*

## Eliot Asinof

# THE ROOKIE (1953)

**T**HE ROOKIE WALKED INTO THE batter's circle behind home plate and listened to the roar of the tremendous crowd. He swung the two big bats over his head, stretching the muscles in his powerful arms, and recorded the deafening noises for his memory. Dropping to one knee, he stroked his favorite piece of shiny ash, and wiped the dirt from the tapered white barrel. He could not resist looking up toward the towering, triple-tiered stadium around him. For the fourth time today he waited there for his turn at bat; each time he would wallow in the exultation that ran through him, repeating under his breath for his senses to enjoy: "You're in the big-time, Mike. . . . At last, you're in the big-time!"

At last . . . after sixteen grueling, sweltering summers in squalid, southern towns. At last . . . after sixteen years, the whole span of a ball-player's life. For a moment, he reveled in the thrill that beat against his insides and almost made him weep. At last . . . he was a Major Leaguer.

But now a hot wave of savage noise rose from the stands, jarring him rudely from his reverie, and brought him back to the sticky climate of this crucial September ball game. He turned to watch Red Schalk fidgeting in the batter's box, then the pitch twisting half-speed to the plate. He saw the hitter's badly timed stride and the ball curve elusively by him, the bat remaining ineptly on his shoulder. The Rookie heard the umpire's callous cry:

"Steee-rike one!"

Mike braced himself for the new roar of the crowd, multiplying the tension in this ninth-inning climax, and considered the crisis in the game. There were two men out, and the tying and winning runs danced helplessly off second and first, itching to hit pay dirt. The game was going down to the wire; it was clearly up to Red Schalk to take it there.

The Rookie added to the bellowing mob behind him, and roared aloud his desperate hopes:

"Keep alive, Red! Keep alive!"

But within him, he knew he meant something else: keep it alive for me . . . for ME! Get on base and leave those runners sitting out there. Selfishly, Mike felt himself begging for the hero's job—to hit that long blow and bust up the game. He transferred his body into Red's, his hands on Red's bat, his power, timing, coordination, and most of all, his will into Red's. To The Rookie, this day was a personal climax, far more important to him that the goddam game. It had to be his day; for after sixteen struggling years to get here, he knew damn well he had it coming to him.

"Mike!" he heard. "The resin. Gimme the resin."

He looked up to see Red walking toward him from the plate. He picked up the resin bag and went to meet him.

"Sonovabitch!" Red muttered under his breath.

"Take it easy, Red," Mike said, trying to steady him; the "veteran" was having it rough. "Get loose."

Red rubbed the resin over his sweaty hands.

"Can't get 'em dry enough . . ."

Scare sweat, The Rookie thought. The guy is scared up there. A chance to be a hero and the guy is scared.

"Take your time, Red. . . ."

"Sonovabitch, Mike . . . can't get loose."

"Take it easy . . ." and he noticed now the guy was shaking. Mike went back to the batter's circle and spat his contempt. He'd give half his pay to be in this guy's spot right now, but the Redhead didn't know whether to piss or go blind. And this was a "bonus baby"—Red Schalk, the new-type ball-player. They had handed him twenty grand for being a high school hero, for hitting .400 against the patsy pitchers, and playing with babies. Twenty Gs for merely signing his lousy name. When Mike signed to play pro ball, they gave him a nickel cigar . . . and he didn't even smoke. He thought back . . . he was just a raw kid out in a Pennsylvania mining town, hating the black mines that threatened to swallow his future. Instead, he had practically lived on the sandlots, driving his natural baseball skills to perfection, hoping to spend the rest of his life with a bat, not a pick, and wear a cap without a flashlight over the peak.

He grunted at his memories, and spat a portion of rich brown tobacco juice skillfully down the length of his extra bat.

"Com'mon, Red!" he hollered, fighting back his bitterness. "Get on that sack!"

Mike watched the pitcher lean into the shadows to pick up the catcher's sign, his intense concentration hidden under the lowered peak. The pitch spun in, an exact facsimile of the previous strike . . . and it tied the Redhead in the exact same knot. Mike groaned helplessly and bit harshly at his lip as the umpire roared again:

"Steerike two!"

Fooled him twice . . . the lousy Redhead . . . fooled the big-time Major Leaguer, over anxious in the clutch like a stinking high school kid.

Red had never even waved his stick. Christ . . . you'd think a guy three years in the big-time would at least know how to get set.

He shivered as an icy wind passed through him, frantic now that everything vital to him seemed so far beyond his control.

He heard Red calling him again.

"Mike. . . . " The voice was low and charged with fear. "Mike. . . . " and he spluttered his confession like a frightened, guilty child: "I . . . I don't wanna hit!"

"What!" Mike snarled, hardly believing, only conscious of something rotten happening. "What! You don't wanna hit?" Then it occurred to him that he had come across this before. The kid had found himself in a crucial spot and hated it. Some punks just weren't cut out for it; they were great only when it didn't count. The hitters with crap in their blood.

Mike looked into the quivering face, amazed at its pallor. He guessed the kid had given up on himself.

"I don't feel good, Mike," Red was saying. "I can't stand up there. . . . "

The Rookie thought of all the drunks he had sobered up; this looked like a tougher job.

"Don't tell that to the Skipper, Red," he said. "I gotta feeling he won't appreciate it."

So now the bottom was falling out; this was supposed to be the hitter who would give him a crack at the big one. Mike felt himself sinking in the field of quicksand . . . down, down he went . . . the towering steel that enclosed it seemed to loom higher, much higher. . . .

"Com'mon, Red," the umpire growled at them. "Let's get the game moving."

Mike grabbed the hitter roughly by the arm. What the hell could he say? "Get back in there and hit or you'll never hit again. Not in this League, anyway." His voice was harsh with anger. "Be tough," he added. "Be tough up there!" And he turned away, spitting the taste of his words. Maybe he oughta pray, too.

Oh you crud, you mighty crud! he muttered under his breath, and he let his memory flash back four wasted years to a city in the Texas League. For there he had first come across Red Schalk, a pink-cheeked, nineteen-year-old bonus-baby out of Georgia. He remembered how they babied him, trying to justify the ridiculous twenty grand investment. He was some big-shot scout's fair-haired boy, the big prospect. Mike had watched them coddle Red all season, letting him nurse his .302 batting average to make it look good. A year later, they moved Red Schalk up to the big-time.

Mike had burned up at the move. Hadn't he outhit Red by a dozen points, and wasn't he a dozen times the glove man? Where were the rewards for his years of consistently good ball-playing? What about the promises they'd made to him . . . year after year? Why doesn't he go up? he demanded to know. Why not him?

Sure, Mike, the Scout had told him; you're a fine ballplayer. But up in the Big Leagues they're after the younger kids. By all rights, you should be up there . . . and if it hadn't been for the war and those years you lost, you would be. Sorry, Mike . . . you know how it is . . . a kid of nineteen has a much longer ride ahead of him. . . .

The plain and simple truth had been made apparent to him; they just didn't want him anymore. He was over thirty by then, and they considered him a secondary piece of property.

Now he was thirty-five, an old man of thirty-five . . . a rookie of thirty-five, playing his first day in the Majors. It did not escape him that he was here by a fluke. The mother club had been riddled with injuries down the stretch, and they decided to use Mike in this crucial September series rather than some green kid. At the last minute, they called him in Texas and flew him up during the night. As he got off the plane in the morning, they hurriedly signed him to a big-league contract. He never even got a chance to get some sleep.

Sixteen years he had plugged his heart out for a crack at the big leagues; when they finally needed him, they threw it in his face.

In the locker room before the game, the Skipper came over to meet him. "You're in the line-up today, Kutner," he said tersely. "Show me something." And he walked away.

The players watched The Rookie smile sourly at this. Those who knew him saw his determination and understood it. To them, it was a matter of winning a pennant, and a few extra thousand bucks to show for it. Oh, that was something, all right. But to this man, it was much more . . . it was a test of a lifetime struggle. They all knew Mike was good, as good as almost any of them—and if the ball had bounced differently, he might have been up there all these years instead of them. But now, at thirty-five, he could be called old. Those who did not know him looked curiously across the room at the signs of his age: his partially bald head, the dark, leathery skin in back of his neck, his heavy, uneven walk . . . and they wondered how many years they had left for themselves. Respectfully, they left him alone while he dressed.

He had waited until they were all out to finish. He laced his shoes tightly and put on his new cap. His uniform was clean and he liked its fresh-sterile smell. With tremendous pride he walked over to the big mirror by the shower room and stood solidly before it. He looked at himself for a long moment, allowing the glow to penetrate his senses. A lush tingling tickled the back of his neck, bringing goose bumps to his skin. He had never felt so wonderful.

"You're here, Mike," he had said out loud. "You finally made it!" Then he clenched his fists as the tears came to his eyes. "You're here, goddamit . . . and you're not going back!"

The umpire's voice brought him out of his reverie.

"Play ball!" he hollered.

The Rookie raised his eyes to Schalk at the plate and watched him feebly wave his bat through the air like he was flagging a train. Red was now an empty shell of a man, a skeleton of bones in a big league uniform, faking through the motions of being a hitter. Look at him, Mike thought. Look at what they picked instead of me! Suddenly, he felt the years of resentment boiling inside him, for here was the sickening symbol of his frustrations. His anger rose furiously to his throat, almost choking him, and he exploded at the Redhead with consummate violence:

"Stand up there like a pro, you goddam yellow punk!" he hollered. "Get on that goddam base!"

At once, he was conscious of what he had done. A ballplayer doesn't blow up that way. That's what you don't do. Instinctively, his mind, his bright, quick baseball mind went back to work for him. He looked out to the pitcher's mound, thinking how much he'd like to be the chucker for this one pitch. If that mug knew the insides of Schalk's guts he'd be laughing out loud. But the pitcher was fingering his own resin bag, and Mike smiled despite himself; the jerk was probably scared too. The Rookie felt like the only veteran in the ballpark.

The pitcher looked for a sign, a studied smile on his face. He'll curve him again, Mike thought. Any decent curve'll get him. Red can't even see anymore . . . just little colored spots in front of his eyes. Count him out, ump . . . Red Schalk, K.O.

The curve spun rapidly in. Red went through the motions, stepping like he knew what he was doing, as if to take his cut. The ball curved from the inside to cut the corner of the plate, but it never got there. It bounded painfully off Red's leg.

"Take yer base!" the umpire bellowed.

Red lay moaning in the dust, rubbing his thigh.

Well, kiss my butt, Mike thought as he went to him, guessing the breaking pitch might have been a good one.

"You OK, Red?" he asked. Maybe the guy did pray at that.

"Yeah, yeah. I'm OK," he said. "It's funny, Mike . . . I never saw it." And he got up, loosening his leg on the way to first.

Mike grinned. It's good you didn't, he thought . . . it's goddam good you didn't. And he turned his concentration quickly to the job before him.

Behind him, the crowd rose to a frenzy at the bases-loaded climax. The Rookie swung the two bats like a windmill and listened to the wild stampede.

It's all yours now; there's nothing left to the day but you. Go back sixteen years, Rookie, and maybe ten thousand turns at bat. None of them matter . . . none of them. Just this one, Mike; just this one, beautiful moment. . . .

He heard the Skipper's voice from the bench, an anti-climax to his mood:

"It's up to you, Kutner. Show me something!"

I'll show you something, you dumb bastard, Mike thought. He tossed away the extra stick and started to dig a foothold in the batter's box. It's all up to you . . . this game, maybe even the big pennant. This is the turn that counted. The other three meant nothing . . . the neat sacrifice bunt, the base on balls, and that long, well-hit fly ball the center-fielder dragged down. They were all routine. This is the spot, Rookie. Blast one and bust up the game!

They were really down to the wire now. All around him there was a tremendous din, a wild persistent yelling that racked his ears. He looked up through the bubbling joy in his heart to face the pitcher. He saw the three runners dance anxiously off their bases. From the bench they were hollering at him: "Com'mon, Mike. Clobber one!"

The pitcher was getting his sign, this time without a smile.

Here we go, Rookie. Tag one and you're a Major Leaguer for the rest of your natural-born life! To Mike, there were no doubts; as sure as he was alive he knew he was going to. He couldn't keep the smile off his face; this was the spot he had waited sixteen years for.

Mike watched the pitcher take a full, slow windup. He cocked his bat menacingly over his shoulder and waited for the throw. It came half-speed, spinning toward the outside corner. He stepped toward the pitch and lashed viciously at the ball with full power. As he finished his pivot, he knew he had gotten only a slice of it. The ball skidded off into the upper grandstand behind him.

"Steee-rike one!" he heard the umpire cry.

He leaned over to pick up dirt, muttering profanities at himself. He was set. He saw it all the way. Yet he hadn't met it squarely. Was it because he was tired? Or too eager? . . . But then he realized this had happened to him too many times over this past year. His memory flashed him pictures of powerful smashes of just such a pitch, years ago. But now he didn't always get around in time. There was something missing; the thin edge of timing and coordination that made the difference had dulled over the years. He swiped viciously at the dirt and sprayed it over the ground in anger, and remembered what the scout had told him in

Texas, four years ago. His age was catching up with him; he was thirty-five and past his prime.

He heard the cries from the other bench now, beamed directly to him over the stamping and screaming of the crowd.

*"Hey, Pop . . . how'd you break in here?"*

He took a moment to adjust his cap and looked squarely into their dugout. They were all on the front step, nervously bellowing at him.

*"Hey, Baldy . . . where's your cane?"*

He stepped back in the box and dug in again. He would like that pitch once more, just to prove he could clobber it. But he knew damn well he wouldn't get it now.

*"Hey, Rookie. Let's see that fine head of skin again!"*

Be set, Mike, and stay loose. This punk has nothing he can throw by you. The ducks are on the pond, Mike, and yours to knock in. It's a picnic, man, a picnic!

He watched the arm swing up and around, the big stride toward the plate, and the little ball spun bullet-speed toward him. It came high and tight, and Mike ducked carefully away from it.

"Steee-rike two!" the ump called.

Mike turned on him in a sudden ferocious rage that raced through him like an electric shock.

"What!" he roared. "It knocked me down! It was a waste pitch!'

"It was in there, buddy. Quit yer crying and get back in there and hit!"

The Rookie slammed the end of his bat against the ground like a sledge hammer, close to the umpire's feet. He was livid.

"No . . . goddamit . . . it knocked me down!"

In a second, the Manager and coaches were there, crowding around the ump, hammering away at him in unsuppressed rage. Not a nice word was spoken.

When the dust had cleared, Mike stood anxiously to the side, trying to collect himself. It was a terrible call, that strike, and it came at a terrible time. It put him way behind the pitcher, making it real tough for him to cut loose. He had to guard that plate now, instead of making the pitcher come in there with it. He couldn't pick out the throw he liked.

Mike thought it was the kind of call an ump would never make on a star. But on a rookie. . . .

"Play ball!" the ump shouted, masking his face, trying to recover his prestige.

Mike turned, his anger still drumming in his gut.

"Take it easy, ump. I got a little something riding on this pitch . . . so take it easy."

The ump lifted his mask and leaned toward him.

"You're pretty sassy for a rookie, buddy."

Sure, Mike thought. There it was.

"Yeah . . . " he said, as sour as he could make it.

"Get up there and hit!"

Behind him he heard the Skipper again.

"To hell with him, Kutner. You got the big one left."

Sure . . . nothing to it. Sorry you had to swallow a call like that, but you still gotta produce. The sacks are loaded and only you can pull out this ball game. That's what you'll get paid for, buddy, and nothing else matters. The stinkin' ump could call another zombie against you, and you're out, just as if you whiffed one, and the game is gone. An hour later, it don't matter anymore that it wasn't your fault. You didn't produce . . . that's what mattered. It's just a big, round K.O. in the papers tomorrow. And because you're thirty-five, you're back in the bush leagues on the first train out.

Then he heard the jockeys from the other bench again.

*"Grampa . . . hey, Grampa! Who does yer grandson play for?"*

*"Get out the rockin' chair . . . here comes Papa Kutner!"*

Mike reached down again to finger some dirt at his feet. He rubbed his hands dry and gripped tightly the narrow handle of his bat. Back in the batter's box, he dug his spikes in position. He faced the pitcher and started thinking baseball again.

Get set, he told himself. Be ready for anything. It's still up to you, Mike. He can't get it by you . . . he can't get it by. . . .

"Ba-a-a-l-d-e-e-eeeeeee!"

The arm swung around again, and Mike's keen eyes followed the movement of the pitcher's hand. His sharp baseball sense picked up a tiny quirk in the pitcher's delivery that clearly indicated curve ball. Mike set himself and moved his body toward the pitch. The ball spun down the inside and started curving late. He pivoted with all his power and met the pitch out front with the fat part of the bat. The sharp crack rang out, beautiful and clear as a bell, and everyone in the park knew that ball was really tagged.

Mike started to first, watching it sail up and up, into the sky, way above the stadium roof, soaring deep toward the left field bleachers. He heard the tremendous, ear-splitting roar of the 50,000 who were a part of it, and the happiness beat glowingly against his ribs. It was the big one! You've done it, Mike . . . you blasted one in the clutch, with the sacks loaded! He rounded first base with tears in his eyes, for he knew, at last, that the world was all his.

As he made his turn, he looked up again to follow the end flight of the ball, wanting to feast on the sight of it disappearing into the seats out there. Suddenly his throat constricted in an agonizing gasp. The ball . . . it wasn't falling right. The wind above the roof had caught it and was pulling it toward the foul line. He followed it down now, sinking deep into the bleachers, but at an angle he could not guess. He saw the foul pole, the tall white shaft; an icy tremor ran through him as the ball fell out of sight into a scramble of spectators.

He never heard the umpire's call. Short of second base, he stopped and turned slowly back to home plate. From some place deep within him, his instincts had called the play: foul ball.

He was right.

It took him a long time to walk back to the plate. He needed all the time he could get now. A sense of doom came over him and he couldn't shake it off. For a moment he thought he'd been feeling it all day, a feeling that luck was down on him, just like always . . . the real luck, luck when you really needed it. Then he realized what he was doing to himself and he cursed his momentary weakness. Just like the Skipper said: Mike, you still got the big one left!

But the thought of trying again somehow depressed him, almost as if he were suddenly very tired. He wondered how much drive he had left in him. For sixteen years he had pushed his body and his spirit, trying with all his heart to get up this far. Now, it seemed to him, his entire effort was to be packed into one brief moment of time. One more pitch, maybe. It must be now . . . there's no more time . . . no more time.

Maybe it was too much to ask of a man.

At the plate, the bat-boy was holding his bat, waiting for him.

"Straighten it out, Mike," he said.

Sure, sure. . . . Stop the wind and straighten it out.

He ran his hand fondly along the end of the bat, subconsciously feeling for the dent. He wished he had more time.

"All right, Kutner," the ump called him. "Batter up!"

Mike played with his belt, trying to stall. His mind was cluttered with doubts and he wanted to shake them loose. Hitting is a state of mind, as important to coordination, timing, and power as a good pair of eyes. He was thinking of too many things now to be a hitter.

The jockeys found it timely to get back on him.

*"Com'mon Pop. Better get back up there before they dig you under!"*

*"Too bad, Baldy. . . . You shot yer wad on a foul ball!"*

Somehow or other he was thinking of all the winter jobs he held over the years. He hated them all . . . gas station attendant, special delivery postman, road gangs . . . they amounted to nothing. Just wasting the winter to get to the spring. After all these years, the whole deal seemed like such a stupid waste.

*"Back to the mines, Pop!"* The jockeys again.

He was about to step in, and it backed him away. "Back to the mines." The words rattled around in his head like loose marbles. It made his head spin as he thought how close he was to it.

"Let's go, Kutner . . . play ball!" The ump was insistent.

Com'mon, Mike. You gotta get up there. You gotta get up there and hit. Suddenly, he leaned over and picked up a tiny pebble. He told himself that unless he put it in his pocket he wouldn't hit. For a moment, he stood there, studying the pebble, debating with himself. It was a foolish superstition and he always rejected them. If you let yourself go, a million little things will deflect you, threaten you, strip you of your will to hit. He had seen guys who became slaves to their petty superstitions. Yet, something almost made him change. Compulsively, he threw the pebble away and stepped up to the plate.

They were ready for him:

*"Yo, Pop. I heard you were in the war . . . which one?"*

He moved his big bat around, trying to loosen the clothing on his shoulders. It didn't seem to set properly. He dug and redug his back foot in the corner of the box. He felt something about his position was different . . . some minute arrangement of his feet, or the balance of his body as he set himself. He watched the pitcher get his sign and his mind began an agonizing conjecture. Would he curve him again . . . half-speed? Would he waste one, or make him cut at something bad? Would he try to throw a hard one by him, under his chin . . . or low outside? It was hard not to guess. Don't guess, he told himself. That's suicide. You're still the hitter. Just be ready . . . be ready.

*"They got a ball club back at the mines, Pop?"*

He cocked his bat over his shoulder and was conscious of the wet pull of his shirt against him. He made a quick movement of his body to release it. It disturbed him, and he thought of stepping out of the box again. Then he remembered the pebble and wondered about superstitions: he regretted not saving it.

*"When ya leave here, turn yer bat in for a pickax!"*

Mike watched the pitcher nod and smile to the catcher. The windup was calm and kept him waiting. It seemed like an endless moment of time.

OK, Mike . . . guard that dish, he told himself. No fear . . . guard that dish. The ball spun lightly off the chucker's fingers and fluttered toward the plate. He saw it start to break, a slow curve breaking toward the outside corner. It didn't look good to him . . . but it might be. In a split second he had to decide, his own judgment shaken by his fear of the umpire. The delicate instrument of timing was shattered, and the balance of his power upset. He stepped toward the pitch and started his swing, lashing at the ball with half a will, half a prayer.

He didn't come near it . . . and the game was over.

For a moment he just stood there, wondering how sick he must have looked. He even tried to guess how far outside the plate the ball had passed.

Then the final thunderous roar of the crowd rose from the stands like a tidal wave, blasting into his ears the consequences of his failure. It was too much for him to take.

"No!" he screamed. "Goddamit . . . NO!" And he beat the plate brutally with his bat, refusing to accept this.

He turned to face the pitcher's mound, swinging his bat like he was ready to hit again, demanding that the game go on.

"Throw the goddam ball!" he hollered savagely. "Throw the goddam ball!"

But their entire team had gathered around the pitcher, slapping his back, clutching and tearing at his triumph. They lifted him to their shoulders to cart him off the field. Mike watched them, letting their spirited laughter bite into him, as if it were aimed at him. He hated them now, the lucky sonovabitchin' pitcher, the lousy jockeys. . . . He stared at them, trying to smear them with his hatred, hoping to provoke one more derisive catcall from them that might unleash his rage and goad him to attack them all. But they never saw him, nor even acknowledged his presence there, and he finally turned away from the plate for the long walk in.

He moved toward the bedlam of the stands now, and saw the screaming faces. A moment ago they were all yours . . . all yours, Mike. They were yelling for you. He looked into the dejection of his dugout and his naked failure came home to him. In a rage, he pulled his bat back, ready to fling it into the crowd, to scatter them and shut them up. He swallowed the top of his anger and held on.

In the stands behind the dugout, they were waiting for him, the harsh faces of the sadistic punks who wallowed in the luxury of a few last kicks at the guy who was down.

"Kutner . . . you stink!"

"You're a bum . . . "

"Ooooooohh . . . what a bum!"

He bristled at their hoots and sneering laughter and wondered how he could get through that gantlet. He gripped his bat tightly as he approached them, trying not to hurry his walk.

"Whatta star! . . . Where'd they pick you up?"

"Back to the Minors, Kutner. . . . "

He felt their stale-beer-spittle spray into his hot face, and he choked on his bubbling rage. A sloppy hand reached over and stole his cap from his head.

"You won't need this no more. . . . "

"Naaah . . . back to the bush leagues!"

He stopped on the bottom step and looked up at them. They taunted him, waving his cap at him, just out of reach. Inside him, suddenly the dam burst, and he flung himself toward the cap, over the dugout and into the stands. In a second he caught the terrified heckler and wrenched the cap from him. With his other hand he started smashing at him in a wild fury, bellowing hoarsely at the top of his lungs.

At once the crowd dispersed, scrambling over each other like scared chickens, and watched in their own terror. The ushers and cops came for him, four of them pulling him off, trying to hold him still, for his rage was only part spent.

They carried him down the steps again, into the dim corridors below the stands, and stood him hard against the wall, just outside the locker room.

"Take it easy, rookie . . . " a cop said, his hands tight on Mike's wrist.

Mike breathed heavily, and looked through the door at the ball-players inside. He saw them, glum and silent on their benches, unlacing their shoes, quietly passing around smokes and cold beer. As he felt the heavy restraint of the cops, he saw Red Schalk among them, close to the door, and their eyes met. His arms were pinned to his side and he tried to wriggle loose.

"Easy, rookie . . . easy . . . " he heard again. "That ain't the way for a Major Leaguer to act. . . . "

The words knifed into him, twisting into his thoughts, and he lowered his eyes from the Redhead's. He wondered how in hell he'd ever be able to go through that door into the locker room again.

*Gerald Beaumont (1886–1926) was born in California and lived in Holly-*
*wood. He was a popular writer of sports stories, which often appeared in* Red-
book *magazine. Beaumont's collected stories on baseball, including "The*
*Crab," were published in his book* Hearts and the Diamond *(1921). His pop-*
*ular collection of stories on horse racing is called* Riders Up! *(1922). Beaumont*
*got many of the ideas for his stories from frequent visits to the racetracks and*
*ballparks of southern California. He served as an official scorer for the old Pa-*
*cific Coast League, which included his home team, the Hollywood Stars.*

*Gerald Beaumont*

# THE CRAB (1920)

**N**OT UNTIL THE ORCHESTRA AT 11:30, with a cheery flourish from
the clarinets, launched into a quaint little melody, did the Crab's expression of disapproval change. Then his eyes sought a velvet curtain
stretched across one end of the room. The drapery parted to admit a slip
of a girl in a pink dress who came gliding down between the tables, slim
white arms swaying in rhythm with her song. The Crab, obeying a sentiment he did not try to analyze, eyed her just as he had done every night
for a week.

Those at the tables who had been there before nudged newcomers and
whispered, "Watch her smile—it's the whole show."

It was a bright little tune—soothing as a lullaby. She sang the second chorus, looking straight at the Crab:

*"Smile a-while, and I'll smile, too,*
*What's the good of feeling blue?*
*Watch my lips—I'll show you how:*
*That's the way—you're smiling now!"*

A spotlight from the balcony darted across the room and encompassed the girl and the man to whom she was singing. Amid general laughter and applause, the Crab squirmed, reddened and achieved a sheepish grin.

The singer passed to other tables, the light playing on her yellow hair and accentuating the slimness of her figure.

*"I'm the Smile Girl, so folks say—*
*Seems like smiles all come my way.*
*Want to smile? I'll show you how:*
*That's the way—you're smiling now."*

People continued smiling and humming to the tuneful melody long after she had declined further encores. The Crab stared into the bottom of his empty glass. His face was still very red. Her fingers had brushed the Crab's sleeve as lightly as a butterfly's wing but he was exalted by the contact.

Coast League fans said of Bill Crowley that if he ever learned to moderate his crabbing, the majors would one day be bidding for the greatest third baseman in history. He was chain lightning on his feet and could hit around .290 in any company. Moreover, he had perfect baseball hands, an arm of steel, and the runner was yet to wear spikes who could scare him into exposing even a corner of the bag if the play was close.

But Bill was a crab by instinct, preference and past performances. He was hard-boiled in the dye of discontent, steeped in irritability—a consistent, chronic, quarrelsome crab, operating apparently with malice aforethought and intent to commit mischief.

Naturally the fans rode him. It is human nature to poke sticks at a crab and turn it over on its back. In time, a crustacean becomes imbued with the idea that it was born to be tormented, hence it moves around with its claws alert for pointed sticks. That was the way with Bill Crowley, third-sacker extraordinary, and kicker plenipotentairy to the court of Brick McGovern, sorrel-topped manager of the Wolves. Looking for trouble, he found it everywhere.

At that, Bill the Crab was not without a certain justification. A third baseman has enough woes without being afflicted with boils on the back of his neck. Such ailments belong by the law of retribution to the outfield. The fact that little pink protuberances appeared every now and then due south from the Crab's collar button, where the afternoon sun could conveniently find them, was further proof that even Providence had joined in the general persecution.

No infielder or outfielder ever threw the ball right to the Crab. It was either too low, or too high, or too late, or on his "meat" hand. There wasn't a scorer on the circuit who knew the definition of a base hit. The only time the umpires were ever on top of the play was when Bill was the runner, and then they had their thumbs in the air before he even hit the dirt.

Under such circumstances there was nothing for the Crab to do but register his emphatic disapproval. This he invariably accomplished by slamming his glove on the ground and advancing on the umpire stiff-legged after the manner of a terrier approaching a strange dog. Had there been hair on the back of his neck, it would have bristled.

The arbiters of the diamond took no chances with the Crab. They waved five fingers at him when he took the first step, and held up both hands when he took the second. If that didn't hold him, they promptly bestowed the Order of the Tin Can by waving the right arm in the general direction of the shower baths. This meant in all a fine of twenty dollars and the familiar line in the sporting extras:

## CROWLEY THROWN OUT FOR CRABBING

In the last game of the season, the Crab distinguished himself by clouting a home run in the first inning with the bases full, but before the contest was over he was led from the park by two policemen, having planted his cleats on the sensitive toes of Umpire Bull Feeney and thereby precipitated the worst riot of the year.

McGovern, astute pilot of a club which had won two pennants, clung to the Crab in the forlorn hope that time and patience might work one of those miracles of the diamond which are within the memory of most veteran managers.

Had any one told the red-headed campaigner that he would yet live to see the day when the Crab would be a spineless thing of milk and water, pulling away from a runner's spikes, flinching under the taunts of the bleachers, accepting meekly the adverse decisions of the men in blue, he would have grinned tolerantly. The Crab might mellow a little with advancing years, but lose his fighting spirit? Not in this world!

It was in the spring of the following year when the team came straggling into camp for the annual conditioning process, and all but the Crab and one or two others had reported, that the Wolves were subjected to a severe jolt.

Rube Ferguson, who had an eye for the dramatic, waited until the gang was at morning batting practice. Then he broke the astounding news.

"The Crab's got himself a wife."

The Wolves laughed.

"*All* right," said Ferguson, "*all* right—you fellows know it all; I'm a liar. The Crab's been married three months. I stood up with him. What's more, you fellows know the girl."

He took advantage of the general paralysis that followed this announcement to sneak up to the plate out of turn. He was still in there swinging when they came to life and rushed him. News is news, but a man's turn at bat, especially after an idle winter, is an inalienable right. Rube clung to his club.

"Three more cuts at the old apple," he bargained, "and I tell you who she is."

They fell back grumbling. Ferguson's last drive screamed into left field and whacked against the fence. Grinning contentedly he surrendered his bat and took his place at the end of the waiting line.

"Not so bad—I could have gone into third on that baby standing up. Trouble with you fellows is you're growing old. Now I—"

Brick McGovern raised a club menacingly.

"Who'd the Crab marry?"

"Keep your shirt on," advised Ferguson. "I'm coming to that. It was the blonde at Steve's place."

"Not the Smile Girl?" The quick objection sprang from a dozen lips. "Not the little queen who sings—not the entertainer?"

Ferguson beamed happily. He had his sensation.

"You said it," he told them. "The Smile Girl is now Mrs. Crab. She married Bill because the whole world was picking on him and it wasn't right. Ain't that a dame for you?"

They were inexpressibly shocked. The Smile Girl—daintiest wisp of cheer in the city—married to the Crab—surliest lump of gloom in baseball. The thing seemed incredible and yet—that was just the sort of girl she was—gravitating toward any one who was in distress. They swore in awed undertones.

"What a bonehead play," sighed Boots Purnell, "what a Joe McGee! Imagine *any* one, let alone the Smile Girl, trying to live with the Crab! Give her an error—oh, give her six!" He made his sorrowful way to the plate, moaning over the appalling blunder.

Rube Ferguson's rich tenor sounded the opening lines of the Smile Girl's own song"

"Smiling puts the blues to flight;
Smiling makes each wrong come right—"

They joined mechanically in the chorus but they did not smile.

Pee-wee Patterson, midget second baseman, expressed what was in every one's mind:

"If anyone can tame the Crab, it's Goldilocks—but I'm betting she slips him his release by June. I wonder will he bring her to camp with him?"

The Crab settled this point himself the following day by showing up—

alone and unchastened. He invited no questions and they forbore to offer any. He was as truculent and peevish as ever. The food was the bunk; someone had the room that he was entitled to; the bushers were too thick for comfort; the weather was "hell," and the new trainer didn't know a "charley horse" from a last year's bunion.

"The Crab's going to have a good year," observed Pee-wee, "twenty bucks says she gives him the gate by the first of June. Who wants it?"

Rube Ferguson whistled thoughtfully.

"If Brick will advance it to me I'll see you," he hazarded. "Some Janes are bears for punishment and the Crab ain't so worse. He made her quit her job and he staked her to a set of furniture and a flat. My wife says they're stuck on one another."

Pee-wee snorted. "Flypaper wouldn't stick to Bill after the first ten minutes." He raised his voice a little in imitation of Bull Feeney addressing the grandstand: "Batt'ries for today's game," he croaked, "the Smile Girl and the Crab. Bon soir, bye-bye, good night."

The Rube grinned. "Sure is a rummy battery," he agreed ruefully, "but the bet stands." He departed in search of McGovern and a piece of the bankroll.

Those of the Wolves who had not already met the Smile Girl, and they were mostly the rookies, learned to know her in the final days of the training season when the Wolves sought their home grounds for the polishing-up process.

She was enough of a child to want to accompany the Crab to the ball park for even the morning workouts and to say pretty things to each one individually. The Crab accomplished the introductions awkwardly, but it was evident that he was very proud of her and that she was very much in love with him.

"Some guys have all the luck," lamented Boots Purnell. "If she ever benches the Crab, I'll be the first one to apply for his job."

At the opening game of the season, the Smile Girl's pink dress and picture hat were conspicuous in the front row of the grandstand just back of third base. Pink for happiness, she always said.

Rube Ferguson confided an important discovery to Brick McGovern and others between innings as they sat in the Wolf dugout.

"The Crab's keeping one eye on the batter and the other on his wife. I don't think he knows there's anybody else in the park. They've got a set of signals. Every time the Crab starts to splutter, she gives him the tip to lay off the rough stuff, and he chokes it back. Pee-wee, you lose!"

The diminutive second-sacker did not reply at once. He was searching wildly for his favorite stick. At length he found it and trotted off for his turn at the plate. He was back shortly, insisting loudly that the "last one was over his head."

"Now about the Crab," he confided to Rube, "everything's coming his way, get me? Wait until we hit the road for a while and the hot weather comes and the ace-in-the-hole boys get to working on him, then we'll see."

The Wolves, always a slow team to round to form because of the many veterans on the roster, trailed along in the second division and swung north in fifth place for their first extended road trip.

Gradually it became apparent to all that Pee-wee Patterson had called the turn on the Crab. He was plainly settling back into his old surly ways, snarling at the umpires, grumbling over the work of the pitchers, and demanding angrily that McGovern get someone behind the bat who didn't have a broken arm—this of Billy Hopper who could handcuff nine third basemen out of ten.

They were on the road four weeks and the Crab's batting average climbed steadily while his temper grew hourly worse. This was characteristic. He seemed able to vent considerable of his spite on the inoffensive leather. It was the nerves of his teammates that suffered.

"What did I tell you?" demanded Patterson, "now when we hit the home grounds next week—the Crab will get the panning of his life and the Smile Girl will break her heart over it. I tell you I'm calling the play!"

Brick McGovern and Rube Ferguson regarded their comrade-at-arms soberly. They felt that he spoke the truth.

"Well," commented Rube, "you can't bench a man that's hitting over .300 just to spare his wife's feelings." And with that understanding, the Crab was retained in the clean-up role.

Most ballplayers have a dislike for one or more cities on the circuit. The Crab's pet aversion was the St. Clair grounds. There, the huge double-decked grandstand, with its lower floor on a level with the infield itself and not forty feet from the foul lines, brought players and spectators into closer contact than was good for either. Back of the heavy screening and paralleling a well-worn path between the home plate and the dugout assigned to the home club, stretched "Sure Thing Row" where men who wagered money in downtown poolrooms before the game congregated like birds of prey to await the outcome.

"Sure Thing Row" ran to checked suits, diamonds and stacks of half dollars, the latter held lightly in one hand and riffled with the thumb and forefinger of the other. It broke no law of the land; it knew its rights and exercised every one of them.

"The Row" maintained a proprietary interest in the Crab. He was theirs by right of discovery. In him they recognized not only the strongest link in the Wolf defense but likewise the weakest. He was an unconscious instrument to be used or not as the odds might require. Now that the Crab was married, the problem was simplified.

It was in the third game of the series that Rube Ferguson, sitting beside Brick McGovern in the dugout while the Wolves werc at bat, reported to his leader what was going on.

"The ace-in-the-hole boys are after the Crab. When he went up to bat just now they were whispering stuff to him about his wife—get me, Brick? They're handing him the laugh about the Smile Girl. He'll blow up before the inning's over."

McGovern nodded. His gnarled and sunscorched hands opened and shut helplessly. "I know," he groaned, "I know—they used to hand it to me like that and if it hadn't been for my wife and kids I'd have done murder twenty times. There's no law against insulting a ballplayer. That goes with the price of admission. They'll not break the Crab's nerve but they'll get him thrown out. Ah!"

The gray-clad figures in the Wolf dugout sprang to their feet. The high-pitched yelp of the timber wolf pierced the clamor, followed by cries of "tear 'em, puppy!"

The Crab had lashed a terrific drive along the right field foul line and was rounding first base in full stride.

McGovern tore for the coaching box with both arms raised, palms outward. Walker in right field had knocked the drive down. He had one of the best arms in the league.

"None out," yelled the Wolf leader, "two bags—play it safe! Back—go back!"

But the Crab had eyes or ears for no one. He was running wild, bent only on showing "Sure Thing Row" he was its master. Blind with rage and excitement he bore down on third base. The ball zipped into the hands of the waiting fielder in plenty of time. The Crab must have known he was out, but he arose from a cloud of dust, wildly denunciatory, and frantic under the jibs of the bleachers and the fox-faced gentry back of the screen.

In the old belligerent way, he stalked after Tim Cahill and grabbed the umpire by the arm.

"You—you—" he foamed.

McGovern dashed out on the diamond but the mischief was already done. Cahill knew his business and he stood for no breach of discipline. Freeing himself from the Crab's clutch, he jerked a thumb in the direction of the clubhouse in center field.

"You're through for the day," he snapped, "off the field or I'll nick you for a ten-spot. Beat it!"

McGovern pulled his infielder away and shoved him in the direction indicated. "Don't be a fool, Bill," he advised, "you were out a mile."

The target for a storm of derisive hoots, the Crab made his way sullenly along the fence and into the clubhouse shadows. Not until he had vanished from sight did the last sibilant hiss die out.

McGovern walked back to the Wolves' pit and shot a quick glance at the Smile Girl sitting in her usual place just back of third. All around her, men were laughing at the Crab's discomfiture. She was smiling bravely but even at that distance he was certain that her chin was quivering.

"Sure Thing Row" settled back contentedly and winked. The Crab and his bludgeon had been eliminated from the crucial game of the series. *The Wolves lost by one run.*

On the last day of June, just before the club left for another long swing around the circle, Rube Ferguson encountered little Patterson in front of the clubhouse. He drew the midget aside and handed him a twenty-dollar bill.

"Much obliged," acknowledged Pee-wee, "what's the idea?"

"The Crab's wife has left him."

"No!"

"Yes. She's been gone three days. She told my wife he came home and beefed because she was sewing something, and she said she could stand his crabbing about everything else but *that*."

The second baseman looked incredulous.

"Seems like somebody's got their signals crossed, don't it?

The Rube shrugged. "What do women always sew? The money's yours."

The little infielder's eyes hardened. "I'm clean," he admitted. "I haven't got a red—but you put that twenty back in your pocket or I'll beat you to death."

Ferguson nodded his comprehension. "I feel that way about it, too. There's something likeable about the Crab but I've never found out what it is. Will he be better or worse now?"

"Does a Crab ever change?" asked Pee-wee.

During the next few weeks it seemed as though Patterson's question could admit of but one answer. The Crab drew if anything a little closer into his shell. He was more morose, more savage in the clubhouse and on the diamond. He snarled his refusals when they offered him the usual hand of poker up in Boots Parnell's hotel room. When they left the club-house in the afternoons, he disappeared and they did not see him until the next morning. They forbore to question him. The ballplayer's code of ethics does not include discussion of domestic averages. While he continued to hit and field as he was doing, he was entitled to behave off the diamond in any way he saw fit.

Not until August when the club was in third place and going like a whirlwind, did the Crab give any indication that he missed the slim little figure in the pink dress who used to blow him kisses from the grandstand.

Then, so gradually that they had difficulty in comprehending the process, something under the Crab's shell began to disintegrate.

It was his hitting–that infallible barometer to a ballplayer's condition, that fell off first. Not that the Crab didn't connect just as frequently as ever, but his swings lacked the old driving power. Outfielders who used to back against the fence when he came up, now moved forward and had no trouble getting under the ball. From fourth place in the batting order he was dropped to sixth and then seventh without result. His huge shoulders seemed devitalized.

Next it was his fielding. He fumbled ground balls that ordinarily would have given him no trouble. He was slow on his feet and erratic in his throwing.

Jiggs Peterson, guardian of the right field pasture, called still another deficiency to the attention of the entire club one afternoon when, in a tight game with the Saints, a runner slid safely into third despite a perfect throw from deep right.

"I had that guy nailed by twenty feet," he complained to the Crab, "and you let him slide into the bag. What's the idea of taking the ball in back of the sack?"

The Crab's only reply was a mumbled, "You peg 'em right and I'll get 'em."

"Jiggs had called the turn," whispered Pee-wee, "the Crab is pulling away from the runner's spikes right along. I don't understand it."

"Nor I," Ferguson responded, "there was a time when he would have broken Jiggs in two for trying to call him like that."

The next day the Crab, seated beside his manager in the dugout, turned suddenly to McGovern.

"Brick–I can't find her–it's August and I can't find her."

McGovern masked his surprise. The Crab's eyes were bloodshot, the lines on his weather-beaten face sunk to unnatural depths. Several times McGovern opened his mouth but the right words did not occur to him.

"I can't find her," reiterated the Crab dully. "I lost her, and I can't find her."

McGovern scraped in the soft dirt with his cleats. He spoke as one man to another. "I'm sorry, Bill, I didn't know just how you felt about it."

The Crab contemplated the palm of a worn-out glove. The muscles of his face twitched.

"I thought it was doll clothes she was sewing, Brick—she's such a kid. Honest to God I thought it was doll's clothes. I never knew different until I read her note. Now you know why I *got* to find her."

The pilot of the four-time pennant winners was again bereft of speech. He nodded slowly.

"She left no address," continued the third baseman. "She thought I was crabbing at her because—" his voice cracked sharply.

The Wolves came trooping noisily in from across the diamond. Their sorrel-topped pilot threw an arm carelessly around the Crab's shoulders.

"The Smile Girl couldn't hold a grudge against anyone," he whispered, "you'll hear from her one of these days. Why, man, any one could see she was nuts about you!"

The Crab's fingers closed on his leader's arm with a grip that made McGovern wince.

"You think so, Brick—on the level?"

"On the level, Bill."

That afternoon the Crab got two hits, the first he had negotiated in a week, but as the fifteenth of August approached, he slumped again, and McGovern benched him and made three unsuccessful attempts to bolster up the one weak spot in his infield. But good third basemen are not lying around loose in the middle of August. The Crab at his worst was better than the newcomers and McGovern put him back in the fray. Two of three major-league scouts who had been attracted by the Crab's hitting and who had lingered in the hope that he would emerge from his slump, packed their grips and went elsewhere. The third man was a product of the school of McGraw. He studied the Crab through half-closed eyelids and—stayed.

With seven weeks of the season still unplayed, the Wolves returned from a southern trip in second place. The fine lines of worry between

McGovern's eyes deepened. He caught himself watching the apathetic figure of the Crab and praying that the third baseman would regain just a little of his old fighting spirit.

And then one afternoon just before the umpire called the Wolves and Tigers together for the opening game of the week, Rube Ferguson, idol of the right field bleachers, tossed a number of neatly folded newspapers into the pit.

"Compliments of 'Pebble Pop,' champion groundkeeper of the world," he told them, "pipe the write-up they gave the old boy."

The Crab opened his paper listlessly, glanced over the tribute to the veteran caretaker, and permitted the pages to slip to the concrete floor of the dugout. He was in the act of thrusting the paper aside with his cleats, when his eye caught a single word in black-face type up near the top of the column on the reverse side of the sporting page. It was his own name. Hypnotically, he picked up the page and stared at it. The words that followed the black-faced capitals burned themselves into his brain.

A sharp ejaculation caused McGovern to look up. The Crab's teeth were chattering.

"What's wrong?"

"N-n-nothing," stammered the Crab. The paper rustled from his nerveless hands. He straightened up, looked around wildly and then walked up and out of the pit—straight as a chalk line to the exit back of first base. With the entire team watching him, open-mouthed, the Crab wrenched savagely at the gate. A special officer drew the bolt, and the third baseman disappeared into the crowd, uniform and all.

Pee-wee Patterson broke the silence.

"I knew it was coming. He's cuckoo. Somebody better follow him."

But Brick McGovern was scanning the paper that the third baseman had dropped.

"Cuckoo, nothing," he exclaimed, "the Crab has found his wife!"

They all saw it then—two lines of agate type that began: "CROW-LEY—"

The paper was eight days old.

A sorrel-topped Irishman with a fighting face, but rather too generous about the middle for perfect condition, plodded up the steps of St. Joseph's Hospital at dusk. One hand grasped a bouquet of pink roses.

"Ah, yes," said the little woman in the office, "second floor of the Annex—Room 41."

McGovern located the room and tapped gently on the white door.

"Come in," chirped a voice.

The pilot of the Wolves turned the knob dubiously and peered into the room.

The Smile Girl was sitting up in bed. Her eyes were bright with the look that comes to a woman who has borne her mate his first man-child. She beckoned to McGovern and then held a pink finger to her lips.

"S-sh!" she whispered, "look!"

In an armchair facing the window and away from the door, McGovern made out a familiar figure, still in uniform. It was rocking gently back and forth, cleats tapping on the linoleum-covered floor, and as it rocked it sang most unmusically to a rose-colored bundle held awkwardly over one shoulder:"

*"Smile awhile—and I'll smile, too,*
*What's the good of feeling blue?*
*Watch my lips—I'll show you how:*
*That's the way—you're smiling now!"*

McGovern blew his nose. The singing stopped abruptly.

"Honey," said the Smile Girl, "bring William, Junior, to me. You've had him for most an hour and I want to show him to Mr. McGovern."

The Crab's cleats click-clacked across the room. He held up the bundle for McGovern's inspection.

"I'd let you hold him, Brick," he confided, "but it's got to be done just a certain way. The nurse put me wise; see—you keep one hand back of the neck and shoulders, so you don't do no fumbling."

McGovern nodded. He deposited the roses on the bed and laid the tip of one pudgy finger ever so lightly on the cheek of the sleeping infant.

"Some kid," he marveled, "*some kid!*"

The Smile Girl emitted a cry of surprise. From an envelope attached to the roses she had extracted a hundred-dollar bill.

"What's that?" demanded the Crab crossly, "what you trying to put over, Brick? I haven't touched a bean of my salary for three months. I don't need—"

"Shut up!" admonished McGovern. "Can't I take an option on the little fellow's services if I want to? Look at those hands, Bill—ain't they made for an infielder—they're yours all over—he's got your eyes and your hair and—"

The baby squirmed and moved its hands restlessly. The lusty wail of a perfectly healthy and hungry man-cub brought a nurse hurrying into the room.

With obvious reluctance, Bill Crowley surrendered his possession. He brushed one hand hastily across his eyes.

"Darn little crab," he said huskily, "he *does* look like me just a little bit, *don't* he, Brick?"

Digger Grimes, base runner par excellence, flashed past first and second in an ever-widening circle and headed for third. He was well between the two bags when Pee-wee Patterson, crouched in short center, took the throw from his old and esteemed friend Rube Ferguson and with a single motion shot the ball, low and a trifle wide of the waiting figure at third.

It was the seventh inning of the last game of the season. Thirty thousand fans in bleachers and grandstand rose to their feet. The play was close, so close that men forgot to breathe. Twenty feet from the bag, the runner made his leap. Spikes flashed in the sunlight menacingly. The Digger was coming in at an angle opposite to the guardian of the bag—charging with his fangs bared!

At the same instant, a heavy-shouldered figure in the familiar uniform of the champion Wolves swept up the ball with one bare hand and flung himself headlong in the path of the plunging runner. The two figures thudded together—threshed a moment in a flurry of arms and legs and then were still.

With his cleats still six inches from the bag, Digger Grimes found himself pinned to the dirt under 180 pounds of inexorable bone and muscle.

Out from a cloud of dust, while the bleachers and grandstand rocked in a tempest of glee, came an indignant bellow:

"He's out—I tell you!—he ain't touched the bag yet—he's out!"

The Crab catapulted to his feet and advanced on Dan McLaughlin. The umpire turned mild blue eyes on the Wolf infielder.

"I called him out," he protested, "what do you want—a written notice?"

The Crab blinked a moment, and stalked back to his position. From under the visor of his cap he shot a swift glance at the crowded benches just back of third. A blur of pink and a smaller blur of blue showed up against the dark background of masculine fandom and told him all he wished to know.

The Crab's chest expanded, as is only proper when a man has got his two hits. Pounding the palm of his worn glove, he dug his cleats into the dirt and set himself for the next play.

"Come on," he called, "get the next man! Ump—it's too bad you only got one lung—can't call a play louder than a whisper, can you? Pipes all rusty, huh? Too bad!"

Over in the Wolf dugout, a red-headed manager who had seen his club climb into the lead in the closing days of the grueling struggle, smiled faintly and stared with unseeing eyes across the diamond. His fingers twisted a telegram that had come to him that morning from New York.

Ten thousand dollars cash and spring delivery is too tempting an offer for any minor-league manager to reject. But there would be a wide hole at third base next year, and Brick McGovern was already wondering how he would ever plug it.

*James G. Thurber (1894–1961) is famous for his stories about people and dogs. Many of his stories appeared in the* New Yorker, *and his major literary works include* My Life and Hard Times *(1933),* The Middle-Aged Man on the Flying Trapeze *(1935), and* My World—and Welcome to It *(1942). The following story is a fine example of Thurber's talent for satirical humor and fantasy. His character Pearl du Monville is a midget who plays baseball. The story is particularly interesting because ten years after it was written fact followed fiction. On August 19, 1951, Bill Veeck, showman owner of the St. Louis Browns, sent Eddie Gaedel, 43 inches tall and weighing 65 pounds, to bat in a game against the Detroit Tigers. Gaedel strode to the plate wearing number* 1/8. *He walked on four straight pitches and was taken out for a pinch runner. Where do you suppose Veeck got the idea to use Eddie Gaedel? You could look it up.*

## *James G. Thurber*

# YOU COULD LOOK IT UP (1941)

IT ALL BEGUN WHEN WE dropped down to C'lumbus, Ohio, from Pittsburgh to play a exhibition game on our way out to St. Louis. It was gettin' on into September, and though we'd been leadin' the league by six, seven games most of the season, we was now in first place by a margin you could 'a' got it into the eye of a thimble, bein' only a half a game ahead of St. Louis. Our slump had given the boys the leapin' jumps, and they was like a bunch a old ladies at a lawn fete with a thunderstorm comin' up, runnin' around snarlin' at each other, eatin' bad and sleepin' worse, and battin' for a team average of maybe .186. Half the time nobody'd speak to nobody else, without it was to bawl 'em out.

Squawks Magrew was managin' the boys at the time, and he was darn near crazy. They called him "Squawks" 'cause when things was goin' bad he lost his voice, or perty near lost it, and squealed at you like a little girl you stepped on her doll or somethin'. He yelled at everybody and wouldn't listen to nobody, without maybe it was me. I'd been trainin' the boys for ten year, and he'd take more lip from me than from anybody else. He knowed I was smarter'n him, anyways, like you're goin' to hear.

This was thirty, thirty-one year ago; you could look it up, 'cause it was the same year C'lumbus decided to call itself the Arch City, on account of a lot of iron arches with electric-light bulbs into 'em which stretched acrost High Street. Thomas Albert Edison sent 'em a telegram, and they was speeches and maybe even President Taft opened the celebration by pushin' a button. It was a great week for the Buckeye capital, which was why they got us out there for this exhibition game.

Well, we just lose a double-header to Pittsburgh, 11 to 5 and 7 to 3, so we snarled all the way to C'lumbus, where we put up at the Chittaden Hotel, still snarlin'. Everybody was tetchy, and when Billy Klinger took a sock at Whitey Cott at breakfast, Whitey threw marmalade all over his face.

"Blind each other, whatta I care?" says Magrew. "You can't see nothin' anyways."

C'lumbus win the exhibition game, 3 to 2, whilst Magrew set in the dugout, mutterin' and cursin' like a fourteen-year-old Scotty. He bad-mouthed everybody on the ball club and he bad-mouthed everybody offa the ball club, includin' the Wright brothers, who, he claimed, had yet to build a airship big enough for any of our boys to hit it with a ball bat.

"I wisht I was dead," he says to me. "I wisht I was in heaven with the angels."

I told him to pull hisself together, 'cause he was drivin' the boys crazy, the way he was goin' on, sulkin' and bad-mouthin' and whinin'. I was older'n he was and smarther'n he was, and he knowed it. I was ten times smarter'n he was about this Pearl du Monville, first time I ever laid eyes on the little guy, which was one of the saddest days of my life.

Now, most people name of Pearl is girls, but this Pearl du Monville was a man, if you could call a fella a man who was only thirty-four, thirty-five inches high. Pearl du Monville was a midget. He was part French and part Hungarian, and maybe even part Bulgarian or somethin'. I can see him now, a sneer on his little pushed-in pan, swingin' a bamboo cane and smokin' a big cigar. He had a gray suit with a big black check into it, and he had a gray felt hat with one of them rainbow-colored hatbands onto it, like the young fellas wore in them days. He talked like he was talkin' into a tin can, but he didn't have no foreign accent. He might 'a' been fifteen or he might 'a' been a hundred, you couldn't tell. Pearl du Monville.

After the game with C'lumbus, Magrew headed straight for the Chittaden bar—the train for St. Louis wasn't goin' for three, four hours—and there he set, drinkin' rye and talkin' to this bartender.

"How I pity me, brother," Magrew was tellin' this bartender. "How I pity me." That was alwuz his favorite tune. So he was settin' there, tellin' this bartender how heartbreakin' it was to be manager of a bunch of blindfolded circus clowns, when up pops this Pearl du Monville outa nowheres.

It give Magrew the leapin' jumps. He thought at first maybe the DTs had come back on him; he claimed he'd had 'em once, and little guys had popped up all around him, wearin' red, white and blue hats.

"Go on, now!" Magrew yells. "Get away from me!"

But the midget clumb up on a chair acrost the table from Magrew and says, "I seen that game today, Junior, and you ain't got no ball club. What you got there, Junior," he says, "is a side show."

"Whatta ya mean, 'Junior'?" says Magrew, touchin' the little guy to satisfy hisself he was real.

"Don't pay him no attention, mister," says the bartender. "Pearl calls everybody 'Junior,' 'cause it alwuz turns out he's a year older'n anybody else."

"Yeh?" says Magrew. "How old is he?"

"How old are you, Junior?" says the midget.

"Who, me? I'm fifty-three," says Magrew.

"Well, I'm fifty-four," says the midget.

Magrew grins and asts him what he'll have, and that was the beginnin' of their beautiful friendship, if you don't care what you say.

Pearl du Monville stood up on his chair and waved his cane around and pretended like he was ballyhooin' for a circus. "Right this way, folks!" he yells. "Come on in and see the greatest collection of freaks in the world! See the armless pitchers, see the eyeless batters, see the in-fielders with five thumbs!" and on and on like that, feedin' Magrew gall and handin' him a laugh at the same time, you might say.

You could hear him and Pearl du Monville hootin' and hollerin' and singin' way up to the fourth floor of the Chattaden, where the boys was packin' up. When it come time to go to the station, you can imagine how disgusted we was when we crowded into the doorway of that bar and seen them two singin' and goin' on.

"Well, well, well," says Magrew, lookin' up and spottin' us. "Look who's here. . . . Clowns, this is Pearl du Monville, a monseer of the old, old school. . . . Don't shake hands with 'em, Pearl, 'cause their fingers is made of chalk and would bust right off in your paws," he says, and he starts guffawin' and Pearl starts titterin' and we stand there givin' 'em the iron eye, it bein' the lowest ebb a ball-club manager'd got hisself down to since the national pastime was started.

Then the midget begun givin' us the ballyhoo. "Come on in!" he says, wavin' his cane. "See the legless base runners, see the outfielders with the butter fingers, see the southpaw with the arm of a little chee-ild!"

Then him and Magrew begun to hoop and holler and nudge each other till you'd of thought this little guy was the funniest guy than even Charlie Chaplin. The fellas filed outa the bar without a word and went on up to the Union Depot, leavin' me to handle Magrew and his new-found crony.

Well, I got 'em outa there finely. I had to take the little guy along, 'cause Magrew had a holt onto him like a vise and I couldn't pry him loose.

"He's comin' along as masket," says Magrew, holdin' the midget in the crouch of his arm like a football. And come along he did, hollerin' and protestin' and beatin' at Magrew with his little fists.

"Cut it out, will ya, Junior?" the little guy kept whinin'. "Come on, leave a man loose, will ya, Junior?"

But Junior kept a holt onto him and begun yellin', "See the guys with the glass arm, see the guys with the cast-iron brains, see the fielders with the feet on their wrists!"

So it goes, right through the whole Union Depot, with people starin' and catcallin', and he don't put the midget down till he gets him through the gates.

"How'm I goin' to go along without no toothbrush?' the midget asts. "What'm I goin' to do without no other suit?" he says.

"Doc here," says Magrew, meanin'me—"doc here will look after you like you was his own son, won't you, doc?"

I give him the iron eye, and he finely got on the train and prob'ly went to sleep with his clothes on.

This left me alone with the midget. "Lookit," I says to him. "Why don't you go on home now? Come mornin', Magrew'll forget all about you. He'll prob'ly think you was somethin' he seen in a nightmare maybe. And he ain't goin' to laugh so easy in the mornin', neither," I says. "So why don't you go on home?"

"Nix," he says to me. "Skiddoo," he says, "twenty-three for you," and he tosses his cane up into the vestibule of the coach and clam'ers on up after it like a cat. So that's the way Pearl du Monville come to go to St. Louis with the ball club.

I seen 'em first at breakfast the next day, settin' opposite each other; the midget playin' "Turkey in the Straw" on the harmonium and Magrew starin' at his eggs and bacon like they was a uncooked bird with its feathers still on.

"Remember where you found this?" I says, jerkin' my thumb at the midget. "Or maybe you think they come with breakfast on these trains," I says, bein' a good hand at turnin' a sharp remark in them days.

The midget puts down the harmonium and turns on me. "Sneeze," he says; "your brains is dusty." Then he snaps a couple drops of water at me from a tumbler. "Drown," he says, tryin' to make his voice deep.

Now, both them cracks is Civil War cracks, but you'd of thought they was brand-new and the funniest than any crack Magrew'd ever heard in his whole life. He started hoopin' and hollerin', and the midget started hoopin' and hollerin', so I walked on away and set down with Bugs Courtney and Hank Metters, payin' no attention to this weak-minded Damon and Phidias acrost the aisle.

Well, sir, the first game with St. Louis was rained out, and there we was facin' a double-header next day. Like maybe I told you, we lose the last three double-headers we play, makin' maybe twenty-five errors in the six games, which is all right for the intimates of a school for the blind, but is disgraceful for the world's champions. It was too wet to go to the zoo, and Magrew wouldn't let us go to the movies, 'cause they flickered so bad in them days. So we just set around, stewin' and frettin'.

One of the newspaper boys come over to take a pitture of Billy Klinger and Whitey Cott shakin' hands–this reporter'd heard about the fight– and whilst they was standin' there, toe to toe, shakin' hands, Billy give a back lunge and a jerk, and throwed Whitey over his shoulder into a corner of the room, like a sack a salt. Whitey come back at him with a chair, and Bethlehem broke loose in that there room. The camera was tromped to pieces like a berry basket. When we finely got 'em pulled apart, I heard a laugh, and there was Magrew and the midget standin' in the door and givin' us the iron eye.

"Wrasslers," says Magrew, cold-like, "that's what I got for a ball club, Mr. du Monville, wrasslers–and not very good wrasslers at that, you ast me."

"A man can't be good at everythin'," says Pearl, "but he oughta be good at somethin'."

This sets Magrew guffawin' again, and away they go, the midget taggin' along by his side like a hound dog and handin' him a fast line of so-called comic cracks.

When we went out to face that battlin' St. Louis club in a double-header the next afternoon, the boys was jumpy as tin toys with keys in their back. We lose the first game, 7 to 2, and are trailin', 4 to 0, when the second game ain't but ten minutes old. Magrew set there like a stone statue, speakin' to nobody. Then, in their half a the fourth, somebody singled to center and knocked in two more runs for St. Louis.

That made Magrew squawk. "I wisht one thing," he says. "I wisht I was manager of a old ladies' sewin' circus 'stead of a ball club."

"Your are, Junior, you are," says a familyer and disagreeable voice.

It was that Pearl du Monville again, poppin' up outa nowheres, swingin' his bamboo cane and smokin' a cigar that's three sizes too big for his face. By this time we'd finely got the other side out, and Hank Metters slithered a bat acrost the ground, and the midget had to jump to keep both his ankles from bein' broke.

I thought Magrew'd bust a blood vessel. "You hurt Pearl and I'll break your neck!" he yelled.

Hank muttered somethin' and went on up to the plate and struck out.

We managed to get a couple runs acrost in our half a the sixth, but they come back with three more in their half a the seventh, and this was too much for Magrew.

"Come on, Pearl," he says. "We're gettin' outa here."

"Where you think you're goin'?" I ast him.

"To the lawyer's again," he says cryptly.

"I didn't know you'd been to the lawyer's once, yet," I says.

"Which that goes to show how much you don't know," he says.

With that, they was gone, and I didn't see 'em the rest of the day, nor know what they was up to, which was a God's blessin'. We lose the nightcap, 9 to 3, and that puts us into second place plenty, and as low in our mind as a ball club can get.

The next day was a horrible day, like anybody that lived through it can tell you. Practice was just over and the St. Louis club was takin' the field, when I hears this strange sound from the stands. It sounds like the nervous whickerin' a horse gives when he smells somethin' funny on the wind. It was the fans ketchin' sight of Pearl du Monville, like you have prob'ly guessed. The midget had popped up onto the field all dressed up in a minacher club uniform, sox, cap, little letters sewed onto his chest, and all. He was swingin' a kid's bat and the only thing kept him from lookin' like a real ballplayer seen through the wrong end of a microscope was this cigar he was smokin'.

Bugs Courtney reached over and jerked it outa his mouth and throwed it away. "You're wearin' that suit on the playin' field," he says to him, severe as a judge. "You go insultin' it and I'll take you out to the zoo and feed you to the bears."

Pearl just blowed some smoke at him which he still has in his mouth.

Whilst Whitey was foulin' off four or five prior to strikin' out, I went on over to Magrew. "If I was as comic as you," I says, "I'd laugh myself to death," I says. "Is that any way to treat the uniform, makin' a mockery out of it?"

"It might surprise you to know I ain't makin' no mockery outa the uniform," says Magrew. "Pearl du Monville here has been made a bone-of-fida member of this so-called ball club. I fixed it up with the front office by long-distance phone."

"Yeh?" I says. "I can just hear Mr. Dillworth or Bart Jenkins agreein' to hire a midget for the ball club. I can just hear 'em." Mr. Dillworth was the owner of the club and Bart Jenkins was the secretary, and they never stood for no monkey business. "May I be so bold as to inquire," I says, "Just what you told 'em?"

"I told 'em," he says, "I wanted to sign up a guy they ain't no pitcher in the league can strike him out."

"Uh-huh," I says, "and did you tell 'em what size of a man he is?"

"Never mind about that," he says. "I got papers on me, made out legal and proper, constitutin' one Pearl du Monville a bone-of-fida member of this former ball club. Maybe that'll shame them big babies into gettin' in there and swingin', knowin' I can replace any one of 'em with a midget, if I have a mind to. A St. Louis lawyer I seen twice tells me it's all legal and proper."

"A St. Louis lawyer would," I says, "seein' nothin' could make him happier that havin' you makin' a mockery outa this one-time baseball outfit," I says.

Well, sir, it'll all be there in the papers of thirty, thirty-one year ago, and you could look it up. The game went along without no scorin' for seven innings, and since they ain't nothin' much to watch but guys poppin' up or strikin' out, the fans pay most of their attention to the goin's-on of Pearl du Monville. He's out there in front a the dugout, turnin' handsprings, balancin' his bat on his chin, walkin' a imaginary line, and so on. The fans clapped and laughed at him, and he ate it up.

So it went up to the last a the eighth, nothin' to nothin', not more'n seven, eight hits all told, and no errors on neither side. Our pitcher gets the first two men out easy in the eighth. Then up come a fella name of Porter or Billings, or some such name, and he lammed one up against the tobacco sign for three bases. The next guy up slapped the first ball out into left for a base hit, and in come the fella from third for the only run of the ball game so far. The crowd yelled, the look a death come onto Magrew's face again, and even the midget quit his tomfoolin'. Their next man fouled out back a third, and we come up for our last bats like a bunch a schoolgirls steppin' into a pool of cold water. I was lower in my mind than I'd been since the day in nineteen-four when Chesbro throwed the wild pitch in the ninth inning with a man on third and lost the pennant for the Highlanders. I knowed something just as bad was goin' to happen, which shows I'm a clairvoyun, or was then.

When Gordy Mills hit out to second, I just closed my eyes. I opened 'em up again to see Dutch Muller standin' on second, dustin' off his pants, him havin' got his first hit in maybe twenty times to the plate. Next up was Harry Loesing, battin' for our pitcher, and he got a base on balls, walkin' on a fourth one you could 'a' combed your hair with.

Then up come Whitey Cott, our lead-off man. He crotches down in what was prob'ly the most fearsome stanch in organized ball, but all he can do is pop out to short. That brung up Billy Klinger, with two down and a man on first and second. Billy took a cut at one you could 'a' knocked a plug hat offa this here Carnera with it, but then he gets sense enough to wait 'em out, and finely he walks, too, fillin' the bases.

Yes, sir, there you are; the tyin' run on third and the winnin' run on second, first a the ninth, two men down, and Hank Metters comin' to the bat. Hank was built like a Pope-Hartford and he couldn't run no faster'n President Taft, but he had five home runs to his credit for the season, and that wasn't bad in them days. Hank was still hittin' better'n anybody else on the ball club, and it was mighty heartenin', seein' him stridin' up toward the plate. But he never got there.

"Wait a minute!" yells Magrew, jumpin' to his feet. "I'm sendin' in a pinch hitter!" he yells.

You could 'a' heard a bomb drop. When a ball-club manager says he's sendin' in a pinch hitter for the best batter on the club, you know and I know and everybody knows he's lost his holt.

"They're goin' to be sendin' the funny wagon for you, if you don't watch out," I says, grabbin' a holt of his arm.

But he pulled away and ran out toward the plate, yellin', "Du Monville battin' for Metters!"

All the fellas begun squawlin' at once, except Hank, and he just stood there starin' at Magrew like he'd gone crazy and was claimin' to be Ty Cobb's grandma or somethin'. Their pitcher stood out there with his hands on his hips and a disagreeable look on his face, and the plate umpire told Magrew to go on and get a batter up. Magrew told him again Du Monville was battin' for Metters, and the St. Louis manager finely got the idea. It brung him outa his dugout, howlin' and bawlin' like he'd lost a female dog and her seven pups.

Magrew pushed the midget toward the plate and he says to him, he says, "Just stand up there and hold that bat on your shoulder. They ain't a man in the world can throw three strikes in there 'fore he throws four balls!" he says.

"I get it, Junior!" says the midget. "He'll walk me and force in the tyin' run!" And he starts on up to the plate as cocky as if he was Willie Keeler.

I don't need to tell you Bethlehem broke loose on that there ball field. The fans got onto their hind legs, yellin' and whistlin', and everybody on the field begun wavin' their arms and hollerin' and shovin'. The plate umpire stalked over to Magrew like a traffic cop, waggin' his jaw and pointin' his finger, and the St. Louis manager kept yellin' like his house was on fire. When Pearl got up to the plate and stood there, the pitcher slammed his glove down onto the ground and started stompin' on it, and they ain't nobody can blame him. He's just walked two normal-sized human bein's, and now here's a guy up to the plate they ain't more'n twenty inches between his knees and his shoulders.

The plate umpire called in the field umpire, and they talked a while, like a couple doctors seein' the bucolic plague or somethin' for the first time. Then the plate umpire come over to Magrew with his arms folded acrost his chest, and he told him to go on and get a batter up, or he'd forfeit the game to St. Louis. He pulled out his watch, but somebody batted it outa his hand in the scufflin', and I thought there'd be a free-for-all, with everybody yellin' and shovin' except Pearl du Monville, who stood up at the plate with his little bat on his shoulder, not movin' a muscle.

Then Magrew played his ace. I seen him pull some papers outa his pocket and show 'em to the plate umpire. The umpire begun lookin' at 'em like they was bills for somethin' he not only never bought it, he never even heard of it. The other umpire studied 'em like they was a death warren, and all this time the St. Louis manager and the fans and the players is yellin' and hollerin'.

Well, sir, they fought about him bein' a midget, and they fought about him usin' a kid's bat, and they fought about where'd he been all season. They was eight or nine rule books brung out and everybody was thumbin' through 'em, tryin' to find out what it says about midgets, but it don't say nothin' about midgets, 'cause this was somethin' never'd come up in the history of the game before, and nobody'd ever dreamed about it, even when they has nightmares. Maybe you can't send no midgets in to bat nowadays, 'cause the old game's changed a lot, mostly for the worst, but you could then, it turned out.

The plate umpire finely decided the contrack papers was all legal and proper, like Magrew said, so he waved the St. Louis players back to their places and he pointed his finger at their manager and told him to quit hollerin' and get on back in the dugout. The manager says the game is percedin' under protest, and the umpire bawls, "Play ball!" over 'n' above the yellin' and booin', him havin' a voice like a hog-caller.

The St. Louis pitcher picked up his glove and beat at it with his fist six or eight times, and then got set on the mound and studied the situation. The fans realized he was really goin' to pitch to the midget, and they went crazy, hoopin' and hollerin' louder'n ever, and throwin' pop bottles and hats and cushions down onto the field. It took five, ten minutes to get the fans quieted down again, whilst our fellas that was on base set down on the bags and waited. And Pearl du Monville kept standin' up there with the bat on his shoulder, like he'd been told to.

So the pitcher starts studyin' the setup again, and you got to admit it was the strangest setup in a ball game since the players cut off their beards and begun wearin' gloves. I wisht I could call the pitcher's name—it wasn't old Barney Pelty nor Nig Jack Powell nor Harry Howell. He was a big right-hander, but I can't call his name. You could look it up. Even in a crotchin' position, the ketcher towers over the midget like the Washington Monument.

The plate umpire tries standin' on his tiptoes, then he tries crotchin' down, and he finely gets hisself into a stanch nobody'd ever seen on a ball field before, kinda squattin' down on his hanches.

Well, the pitcher is sore as a old buggy horse in fly time. He slams in the first pitch, hard and wild, and maybe two foot higher'n the midget's head.

"Ball one!" hollers the umpire over 'n' above the racket, 'cause everybody is yellin' worsten ever.

The ketcher goes on out toward the mound and talks to the pitcher and hands him the ball. This time the big right-hander tries a under-shoot, and it comes in a little closer, maybe no higher'n a foot, foot and a half above Pearl's head. It would 'a' been a strike with a human bein' in there, but the umpire's got to call it, and he does.

"Ball two!" he bellers.

The ketcher walks on out to the mound again, and the whole infield comes over and gives advice to the pitcher about what they'd do in a case like this, with two balls and no strikes on a batter that ought be in a bottle of alcohol 'stead of up there at the plate in a big-league game between the teams that is fightin' for first place.

For the third pitch, the pitcher stands there flat-footed and tosses up the ball like he's playin' ketch with a little girl.

Pearl stands there motionless as a hitchin' post, and the ball comes in big and slow and high—high for Pearl, that is, it bein' about on a level with his eyes, or a little higher'n a grown man's knees.

They ain't nothin' else for the umpire to do, so he calls, "Ball three!"

Everybody is onto their feet, hoopin' and hollerin', as the pitcher sets to throw ball four. The St. Louis manager is makin' signs and faces like he was a contorturer, and the infield is givin' the pitcher some more advice about what to do this time. Our boys who was on base stick right onto the bag, runnin' no risk of bein' nipped for the last out.

Well, the pitcher decides to give him a toss again, seein' he come closer with that than with a fast ball. They ain't nobody ever seen a slower ball throwed. It come in big as a balloon and slower'n any ball ever throwed before in the major leagues. It come right in over the plate in front of Pearl's chest, lookin' prob'ly big as a full moon to Pearl. They ain't never been a minute like the minute that followed since the United States was founded by the Pilgrim grandfathers.

Pearl du Monville took a cut at that ball, and he hit it! Magrew give a groan like a poleaxed steer as the ball rolls out in front a the plate into fair territory.

"Fair ball!" yells the umpire, and the midget starts runnin' for first, still carryin' that little bat, and makin maybe ninety foot an hour. Bethlehem breaks loose on that ball field and in them stands. They ain't never been nothin' like it since creation was begun.

The ball's rollin' slow, on down toward third, goin' maybe eight, ten foot. The infield comes in fast and our boys break from their bases like hares in a brush fire. Everybody is standin' up, yellin' and hollerin', and Magrew is tearin' his hair outa his head, and the midget is scamperin' for first with all the speed of one of them little dashhounds carryin' a satchel in his mouth.

The ketcher gets to the ball first, but he boots it on out past the pitcher's box, the pitcher fallin' on his face tryin' to stop it, the shortstop sprawlin' after it full length and zaggin' it on over toward the second baseman, whilst Muller is scorin' with the tyin' run and Loesing is roundin' third with the winnin' run. Ty Cobb could 'a' made a three-bagger outa that bunt, with everybody fallin' over theirself tryin' to pick the ball up. But Pearl is still maybe fifteen, twenty feet from the bag, toddlin' like a baby and yeepin' like a trapped rabbit, when the second baseman finely gets a holt of that ball and slams it over to first. The first baseman ketches it and stomps on the bag, the base umpire waves Pearl out, and there goes your old ball game, the craziest ball game ever played in the history of the organized world.

Their players start runnin' in, and then I see Magrew. He starts after Pearl, runnin' faster'n any man ever run before. Pearl sees him comin' and runs behind the base umpire's legs and gets a holt onto 'em. Magrew comes up, pantin' and roarin', and him and the midget plays ring-around-a-rosy with the umpire, who keeps shovin' at Magrew with one hand and tryin' to slap the midget loose from his legs with the other.

Finely Magrew ketches the midget, who is still yeepin' like a stuck sheep. He gets holt of that little guy by both his ankles and starts whirlin' him round and round his head like Magrew was a hammer thrower and Pearl was the hammer. Nobody can stop him without gettin' their head knocked off, so everybody just stands there and yells. Then Magrew lets the midget fly. He flies on out toward second, high and fast, like a human home run, headed for the soap sign in center field.

Their shortstop tries to get to him, but he can't make it, and I knowed the little fella was goin' to bust to pieces like a dollar watch on a asphalt street when he hit the ground. But it so happens their center fielder is just crossin' second, and he starts runnin' back, tryin' to get under the midget, who had took to spiralin' like a football 'stead of turnin' head over foot, which give him more speed and more distance.

I know you never seen a midget ketched, and you prob'ly never even seen one throwed. To ketch a midget that's been throwed by a heavy-muscled man and is flyin' through the air, you got to run under him and with him and pull your hands and arms back and down when you ketch him, to break the compact of his body, or you'll bust him in two like a matchstick. I seen Bill Lange and Willie Keeler and Tris Speaker make some wonderfull ketches in my day, but I never seen nothin' like that center fielder. He goes back and back and still further back and he pulls that midget down outa the air like he was liftin' a sleepin' baby from a cradle. They wasn't a bruise onto him, only his face was the color of cat's meat and he ain't got no air in his chest. In his excitement, the base umpire, who was runnin' back with the center fielder when he ketched Pearl, yells, "Out!" and that give hysteries to the Bethlehem which was ragin' like Niagry on that ball field.

Everybody was hoopin' and hollerin' and yellin' and runnin', with the fans swarmin' onto the field, and the cops tryin' to keep order, and some guys laughin' and some of the women fans cryin', and six or eight of us holdin' onto Magrew to keep him from gettin' at that midget and finishin' him off. Some of the fans picks up the St. Louis pitcher and the center fielder, and starts carryin' 'em around on their shoulders, and they was the craziest goin's-on knowed to the history of organized ball on this side of the 'Lantic Ocean.

I seen Pearl du Monville strugglin' in the arms of a lady fan with a ample bosom, who was laughin' and cryin' at the same time, and him beatin' at her with his little fists and bawlin' and yellin'. He clawed his way loose finely and disappeared in the forest of legs which made that ball field look like it was Coney Island on a hot summer's day.

That was the last I ever seen of Pearl du Monville. I never seen hide nor hair of him from that day to this, and neither did nobody else. He just vanished into the thin of the air, as the fella says. He was ketched for the final out of the ball game and that was the end of him, just like it was the end of the ball game, you might say, and also the end of our losin' streak, like I'm goin' to tell you.

That night we piled onto a train for Chicago, but we wasn't snarlin' and snappin' any more. No, sir, the ice was finely broke and a new spirit come into that ball club. The old zip come back with the disappearance of Pearl du Monville out back a second base. We got to laughin' and talkin' and kiddin' together, and 'fore long Magrew was laughin' with us. He got a human look onto his pan again, and he quit whinin' and complainin' and wishtin' he was in heaven with the angels.

Well, sir, we wiped up that Chicago series, winnin' all four games, and

JAMES G. THURBER

makin' seventeen hits in one of 'em. Funny thing was, St. Louis was so shook up by that last game with us, they never did hit their stride again. Their center fielder took to misjudgin' everything that come his way, and the rest a the fellas followed suit, the way a club'll do when one guy blows up.

"Fore we left Chicago, I and some of the fellas went out and bought a pair of them little baby shoes, which we had 'em golded over and give 'em to Magrew for a souvenir, and he took it all in good spirit. Whitey Cott and Billy Klinger made up and was fast friends again, and we hit our home lot like a ton of dynamite and they was nothin' could stop us from then on.

I don't recollect things as clear as I did thirty, forty year ago. I can't read no fine print no more, and the only person I got to check with on the golden days of the national pastime, as the fella says, is my friend, old Milt Kline, over in Springfield, and his mind ain't as strong as it once was.

He gets Rube Waddell mixed up with Rube Marquard, for one thing, and anybody does that oughta be put away where he won't bother nobody. So I can't tell you the exact margin we win the pennant by. Maybe it was two and a half games, or maybe it was three and a half. But it'll all be there in the newpapers and record books of thirty, thirty-one year ago and, like I was sayin', you could look it up.

*Michael Chabon was born in 1965 in New York City and now lives in Los Angeles. His most recent book is* Wonder Boy *(1995). Chabon's gifts as a young writer came to light in his first book,* The Mysteries of Pittsburgh *(1988), a novel about a summer in the life of a gangster's son who is coming to grips with his identity. His second book,* A Model World and Other Stories *(1991), includes the baseball story "Smoke," which was originally published in the New Yorker. "Smoke" is about a pitcher of diminishing skills who attends the funeral of his catcher.*

## *Michael Chabon*

# SMOKE (1990)

**I**T WAS A FRIGID MAY morning at the end of a freak cold snap that killed all the daffodils on the lawns of the churches of Pittsburgh. Matt Magee sat in the front seat of his old red Metropolitan, struggling with the French cuffs of his best shirt. This was a deliberate and calm struggle. He did not relish the prospect of Drinkwater's funeral, and he was in no hurry to go in. He had already sat and fiddled and listened to the radio and rubbed lovingly at his left shoulder for ten minutes in the parking lot of St. Stephen's, watching the other mourners and the media arrive. Magee was not all that young anymore, and it seemed to him that he had been to a lot of funerals.

On the evening that Eli Drinkwater wrecked his Fleetwood out on Mt. Nebo Road, Magee had been sent down to Buffalo after losing his third consecutive start, in the second inning, when he got a fastball up to a good right-handed hitter with the bases loaded and nobody out. He'd walked two batters and hit a third on the elbow, and then he had thrown the bad pitch after shaking off Drinkwater's sign for a slider, because he was so nervous about walking in a run.

Eli Drinkwater had been a scholarly catcher, a redoubtable batsman, and a kind, affectionate person, but as Magee lost his stuff their friendship had deteriorated into the occasional beer at the Post Tavern and terse expressions of pity and shame. Little Coleman Drinkwater was Magee's godson, but he hadn't seen the boy in nearly four years. It was the necessity of encountering Drinkwater's widow and son at the funeral, along with his erstwhile teammates, that kept Magee hunched over behind the wheel of his car in an empty corner of the church parking lot, rolling his cuffs and unrolling them, as the car filled with the varied exhalations of his body. For eleven and a half hours now, he'd been working on a quart of Teacher's. He was not attempting to get roaring drunk, or to assuage his professional disgrace and the sorrow of Drinkwater's death, but with care and a method to poison himself. It was not only from Drinkwater that he had drifted apart in recent years; he seemed to have simply drifted apart, like a puff of breath. He was five years past his best season, and his light was on the verge of winking out.

At last Magee started to shiver in the cold. He fastened his pink tourmaline cufflinks, turned off the radio, and climbed out of the car. He was nearly six feet five, and it always gave other people a good deal of pleasure to watch him unfold himself out of the tiny Metropolitan. According to the settlement of his divorce from his wife, Elaine, he had ended up with it, even though it had been hers before. Elaine had ended up with everything else. Thanks to a bad investment Magee had made in an ill-fated chain of baseball-themed, combination laundromat-and-crab-houses, this consisted of less than seventy-one thousand dollars, a king-size mobile home in Monroeville with a dish and a Jacuzzi bathtub, and a five-year-old Shar-Pei with colitis. Magee retrieved his sober charcoal suit jacket and navy tie from the minute rear bench of the Metropolitan and slowly knotted the necktie. The tie had white clocks on it, and the suit was flecked with a paler gray. He had lost his overcoat—a Hart Schaffner & Marx—on the flight down to Florida that spring, and had hoped he wouldn't be needing one again. Just before Magee slammed the car door, he paused a moment to study his two small suitcases, side by side on the passenger seat, and allowed himself to imagine carrying them to any one of a thousand destinations other than Buffalo, New York. Then he checked his hair in the window, patted it in two places, and headed across the parking lot toward the handsome stone church.

It was warm inside St. Stephen's, and there was a wan smell of woollens and paper-whites and old furniture polish. Magee took up a place behind the last row of pews, over by the far wall, among some reporters he knew well enough to hope that they would not be embarrassed to see him. The arrangements for the funeral had been made without fanfare, and although the church was filled from front to back, there were still not as many people as Magee had expected. The minister, a handsome old man in a gilded chasuble, murmured out over the scattered heads of Drinkwater's family and teammates. There was to be a memorial ceremony later in the week which ought to pack them in. By then the newspaper eulogies would have worked their way past shock and fond anecdote and begun to put the numbers together, and people would see what they had lost. Drinkwater had led the league in home runs the past two years, and his on-base average over that period was .415. He had walked three times as often as he struck out, and had last year broken the season record for bases stolen by a catcher—not that this had been all that difficult. The lifetime won-lost percentage for games he had caught, which to Magee's mind was the most important statistic of all, was close to .600; had he not been required to catch most of the fifty-odd games Magee had lost during that period, it would have been even better. Drinkwater had been cut down in his prime, all right. And that was what the numbers would show.

"Too bad it couldn't have been you instead of him," said a gravelly female voice at his ear. He turned, startled at hearing his own thought echoed aloud. It was Beryl Zmuda, in a fur coat, and she was only kidding, in her gravelly way. Beryl was a sports columnist for the Erie morning paper, and she had known Magee ever since Magee had come up in that city, with the Cardinals organization. A laudatory article by Beryl, written after Magee's first professional shutout, had gotten things rolling for him eleven years before. In that game Magee had struck out nine batters in a row and made the last out himself by bare-handing a line drive. No one was more disappointed by what had become of Magee's career than Beryl Zmuda.

"Hey, Ber," said Magee in a whisper. "When do I get to go to your funeral?"

"It was last year. You missed it." She did not trouble to whisper. She wore a myrtle-green hat with a heron feather which he had seen many times before. "You look terrible. But as usual that's a lovely suit."

"Thanks."

They shook hands and then Magee bent down to kiss her. She sniffled and leaned forward to accept his kiss. Her pointed nose was still red from the cold, and he found her cheeks a little wet. The sable coat felt delightful and smelled both of warm fur and of Quelques Fleurs, and he had to force himself to let go of her. They had slept together for two months during the minor-league season of 1979, and Magee still held a fond regard for her. Her uncle had been a wartime pitcher for the St. Louis Browns; she knew baseball, especially pitchers, and she could write a nice line. Because of her name, she favored the color green, and under the coat her funeral suit was a worn gabardine the sombre hue of winter seawater.

"What a shame it is," he said, wiping at his own eyes. Magee was a sucker for weeping women, and lachrymose when he had been drinking.

"He had a great April," said Beryl. Her Pittsburgh accent was flat and angular. She had fifteen years on Magee, and it was starting to tell. Her hair, blond as an ashwood hat, was entirely the product of technology now, and her face was looking papery and translucent and pinched at the corners. But she still had nice legs with the pomaceous calves of a Pittsburgh girl. She had been raised on the steep staircases of Mt. Washington.

"He did," said Magee. "Three-thirty-one with seven home runs and eighteen ribbies."

"Hey, how about you?" She looked him up and down as though he had just gotten out of the hospital. "How's the arm?"

He shrugged; the arm was fine. Magee had a problem with his mechanics. He had become balky and as wild as a loose fire hose. Although on the hill he felt the same as he had since the age of fourteen, jangling and irritable and clear-headed, some invisible element of his delivery had changed. The coaches felt that it was the fault of his right foot, which seemed to have grown half a shoe size in recent years. Whatever the cause, he could no longer find what Eli Drinkwater had called the wormhole. Drinkwater had picked up this term from Dr. Carl Sagan's television program. A pitched ball passing through the wormhole disappeared for an instant and then reappeared somewhere else entirely, at once right on target and nowhere near where it ought to be, halfway across the galaxy, right on the edge of the paint. Magee's repeated, multiseasonal failure to find the wormhole had bred fear, and fear caution; he had undergone some horrendous shellings.

"It's fine," said Magee, rubbing his left shoulder. "I'm going up to Buffalo this afternoon. Right after this." He nodded in the general direction of the altar, before which sat the closed casket that held the body of Eli Drinkwater. It was a fancy black casket, whose size and finish and trim recalled those of the massive American automobiles its occupant had preferred.

The pastor finished his bit, and Gamble Wicklow, the Pittsburgh manager, rose to his feet and approached the pulpit. He was an eloquent speaker with a degree in law from Fordham—his sending down of Magee had been a masterpiece of regret and paternal solicitude—but he looked tired and elderly today. Magee could not make out what he was saying. Gamble had been sitting beside Roxille Drinkwater, in the foremost pew, and now there was a gap between Roxille and little Coleman. The sight of this gap was poignant, and Magee looked away.

"Will you look at that," said Beryl. She went up on tiptoe to get a clearer view.

MICHAEL CHABON

"I can't," said Magee.

"Look how Roxille's looking at that casket."

The reporters on either side of them, saddened, serious as the occasion required, were still rapacious and insatiable. They turned toward the grieving widow with the simultaneity of starlings taking wing. There was indeed something odd in the face and the posture of Roxille Drinkwater. Roxille was a pretty woman, a little heavy. Her russet hair was pulled tightly against her head and tied at the back. She wore no veil, and the look in her eyes was angry and complicated, but Magee thought he recognized it. Her husband had blown away, out of her life, like an empty wrapper, like a cloud of smoke. She was wondering how she could ever have thought he was real. As Magee watched she began to rock a little in the pew, back and forth. It was hardly noticeable at first, but as Wicklow's voice rose to praise her dead husband for his constancy and steadiness, and to foretell the endurance of his presence in the game, Roxille's rocking gathered force, and Magee knew he would have to do something.

Once, on an airplane, Magee had seen Roxille lose it. It had been during a night flight from New York, where Drinkwater had gone to collect an award, to Pittsburgh, aboard a careering, rattling, moaning little two-propeller plane. Roxille had begun by rocking in her seat, rocking, and staring into the darkness outside the window of the plane. She had finished by shrieking and praying aloud, and then slapping a stewardess who attempted to calm her down. Now the people sitting in the pews around Roxille exchanged worried looks. Joey Puppo, the GM, was frowning, and glancing frequently toward the reporters, who had begun to mutter and click their tongues. Magee saw that she intended, whether she knew it or not, to hurl herself across the gleaming black lid of the coffin.

"She won't do it," said Beryl, in a voice that just qualified as a whisper. She had little esteem for other women, in particular for baseball wives.

"This is a funeral," said a television sports reporter, a former outfielder named Leon Lamartine who once at Wrigley had knocked one of

Magee's sliders—a high, hard one that was not quite hard enough—out onto Waveland Avenue, under a rosebush and into pictures that were shown on national TV. His tone seemed to imply not that decorum would prevent Roxille from doing something outrageous but that anything was possible at funerals.

"Hey, c'mon, you guys," said Magee. "Keep it down." But he cracked his knuckles and worked his shoulder blades a couple of times, just in case.

Gamble Wicklow was winding down now. His chin had settled into his chest, and he was commending the departed soul of Eli Drinkwater to the Man in charge of putting together the Great Roster in the Sky. Roxille licked her lips. Her eyelids fluttered. She reached out tentatively toward the stylish coffin. Three dozen cameras and recording devices turned upon her. Magee moved.

"Where you going, Matty?" said Beryl, whirling. "Oh, my. Oh, my."

". . . now that Eli Drinkwater has forever become, as I think we may truly say, All-Star," said Gamble Wicklow, putting a period to his elegy with a sad smile.

"I told you," Leon Lamartine said, pointing.

Magee had delayed too long—his timing was irrevocably off—and his initial smooth glide down the aisle toward the first pew became a two-way foot race as Gamble stepped down from the pulpit. Magee was forced to run while pretending that he was still walking, all the time trying to keep his head down and remain inconspicuous. The result was an unintentional but skilled approximation of the gait of Groucho Marx. Only the fact that Gamble and the next eulogist collided by the entrance to the chancel allowed Magee to occupy Gamble's place in the pew. Magee put his left arm around Roxille, as though to comfort her, and wrestled her back into her seat.

"Take it easy," said Magee in his softest voice.

When Gamble Wicklow saw that Magee had usurped his seat, he frowned, gave an odd little wave, then turned and trudged managerially up the aisle. His suit was of old tweed and fit him ill. The nave of St. Stephen's filled with rumor and alarm and a faint, funereal laughter.

"Magee. Oh, Magee. What in the hell am I going to do?" Roxille said quietly. Her voice was almost inaudible when when said the word "hell." Her eyes wcre bloodshot and lively. She was not really looking at Magee but around him, at her son, who had turned and clambered to his knees in the pew to see what was going on back there among the cameras. Coleman had grown to be a good-looking little boy, long-limbed and as dark as his father. His hair had been cut very short, and, according to the fashion, a design had been carved into the stubble at the side of his head; it looked like a couple of eyeballs.

Magee put his hand on Roxille's forearm. She had on an expensive-looking black knit dress with a black lace collar and noticeable gores. She smelled of Castile soap.

"I don't know, Roxie," he said. He blushed. He felt very out of place, here in the front row, and he was ashamed to have gone so long without visiting or speaking to her, but he was glad that he had kept her off national TV. "You'll get along."

Roxille shuddered and took a deep breath. She closed her wild eyes and then opened them carefully. The minister had regained the pulpit and managed, by dint of looking pale and disappointed, to quiet the murmuring. He then introduced the next eulogist, a writer from *Sports Illustrated*. This man had started out working at the same Erie newspaper as Beryl, and not all that long ago. He was talented and he had done well for himself. Beryl hated him, in a good-humored way, and this led Magee to wonder why he had not hated Eli Drinkwater, whose fortunes had begun to rise so soon after Magee lost sight of the wormhole. He looked at Drinkwater's coffin, now no more than a few feet away from him. The Teacher's had worn off, and all at once he felt incurably tired. It occurred to him that you could probably tell a joke whose punch line involved a choice between being dead and being outrighted to Buffalo. It didn't seem like much of a choice, but he supposed that Buffalo held a slight edge. On the other hand, at least Drinkwater didn't have to know that he had died.

He had the vague impression that something was disturbing his exhaustion and then realized that it was Coleman Drinkwater, pulling on his sleeve. The little boy pointed at the coffin. He was watching it as though he had been told that it was going to perform a trick.

"Is my daddy in there?" he said, in a clear, thin, terribly normal voice.

Magee and Coleman looked at each other for what became several seconds. Magee, who had no children, searched for the correct answer. He wanted to say something that would be fair to Coleman and yet would not make him afraid. He wished that his head were clearer and that he were not so damn tired. He felt as though everyone in the church were waiting on his reply. His forehead grew damp and he opened his mouth, but he said nothing. Finally, helpless, he put an arm around Coleman's small shoulders, and turned back to the speaker in the pulpit. The little boy suffered his godfather's arm upon him, and as the funeral dragged on he even rested his head against Magee's rib cage. Presently he fell asleep.

After a while, Magee himself, who had been awake for some thirty-two hours, drifted into an easy sleep. He dreamed his usual dream, the one in which he had found his stuff again and was on the mound at Three Rivers throwing seven different kinds of smoke. The sunshine was fragrant and the grass brilliant. When he awoke, feeling refreshed, the funeral was over and the coffin had already been wheeled out. Beryl was standing in front of him, her arms folded, looking as she had once looked on bailing him out of the Erie County Prison. Magee smiled, rubbed his eyes, and then realized that Coleman and Roxille had gone. He spun around in time to see the little boy being towed by his mother out the front door of the church. Coleman smiled across the empty pews at Magee, who saw from this distance that the design shaved into the side of the little boy's head was not two eyeballs. It was Eli Drinkwater's uniform number, the double zero.

"Poor kid," said Beryl. "I heard what he asked you. God. I almost lost it."

"I know," said Magee, scratching his chin. He could not seem to remember what his reply had been, or if he had said anything at all.

"So," said Beryl, sitting down beside him and taking hold of his throwing hand. She began, with a firm, nursely touch, to massage it. The backs of her hands hadn't aged very much at all, and Magee, feeling nostalgic, watched them for a while as they worked him over. A soft lock of her platinum hair brushed against his cheek. "So. What are you going to do? Buffalo? You're really going to let them do that to you?"

"I want to pitch, Ber. I have to get my mechanics back. I think it'll be a little easier in Triple A."

Beryl tightened her grasp on his hand and looked at him. Her face was neither incredulous nor mocking; she only bit her lip and wrinkled the bridge of her nose. Beryl's nose, though small, could be expressive of great sadness.

"Magee," she said. "Matty. Maybe I'm wrong to even put this thought in your head. I know how hard you're trying, Matty, but—what if they're just gone, baby?" Her voice cracked sweetly as she said this. "Have you ever thought of that?"

Magee withdrew his pitching hand and flexed it a couple of times. He watched it with a puzzled expression, as though it were a new model, of uncertain capacity. Then he looked away from it, up toward the ceiling of the church, and tried, for the last time, to remember if he had answered Coleman Drinkwater, and what he had told him.

"Yes," he said to the empty choir.

*Originally published in* Collier's *magazine, W. C. Heinz's story "One Throw" is a wonderful morality play on the diamond. It's about a highly talented young shortstop who is stuck in the low minors playing for an unfeeling manager. What if he makes a bad throw to goad the manager into shoving him up to a higher league? Heinz is the author of the highly acclaimed sports novel,* The Professional *(1958).*

*W. C. Heinz*

# ONE THROW
# (1950)

CHECKED INTO A HOTEL called the Olympia, which is right on the main street and the only hotel in the town. After lunch I was hanging around the lobby, and I got to talking to the guy at the desk. I asked him if this wasn't the town where that kid named Maneri played ball.

"That's right," the guy said. "He's a pretty good ballplayer."

"He should be," I said. "I read that he was the new Phil Rizzuto."

"That's what they said," the guy said.

"What's the matter with him?" I said. "I mean if he's such a good ballplayer what's he doing in this league?"

"I don't know," the guy said. "I guess the Yankees know what they're doing."

"He's a nice kid," the guy said. "He plays good ball, but I feel sorry for him. He thought he'd be playing for the Yankees soon, and here he is in this town. You can see it's got him down."

"He lives here in this hotel?"

"That's right," the guy said. "Most of the older ballplayers stay in rooming houses, but Pete and a couple other kids live here."

He was leaning on the desk, talking to me and looking across the hotel lobby. He nodded his head. "This is a funny thing," he said. "Here he comes now."

The kid had come through the door from the street. He had on a light gray sport shirt and a pair of gray flannel slacks.

I could see why, when he showed up with the Yankees in spring training, he made them all think of Rizzuto. He isn't any bigger than Rizzuto, and he looks just like him.

"Hello, Nick," he said to the guy at the desk.

"Hello, Pete," the guy at the desk said. "How goes it today?"

"All right," the kid said but you could see he was exaggerating.

"I'm sorry, Pete," the guy at the desk said, "but no mail today."

"That's all right, Nick," the kid said. "I'm used to it."

"Excuse me," I said, "but you're Pete Maneri?"

"That's right," the kid said, turning and looking at me.

"Excuse me," the guy at the desk said, introducing us. "Pete, this is Mr. Franklin."

"Harry Franklin," I said.

"I'm glad to know you," the kid said, shaking my hand.

"I recognize you from your pictures," I said.

"Pete's a good ballplayer," the guy at the desk said.

"Not very," the kid said.

"Don't take his word for it, Mr. Franklin," the guy said.

"I'm a great ball fan," I said to the kid. "Do you people play tonight?"

"We play two games," the kid said.

"The first game's at six o'clock," the guy at the desk said. "They play pretty good ball."

"I'll be there," I said. "I used to play a little ball myself."

"You did?" the kid said.

"With Columbus," I said. "That's twenty years ago."

"Is that right?" the kid said. . . .

That's the way I got to talking with the kid. They had one of those pine-paneled taprooms in the basement of the hotel, and we went down there. I had a couple and the kid had a Coke, and I told him a few stories and he turned out to be a real good listener.

"But what do you do now, Mr. Franklin?" he said after a while.

"I sell hardware," I said. "I can think of some things I'd like better, but I was going to ask you how you like playing in this league."

"Well," the kid said, "I suppose it's all right. I guess I've got no kick coming."

"Oh, I don't know," I said. "I understand you're too good for this league. What are they trying to do to you?"

"I don't know," the kid said. "I can't understand it."

"What's the trouble?"

"Well," the kid said, "I don't get along very well here. I mean there's nothing wrong with my playing. I'm hitting .365 right now. I lead the league in stolen bases. There's nobody can field with me, but who cares?"

"Who manages this ball club?"

"Al Dall," the kid said. "You remember, he played in the outfield for the Yankees for about four years."

"I remember."

"Maybe he is all right," the kid said, "but I don't get along with him. He's on my neck all the time."

"Well," I said, "that's the way they are in the minors sometimes. You have to remember the guy is looking out for himself and his ball club first. He's not worried about you."

"I know that," the kid said. "If I get the big hit or make the play he never says anything. The other night I tried to take second on a loose ball and I got caught in the run-down. He bawls me out in front of everybody. There's nothing I can do."

"Oh, I don't know," I said. "This is probably a guy who knows he's got a good thing in you, and he's looking to keep you around. You people lead the league, and that makes him look good. He doesn't want to lose you to Kansas City or the Yankees."

"That's what I mean," the kid said. "When the Yankees sent me down here they said, 'Don't worry. We'll keep an eye on you.' So Dall never sends a good report on me. Nobody ever comes down to look me over. What chance is there for a guy like Eddie Brown or somebody like that coming down to see me in this town?"

"You have to remember that Eddie Brown's the big shot," I said, "the great Yankee scout."

"Sure," the kid said. "I never even saw him, and I'll never see him in this place. I have an idea that if they ever ask Dall about me he keeps knocking me down."

"Why don't you go after Dall?" I said. "I had trouble like that once myself, but I figured out a way to get attention."

"You did?" the kid said.

"I threw a couple of balls over the first baseman's head," I said. "I threw a couple of games away, and that really got the manager sore. I was lousing up his ball club and his record. So what does he do? He blows the whistle on me, and what happens? That gets the brass curious, and they send down to see what's wrong."

"Is that so?" the kid said. "What happened?"

"Two weeks later," I said, "I was up with Columbus."

"Is that right?" the kid said.

"Sure, I said, egging him on. "What have you got to lose?"

"Nothing," the kid said. "I haven't got anything to lose."

"I'd try it," I said.

"I might try it," the kid said. "I might try it tonight if the spot comes up."

I could see from the way he said it that he was madder than he'd said. Maybe you think this is mean to steam a kid up like this, but I do some strange things.

"Take over," I said. "Don't let this guy ruin your career."

"I'll try it," the kid said. "Are you coming out to the park tonight?"

"I wouldn't miss it," I said. "This will be better than making out route sheets and sales orders."

It's not much ballpark in this town—old wooden bleachers and an old wooden fence and about four hundred people in the stands. The first game wasn't much either, with the home club winning something like 8 to 1.

The kid didn't have any hard chances, but I could see he was a ballplayer, with a double and a couple of walks and a lot of speed.

The second game was different, though. The other club got a couple of runs and then the home club picked up three runs in one, and they were in the top of the ninth with a 3–2 lead and two outs when the pitching began to fall apart and they loaded the bases.

I was trying to wish the ball down to the kid, just to see what he'd do with it, when the batter drives one on one big bounce to the kid's right.

The kid was off for it when the ball started. He made a backhand stab and grabbed it. He was deep now, and he turned in the air and fired. If it goes over the first baseman's head, it's two runs in and a panic—but it's the prettiest throw you'd want to see. It's right on a line, and the runner is out by a step, and it's the ball game.

I walked back to the hotel, thinking about the kid. I sat around the lobby until I saw him come in, and then I walked toward the elevator like I was going to my room, but so I'd meet him. And I could see he didn't want to talk.

"How about a Coke?" I said.

"No," he said. "Thanks, but I'm going to bed."

"Look," I said. "Forget it. You did the right thing. Have a Coke."

We were sitting in the taproom again. The kid wasn't saying anything.

"Why didn't you throw that ball away?" I said.

"I don't know," the kid said. "I had it in my mind before he hit it, but I couldn't."

"Why?"

"I don't know why."

"I know why," I said.

The kid didn't say anything. He just sat looking down.

"Do you know why you couldn't throw that ball away?" I said.

"No," the kid said.

"You couldn't throw that ball away," I said, "because you're going to be a major-league ballplayer someday."

The kid just looked at me. He had that same sore expression.

"Do you know why you're going to be a major-league ballplayer?" I said.

The kid was just looking down again, shaking his head. I never got more of a kick out of anything in my life.

"You're going to be a major-league ballplayer," I said, "because you couldn't throw that ball away, and because I'm not a hardware salesman and my name's not Harry Franklin."

"What do you mean?" the kid said.

"I mean," I explained to him, "that I tried to needle you into throwing that ball away because I'm Eddie Brown."

*This is Ring Lardner's second story in the book. Lardner, a celebrated sports-writer, syndicated columnist, and writer of short stories, knew baseball play-ers as well as any writer ever has. He lived with them in training camps, on trains, in hotels, at home, and on the road. "My Roomy" draws on this expe-rience. Its humor and sarcasm could only come from someone who has been there. As with his other stories, Lardner writes in the slang commonly used by early players, providing a quaint realism to his prose.*

*Ring Lardner*

# MY ROOMY (1914)

## 1

**N**O—I AIN'T SIGNED FOR next year; but there won't be no trouble about that. The dough part of it is all fixed up. John and me talked it over and I'll sign as soon as they send me a contract. All I told him was that he'd have to let me pick my own roommate after this and not sic no wild man on to me.

You know I didn't hit much the last two months o' the season. Some o' the boys, I notice, wrote some stuff about me gettin' old and losin' my battin' eye. That's all bunk! The reason I didn't hit was because I wasn't gettin' enough sleep. And the reason for that was Mr. Elliott.

He wasn't with us after the last part o' May, but I roomed with him long enough to get the insomny. I was the only guy in the club game enough to stand for him; but I was sorry afterward that I done it, because it sure did put a crimp in my little old average.

And do you know where he is now? I got a letter today and I'll read it to you. No—I guess I better tell you somethin' about him first. You fellers never got acquainted with him and you ought to hear the dope to understand the letter. I'll make it as short as I can.

He didn't play in no league last year. He was with some semi-pros over in Michigan and somebody writes John about him. So John send Needham over to look at him. Tom stayed there Saturday and Sunday, and seen him work twice. He was playin' the outfield, but as luck would have it they wasn't a fly ball hit in his direction in both games. A base hit was made out his way and he booted it, and that's the only report Tom could get on his fieldin'. But he wallops two over the wall in one day and they catch two line drives off him. The next day he gets four blows and two o' them is triples.

So Tom comes back and tells John the guy is a whale of a hitter and fast as Cobb, but he don't know nothin' about his fieldin'. Then John signs him to a contract—twelve hundred or somethin' like that. We'd been in Tampa a week before he showed up. Then he comes to the hotel and just sits round all day, without tellin' nobody who he was. Finally the bellhops was going to chase him out and he says he's one o' the ballplayers. Then the clerk gets John to go over and talk to him. He tells John his name and says he hasn't had nothin' to eat for three days, because he was broke. John told me afterward that he'd drew about three hundred in advance—last winter sometime. Well, they took him in the dinin' room and they tell me he inhaled about four meals at once. That night they roomed him with Heine.

Next mornin' Heine and me walks out to the grounds together and Heine tells me about him. He says:

"Don't never call me a bug again. They got me roomin' with the champion o' the world."

"Who is he?" I says.

"I don't know and I don't want to know," says Heine; "but if they stick him in there with me again I'll jump to the Federals. To start with, he ain't got no baggage. I ast him where his trunk was and he says he didn't have none. Then I ast him if he didn't have no suitcase, and he says: 'No. What do you care?' I was goin' to lend him some pajamas, but he put on the shirt o' the uniform John give him last night and slept in that. He was asleep when I got up this mornin'. I seen his collar layin' on the dresser and it looked like he had wore it in Pittsburgh every day for a year. So I threwed it out the window and he comes down to breakfast with no collar. I ast him what size collar he wore and he says he didn't want none, because he wasn't goin' out nowheres. After breakfast he beat it up to the room again and put on his uniform. When I got up there he was lookin' in the glass at himself, and he done it all the time I was dressin'."

When we got out to the park I got my first look at him. Pretty good-lookin' guy, too, in his unie—big shoulders and well put together; built somethin' like Heine himself. He was talkin' to John when I come up.

"What position do you play?" John was askin' him.

"I play anywheres," says Elliott.

"You're the kind I'm lookin' for," says John. Then he says: "You was an outfielder up there in Michigan, wasn't you?"

"I don't care where I play," says Elliott.

John sends him to the outfield and forgets all about him for a while. Pretty soon Miller comes in and says:

"I ain't goin' to shag for no bush outfielder!"

John ast him what was the matter, and Miller tells him that Elliott ain't doin' nothin' but just standin' out there; that he ain't makin' no attemp' to catch the fungoes, and that he won't even chase 'em. Then John starts watchin' him, and it was just like Miller said. Larry hit one pretty near in his lap and he stepped out o' the way. John calls him in and ast him:

"Why don't you go after them fly balls?"

"Because I don't want 'em," says Elliott.

John gets sarcastic and says:

"What do you want? Of course we'll see that you get anythin' you want!"

"Give me a ticket back home," says Elliott.

"Don't you want to stick with the club?" says John, and the busher tells him, no, he certainly did not. Then John tells him he'll have to pay his own fare home and Elliott don't get sore at all. He just says:

"Well, I'll have to stick, then—because I'm broke."

We was havin' battin' practice and John tells him to go up and hit a few. And you ought to of seen him bust 'em!

Lavender was in there workin' and he'd been pitchin' a little all winter, so he was in pretty good shape. He lobbed one up to Elliott, and he hit it 'way up in some trees outside the fence—about a mile, I guess. Then John tells Jimmy to put somethin' on the ball. Jim comes through with one of his fast ones and the kid slams it agin the right-field wall on a line.

"Give him your spitter!" yells John, and Jim handed him one. He pulled it over first base so fast that Bert, who was standin' down there, couldn't hardly duck in time. If it'd hit him it'd killed him.

Well, he kep' on hittin' everthin' Jim give him—and Jim had somethin' too. Finally John gets Pierce warmed up and sends him out to pitch, tellin' him to hand Elliott a flock o' curve balls. He wanted to see if left-handers was goin' to bother him. But he slammed 'em right along, and I don't b'lieve he hit more'n two the whole mornin' that wouldn't of been base hits in a game.

They sent him out to the outfield again in the afternoon, and after a lot o' coaxin' Leach got him to go after fly balls; but that's all he did do—just go after 'em. One hit him on the bean and another on the shoulder. He run back after the short ones and 'way in after the ones that went over his head. He catched just one—a line drive that he couldn't get out o' the way of; and then he acted like it hurt his hands.

I come back to the hotel with John. He ast me what I thought of Elliott.

"Well," I says, "he'd be the greatest ballplayer in the world if he could just play ball. He sure can bust 'em."

John says he was afraid he couldn't never make an outfielder out o' him. He says:

"I'll try him on the infield to-morrow. They must be some place he can play. I never seen a lefthand hitter that looked so good agin lefthand pitchin'—and he's got a great arm; but he acts like he'd never saw a fly ball."

Well, he was just as bad on the infield. They put him at short and he was like a sieve. You could of drove a hearse between him and second base without him gettin' near it. He'd stoop over for a ground ball about the time it was bouncin' up agin the fence; and when he'd try to cover the bag on a peg he'd trip over it.

They tried him at first base and sometimes he'd run 'way over in the coachers' box and sometimes out in right field lookin' for the bag. Once Heine shot one across at him on a line and he never touched it with his hands. It went bam! right in the pit of his stomach—and the lunch he'd ate didn't do him no good.

Finally John just give up and says he'd have to keep him on the bench and let him earn his pay by bustin' 'em a couple o' times a week or so. We all agreed with John that this bird would be a whale of a pinch hitter—and we was right too. He was hittin' 'way over five hundred when the blowoff come, along about the last o' May.

# 2

Before the trainin' trip was over, Elliott had roomed with pretty near everybody in the club. Heine raised an awful holler after the second night down there and John put the bug in with Needham. Tom stood him for three nights. Then he doubled up with Archer, and Schulte, and Miller, and Leach, and Saier—and the whole bunch in turn, averagin' about two nights with each one before they put up a kick. Then John tried him with some o' the youngsters, but they wouldn't stand for him no more'n the others. They all said he was crazy and they was afraid he'd get violent some night and stick a knife in 'em.

He always insisted on havin' the water run in the bathtub all night, because he said it reminded him of the sound of the dam near his home. The fellers might get up four or five times a night and shut off the faucet, but he'd get right up after 'em and turn it on again. Carter, a big bush pitcher from Georgia, started a fight with him about it one night, and Elliott pretty near killed him. So the rest o' the bunch, when they'd saw

Carter's map next mornin', didn't have the nerve to do nothin' when it come their turn.

Another o' his habits was the thing that scared 'em, though. He'd brought a razor with him—in his pocket, I guess—and he used to do his shavin' in the middle o' the night. Instead o' doin' it in the bathroom he'd lather his face and then come out and stand in front o' the lookin'-glass on the dresser. Of course he'd have all the lights turned on, and that was bad enough when a feller wanted to sleep; but the worst of it was that he'd stop shavin' every little while and turn round and stare at the guy who was makin' a failure o' tryin' to sleep. Then he'd wave his razor round in the air and laugh, and begin shavin' agin. You can imagine how comf'table his roomies felt!

John had bought him a suitcase and some clothes and things, and charged 'em up to him. He'd drew so much dough in advance that he didn't have nothin' comin' till about June. He never thanked John and he'd wear one shirt and one collar till some one throwed 'em away.

Well, we finally gets to Indianapolis, and we was goin' from there to Cincy to open. The last day in Indianapolis John come and ast me how I'd like to change roomies. I says I was perfectly satisfied with Larry. Then John says:

"I wisht you'd try Elliott. The other boys all kicks on him, but he seems to hang round you a lot and I b'lieve you could get along all right."

"Why don't you room him alone?" I ast.

"The boss or the hotels won't stand for us roomin' alone," says John. "You go ahead and try it, and see how you make out. If he's too much for you let me know; but he likes you and I think he'll be diff'rent with a guy who can talk to him like you can."

So I says I'd tackle it, because I didn't want to throw John down. When we got to Cincy they stuck Elliott and me in one room, and we was together till he quit us.

# 3

I went to the room early that night, because we was goin' to open next day and I wanted to feel like somethin'. First thing I done when I got undressed was turn on both faucets in the bathtub.

They was makin' an awful racket when Elliott finally come in about midnight. I was layin' awake and I opened right up on him. I says:

"Don't shut off that water, because I like to hear it run."

Then I turned over and pretended to be asleep. The bug got his clothes off, and then what did he do but go in the bathroom and shut off the water! Then he come back in the room and says:

"I guess no one's goin' to tell me what to do in here."

But I kep' right on pretendin' to sleep and didn't pay no attention. When he'd got into his bed I jumped out o' mine and turned on all the lights and begun stroppin' my razor. He says:

"What's comin' off?"

"Some o' my whiskers," I says. "I always shave along about this time."

"No, you don't!" he says. "I was in your room one mornin' down in Louisville and I seen you shavin' then."

"Well," I says, "the boys tell me you shave in the middle o' the night; and I thought if I done all the things you do mebbe I'd get so's I could hit like you."

"You must be superstitious!" he says. And I told him I was. "I'm a good hitter," he says, "and I'd be a good hitter if I never shaved at all. That don't make no diff'rence."

"Yes, it does," I says. "You prob'ly hit good because you shave at night; but you'd be a better fielder if you shaved in the mornin'."

You see, I was tryin' to be just as crazy as him—though that wasn't hardly possible.

"If that's right," says he, "I'll do my shavin' in the mornin'—because I seen in the papers where the boys says that if I could play the outfield like I can hit I'd be as good as Cobb. They tell me Cobb gets twenty thousand a year."

"No," I says; "he don't get that much—but he gets about ten times as much as you do."

"Well," he says, "I'm goin' to be as good as him, because I need the money."

"What do you want with money?" I says.

He just laughed and didn't say nothin'; but from that time on the water didn't run in the bathtub nights and he done his shavin' after breakfast. I didn't notice, though, that he looked any better in fieldin' practice.

# 4

It rained one day in Cincy and they trimmed us two out o' the other three; but it wasn't Elliott's fault.

They had Larry beat four to one in the ninth innin' o' the first game. Archer gets on with two out, and John sends my roomy up to hit—though Benton, a lefthander, is workin' for them. The first thing Benton serves up there Elliott cracks it a mile over Hobby's head. It would of been good for three easy—only Archer—playin' safe, o' course—pulls up at third base. Tommy couldn't do nothin' and we was licked.

The next day he hits one out o' the park off the Indian; but we was 'way behind and they was nobody on at the time. We copped the last one without usin' no pinch hitters.

I didn't have no trouble with him nights durin' the whole series. He come to bed pretty late while we was there and I told him he'd better not let John catch him at it.

"What would he do?" he says.

"Fine you fifty," I says.

He can't fine me a dime," he says, "because I ain't got it."

Then I told him he'd be fined all he had comin' if he didn't get in the hotel before midnight; but he just laughed and says he didn't think John had a kick comin' so long as he kep' bustin' the ball.

"Some day you'll go up there and you won't bust it," I says.

"That'll be an accident," he says.

That stopped me and I didn't say nothin'. What could you say to a guy who hated himself like that?

The "accident" happened in St. Louis the first day. We needed two runs in the eighth and Saier and Brid was on, with two out. John tells Elliott to go up in Pierce's place. The bug goes up and Griner gives him two bad balls—'way outside. I thought they was goin' to walk him—and it looked like good jud'gment, because they'd heard what he done in Cincy. But no! Griner comes back with a fast one right over and Elliott pulls it down the right foul line, about two foot foul. He hit it so hard you'd of thought they'd sure walk him then; but Griner gives him another fast one. He slammed it again just as hard, but foul. Then Griner gives him one 'way outside and it's two and three. John says, on the bench:

"If they don't walk him now he'll bust that fence down."

I thought the same and I was sure Griner wouldn't give him nothin' to hit; but he come with a curve and Rigler calls Elliott out. From where we sat the last one looked low, and I thought Elliott'd make a kick. He come back to the bench smilin'.

John starts for his position, but stopped and ast the bug what was the matter with that one. Any busher I ever knowed would of said, "It was too low," or "It was outside," or "It was inside." Elliott says:

"Nothin' at all. It was right over the middle."

"Why didn't you bust it, then?" says John.

"I was afraid I'd kill somebody," says Elliott, and laughed like a big boob.

John was pretty near chokin'.

"What are you laughin' at?" he says.

"I was thinkin' of a nickel show I seen in Cincinnati," says the bug.

"Well," says John, so mad he couldn't hardly see, "that show and that laugh'll cost you fifty."

We got beat, and I wouldn't of blamed John if he'd fined him his whole season's pay.

Up 'n the room that night I told him he'd better cut out that laughin' stuff when we was gettin' trimmed or he never would have no pay day. Then he got confidential.

"Pay day wouldn't do me no good," he says. "When I'm all squared up with the club and begin to have a pay day I'll only get a hundred bucks at a time, and I'll owe that to some o' you fellers. I wisht we could win the pennant and get in on that World's Series dough. Then I'd get a bunch at once."

"What would you do with a bunch o' dough?" I ast him.

"Don't tell nobody, sport," he says; "but if I ever get five hundred at once I'm goin' to get married."

"Oh!" I says. "And who's the lucky girl?"

"She's a girl up in Muskegon," says Elliott; "and you're right when you call her lucky."

"You don't like yourself much, do you?" I says.

"I got reason to like myself," says he. "You'd like yourself, too, if you could hit 'em like me."

"Well," I says, "you didn't show me no hittin' to-day."

"I couldn't hit because I was laughin' too hard," says Elliott.

"What was it you was laughin' at?" I says.

"I was laughin' at that pitcher," he says. "He thought he had some-thin' and he didn't have nothin'."

"He had enough to whiff you with," I says.

"He didn't have nothin'!" says he again. "I was afraid if I busted one off him they'd can him, and then I couldn't never hit agin him no more."

Naturally I didn't have no comeback to that. I just sort o' gasped and got ready to go to sleep; but he wasn't through.

"I wisht you could see this bird!" he says.

"What bird?" I says.

"This dame that's nuts about me," he says.

"Good-looker?" I ast.

"No," he says; "she ain't no bear for looks. They ain't nothin' about her for a guy to rave over till you hear her sing. She sure can holler some."

"What kind o' voice has she got?" I ast.

"A bear," says he.

"No," I says; "I mean is she a barytone or an air?"

"I don't know," he says; "but she's got the loudest voice I ever hear on a woman. She's pretty near got me beat."

"Can you sing?" I says; and I was sorry right afterward that I ast him that question.

I guess it must of been bad enough to have the water runnin' night after night and to have him wavin' that razor round; but that couldn't of been nothin' to his singin'. Just as soon as I'd pulled that boner he says, "Listen to me!" and starts in on 'Silver Threads Among the Gold.' Mind you, it was after midnight and they was guests all round us tryin' to sleep!

They used to be noise enough in our club when we had Hofman and Sheckard and Richie harmonizin'; but this bug's voice was louder'n all o' theirn combined. We once had a pitcher named Martin Walsh—brother o' Big Ed's—and I thought he could drownd out the Subway; but this guy made a boiler factory sound like Dummy Taylor. If the whole hotel wasn't awake when he'd howled the first line it's a pipe they was when he cut loose, which he done when he come to "Always young and fair to me." Them words could of been heard easy in East St. Louis.

He didn't get no encore from me, but he goes right through it again—or starts to. I knowed somethin' was goin' to happen before he finished—and somethin' did. The night clerk and the house detective come bangin' at the door. I let 'em in and they had plenty to say. If we made another sound the whole club'd be canned out o' the hotel. I tried to salve 'em, and I says:

"He won't sing no more."

But Elliott swelled up like a poisoned pup.

"Won't I?" he says. "I'll sing all I want to."

"You won't sing in here," says the clerk.

"They ain't room for my voice in here anyways," he says. "I'll go out-doors and sing."

And he puts his clothes on and ducks out. I didn't make no attemp' to stop him. I heard him bellowin' 'Silver Threads' down the corridor and down the stairs, with the clerk and the dick chasin' him all the way and tellin' him to shut up.

Well, the guests make a holler the next mornin'; and the hotel people tells Charlie Williams that he'll either have to let Elliott stay somewheres else or the whole club'll have to move. Charlie tells John, and John was thinkin' o' settlin' the question by releasin' Elliott.

I guess he'd about made up his mind to do it; but that afternoon they had us three to one in the ninth, and we got the bases full, with two down and Larry's turn to hit. Elliott had been sittin' on the bench sayin' nothin'.

"Do you think you can hit one today?" says John.

"I can hit one any day," says Elliott.

"Go up and hit that lefthander, then," says John, "and remember there's nothin' to laugh at."

Sallee was workin'—and workin' good; but that didn't bother the bug. He cut into one, and it went between Oakes and Whitted like a shot. He come into third standin' up and we was a run to the good. Sallee was so sore he kind o' forgot himself and took pretty near his full wind-up pitchin' to Tommy. And what did Elliott do but steal home and get away with it clean!

Well, you couldn't can him after that, could you? Charlie gets him a room somewheres and I was relieved of his company that night. The next evenin' we beat it for Chi to play about two weeks at home. He didn't tell nobody where he roomed there and I didn't see nothin' of him, 'cep' out to the park. I ast him what he did with himself nights and he says:

"Same as I do on the road—borrow some dough some place and go to the nickel shows."

"You must be stuck on 'em," I says.

"Yes," he says; "I like the ones where they kill people—because I want to learn how to do it. I may have that job some day."

"Don't pick on me," I says.

"Oh," says the bug, "you never can tell who I'll pick on."

It seemed as if he just couldn't learn nothin' about fieldin', and finally John told him to keep out o' the practice.

"A ball might hit him in the temple and croak him," says John.

But he busted up a couple o' games for us at home, beatin' Pittsburgh once and Cincy once.

# 5

They give me a great big room at the hotel in Pittsburgh; so the fellers picked it out for the poker game. We was playin' along about ten o'clock one night when in come Elliott–the earliest he'd showed up since we'd been roomin' together. They was only five of us playin' and Tom ast him to sit in.

"I'm busted," he says.

"Can you play poker?" I ast him.

"They's nothin' I can't do!" he says. "Slip me a couple o' bucks and I'll show you."

So I slipped him a couple o' bucks and honestly hoped he'd win, because I knowed he never had no dough. Well, Tom dealt him a hand and he picks it up and says:

"I only got five cards."

"How many do you want?" I says

"Oh," he says, "if that's all I get I'll try to make 'em do."

The pot was cracked and raised, and he stood the raise. I says to myself: "There goes my two bucks!" But no–he comes out with three queens and won the dough. It was only about seven bucks; but you'd of thought it was a million to see him grab it. He laughed like a kid.

"Guess I can't play this game!" he says; and he had me fooled for a minute–I thought he must of been kiddin' when he complained of only havin' five cards.

He copped another pot right afterward and was sittin' there with about eleven bucks in front of him when Jim opens a roodle pot for a buck. I stays and so does Elliott. Him and Jim both drawed one card and I took three. I had kings or queens–I forget which. I didn't help 'em none; so when Jim bets a buck I throws my hand away.

"How much can I bet?" says the bug.

"You can raise Jim a buck if you want to," I says.

So he bets two dollars. Jim comes back at him. He comes right back at Jim. Jim raises him again and he tilts Jim right back. Well, when he'd boosted Jim with the last buck he had, Jim says:

"I'm ready to call. I guess you got me beat. What have you got?"

"I know what I've got, all right," says Elliott. "I've got a straight." And he throws his hand down. Sure enough, it was a straight, eight high. Jim pretty near fainted and so did I.

The bug had started pullin' in the dough when Jim stops him.

"Here! Wait a minute!" says Jim. "I thought you had somethin'. I filled up." Then Jim lays down his nine full.

"You beat me, I guess," says Elliott, and he looked like he'd lost his last friend.

"Beat you?" says Jim. "Of course I beat you! What did you think I had?"

'Well," says the bug, "I thought you might have a small flush or some-thin'."

When I regained consciousness he was beggin' for two more bucks.

"What for?" I says. "To play poker with? You're barred from the game for life!"

"Well," he says, "if I can't play no more I want to go to sleep, and you fellers will have to get out o' this room."

Did you ever hear o' nerve like that? This was the first night he'd came in before twelve and he orders the bunch out so's he can sleep! We politely suggested to him to go to Brooklyn.

Without sayin' a word he starts in on his 'Silver Threads'; and it wasn't two minutes till the game was busted up and the bunch–all but me–was out o' there. I'd of beat it too, only he stopped yellin' as soon as they'd went.

"You're some buster!" I says. "You bust up ball games in the afternoon and poker games at night."

"Yes," he says; "that's my business–bustin' things."

And before I knowed what he was about he picked up the pitcher of ice-water that was on the floor and throwed it out the window–through the glass and all.

Right then I give him a plain talkin' to. I tells him how near he come to gettin' canned down in St. Louis because he raised so much Cain singin' in the hotel.

"But I had to keep my voice in shape," he says. "If I ever get dough enough to get married the girl and me'll go out singin' together."

"Out where?" I ast.

"Out on the vaudeville circuit," says Elliott.

"Well," I says, "if her voice is like yours you'll be wastin' money if you travel round. Just stay up in Muskegon and we'll hear you, all right!"

I told him he wouldn't never get no dough if he didn't behave himself. That, even if we got in the World's Series, he wouldn't be with us—unless he cut out the foolishness.

"We ain't goin' to get in no World's Series," he says, "and I won't never get a bunch o' money at once; so it looks like I couldn't get married this fall."

Then I told him we played a city series every fall. He'd never thought o' that and it tickled him to death. I told him the losers always got about five hundred apiece and that we were about due to win it and get about eight hundred. "But," I says, "we still got a good chance for the old pennant; and if I was you I wouldn't give up hope o' that yet—not where John can hear you, anyway."

"No," he says, "we won't win no pennant, because he won't let me play reg'lar; but I don't care so long as we're sure o' that city-series dough."

"You ain't sure of it if you don't behave," I says.

"Well," says he, very serious, "I guess I'll behave." And he did—till we made our first Eastern trip.

# 6

We went to Boston first, and that crazy bunch goes out and piles up a three-run lead on us in seven innin's the first day. It was the pitcher's turn to lead off in the eighth, so up goes Elliott to bat for him. He kisses the first thing they hands him for three bases; and we says, on the bench: "Now we'll get 'em!"—because, you know, a three-run lead wasn't nothin' in Boston.

"Stay right on that bag!" John hollers to Elliott.

Mebbe if John hadn't said nothin' to him everythin' would of been all right; but when Perdue starts to pitch the first ball to Tommy, Elliott starts to steal home. He's out as far as from here to Seattle.

If I'd been carryin' a gun I'd of shot him right through the heart. As it was, I thought John'd kill him with a bat, because he was standin' there with a couple of 'em, waitin' for his turn; but I guess John was too stunned to move. He didn't even seem to see Elliott when he went to the bench. After I'd cooled off a little I says:

"Beat it and get into your clothes before John comes in. Then go to the hotel and keep out o' sight."

When I got up in the room afterward, there was Elliott, lookin' as innocent and happy as though he'd won fifty bucks with a pair o' treys.

"I thought you might of killed yourself," I says.

"What for?" he says.

"For that swell play you made," says I.

"What was the matter with the play?" ast Elliott, surprised. "It was all right when I done it in St. Louis."

"Yes," I says; "but they was two out in St. Louis and we wasn't no three runs behind."

"Well," he says, "if it was all right in St. Louis I don't see why it was wrong here."

"It's a diff'rent climate here," I says, too disgusted to argue with him.

"I wonder if they'd let me sing in this climate?" says Elliott.

"No," I says. "Don't sing in this hotel, because we don't want to get fired out o' here–the eats is too good."

"All right," he says. "I won't sing." But when I starts down to supper he says: "I'm li'ble to do somethin' worse'n sing."

He didn't show up in the dinin' room and John went to the boxin' show after supper; so it looked like him and Elliott wouldn't run into each other till the murder had left John's heart. I was glad o' that–because a Mass'chusetts jury might not consider it justifiable hommercide if one guy croaked another for givin' the Boston club a game.

I went down to the corner and had a couple o' beers; and then I come straight back, intendin' to hit the hay. The elevator boy had went for a drink or somethin', and they was two old ladies already waitin' in the car when I stepped in. Right along after me comes Elliott.

"Where's the boy that's supposed to run this car?" he says. I told him the boy'd be right back; but he says: "I can't wait. I'm much too sleepy."

And before I could stop him he'd slammed the door and him and I and the poor old ladies was shootin' up.

"Let us off at the third floor, please!" says one o' the ladies, her voice kind o' shakin'.

"Sorry, madam," says the bug; "but this is a express and we don't stop at no third floor."

I grabbed his arm and tried to get him away from the machinery; but he was as strong as a ox and he throwed me agin the side o' the car like I was a baby. We went to the top faster'n I ever rode in an elevator before. And then we shot down to the bottom, hittin' the bumper down there so hard I thought we'd be smashed to splinters.

The ladies was too scared to make a sound durin' the first trip; but while we was goin' up and down the second time—even faster'n the first—they begun to scream. I was hollerin' my head off at him to quit and he was makin' more noise than the three of us—pretendin' he was the locomotive and the whole crew o' the train.

Don't never ask me how many times we went up and down! The women fainted on the third trip and I guess I was about as near it as I'll ever get. The elevator boy and the bellhops and the waiters and the night clerk and everybody was jumpin' round the lobby screamin'; but no one seemed to know how to stop us.

Finally—on about the tenth trip, I guess—he slowed down and stopped at the fifth floor, where we was roomin'. He opened the door and beat it for the room, while I, though I was tremblin' like a leaf, run the car down to the bottom.

The night clerk knowed me pretty well and knowed I wouldn't do nothin' like that; so him and I didn't argue, but just got to work together to bring the old women to. While we was doin' that Elliott must of run down the stairs and slipped out o' the hotel, because when they sent the officers up to the room after him he'd blowed.

They was goin' to fire the club out; but Charlie had a good stand-in with Amos, the proprietor, and he fixed it up to let us stay—providin' Elliott kep' away. The bug didn't show up at the ballpark next day and we didn't see no more of him till we got on the rattler for New York.

Charlie and John both bawled him, but they give him a berth–an up-per–and we pulled into the Grand Central Station without him havin' made no effort to wreck the train.

# 7

I'd studied the thing pretty careful, but hadn't come to no conclusion. I was sure he wasn't no stew, because none o' the boys had ever saw him even take a glass o' beer, and I couldn't never detect the odor o' booze on him. And if he'd been a dope I'd of knew about it–roomin' with him.

There wouldn't of been no mystery about it if he'd been a lefthand pitcher–but he wasn't. He wasn't nothin' but a whale of a hitter and he throwed with his right arm. He hit lefthanded, o'course; but so did Saier and Brid and Schulte and me, and John himself; and none of us was violent. I guessed he must of been just a plain nut and li'ble to break out any time.

They was a letter waitin' for him at New York, and I took it, intendin' to give it to him at the park, because I didn't think they'd let him room at the hotel; but after breakfast he come up to the room, with his suitcase. It seems he'd promised John and Charlie to be good, and made it so strong they b'lieved him.

I give him his letter, which was addressed in a girl's writin' and come from Muskegon.

"From the girl?" I says.

"Yes," he says; and, without openin' it, he tore it up and throwed it out the window.

"Had a quarrel?" I ast.

"No, no," he says; "but she can't tell me nothin' I don't know already. Girls always writes the same junk. I got one from her in Pittsburgh, but I didn't read it."

"I guess you ain't so stuck on her," I says.

He swells up and says:

"Of course I'm stuck on her! If I wasn't, do you think I'd be goin' round with this bunch and gettin' insulted all the time? I'm stickin' here because o' that series dough, so's I can get hooked."

"Do you think you'd settle down if you was married?" I ast him.

"Settle down?" he says. "Sure, I'd settle down. I'd be so happy that I wouldn't have to look for no excitement."

Nothin' special happened that night 'cep' that he come in the room about one o'clock and woke me up by pickin' up the foot o' the bed and droppin' it on the floor, sudden-like.

"Give me a key to the room," he says.

"You must of had a key," I says, "or you couldn't of got in."

"That's right!" he says, and beat it to bed.

One o' the reporters must of told Elliott that John had ast for waivers on him and New York had refused to waive, because next mornin' he come to me with that dope.

"New York's goin' to win this pennant!" he says.

"Well," I says, "they will if some one else don't. But what of it?"

"I'm goin' to play with New York," he says, "so's I can get the World's Series dough."

"How you goin' to get away from this club?" I ast.

"Just watch me!" he says. "I'll be with New York before this series is over."

Well, the way he goes after the job was original, anyway. Rube'd had one of his good days the day before and we'd got a trimmin'; but this second day the score was tied up at two runs apiece in the tenth, and Big Jeff'd been wabblin' for two or three innin's.

Well, he walks Saier and me, with one out, and Mac sends for Matty, who was warmed up and ready. John sticks Elliott in Brid's place and the bug pulls one into the right-field stand.

It's a cinch McGraw thinks well of him then, and might of went after him if he hadn't went crazy the next afternoon. We're tied up in the ninth and Matty's workin'. John sends Elliott up with the bases choked; but he doesn't go right up to the plate. He walks over to their bench and calls McGraw out. Mac tells us about it afterward.

"I can bust up this game right here!" says Elliott.

"Go ahead," says Mac; "but be careful he don't whiff you." Then the bug pulls it.

"If I whiff," he says, "will you get me on your club?"

"Sure!" says Mac, just as anybody would.

By this time Bill Koem was hollerin' about the delay; so up goes Elliott and gives the worst burlesque on tryin' to hit that you ever see. Matty throws one a mile outside and high and the bug swings like it was right over the heart. Then Matty throws one at him and he ducks out o' the way—but swings just the same. Matty must of been wise by this time, for he pitches one so far outside that the Chief almost has to go to the coachers' box after it. Elliott takes his third healthy and runs through the field down to the clubhouse.

We got beat in the eleventh; and when we went in to dress he has his street clothes on. Soon as he seen John comin' he says: "I got to see McGraw!" And he beat it.

John was goin' to the fights that night; but before he leaves the hotel he had waivers on Elliott from everybody and had sold him to Atlanta.

"And," says John, "I don't care if they pay for him or not."

My roomy blows in about nine and got the letter from John out of his box. He was goin' to tear it up, but I told him they was news in it. He opens it and reads where he's sold. I was still sore at him; so I says:

"Thought you was goin' to get on the New York club?"

"No," he says. "I got turned down cold. McGraw says he wouldn't have me in his club. He says he'd had Charlie Faust—and that was enough for him."

He had a kind o' crazy look in his eyes; so when he starts up to the room I follows him.

"What are you goin' to do now?" I says.

"I'm goin' to sell this ticket to Atlanta," he says, "and go back to Muskegon, where I belong."

"I'll help you pack," I says.

"No," says the bug. "I come into this league with this suit o' clothes and a collar. They can have the rest of it." Then he sits down on the bed and begins to cry like a baby. "No series dough for me," he blubbers, "and no weddin' bells! My girl'll die when she hears about it!"

Of course that made me feel kind o' rotten, and I says:

"Brace up, boy! The best thing you can do is go to Atlanta and try hard. You'll be up here again next year."

"You can't tell me where to go!" he says, and he wasn't cryin' no more. "I'll go where I please—and I'm li'ble to take you with me."

I didn't want no argument, so I kep' still. Pretty soon he goes up to the lookin'-glass and stares at himself for five minutes. Then, all of a sudden, he hauls off and takes a wallop at his reflection in the glass. Naturally he smashed the glass all to pieces and he cut his hand somethin' awful.

Without lookin' at it he come over to me and says: "Well, good-by, sport!"—and holds out his other hand to shake. When I starts to shake with him he smears his bloody hand all over my map. Then he laughed like a wild man and run out o' the room and out o' the hotel.

# 8

Well, boys, my sleep was broke up for the rest o' the season. It might of been because I was used to sleepin' in all kinds o' racket and excitement, and couldn't stand for the quiet after he'd went—or it might of been because I kep' thinkin' about him and feelin' sorry for him.

I of'en wondered if he'd settle down and be somethin' if he could get married; and finally I got to b'lievin' he would. So when we was dividin' the city series dough I was thinkin' of him and the girl. Our share o' the money—the losers', as usual—was twelve thousand seven hundred sixty bucks or somethin' like that. They was twenty-one of us and that meant six hundred seven bucks apiece. We was just goin' to cut it up that way when I says:

"Why not give a divvy to poor old Elliott?"

About fifteen of 'em at once told me that I was crazy. You see, when he got canned he owed everybody in the club. I guess he'd stuck me for the most—about seventy bucks—but I didn't care nothin' about that. I knowed he hadn't never reported to Atlanta, and I thought he was prob'ly busted and a bunch o' money might make things all right for him and the other songbird.

I made quite a speech to the fellers, tellin' 'em how he'd cried when he left us and how his heart'd been set on gettin' married on the series dough. I made it so strong that they finally fell for it. Our shares was cut to five hundred eighty apiece, and John sent him a check for a full share.

For a while I was kind o' worried about what I'd did. I didn't know if I was doin' right by the girl to give him the chance to marry her.

He'd told me she was stuck on him, and that's the only excuse I had for tryin' to fix it up between 'em; but, b'lieve me, if she was my sister or a friend o' mine I'd just as soon of had her manage the Cincinnati Club as marry that bird. I thought to myself:

"If she's all right she'll take acid in a month—and it'll be my fault; but if she's really stuck on him they must be somethin' wrong with her too, so what's the diff'rence?"

Then along comes this letter that I told you about. It's from some friend of hisn up there—and they's a note from him. I'll read 'em to you and then I got to beat it for the station:

Dear Sir: They have got poor Elliott locked up and they are goin' to take him to the asylum at Kalamazoo. He thanks you for the check, and we will use the money to see that he is made comf'table.

When the poor boy come back here he found that his girl was married to Joe Bishop, who runs a soda fountain. She had wrote to him about it, but he did not read her letters. The news drove him crazy—poor boy—and he went to the place where they was livin' with a baseball bat and very near killed 'em both. Then he marched down the street singin' 'Silver Threads Among the Gold' at the top of his voice. They was goin' to send him to prison for assault with intent to kill, but the jury decided he was crazy.

He wants to thank you again for the money.

Yours truly,

Jim—

I can't make out his last name—but it don't make no diff'rence. Now I'll read you his note:

Old Roomy: I was at bat twice and made two hits; but I guess I did not meet 'em square. They tell me they are both alive yet, which I did not mean 'em to be. I hope they got good curve-ball pitchers where I am goin'. I sure can bust them curves—can't I, sport?

Yours,

B. Elliott.

P.S.—the B stands for Buster.

That's all of it, fellers; and you can see I had some excuse for not hittin'. You can also see why I ain't never goin' to room with no bug again—not for John or nobody else!

*Ashley Buck's poignant story "A Pitcher Grows Tired" was originally published in* Esquire *magazine. It's about an aging pitcher, still sharp but realizing his baseball mortality and hanging on to a fleeting career. This is a real nostalgia piece.*

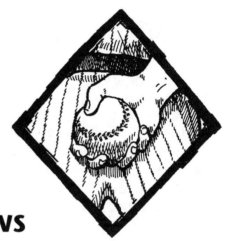

## *Ashley Buck*

# A PITCHER GROWS TIRED (1946)

**R**ODKIN WALKED ACROSS THE FIELD to the clubhouse. Burke and Peck were beside him. The crowd gathered close around and it was difficult to move. They pulled at Rodkin's uniform and slapped his back. Once he had liked that in a crowd. His heart liked it now, but their friendly grasping wore his body to exhaustion. They came to the edge of the field and walked under the bleachers and into the clubhouse. Inside there was an odor of sweat, dust, liniments and steam from the hot showers. Rodkin liked the smell: strong, human, earthly. It was a smell you never forgot and during the long winters when there was no baseball you got lonely for the smell and wanted to bring it back.

The players laughed and hurried to get dressed. They spoke of the splendid game Rodkin had pitched. He wondered if they knew how fortunate he had been. If Blake had known how tired he was he would not have been overanxious. He would have waited. Blake and others would not always be young and inexperienced.

Rodkin did not hurry. He sat down and slowly unlaced his shoes. His hands shook. All the strength was gone from them. Peck spoke to him, low, not wanting anyone else to hear: "You still got plenty of guts. You've always had the heart."

Rodkin kept his eyes on his shoes: "And I have plenty on the ball too."

"Yes," said Peck.

"I can put it anywhere Burke says."

"I know that."

There was a silence. Rodkin slipped off his shirt. The muscles in his shoulders throbbed like hearts. His eyes never met Peck's.

"You got the guts," said Peck. "I never knew you had so much. You looked like a million dollars in there."

"Yeah," said Rodkin.

"And you felt like two cents."

"I was all right."

"You were fine."

Peck moved away. There was a gnawing feeling in Rodkin's chest, a dull pressure at the back of his head.

The players left the building and only the trainer, Rodkin and Joie remained. Rodkin lay upon the table. He closed his eyes and let his body relax. It was a pleasant feeling that brought a soft ache to his stomach. He seemed to sink into nothingness.

"Take it easy," he told the trainer.

"I've taken it easy for years," said Hank.

Hank took more time to rub down Rodkin than he did anyone else. Rodkin knew this. The massaging hurt. Not a painful hurt; only the hurt of wanting to be hurt, wanting the body gently tortured for the relief that came afterward; for the fine feeling after the fingers left the sore spots.

"You and Burke won today's game with your heads," said Hank.

"Yes," said Rodkin.

"Your arm had nothing to do with it," said Hank.

"Burke's smart."

"You're smart too," said Hank. "You've always been smart."

"No one is smarter than Mr. Rodkin," said Joie.

Rodkin opened his eyes. He had forgotten Joie was there. "Forget the Mister, Joie. I'm only one of the players."

"No, you're not."

You're anything but that," said Hank.

"Why do you call me Mister, Joie?"

"It's like I told you. There are ballplayers you call by their first names, ballplayers you call by nick names and then there are the ones you call Mister. You couldn't call them anything else."

"And I'm a Mister?"

"Yes."

"If you had known Ty Cobb, what would he have been?"

"Mister Cobb."

"He was the very best, Joie. There's never been a player as great."

"You're as great a pitcher as he was an outfielder."

A strange look passed between Rodkin and Hank. Rodkin closed his eyes and turned his head away from Joie. He spoke softly: "Thanks, Joie. That's the nicest thing ever said to me. As great as Cobb."

A calmness settled over the clubhouse. The only sound was Hank's hands rubbing Rodkin's body.

Joie sat thinking. He spoke: "Cobb could hit even when he quit baseball, couldn't he, Mr. Rodkins?"

"He was always dangerous. Even at the end his eyes were sharp and few players hit better."

"It was his legs, wasn't it? He wasn't fast anymore?"

"That's right. He wasn't fast. He played his last two years in the outfield on a dime."

"But he could still hit?"

"Always."

"Damn the legs," said Joie. "Damn them!"

"Even at the finish he was beautiful to watch. He had a sixth sense. Speaker had it too. They knew where to play a ball. I've seen them not have to move two feet to take a line drive. Their legs lasted longer than most legs do."

"They were the last word," said Hank. "They had everything."

"Everything," said Rodkin.

"I never saw either of them," said Joie.

"Then you've never seen the outfield played," said Hank. "And if you never saw Sisler, you've never seen first base played either."

"That's right," said Rodkin.

"I've missed those things," said Joie, "but I've seen Mr. Rodkin pitch and that makes up for them."

A silence. Joie walked over to the table and put his hand on Rodkin's back: "How do you feel?"

"Fine."

"You're not tired?"

"No. I'm not tired."

"You pitched a swell game today."

"Thanks, Joie."

"I have to run along. I'll see you tomorrow."

"Yes."

"Goodbye."

"Goodbye."

Hank's hands never left Rodkin's body. His fingers worked in and out between the muscles. Rodkin's tiredness went away.

"OK," said Hank.

"OK," said Rodkin. He got off the table and began to dress.

"You should have married," said Hank. "A ballplayer needs a wife."

"I've never been able to find a girl who sees baseball as I do."

"It's not too late."

"Yes it is."

"More women come to the games every day."

"It's a fad," said Rodkin. "Few really like it."

"My wife likes it."

"She's different."

"When you stop winning games Joie's heart will break."

"We all stop sometime," said Rodkin.

Hank spoke, casually, quietly: "Some pitchers pitch years with their heads."

"Yes."

"I've known pitchers who stayed around two and three years that didn't have a thing on the ball—just brains."

"Johnson pitched a long time like that."

"Yeah, and Alexander too," said Hank. "If a pitcher keeps getting smarter and doesn't bear down too hard—except in the pinches—he could stay around as long as Quinn did. He was near fifty before he left the majors."

"He was a spitball pitcher."

"That makes no difference. He had nerve and a head. You have them too."

They looked at each other. Rodkin lowered his eyes. He slipped on his coat. "So long," he said.

"So long," said Hank.

Rodkin walked out of the clubhouse. He wanted to see the park again. He wanted to go back a long way. He stood in deep rightfield and looked across the diamond to home plate. A great stillness lay over the field and stands. There is no lonelier place in the world than a ball park when the crowd has gone and it is cleaned out and in the west the day swiftly dying and nothing remains but a quietness that seems to speak. Inside Rodkin was filled with an emptiness. An aching loneliness started at the pit of his stomach and crept slowly upward past his chest, lingering in his throat. Whenever he spoke of those men a dullness came to him. Once there had been something and now that thing was gone. Once, long ago, he had pitched to those men and now they were no more. He remembered Cobb standing at the plate, kidding him, calling him a dumb rookie. Cobb was nearing the tiring age then. Who was it that said Cobb's only weakness was a walk? It was true anyway.

His eyes went to the green of the outfield. Speaker, Hooper and Cobb were ghosts running swiftly to catch long low drives. Their figures were silhouetted against the blue horizon: satyrs racing gracefully over the fresh spring earth to catch a white ball no larger than their closed hand. They had been great men and great players. Rodkin wanted to pitch to them again, but they had gotten tired and gone away. Their hearts had remained enthusiastic but not their bodies. He too was tired and like them would some day go away. He felt fine after the rubdown, but knew he would not be able to pitch any real ball for four days. Peck would not ask him to pitch until then. Peck was saving him. Rodkin wanted to be saved. Baseball was a part of him and he could not imagine what he would do without it. There is a difference in liking to see it played and in liking to play it. He wanted to play it forever—to pitch big-league ball until he died. The great players he loved were gone, but every spring would bring new players and like young Blake some would stay and grow older and become smart, that is, if they had the courage and were thoughtful and listened to what was told them and did not dissipate too much. They would stand before Rodkin with confidence, the crowd roaring or sitting in hushed stillness, and it would be their thinking against his. There would always be young players staring into the sun, dreaming of being as great as Cobb or Sisler, and maybe, one or two would reach that goal and he would then be too old to pitch to them.

And Burke? Burke must be tired. But he wasn't. Not until he straightened up a trifle to throw to second base. He would then be tired and the afternoons seem long and endless. And shortly after that time he would find there was to be no more afternoons. Rodkin never wanted to see that day. . . . To wipe the vision away he sank the palms of his hands against his eyelids.

He moved slowly away. All days wouldn't be like today. He could stay a long time if he pitched with his head. He could stay for another three years—maybe four. He would have to be careful. He would have to be smart.

*Damon Runyon (1880–1946) was widely recognized as the greatest news-*
*paper reporter in the country. Born in Manhattan, Kansas, his formal educa-*
*tion extended only through the sixth grade. Runyon's initial fame was as a*
*columnist for the old* New York American *and nationally syndicated writer for*
*the Hearst Newspaper chain. He became a man about town in New York,*
*playing the horses and chumming with the likes of boxer Jack Dempsey and*
*Giants manager John McGraw. Both a humorist and dramatic writer, Runyon*
*is one of the best short-story writers ever. Many of his fictional creations are*
*New York-talking guys of shady character with rough grammar, a genre that*
*is called* Runyonesque. *Among his best-known works are the trilogy of col-*
*lected stories:* Guys and Dolls *(1929),* Money From Home *(1931), and* Blue
Plate Special *(1931).*

*Damon Runyon*

# BASEBALL HATTIE
# (1954)

**I**T COMES ON SPRINGTIME, AND the little birdies are singing in the trees
in Central Park, and the grass is green all around and about, and I am at
the Polo Grounds on the opening day of the baseball season, when who
do I behold but Baseball Hattie. I am somewhat surprised at this spec-
tacle, as it is years since I see Baseball Hattie, and for all I know she long
ago passes to a better and happier world. But there she is, as large as life,
and in fact twenty pounds larger, and when I call the attention of Armand Fibleman, the gambler, to her he gets up and tears right out of the
joint as if he sees a ghost, for if there is one thing Armand Fibleman

loathes and despises, it is a ghost. I can see that Baseball Hattie is greatly changed, and to tell the truth, I can see that she is getting to be nothing but an old bag. Her hair that is once as black as a yard up a stovepipe is gray, and she is wearing gold-rimmed cheaters, although she seems to be pretty well dressed and looks as if she may be in the money a little bit, at that.

But the greatest change in her is the way she sits there very quiet all afternoon, never once opening her yap, even when many of the customers around her are claiming that Umpire William Klem is Public Enemy No. 1 to 16 inclusive, because they think he calls a close one against the Giants. I am wondering if maybe Baseball Hattie is stricken dumb somewhere back down the years, because I can remember when she is usually making speeches in the grandstand in favor of hanging such characters as Umpire William Klem when they call close ones against the Giants. But Hattie just sits there as if she is in a church while the public clamor goes on about her, and she does not as much as cry out robber, or even you big bum at Umpire William Klem. I see many a baseball bug in my time, male and female, but without doubt the worst bug of them all is Baseball Hattie, and you can say it again. She is most particularly a bug about the Giants, and she never misses a game they play at the Polo Grounds, and in fact she sometimes bobs up watching them play in other cities, which is always very embarrassing to the Giants, as they fear the customers in these cities may get the wrong impression of New York womanhood after listening to Baseball Hattie awhile.

The first time I ever see Baseball Hattie to pay any attention to her is in Philadelphia, a matter of twenty-odd years back, when the Giants are playing a series there, and many citizens of New York, including Armand Fibleman and myself, are present, because the Philadelphia customers are great hands for betting on baseball games in those days, and Armand Fibleman figures he may knock a few of them in the creek. Armand Fibleman is a character who will bet on baseball games from who-laid-the-chunk, and in fact he will bet on anything whatever, because Armand Fibleman is a gambler by trade and has been such since infancy. Personally, I will not bet you four dollars on a baseball game, because in the first place I am not apt to have four dollars, and in the second place I consider horse races a much sounder investment, but I often go around and about with Armand Fibleman, as he is a friend of mine, and sometimes he gives me a little piece of one of his bets for nothing.

Well, what happens in Philadelphia but the umpire forfeits the game in the seventh inning to the Giants by a score of nine to nothing when the Phillies are really leading by five runs, and the reason the umpire takes this action is because he orders several of the Philadelphia players to leave the field for calling him a scoundrel and a rat and a snake in the grass, and also a baboon, and they refuse to take their departure, as they still have more names to call him. Right away the Philadelphia customers become infuriated in a manner you will scarcely believe, for ordinarily a Philadelphia baseball customer is as quiet as a lamb, no matter what you do to him, and in fact in those days a Philadelphia baseball customer is only considered as somebody to do something to.

But these Philadelphia customers are so infuriated that they not only chase the umpire under the stand, but they wait in the street outside the baseball orchard until the Giants change into their street clothes and come out of the clubhouse. Then the Philadelphia customers begin pegging rocks, and one thing and another, at the Giants, and it is a most exciting and disgraceful scene that is spoken of for years afterwards. Well, the Giants march along toward the North Philly station to catch a train for home, dodging the rocks and one thing and another the best they can, and wondering why the Philadelphia gendarmes do not come to the rescue, until somebody notices several gendarmes among the customers doing some of the throwing themselves, so the Giants realize that this is a most inhospitable community, to be sure.

Finally all of them get inside the North Philly station and are safe, except a big, tall, left-handed pitcher by the name of Haystack Duggeler, who just reports to the club the day before and who finds himself surrounded by quite a posse of these infuriated Philadelphia customers, and who is unable to make them understand that he is nothing but a rookie, because he has a Missouri accent, and besides, he is half paralyzed with fear. One of the infuriated Philadelphia customers is armed with a brick-

matter who is pitching, she puts on extra steam when Haystack is bending them over, and it is quite an experience to hear her crying lay them in there, Haystack, old boy, and strike this big tramp out, Haystack, and other exclamations of a similar nature, which please Haystack quite some, but annoy Baseball Hattie's neighbors back of third base, such as Armand Fibleman, if he happens to be betting on the other club.

A month before the close of his first season in the big league, Haystack Duggeler gets so ornery that Manager Mac suspends him, hoping maybe it will cause Haystack to do a little thinking, but naturally Haystack is unable to do this, because he has nothing to think with. About a week later, Manager Mac gets to noticing how he can use a few ball games, so he starts looking for Haystack Duggeler, and he finds him tending bar on Eighth Avenue with his uniform hung up back of the bar as an advertisement. The baseball writers speak of Haystack as eccentric, which is a polite way of saying he is a screwball, but they consider him a most unique character and are always writing humorous stories about him, though any one of them will lay you plenty of nine to five that Haystack winds up an umbay. The chances are they will raise their price a little, as the season closes and Haystack is again under suspension with cold weather coming on and not a dime in his pants pockets.

It is sometime along in the winter that Baseball Hattie hauls off and marries Haystack Duggeler, which is a great surprise to one and all, but not nearly as much of a surprise as when Hattie closes her boarding and rooming house and goes to live in a little apartment with Haystack Duggeler up on Washington Heights.

It seems that she finds Haystack one frosty night sleeping in a hallway, after being around slightly mulled up for several weeks, and she takes him to her home and gets him a bath and a shave and a clean shirt and two boiled eggs and some toast and coffee and a shot or two of rye whiskey, all of which is greatly appreciated by Haystack, especially the rye whiskey. Then Haystack proposes marriage to her and takes a paralyzed oath that if she becomes his wife he will reform, so what with loving Haystack anyway, and with the fix commencing to request more dough off the boarding-and-rooming-house business than the business will stand, Hattie takes him at his word, and there you are. The baseball writers are wondering what Manager Mac will say when he hears these tidings, but all Mac says is that Haystack cannot possibly be any worse married than he is single-o, and then Mac has the club office send the happy couple a little paper money to carry them over the winter. Well, what happens but a great change comes over Haystack Duggeler. He stops bending his elbow and helps Hattie cook and wash the dishes, and holds her hand when they are in the movies, and speaks of his love for her several times a week, and Hattie is as happy as nine dollars' worth of lettuce. Manager Mac is so delighted at the change in Haystack that he has the club office send over more paper money, because Mac knows that with Haystack in shape he is sure of twenty-five games, and maybe the pennant.

In late February, Haystack reports to the training camp down South still as sober as some judges, and the other ballplayers are so impressed by the change in him that they admit him to their poker game again. But of course it is too much to expect a man to alter his entire course of living all at once, and it is not long before Haystack discovers four nines in his hand on his own deal and breaks up the game.

He brings Baseball Hattie with him to the camp, and this is undoubtedly a slight mistake, as it seems the old rumor about her boarding-and-rooming-house business gets around among the ever-loving wives of the other players, and they put on a large chill for her. In fact, you will think Hattie has the smallpox. Naturally, Baseball Hattie feels the frost, but she never lets on, as it seems she runs into many bigger and better frosts than this in her time. Then Haystack Duggeler notices it, and it seems that it makes him a little peevish toward Baseball Hattie, and in fact it is said that he gives her a slight pasting one night in their room, partly because she has no better social standing and partly because he is commencing to cop a few sneaks on the local corn now and then, and Hattie chides him for same.

Well, about this time it appears that Baseball Hattie discovers that she is going to have a baby, and as soon as she recovers from her astonishment, she decides that it is to be a boy who will be a great baseball player, maybe a pitcher, although Hattie admits she is willing to compromise on a good second basemen. She also decides that his name is to be Derrill Duggeler, after his paw, as it seems Derrill is Haystack's real name, and he is only called Haystack because he claims he once makes a living stacking hay, although the general opinion is that all he ever stacks is cards. It is really quite remarkable what a belt Hattie gets out of the idea of having this baby, though Haystack is not excited about the matter. He is not paying much attention to Baseball Hattie by now, except to give her a slight pasting now and then, but Hattie is so happy about the baby that she does not mind these pastings.

Haystack Duggeler meets up with Armand Fibleman along in midsummer. By this time, Haystack discovers horse racing and is always making bets on the horses, and naturally he is generally broke, and then I commence running into him in different spots with Armand Fibleman, who is now betting higher than a cat's back on baseball games.

It is late August, and the Giants are fighting for the front end of the league, and an important series with Brooklyn is coming up, and everybody knows that Haystack Duggeler will work in anyway two games of the series, as Haystack can generally beat Brooklyn just by throwing his glove on the mound. There is no doubt but what he has the old Indian sign on Brooklyn, and the night before the first game, which he is sure to work, the gamblers along Broadway are making the Giants two-to-one favorites to win the game.

This same night before the game, Baseball Hattie is home in her little apartment on Washington Heights waiting for Haystack to come in and eat a delicious dinner of pigs' knuckles and sauerkraut, which she personally prepares for him. In fact, she hurries home right after the ball game to get this delicacy ready, because Haystack tells her he will surely come home this particular night, although Hattie knows he is never better than even money to keep his word about anything. But sure enough, in he comes while the pigs' knuckles and sauerkraut are still piping hot, and Baseball Hattie is surprised to see Armand Fibleman with him, as she knows Armand backwards and forwards and does not care much for him, at that. However, she can say the same thing about four million other characters in this town, so she makes Armand welcome, and they sit down and put on the pigs' knuckles and sauerkraut together, and a pleasant time is enjoyed by one and all. In fact, Baseball Hattie puts herself out to entertain Armand Fibleman, because he is the first guest Haystack ever brings home.

Well, Armand Fibleman can be very pleasant when he wishes, and he speaks very nicely to Hattie. Naturally, he sees that Hattie is expecting, and in fact he will have to be blind not to see it, and he seems greatly interested in this matter and asks Hattie many questions, and Hattie is delighted to find somebody to talk to about what is coming off with her, as Haystack will never listen to any of her remarks on the subject. So Armand Fibleman gets to hear all about Baseball Hattie's son, and how he is to be a great baseball player, and Armand says is that so, and how nice, and all this and that, until Haystack Duggeler speaks up as follows, and to wit:

"Oh, dag-gone her son!" Haystack says. "It is going to be a girl, anyway, so let us dismiss this topic and get down to business. Hat," he says, "you fan yourself into the kitchen and wash the dishes, while Armand and me talk."

So Hattie goes into the kitchen, leaving Haystack and Armand sitting there talking, and what are they talking about but a proposition for Haystack to let the Brooklyn club beat him the next day so Armand Fibleman can take the odds and clean up a nice little gob of money, which he is to split with Haystack. Hattie can hear every word they say, as the kitchen is next door to the dining room where they are sitting, and at first she thinks they are joking, because at this time nobody ever even as much as thinks of skulduggery in baseball, or anyway, not much. It seems that at first Haystack is not in favor of the idea, but Armand Fibleman keeps mentioning money that Haystack owes him for bets on the horse races, and he asks Haystack how he expects to continue betting on the races without fresh money, and Armand also speaks of the great injustice that is being done Haystack by the Giants in not paying him twice the salary he is getting, and how the loss of one or two games is by no means such a great calamity.

Well, finally Baseball Hattie hears Haystack say all right, but he wishes a thousand dollars then and there as a guarantee, and Armand Fibleman says this is fine, and they will go downtown and he will get the money at once, and now Hattie realizes that maybe they are in earnest, and she pops out of the kitchen and speaks as follows:

"Gentlemen," Hattie says, "you seem to be sober, but I guess you are drunk. If you are not drunk, you must both be daffy to think of such a thing as phenagling around with a baseball game."

"Hattie," Haystack says, "kindly close your trap and go back in the kitchen, or I will give you a bust in the nose."

And with this he gets up and reaches for his hat, and Armand Fibleman gets up, too, and Hattie says like this:

"Why, Haystack," she says, "you are not really serious in this matter, are you?"

"Of course I am serious," Haystack says. "I am sick and tired of pitching for starvation wages, and besides, I will win a lot of games later on to make up for the one I lose tomorrow. Say," he says, "these Brooklyn bums may get lucky tomorrow and knock me loose from my pants, anyway, no matter what I do, so what difference does it make?"

"Haystack," Baseball Hattie says, "I know you are a liar and a drunkard and a cheat and no account generally, but nobody can tell me you will sink so low as to purposely toss off a ball game. Why, Haystack, baseball is always on the level. It is the most honest game in all this world. I guess you are just ribbing me, because you know how much I love it."

"Dry up!" Haystack says to Hattie. "Furthermore, do not expect me home again tonight. But anyway, dry up."

"Look, Haystack," Hattie says, "I am going to have a son. He is your son and my son, and he is going to be a great ballplayer when he grows up, maybe a greater pitcher than you are, though I hope and trust he is not left-handed. He will have your name. If they find out you toss off a game for money, they will throw you out of baseball and you will be disgraced. My son will be known as the son of a crook, and what chance will he have in baseball? Do you think I am going to allow you to do this to him, and to the game that keeps me from going nutty for marrying you?"

Naturally, Haystack Duggeler is greatly offended by Hattie's crack about her son being maybe a greater pitcher than he is, and he is about to take steps, when Armand Fibleman stops him. Armand Fibleman is commencing to be somewhat alarmed at Baseball Hattie's attitude, and he gets to thinking that he hears that people in her delicate condition are often irresponsible, and he fears that she may blow a whistle on this enterprise without realizing what she is doing. So he undertakes a few soothing remarks to her. "Why, Hattie," Armand Fibleman says, "nobody can possibly find out about this little matter, and Haystack will have enough money to send your son to college, if his markers at the race track do not take it all. Maybe you better lie down and rest awhile," Armand says.

But Baseball Hattie does not as much as look at Armand, though she goes on talking to Haystack. "They always find out thievery, Haystack," she says, "especially when you are dealing with a fink like Fibleman. If you deal with him once, you will have to deal with him again and again, and he will be the first to holler copper on you, because he is a stool pigeon in his heart."

"Haystack," Armand Fibleman says, "I think we better be going."

"Haystack," Hattie says, "you can go out of here and stick up somebody or commit a robbery or a murder, and I will still welcome you back and stand by you. But if you are going out to steal my son's future, I advise you not to go."

"Dry up!" Haystack says. "I am going."

"All right, Haystack," Hattie says, very calm. "But just step into the kitchen with me and let me say one little word to you by yourself, and then I will say no more." Well, Haystack Duggeler does not care for even just one little word more, but Armand Fibleman wishes to get this disagreeable scene over with, so he tells Haystack to let her have her word, and Haystack goes into the kitchen with Hattie, and Armand cannot

DAMON RUNYON

hear what is said, as she speaks very low, but he hears Haystack laugh
heartily and then Haystack comes out of the kitchen, still laughing, and
tells Armand he is ready to go.

As they start for the door, Baseball Hattie outs with a long-nosed .38-
caliber Colt's revolver, and goes root-a-toot-toot with it, and the next
thing anybody knows, Haystack is on the floor yelling bloody murder,
and Armand Fibleman is leaving the premises without bothering to
open the door. In fact, the landlord afterwards talks some of suing
Haystack Duggeler because of the damage Armand Fibleman does to the
door. Armand himself afterwards admits that when he slows down for a
breather a couple of miles down Broadway he finds splinters stuck all
over him.

Well, the doctors come, and the gendarmes come, and there is great
confusion, especially as Baseball Hattie is sobbing so she can scarcely
make a statement, and Haystack Duggeler is so sure he is going to die
that he cannot think of anything to say except oh-oh-oh, but finally the
landlord remembers seeing Armand leave with his door, and everybody
starts questioning Hattie about this until she confesses that Armand is
there all right, and that he tries to bribe Haystack to toss off a ball game,
and that she then suddenly finds herself with a revolver in her hand, and
everything goes black before her eyes, and she can remember no more
until somebody is sticking a bottle of smelling salts under her nose. Naturally, the newspaper reporters put two and two together, and what they
make of it is that Hattie tries to plug Armand Fibleman for his rascally
offer, and that she misses Armand and gets Haystack, and right away
Baseball Hattie is a great heroine, and Haystack is a great hero, though
nobody thinks to ask Haystack how he stands on the bribe proposition,
and he never brings it up himself.

And nobody will ever offer Haystack any more bribes, for after the
doctors get through with him he is shy a left arm from the shoulder
down, and he will never pitch a baseball again, unless he learns to pitch
right-handed. The newspapers make quite a lot of Baseball Hattie protecting the fair name of baseball. The National League plays a benefit
game for Haystack Duggeler and presents him with a watch and a purse

of twenty-five thousand dollars, which Baseball Hattie grabs away from him, saying it is for her son, while Armand Fibleman is in bad with one and all.

Baseball Hattie and Haystack Duggeler move to the Pacific Coast, and this is all there is to the story, except that one day some years ago, and not long before he passes away in Los Angeles, a respectable grocer, I run into Haystack when he is in New York on a business trip, and I say to him like this:

"Haystack," I say, "it is certainly a sin and a shame that Hattie misses Armand Fibleman that night and puts you on the shelf. The chances are that but for this little accident you will hang up one of the greatest pitching records in the history of baseball. Personally," I say, "I never see a better left-handed pitcher."

"Look," Haystack says. "Hattie does not miss Fibleman. It is a great newspaper story and saves my name, but the truth is she hits just where she aims. When she calls me into the kitchen before I start out with Fibleman, she shows me a revolver I never before know she has, and says to me, 'Haystack,' she says, 'if you leave with this weasel on the errand you mention, I am going to fix you so you will never make another wrong move with your pitching arm. I am going to shoot it off for you.'

"I laugh heartily," Haystack says. "I think she is kidding me, but I find out different. By the way," Haystack says, "I afterwards learn that long before I meet her, Hattie works for three years in a shooting gallery at Coney Island. She is really a remarkable broad," Haystack says.

I guess I forget to state that the day Baseball Hattie is at the Polo Grounds she is watching the new kid sensation of the big leagues, Derrill Duggeler, shut out Brooklyn with three hits.

He is a wonderful young left-hander.

*Herbert Warren Wind is a preeminent authority on golf and tennis. Primarily a nonfiction writer, his well-known books include* The Complete Golfer *(1954),* The Gilded Age of Sport *(1961), and* Game, Set, and Match *(1979). Wind wrote an outstanding baseball yarn in "The Masters Touch." The "master" in the story is a wily general manager, Calvin Shepard, who keeps a keen eye on his minor-league prospects. Trouble is, one of his finest talents is head over heels in love with a beautiful movie star of dubious reputation. As love blooms the player's batting average plummets. Can Shepard save the day?*

## Herbert Warren Wind

# THE MASTER'S TOUCH (1951)

CALVIN COWLEY SHEPARD WAS METHODICALLY going through the mail stacked on his desk. He owned the largest desk in organized baseball—a foot longer and nine inches wider than Branch Rickey's by actual measurement. It was a fine July morning, the air exceptionally cool and dry for the Atlantic seaboard in summer, Shepard was thinking as he savored a testimonial from the local Elks Club to the effect that C. C. Shepard was the smartest man in the major leagues.

Reluctantly, he went on to the next letter, a routine report from the secretary of the Redlands farm team. The weather suddenly changed.

The severe granite contours of his face became sharper and deeper as Shepard impatiently jabbed at a buzzer on his desk.

By the time his secretary, Ray Bell, came hurrying in, Shepard looked like the Old Man of the Mountain after a rough storm.

"You're not ready to see the press yet, are you?" Ray asked. He was a slim young man in his early thirties, who spoke, as did Shepard, with slight traces of a Vermont twang.

"No, my boy, I'm not ready to see the press," Shepard said with what was supposed to be elegant sarcasm. "I see them at ten o'clock. I know that. I don't need any coaching." He paused for a moment. "I've just been reading the report from Redlands. Do you know what Walter Eamons is batting?"

"It was .274 on last month's report," Ray answered. "Probably up around .280, .285 by now. I wouldn't worry about Eamons."

"Well, for your information," Shepard said slowly, "our Mr. Eamons is now pounding the ball at a robust .221. That boy ever hit below .340 for us?"

Ray fingered his brow. "No. He was over .370 those two years in the Kitty League. Last year at Redlands, let's see—" He broke off. "Think it was .362."

Shepard leaned over and pushed one button in a battery of sixteen attached to his desk. A glass panel at the far end of the office was jerkily lighted by fluorescent tubing. At the top of the panel, *Redlands* was printed in red; beneath the name of the club, in black, the roster of players. Fifteen similar panels, each devoted to a different farm team, formed unbroken murals along the two windowless walls of the office. The installation of this equipment had been one of Shepard's first moves after he'd bought his major-league franchise, and he derived a sense of power from pressing his buttons and watching the panels light up like a pinball machine in the hands of a true artist.

"I've won three pennants in the five years I've been in baseball," Shepard resumed, slightly appeased by the panel's obedience to his wishes. "How did I do it? By building up the best organization in the game. Not a single personal relation of mine is on the payroll. How come, then, I'm only now getting word that the best prospect we own is miles off the beam?"

"You saw that note about Eamons, didn't you—the one in last month's report from Redlands?" Ray asked him. "That line about possible woman trouble."

"Woman trouble!" Shepard cut in scornfully. "How can you live and not have woman trouble! That doesn't tell me a thing. It seems that any time I want the dope on anything, I've got to get it myself. Add Redlands to the itinerary on tomorrow's trip. Tell McCrillis to get packed. I'll want both of you. And *now* you may show the gentlemen of the press in."

Late Friday afternoon, Shepard and his aides deplaned at San Bernardino and proceeded directly to the Arrowhead Springs Hotel, a plush oasis perched on the foothills of the mountains above the arid valley. Shepard had been pushing himself hard for three days but his labors had paid off in results. In Topeka, Shepard and McCrillis, his chief scout, had watched Whitey Kravchek pitch a four-hit shutout. Sid Sandler, the young left-hander with Portland, had also impressed them as having the stuff to make the big jump to the majors.

As McCrillis put it, both youngsters had a little more to learn before they were finished pitchers, but just as they were, they would probably help the club a lot more than those two base-on-balls philanthropists, Al Marineau and Blitz Baker.

With his pitching problem nicely under control, Shepard took things easy during dinner and limited himself to two long-distance calls. In addition, he made one local call, instructing Emil Hochstetter, the old Cincinnati outfielder who managed Redlands, to meet him at nine o'clock sharp on the hotel's outdoor terrace. After lighting his old cherrywood pipe, Shepard felt so pleasantly in tune with his private universe that the thought of calling a conference of the local sports writers never entered his mind.

Somewhat under the spell of the palms and a few planter's punches, Shepard and his entourage, supplemented by Hochstetter, relaxed contentedly on the terrace. They did not stop talking baseball, however, until their attention was arrested by the entrance of a tall, handsome girl whom the headwaiter guided to a table directly across the dance floor from theirs. She wore a white dress over her tan, and had whatever it is that makes people rest their drinks on the table and stare. The four baseball men looked her over as closely as they would a promising left-hander.

"Now there's the sort of girl I like!" Shepard exclaimed.

"That's very big of you," Ray said. "I thought you were an antiglamour man, boss. That girl's loaded with it."

"*Honest* glamour," Shepard said, correcting him. "That tan, for example. That isn't one of those beauty-parlor jobs. None of that grapefruit-colored hair, either. There're a lot of other tips if you know what to look for. I can tell you all about that girl."

"Like what?"

"Well, first, she's in the movies."

"That's like saying that a guy who's just fanned Kiner, Musial and Robinson is in baseball."

Shepard refused to be thrown off stride. "She's obviously an outdoor girl," he continued calmly. "Plays good tennis, rides horseback well. She's an intelligent girl, levelheaded. Probably from a solid middle-class family. I'd guess that she comes of good old New England stock."

Ray whipped out a notebook and pretended to take notes.

"I don't see what's so amusing," Shepard said to him. "I happen to be able to judge women as accurately as I can judge ballplayers. I can sense these things, just the way I knew that Eamons belonged in center field, not at shortstop."

At almost the exact moment his name was mentioned, Walter Eamons was making his way through the tables at the far end of the terrace. The four baseball men, spotting the rangy towhead immediately, watched him pick a zigzag path to the table where the level-headed girl from the solid New England family was sitting. She and the outfielder greeted each other with the sort of kiss that can be seen nowadays only in foreign movies.

"I can see it all now," Shepard said, beaming benevolently. "It's as simple as two and two. The boy's in love. No wonder he's not hitting."

"With a dish like that around, he's lucky to be able to find his way to the ballpark," Ray said.

"Don't be cynical," Shepard said. "I wish all my players picked girls like that! Say, Emil," he said, turning to Hochstetter, "the next time you people refer to 'woman trouble' in a report, you've got to be more specific—much more specific."

"Would you like to meet her, Shep?" Hochstetter asked.

When Shepard said he would, Hochstetter padded slowly across the dance floor and returned shortly with the model young couple, smiling, in tow.

"I recognized you, all right, Mr. Shepard," Walter Eamons said as Shepard and his aides stood up to welcome him. "I didn't think you'd remember me. That's why I didn't come over."

"Of course I do," Shepard assured him. He grasped the outfielder's hand. "It's nice seeing you, Walter. Who's the lovely young lady?"

"Mr. Shepard, I'd like you to meet my fiancée, Priscilla Summers," Eamons said awkwardly, as if he had memorized the line. "We're engaged," he explained.

Miss Summers, who had been restricting herself to a smile of general cordiality, turned on the full wattage as she received the congratulations of the three baseball men. "My, you have a strong grip!" she purred to Jim McCrillis.

"Used to catch," McCrillis replied shyly.

"I've heard a lot about *you*, Mr. Shepard," Priscilla Summers continued. "You look much younger than your pictures."

Shepard took the compliment gracefully. "You're an extremely fortunate young man, Walter," he said, dropping his voice to a judicial pitch. "When's the big day?"

Eamons looked at his fiancée for guidance. "Sometime after the end of the season," she answered for them.

Shepard thought that was fine, just fine. "You kids run along now," he said. "No sense spending your time with a bunch of old fogies when you've got better things to do. I'll see you at the ballpark, Walter."

"Peach of a girl," Shepard said approvingly to Hochstetter, when the young couple had gone off to dance. "Real New England type. It's a pity, though, they couldn't have fallen in love during the off season. That's a small matter, really. Next spring the boy will be himself again."

"I don't think so," Hochstetter said shortly.

Shepard stiffened. "You don't think what?"

Hochstetter looked at his boss as if Shepard were a pitcher to whom he was going to have to break the bad news that he was yanking him. "I don't think Eamons will be any good next year, or the year after, or any year, if he marries that girl."

"Emil—" Shepard's smile was patronizing—"I don't think you know women."

"I don't claim to, Shep. But I know a hell of a lot more about this customer than you do. I wanted to tell you about her, but you didn't give me a chance. Get the picture now. She comes down to this hotel from Hollywood for the weekend. This is five, six weeks ago. She's with another actress friend. They decide they'll kill the afternoon by watching a ball game. They get themselves a couple of box seats, in the section where the players' wives sit. I got this from Lefty Blake's wife. She was sitting in the row behind them. To make a long story short, this Summers babe spots Eamons and she goes for him—"

"But he wasn't hitting," Shepard objected.

"From a woman's point of view, Eamons ain't a good outfielder or a lousy outfielder or any other kind of an outfielder," Hochstetter said. "He's a big, good-looking kid with a build. Well, round about the fourth, when he's leaning against the bat rack, she stands up and looks him over like he was a bull at a country fair. Then she announces to her friend, just as cool as you like, 'I think I want that boy.' Blake's wife told me all about it."

Shepard stared for a long minute at his pipe. "What do you know about this girl's background?" he finally asked.

"Nothing much," Hochstetter replied. "All I know, Shep, is the kid's been no good to the team since she got hold of him. She's down here every weekend, so he can't keep his mind on his work Friday, Saturday, or Sunday. Tuesday and Wednesday he's still in a fog, dreaming about the weekend. Thursday he's off on a new fog, counting the hours till she shows up on Friday."

Shepard sat silent for several minutes. Then he turned, as he did whenever his intuitive powers had let him down, to the extreme opposite pole of operation: the meticulous collecting of facts and figures with which his problem could be worked out as unemotionally as an algebraic equation. "Ray," Shepard snapped in a weak imitation of his best bark, "I want you to get up to Hollywood immediately and dig up a full dossier on Priscilla Summers. I want you back by nine tomorrow night."

"You mean you want me to leave right now?"

"That's exactly what I mean. Now get moving."

On Saturday, Shepard pushed himself through, what was, for him, an unsatisfyingly slow morning. He leafed through the special reports his office had airmailed: the team was just barely holding on to third place—something he didn't need to be told. He conferred with McCrillis on minor problems that had arisen at Topeka and Portland, and, after a short call at Lefty Blake's house on the way to the ballpark, lunched with the club secretary and was interviewed by the local reporters. After lunch he tried to rouse himself from his lethargy by okaying plans for a new scoreboard and taking batting practice with the team, but his mind was not on his work. Just before game time he motioned Walter Eamons over to his box.

"You weren't getting much of that ball during batting practice," Shepard said, in a more severe tone than he had meant to use.

"Yeah, I was kinda poppin' 'em up," Eamons said. His face took on a look of concern. "You feeling all right, Mr. Shepard?"

Shepard stared at him.

"You don't look so good as last night," Eamons went on. "You eat something that didn't agree with you?"

"I'll worry about my own digestion," Shepard sputtered. He tried to calm himself. "I'm certain I'd feel a hundred percent better, Walter, if you started to play the ball we know you're capable of. Do you know you're batting .221?"

"I just can't seem to get a good piece of the ball," Eamons answered. He broke out in a grin, as if a very funny thought had just struck him. "That ball keeps getting smaller and smaller, Mr. Shepard. Right now it looks about as tiny as . . ."

Eamons's voice traled off as his eyes focused on something over Shepard's left shoulder. He blew a kiss in that direction. Shepard turned. Priscilla Summers, her fingers pressed against her lips, was undulating down the aisle. Shepard scrutinized the faraway look in Eamons's eyes as Priscilla walked toward them. The boy was a goner, Shepard realized, scarcely recognizable as the same lean athlete who had shown such spirit at the training camp that Shepard had soberly appraised him to a newspaperman as "one of those aggressive, old-time ballplayers who can hit, field, throw and run those bases, a true competitor, possibly another Cobb." In the shape he was in, Eamons wasn't fit to carry Cobb's Coca-Cola stock, let alone his glove.

Shepard held his guard high. He just grunted when Priscilla greeted him with a warm smile and repeated her observation that photographs failed to do justice to his youthful appearance. "Walter," Shepard said curtly, as Eamons rested his elbows on the railing before the box, "I think you'd better get out in center field. The game's ready to begin."

"Now, darling," Priscilla cautioned the outfielder, patting him on the hand, "It's a terribly hot day, so don't play too hard. I've got a wonderful evening plannned for us, and I don't want you to be all worn out. We're—"

"Walter, you're holding up the game," Shepard interrupted. "Miss Summers," he continued firmly, as Eamons trotted out to center field, "I don't know if you realize this or not, but all this high living and late hours—well, it's hurting the boy. I don't think you have Walter's best interests at heart."

"I think I'm a better judge of what's good for Walter than you are," Priscilla answered. "Anyhow, I don't see how what happens between Walter and me is any business of yours."

"It most certainly *is* my business," Shepard said. "Women like you don't care who you fool around with. It doesn't mean a thing to you that you're ruining the career of one of the best young ballplayers in the country. No, I can see it doesn't."

Priscilla measured Shepard coolly. "Get this through that great brain of yours, Grandpa," she said. "I don't give a damn about you and your precious baseball. If I want to marry that outfielder of yours or whatever he is, I'm going to, and there's nothing you or anybody else can do about it. Do I make myself clear?"

"You won't talk so bold tomorrow," Shepard fumed. "I've got a man in Hollywood getting the dope on you right now. You won't marry Walter Eamons. I'll see to it you won't."

"Like to bet on that?"

Shepard, barely in control of himself, pushed by Priscilla and marched out of the box.

Ray Bell knocked on the door of Shepard's suite and walked in.

"You're back earlier than I expected," Shepard said. "Let's have it."

"She was easier to check on than I thought she'd be. Everyone in Hollywood seems to know Priscilla Summers," Ray explained as he riffled through his notebook. "You were right on some things and wrong on others. Her real name *is* Priscilla Summers. She *does* come from New England. Worcester, Mass. After that, your diagnosis isn't so hot."

"I'm not paying you to tell me how stupid I am," Shepard growled. "Cut the baloney and get on with it."

"OK. I'll give it to you quick. She's been in Hollywood not quite two years. Been in two movies. They haven't been released yet, but everbody who's seen the previews says she's going to get somewhere. Clean-cut sex appeal. Okay, going back to the beginning. Born Worcester, 1927. Father managed a movie house. Nothing but the usual studio fiction on her till 1946, year she hit New York. Made a big splash as a model. She was a blonde then. That's not important, but I thought you'd like to know. The tan is real, though. She's been on location the last six weeks, making a Western."

"*Private* life," Shepard said.

"Just coming to that. She's been married twice. First time to a light-heavyweight fighter I never heard of. Lasted less than a year. Second time to a pro football player. She's known about town as a pretty predatory gal. Specializes in athletes, the way other women do in artists or millionaires. Just now getting around to baseball, I guess. Let's see, what else? Well, she's five-six and weighs one-nineteen and–"

"Bats right-handed and throws with both hands," Shepard broke in. "That's enough, Ray." He made an effort to smile that didn't quite come off. "I don't want any cracks out of you about how I ought to stick to judging ballplayers," he muttered. "I can handle this baby. Watch me."

Shepard paced the floor for a minute or two, and then directed Ray to summon Jim McCrillis to the room.

"All right. I've got it all figured out," Shepard announced when McCrillis arrived. "We're going to call up Kravchek and Sandler. We'll send Marineau down to Topeka. They need a pitcher. I was going to give Portland Blitz Baker in exchange for Sandler, but I'm going to bring Blitz to Redlands instead. In a hot, dry climate, Blitz has a better chance of getting his arm back. Get the paperwork started on this, Ray. One other thing: We're going to bring up Eamons."

Ray jerked his head up from his note-taking.

"I don't see what else we can do," Shepard said defensively. "I suppose we could transfer Eamons to one of the other farms, but I'd feel safer having him where I can keep an eye on him myself. We're dealing with a pretty unscrupulous woman." A new thread of anxiety crept into his voice: "Jim, you go out and round up Eamons right this minute. Get a double room in the hotel for tonight and stay with him. We're starting home first thing tomorrow, and I want that boy on the plane."

On Labor Day, C. C. Shepard's team propelled itself into a tie for first place by taking both ends of a doubleheader. Sandler and Kravchek were the winning pitchers. They had led the team's drive to the top, and the pro-Shepard press cited their arrival in the nick of time as one further evidence of C. C.'s peerless masterminding. As was to be expected, the reporters who didn't like Shepard glossed over the remarkable showings of Sandler and Kravchek—they had won eight games between them—and lambasted Shepard for bringing up Walter "Cantaloupe" Eamons, who had succeeded in losing two games all by himself and could easily have lost more if he'd been given the opportunity.

In an important game against Boston, for example, Eamons had been inserted in the line-up in the seventh inning for defensive purposes. In the ninth, although the sun had been down for twenty minutes, for some reason he was still wearing his sunglasses. This may have accounted in part for the improbable demonstration he had put on in attempting to field a hard-hit drive that the average big-league outfielder could have handled with little or no trouble. Eamons had misjudged the sinking liner, and the ball had skidded between his legs on its first low bounce, hit the fence behind him, and rebounded right through his legs a second time.

Eamons had previously been relieved from his pinch-hitting duties after popping up three times and fanning twice. He reminded very few people of Cobb.

Off the field, Eamons dwelt in a similar fog. During his first weeks in the East, it was simply the usual haziness that enshrouds the lovesick. Then it thickened into a depression. During the last two weeks in August, Eamons, who had been hearing from Priscilla at least once a day, received no word whatever from her. His increasingly desperate phone calls to the West Coast had also gone unanswered. Jim McCrillis did everything he could to cheer up the forlorn outfielder. Assigned by Shepard to stay on as Eamons's twenty-four-hour companion, McCrillis took him to a Western movie each night and dined him at the best rathskillers. In their hotel room, he listened patiently to the boy's lamentations.

On Labor Day evening, McCrillis reported to Shepard that the situation had become impossible. "And damn' unpleasant, too," he added. "I can't tell the boy why he hasn't heard from that girl. I think he knows she's dropped him. He just can't bring himself to face it."

"He'll have to eventually. Then he'll start to mend," Shepard told him. "Stick with it, Jim."

The Saturday after Labor Day, Eamons pulled another "Eamons," as his boners were now being called. In the fourth inning, he was sent in as a pinch runner, a seemingly foolproof assignment. Eamons found a way, though. No one told him to steal second, but on the third pitch he was off like a hare.

He flashed down the base line with a terrific burst of speed, and had the base stole before the catcher went through the motions of making his throw. The only trouble was that second base was already occupied by a teammate. This teammate, of course, was not prepared to jump for third, and Eamons was tagged for the rally-killing out. If there was a bright side to the incident, it was that Eamons didn't have to be used again in the game.

Shepard witnessed this "Eamons" from the center-field bleachers. He made it a practice to mingle with the fans in the bleachers from time to time in order to get, as he phrased it, "a true and undistorted picture of the real fan's attitude toward the team and the administration." On these expeditions, Shepard diguised himself in a baggy suit and dark glasses, and pulled the brim of an old hat down low over his forehead. Now and then a fan penetrated Shepard's disguise, but for the most part his identity went unsuspected. It was a bittersweet triumph. It pleased him to be a successful masquerader, but at the same time he was always hoping that, in spite of his efforts to conceal his face and figure, he would be so well-known to an adoring public that they could spot him in a suit of armor with the visor shut.

"Mr. Shepard," he heard a voice saying in hushed tones as he sat in the bleachers, wondering when the fans would quiet down about Eamons's latest blunder and stop accusing C. C. Shepard of throwing away a pennant. He turned his head cautiously. It was Ray.

"Priscilla Summers wants to see you," Ray whispered excitedly in his ear. "She's up at the top of the bleachers."

Shepard's jaw sagged.

"She showed up at your box," Ray went on. "I would have brushed her off but I was afraid she'd get to Eamons."

Shepard tugged the brim of his hat down and followed Ray up the aisle of concrete steps. His mind worked furiously to bring this unsettling turn of events into some sort of focus.

Priscilla Summers sat, with her legs casually crossed, in the last row of the bleachers. She was wearing dark glasses, too. They hid the expression in her eyes, but the line of her mouth showed she was in an aggressive mood.

Shepard removed his hat in an elaborate gesture of mock courtesy. "I hope you didn't come all this distance," he said, "just to tell me I'm looking much more handsome than my recent photographs."

"Is that a nice way to speak to one of your greatest admirers?" she cooed. They faced each other like ancient foes. "I just happened to be in town," she went on coolly. "Publicity. One of my pictures opens here next week. We're greasing the wheels."

"And you came all the way out to the ballpark to give me a pair of free tickets."

"Ah, you're a cute boy," she laughed. "No, I've got news for you. Personal news. I wanted to tell you I'm going to marry one of your players next Wednesday."

Shepard tried to steady himself by clutching wildly for Ray's arm.

"I knew you'd be delighted to hear that," Priscilla smiled.

"How'd you ever work that, young lady?" Shepard sputtered feebly. "You haven't seen Eamons for a month. You haven't written him in over two weeks. You–"

"Oh, I'm not marrying Walter," she interrupted. "I'm going to marry Blitz Baker."

Shepard's instinct told him to cover up, fast. The important thing was for Priscilla to believe she had triumphed gloriously and completely. He made a titanic effort not to register the feeling of relief that surged through every fiber of his body. It was only Blitz Baker. A washed-up pitcher. Won four, lost nine. Whew! A cheap price to pay when it could have been Eamons.

"I've got to hand it to you," he said, as if he were standing gallant in defeat. "You're a faster worker than I bargained for."

"Just call me Shep," Priscilla said with frosty sarcasm. She stood up to leave. "How do you like finishing second, Grandpa?"

Shepard watched her as she disappeared down the runway exit. He shocked Ray by leading him back to the office for a good stiff drink. When his nerves had slowed down to a bumpy trot after he'd had three fingers of Scotch, Shepard peeled off his disguise and climbed back into his regular clothes. The telephone rang just as he was leaving for home. It was McCrillis, calling from the players' dressing room. He wanted to know if Shepard had seen the story in the afternoon papers about Blitz Baker and Priscilla Summers.

Shepard described the meeting in the bleachers. "I was going to call you, Jim," he said, his voice still husky with tension. "Do you think we should tell Eamons or try to keep it from him?"

"He knows about it," McCrillis said. "Somebody showed him the paper."

"How'd he take it?"

"Hard, Shep, awful hard. He's been in the shower for over a half hour. I think he's waiting till everybody goes."

"Watch him close," Shepard said to McCrillis. "Don't let him out of your sight."

Refreshed by a good night's sleep and some glowing write-ups in the morning papers, Shepard arrived at the ballpark shortly after nine on Sunday morning. His footsteps, the only sound in the vast hush of the stadium, echoed strangely as he strode through the rotunda where, three hours later, thousands would be clamoring around the ticket booths. He unlocked a gate next to the turnstiles, and was striding down the passageway under the stands when he was startled by what seemed to be the sound of bat meeting ball. He heard it again as he hurried up the nearest ramp. Probably some kids who'd stowed away over Saturday night.

He stopped short when he came to the head of the ramp, behind first base, and tried to make some sense out of the baffling scene on the diamond below him. Jim McCrillis stood on the pitcher's mound, with thirty or so practice balls scattered around him. He was pitching to Eamons. *Whack!* Shepard watched a long belt sail all the way to the wall in right center. That's the way he used to cut, thought Shepard. McCrillis picked up another ball. Into the motion. *Whack!* Shepard lowered himself into a chair and gazed at the ghostly batting practice.

Eamons slammed the last pitch against the scoreboard in dead-center field and hustled down the first-base line and on into the outfield. He picked up a ball near the wall, wheeled, and fired it in to home plate, where McCrillis stood. Eamons picked up another ball, wheeled and fired again.

McCrillis had just handled the fourth throw from the outfield when, out of the corner of his eye, he caught sight of Shepard making his way through the boxes. McCrillis cupped his glove and bare hand to his mouth and hollered to Eamons to hold it up.

Shepard clambered awkwardly over the railing and on to the field. "What goes on here, anyway?" he shouted as he walked toward the plate.

"He wanted some practice," McCrillis said, panting a little. He looked as if he had just caught both games of a double header. "Got me out of bed at—"

"Watch your head!" Eamons's voice carried pugnaciously from the far reaches of the outfield. A rifle-shot throw kicked off the turf near the pitcher's mound. McCrillis and Shepard hit the dirt just in time, and the ball banged against the backstop. The two men dusted themselves off and moved a safe distance down the first-base line.

"He's been like that all morning. You can't do anything with him," McCrillis grumbled as the bombardment of baseballs continued. "One extreme to the other. Last night, he was like a wounded deer. Pitiful. Fell asleep right after supper. He couldn't eat any. Fell asleep with all his clothes on, in a chair. This morning—whango! I'm living with a madman. He pulls me out of bed at six o'clock. Yanks the blankets off and tells me to shut up when I ask him what's the matter. He needs some practice, he tells me; we're going to the ballpark. We've been out here three hours. He wouldn't even let me get some breakfast."

A bounding ball zipped by McCrillis's knee. He started to yell something to Eamons and then decided it was a waste of time. "When he comes in now," McCrillis complained, "I'll have to pitch that whole batch to him again or hit him fungoes. I don't mind that. But he's got no right to be sore at me. I'm not Priscilla Summers."

"I think you hit it there," Shepard said absently. He had been listening with one ear, trying to put the parts together. "He's going to take it out on everyone for a while, Jim. He's going to show the world."

Shepard and McCrillis were collecting the balls in front of the backstop and rolling them toward the pitcher's mound when Eamons came jogging in from the outfield. Shepard greeted him warmly: "Good morning, Walter."

Eamons glowered at Shepard for a moment. He spat a slug of tobacco juice an inch over Shepard's shoe and walked on to pick up a bat.

Shepard dug an elbow into McCrillis's ribs. "We've got a ballplayer again," he said.

During the week that followed, Eamons treated opposing pitchers with no more respect than he had Shepard. He delivered twice as a pinch hitter, and was given a crack at the starting line-up. In the final six games of the team's home stand, he collected twelve hits in twenty-six times at bat, stole three bases, and was impeccable in the field. His one-man rampage was the spearhead of the drive that sent the team four full games in front as it headed west to play the last twelve games on the schedule.

"And that, gentlemen," C. C. Shepard announced with a crackle of self-congratulation, "is how it worked out—precisely as we planned it." He watched the faces of the reporters whom he had summoned when the news had come through from Chicago that his team had clinched the pennant. Even his severest critics, Shepard could see, had been impressed by his account of how he had coped with his difficult midsummer problems.

Shepard basked for a moment in the admiration of his audience. "I just happen to have the ability to size up women," he went on. "Five minutes after I met this actress, I had her number. I knew Blitz Baker was exactly the type she'd go for. That's why I sent Blitz to Redlands. In two weeks she had forgotten all about Eamons. You know the rest, gentlemen. Last week she and Blitz were married. I'm afraid this will mean the finish of Blitz's baseball career. My guess, gentlemen, is that he'll be lucky to be pitching Class-D ball next year."

Ray, standing beside his boss, studied Shepard's face as he warmed up to the subject of Walter Eamons's great future. It struck Ray that he had never seen Shepard's craggy features composed in an expression of such radiant bliss.

The telephone rang, and Shepard motioned for Ray to take it.

"Who was it?" Shepard asked as Ray hung up.

"Nothing important, Mr. Shepard," Ray answered casually.

"Well, who was it?" Shepard asked again.

"Just Hochstetter," Ray said. "Nothing urgent."

"He wouldn't call me up just to congratulate me on the pennant," Shepard persisted. "What was on his mind, Ray?"

"Just some news about Blitz Baker."

"What did he do? Quit the team?" Shepard asked with a wise twinkle.

"Well, if you must know," Ray said, as if he were being pushed into something against his better judgment, "Hochstetter wanted to tell you that Blitz just pitched a no-hitter and struck out eleven men."

"As I was saying, gentlemen," Shepard resumed quickly, "this Eamons will be even better next year. With proper handling, I predict he'll develop into another Cobb. You can quote me on that."

*Garrison Keillor's tales of small-town America include runaway best sellers like* Lake Wobegone Days *(1985) and* Leaving Home *(1987). He has written many popular short stories for the* New Yorker *and the* Atlantic Monthly, *which have been collected into his books,* Happy to Be Here *(1982),* We Are Still Married *(1990), and* The Book of Guys: Stories *(1993). "What Did We Do Wrong?" originally appeared in the* New Yorker. *It gives us Annie Szemanski, the first woman to play in the major leagues.*

## *Garrison Keillor*

# WHAT DID WE DO WRONG? (1985)

THE FIRST WOMAN TO REACH the big leagues said she wanted to be treated like any other rookie, but she didn't have to worry about that. The Sparrows nicknamed her Chesty and then Big Numbers the first week of spring training, and loaded her bed at the Ramada with butterscotch pudding. Only the writers made a big thing about her being the First Woman. The Sparrows treated her like dirt.

Annie Szemanski arrived in camp fresh from the Federales League of Bolivia, the fourth second baseman on the Sparrows roster, and when Drayton stepped in a hole and broke his ankle Hemmie put her in the lineup, hoping she would break hers. "This was the front office's bright idea," he told the writers. "Off the record, I think it stinks." But when she got in she looked so good that by the third week of March she was a foregone conclusion. Even Hemmie had to admit it. A .346 average tells no lies. He disliked her purely because she was a woman—there was nothing personal about it. Because she was a woman, she was given the manager's dressing room, and Hemmie had to dress with the team. He was sixty-one, a heavyweight, and he had a possum tattooed on his belly alongside the name "Georgene," so he was shy about taking his shirt off in front of people. He hated her for making it necessary. Other than that, he thought she was a tremendous addition to the team.

Asked how she felt being the first woman to make a major-league team, she said, "Like a pig in mud," or words to that effect, and then turned and released a squirt of tobacco juice from the wad of rum-soaked plug in her right cheek. She chewed a rare brand of plug called Stuff It, which she learned to chew when she was playing Nicaraguan summer ball. She told the writers, "They were so mean to me down there you couldn't write it in your newspaper. I took a gun everywhere I went, even to bed. *Especially* to bed. Guys were after me like you can't believe. That's when I started chewing tobacco—because no matter how bad anybody treats you, it's not as bad as this. This is the worst chew in the world. After this, everything else is peaches and cream." The writers elected Gentleman Jim, the Sparrow's P. R. guy, to bite off a chunk and tell them how it tasted, and as he sat and chewed it tears ran down his old sunburnt cheeks and he couldn't talk for a while. Then he whispered, "You've been chewing this for two years? God, I had no idea it was so hard to be a woman."

When thirty-two thousand fans came to Cold Spring Stadium on April 4th for Opening Day and saw the scrappy little freckle-faced woman with tousled black hair who they'd been reading about for almost two months, they were dizzy with devotion. They chanted her name and waved Annie flags and Annie caps ($8.95 and $4.95) and held up hand-painted bedsheets ("EVERY DAY IS LADIES' DAY," "A WOMAN'S PLACE—AT SECOND BASE," "E.R.A. & R.B.I." "THE

GAME AIN'T OVER TILL THE BIG LADY BATS"), but when they saw No. 18 trot out to second with a load of chew as big as if she had the mumps it was a surprise. Then, bottom of the second, when she leaned over in the on-deck circle and dropped a stream of brown juice in the sod, the stadium experienced a moment of thoughtful silence.

One man in Section 31 said, "Hey, what's the beef? She can chew if she wants to. This is 1987. Grow up."

"I guess you're right," his next-seat neighbor said. "My first reaction was nausea, but I think you're right."

"Absolutely. She's a woman, but, more than that, she's a *person.*"

Other folks said, "I'm with you on that. A woman can carry a quarter pound of chew in her cheek and spit in public, same as any man—why should there be any difference?"

*And yet.* Nobody wanted to say this, but the plain truth was that No. 18 was not handling her chew well at all. Juice ran down her chin and dripped onto her shirt. She's bit off more than she can chew, some people thought to themselves, but they didn't want to say that.

Arnie (the Old Gardener) Brixius mentioned it ever so gently in his "Hot Box" column the next day:

> It's only this scribe's opinion, but isn't it about time baseball cleaned up its act and left the tobacco in the locker? Surely big leaguers can go two hours without nicotine. Many a fan has turned away in disgust at the sight of grown men (and now a member of the fair sex) with a faceful, spitting gobs of the stuff in full view of paying customers. Would Frank Sinatra do this onstage? Or Anne Murray? Nuff said.

End of April, Annie was batting .278, with twelve R.B.I.s, which for the miserable Sparrows was stupendous, and at second base she was surprising a number of people, including base runners who thought she'd be a pushover on the double play. A runner heading for second quickly found out that Annie had knees like ballpeen hammers and if he tried to eliminate her from the play she might eliminate him from the rest of the week. One night, up at bat against the Orioles, she took a step toward the mound after an inside pitch and yelled some things, and when the dugouts emptied she was in the thick of it with men who had never been walloped by a woman before. The home-plate ump hauled her off a guy she was pounding the cookies out of, and a moment later he threw her out of the game for saying things to him, he said, that he had never heard in his nineteen years of umpiring. ("Like what, for example?" writers asked. "Just tell us one thing." But he couldn't; he was too upset.)

The next week, the United Baseball Office Workers local passed a resolution in support of Annie, as did the League of Women Voters and the Women's Softball Caucus, which stated, "Szemanski is a model for all women who are made to suffer guilt for their aggressiveness, and we declare our solidarity with her heads-up approach to the game. While we feel she is holding the bat too high and should bring her hips into her swing more, we're behind her one hundred percent."

Then, May 4th, at home against Oakland—seventh inning, two outs, bases loaded—she dropped an easy pop-up and three runs came across home plate. The fans sent a few light boos her way to let her know they were paying attention, nothing serious or overtly political, just some folks grumbling, but she took a few steps toward the box seats and yelled something at them that sounded like—well, like something she shouldn't have said, and after the game she said some more things to the writers that Gentleman Jim pleaded with them not to print. One of them was Monica Lamarr, of the *Press,* who just laughed. She said, "Look. I spent two years in the Lifestyles section writing about motherhood vs. career and the biological clock. Sports is my way out of the gynecology ghetto, so don't ask me to eat this story. It's a hanging curve and I'm going for it. I'm never going to write about day care again." And she wrote it:

SZEMANSKI RAPS FANS AS "SMALL PEOPLE" AFTER DUMB ERROR GIVES GAME TO A'S

FIRST WOMAN ATTRIBUTES BOOS TO SEXUAL INADEQUACY IN STANDS

Jim made some phone calls and the story was yanked and only one truckload of papers went out with it, but word got around, and the next night, though Annie went three for four, the crowd was depressed, and even when she did great the rest of the home stand, and became the first woman to hit a major-league triple, the atmosphere at the ballpark was one of moodiness and deep hurt. Jim went to the men's room one night and found guys standing in line there, looking thoughtful and sad. One of them said, "She's a helluva ballplayer," and other guys murmured that yes, she was, and they wouldn't take anything away from her, she was great and it was wonderful that she had opened up baseball to women, and then they changed the subject to gardening, books, music, aesthetics, anything but baseball. They looked like men who had been stood up.

Gentleman Jim knocked on her door that night. She wore a blue chenille bathrobe flecked with brown tobacco-juice stains, and her black hair hung down in wet strands over her face. She spat into a Dixie cup she was carrying. "Hey! How the Fritos are you? I haven't seen your Big Mac for a while," she said, sort of. He told her she was a great person and a great ballplayer and that he loved her and wanted only the best for her, and he begged her to apologize to the fans. "Make a gesture— *anything*. They *want* to like you. Give them a chance to like you."

She blew her nose into a towel. She said that she wasn't there to be liked, she was there to play ball.

It was a good road trip. The Sparrows won five out of ten, lifting their heads off the canvas, and Annie raised her average to .291 and hit the first major-league home run ever by a woman, up into the left-field screen at Fenway. Sox fans stood and cheered for fifteen minutes. They whistled, they stamped, they pleaded, the Sparrows pleaded, umpires pleaded, but she refused to come out and tip her hat until the public-address announcer said, "No. 18, please come out of the dugout and take a bow. No. 18, the applause is for you and is not intended as patronizing in any way," and then she stuck her head out for 1.5 seconds and did not tip but only touched the brim. Later, she told the writers that just because people had expectations didn't mean she had to fulfill them— she used other words to explain this, but her general drift was that she didn't care very much about living up to anyone else's image of her, and if anyone thought she should, they could go watch wrist wrestling.

The forty thousand who packed Cold Spring Stadium June 6th to see the Sparrows play the Yankees didn't come for a look at Ron Guidry. Banners hung form the second deck: "WHAT DID WE DO WRONG?" and "ANNIE COME HOME" and "WE LOVE YOU, WHY DO YOU TREAT US THIS WAY?" and "IF YOU WOULD LIKE TO DISCUSS THIS IN A NON-CONFRONTATIONAL, MUTUALLY RESPECTFUL WAY, MEET US AFTER THE GAME AT GATE C." It was Snapshot Day, and all the Sparrows appeared on the field for photos with the fans except you know who. Hemmie begged her to go. "You owe it to them," he said.

"Owe?" she said. "*Owe?*"

"Sorry, wrong word," he said. "What if I put it this way: it's a sort of tradition."

"*Tradition?*" she said. "I'm supposed to worry about *tradition?*"

That day, she became the first woman to hit .300. A double in the fifth inning. The scoreboard flashed the message, and the crowd gave her a nice hand. A few people stood and cheered, but the fans around them told them to sit down. "She's not that kind of person," they said. "Cool it. Back off." The fans were trying to give her plenty of space. After the game, Guidry said, "I really have to respect her. She's got that small strike zone and she protects it well, so she makes you pitch to her." She said, "Guidry? Was that his name? I didn't know. Anyway, he didn't show me much. He throws funny, don't you think? He reminded me a little bit of a southpaw I saw down in Nicaragua, except she threw inside more."

All the writers were there, kneeling around her. One of them asked if Guidry had thrown her a lot of sliders.

She gave him a long, baleful look. "Jeez, you guys are out of shape," she said. "You're wheezing and panting and sucking air, and you just took the elevator *down* from the press box. You guys want to write about sports you ought to go into training. And then you ought to learn how to recognize a slider. Jeez, if you were writing about agriculture, would you have to ask someone if those were Holsteins?"

Tears came to the writer's eyes. "I'm trying to help," he said. "Can't you see that? Don't you know how much we care about you? Sometimes I think you put up this tough exterior to hide your own insecurity."

She laughed and brushed the wet hair back from her forehead. "It's no exterior," she said as she unbuttoned her jersey. "It's who I am." She peeled off her socks and stepped out to her cubicle a moment later, sweaty and stark naked. The towel hung from her hand. She walked slowly around them. "You guys learned all you know about women thirty years ago. That wasn't me back then, that was my mother." The writers bent over their notepads, writing down every word she said and punctuating carefully. Gentleman Jim took off his glasses. "My mother was a nice lady, but she couldn't hit the curve to save her Creamettes," she went on. "And now, gentlemen, if you'll excuse me, I'm going to take a shower." They pored over their notes until she was gone, and then they piled out into the hallway and hurried back to the press elevator.

Arnie stopped at the Shortstop for a load of Martinis before he went to the office to write the "Hot Box," which turned out to be about love:

> Baseball is a game but it's more than a game, baseball is people, dammit, and if you are around people you can't help but get involved in their lives and care about them and then you don't know how to talk to them or tell them how much you care and how come we know so much about pitching and we don't know squat about how to communicate? I guess that is the question.

The next afternoon, Arnie leaned against the batting cage before the game, hung over, and watched her hit line drives, fifteen straight, and each one made his head hurt. As she left the cage, he called over to her. "Later," she said. She also declined a pregame interview with Joe Garagiola, who had just told his NBC "Game of the Week" television audience, "This is a city in love with a little girl named Annie Szemanski," when he saw her in the dugout doing deep knee bends. "Annie! Annie!" he yelled over the air. "Let's see if we can't get her up here," he told the home audience. "Annie! Joe Garagiola!" She turned her back to him and went down into the dugout.

That afternoon, she became the first woman to steal two bases in one inning. She reached first on a base on balls, stole second, went to third on a sacrifice fly, and headed for home on the next pitch. The catcher came out to make the tag, she caught him with her elbow under the chin, and when the dust cleared she was grinning at the ump, the catcher was sprawled in the grass trying to inhale, and the ball was halfway to the backstop.

The TV camera zoomed in on her, head down, trotting toward the dugout steps, when suddenly she looked up. Some out-of-town fan had yelled at her from the box seats. ("A profanity which also refers to a female dog," the *News* said.) She smiled and, just before she stepped out of view beneath the dugout roof, millions observed her right hand uplifted in a familiar gesture. In bars around the country, men looked at each other and said, "Did she do what I think I saw her do? She didn't do that, did she?" In the booth, Joe Garagiola was observing that it was a clean play, that the runner has a right to the base path, but when her hand appeared on the screen he stopped. At home, it sounded as if he had been hit in the chest by a rock. The screen went blank, then went to a beer commercial. When the show resumed, it was the middle of the next inning.

On Monday, for "actions detrimental to the best interests of baseball," Annie was fined a thousand dollars by the Commissioner and suspended for two games. He deeply regretted the decision, etc. "I count myself among her most ardent fans. She is good for baseball, good for the cause of equal rights, good for America." He said he would be happy to suspend the suspension if she would make a public apology, which would make him the happiest man in America.

Gentleman Jim went to the bank Monday afternoon and got the money, a thousand dollars, in a cashier's check. All afternoon, he called Annie's number over and over, waiting thirty and forty rings, then trying again. He called from a pay phone at the Stop 'N' Shop, next door to the Cityview Apartments, where she lived, and between calls he sat in his car and watched the entrance, waiting for her to come out. Other men were parked there, too, in front, and some in back—men with Sparrows bumper stickers. After midnight, about eleven of them were left. "Care to share some onion chips and clam dip?" one guy said to another guy. Pretty soon all of them were standing around the trunk of the clam-dip guy's car, where he also had a case of beer.

"Here, let me pay you something for this beer," said a guy who had brought a giant box of pretzels.

"Hey, no. Really. It's just good to have other guys to talk to tonight," said the clam-dip owner.

"She changed a lot of very basic things about the whole way that I look at myself as a man," the pretzel guy said quietly.

"I'm in public relations," said Jim, "but even I don't understand all that she has meant to people."

"How can she do this to us?" said a potato-chip man. "All the love of the fans, how can she throw it away? Why can't she just play ball?"

Annie didn't look at it that way. "Pall Mall! I'm not going to crawl just because some Tootsie Roll says crawl, and if they don't like it, then Ritz, they can go Pepsi their Hostess Twinkies," she told the writers as she cleaned out her locker on Tuesday morning. They had never seen the inside of her locker before. It was stuffed with dirty socks, half unwrapped gifts from admiring fans, a set of ankle weights, and a small silver-plated pistol. "No way I'm going to pay a thousand dollars, and if they expect an apology—well, they better send out for lunch, because it's going to be a long wait. Gentlemen, goodbye and hang on to your valuable coupons." And she smiled her most winning smile and sprinted up the stairs to collect her paycheck. They waited for her outside the Sparrows office, twenty-six men, and then followed her down the ramp and out of Gate C. She broke into a run and disappeared into the lunchtime crowd on West Providence Avenue, and that was the last they saw of her—the woman of their dreams, the love of their lives, carrying a red gym bag, running easily away from them.

*Although Ring Lardner was personally articulate, modest, and somewhat prudish, his fictional baseball players are usually just the opposite. In his later short stories, Lardner branched out to other sports and aspects of the American scene and character. This widened his popularity and burnished his image as one of the great American writers. His books, many of which are collections of his short stories, include* You Know Me, Al *(1916),* Round Up *(1929),* The Big Town *(1925), and the* Collected Stories of Ring Lardner *(1941).*

*Ring Lardner*

# HORSESHOES
# (1914)

THE SERIES ENDED TUESDAY, BUT I had stayed in Philadelphia an extra day on the chance of there being some follow-up stuff worth sending. Nothing had broken loose; so I filed some stuff about what the Athletics and Giants were going to do with their dough, and then caught the eight o'clock train for Chicago.

Having passed up supper in order to get my story away and grab the train, I went to the buffet car right after I'd planted my grips. I sat down at one of the tables and ordered a sandwich. Four salesmen were playing rum at the other table and all the chairs in the car were occupied; so

RING LARDNER

it didn't surprise me when somebody flopped down in the seat opposite me.

I looked up from my paper and with a little thrill recognized my companion. Now I've been experting round the country with ballplayers so much that it doesn't usually excite me to meet one face to face, even if he's a star. I can talk with Tyrus without getting all fussed up. But this particular player had jumped from obscurity to fame so suddenly and had played such an important though brief part in the recent argument between the Macks and McGraws that I couldn't help being a little awed by his proximity.

It was none other than Grimes, the utility outfielder Connie had been forced to use in the last game because of the injury to Joyce—Grimes, whose miraculous catch in the eleventh inning had robbed Parker of a home run and the Giants of victory, and whose own homer—a fluky one—had given the Athletics another World's Championship.

I had met Grimes one day during the spring he was with the Cubs, but I knew he wouldn't remember me. A ballplayer never recalls a reporter's face on less than six introductions or his name on less than twenty. However, I resolved to speak to him, and had just mustered sufficient courage to open a conversation when he saved me the trouble.

"Whose picture have they got there?" he asked, pointing to my paper.

"Speed Parker's," I replied.

"What do they say about him?" asked Grimes.

"I'll read it to you," I said:

'Speed Parker, McGraw's great third baseman, is ill in a local hospital with nervous prostration, the result of the strain of the World's Series, in which he played such a stellar role. Parker is in such a dangerous condition that no one is allowed to see him. Members of the New York team and fans from Gotham called at the hospital today, but were unable to gain admittance to his ward. Philadelphians hope he will recover speedily and will suffer no permanent ill effects from his sickness, for he won their admiration by his work in the series, though he was on a rival team. A lucky catch by Grimes, the Athletics' substitute outfielder, was all that prevented Parker from winning the title for New York. According to Manager Mack, of the champions, the series would

222

have been over in four games but for Parker's wonderful exhibition of nerve and—'

"That'll be a plenty," Grimes interrupted. "And that's just what you might expect from one o' them doughheaded reporters. If all the baseball writers was where they belonged they'd have to build a annex to Matteawan."

I kept my temper with very little effort—it takes more than a peevish ballplayer's remarks to insult one of our fraternity; but I didn't exactly understand his peeve.

"Doesn't Parker deserve the bouquet?" I asked.

"Oh, they can boost him all they want to," said Grimes; "but when they call that catch lucky and don't mention the fact that Parker is the luckiest guy in the world, somethin' must be wrong with 'em. Did you see the serious?"

"No," I lied glibly, hoping to draw from him the cause of his grouch.

"Well," he said, "you sure missed somethin'. They never was a serious like it before and they won't never be one again. It went the full seven games and every game was a bear. They was one big innin' every day and Parker was the big cheese in it. Just as Connie says, the Ath-a-letics would of cleaned 'em in four games but for Parker; but it wasn't because he's a great ballplayer—it was because he was born with a knife, fork and spoon in his mouth, and a rabbit's foot hung round his neck.

"You may not know it, but I'm Grimes, the guy that made the lucky catch. I'm the guy that won the serious with a hit—a home-run hit; and I'm here to tell you that if I'd had one-tenth o' Parker's luck they'd of heard about me long before yesterday. They say my homer was lucky. Maybe it was; but, believe me, it was time things broke for me. They been breakin' for him all his life."

"Well," I said, "his luck must have gone back on him if he's in a hospital with nervous prostration."

"Nervous prostration nothin'," said Grimes. "He's in a hospital because his face is all out o' shape and he's ashamed to appear on the street. I don't usually do so much talkin' and I'm ravin' a little to-night because I've had a couple o' drinks; but—"

"Have another," said I, ringing for the waiter, "and talk some more."

"I made two hits yesterday," Grimes went on, "but the crowd only seen one. I busted up the game and the serious with the one they seen. The one they didn't see was the one I busted up a guy's map with—and Speed Parker was the guy. That's why he's in a hospital. He may be able to play ball next year; but I'll bet my share o' the dough that McGraw won't reco'nize him when he shows up at Marlin in the spring."

"When did this come off?" I asked. "And why?"

"It come off outside the clubhouse after yesterday's battle," he said; "and I hit him because he called me a name—a name I won't stand for from him."

"What did he call you?" I queried, expecting to hear one of the delicate epithets usually applied by conquered to conqueror on the diamond.

"'Horseshoes!'" was Grimes' amazing reply.

"But, good Lord!" I remonstrated, "I've heard of ballplayers calling each other that, and Lucky Stiff, and Fourleaf Clover, ever since I was a foot high, and I never knew them to start fights about it."

"Well," said Grimes, "I might as well give you all the dope; and then if you don't think I was justified I'll pay your fare from here to wherever you're goin'. I don't want you to think I'm kickin' about trifles—or that I'm kickin' at all, for that matter. I just want to prove to you that he didn't have no license to pull that Horseshoes stuff on me and that I only give him what was comin' to him."

"Go ahead and shoot," said I.

"Give us some more o' the same," said Grimes to the passing waiter. And then he told me about it.

Maybe you've heard that me and Speed Parker was raised in the same town—Ishpeming, Michigan. We was kids together, and though he done all the devilment I got all the lickin's. When we was about twelve years old Speed throwed a rotten egg at the teacher and I got expelled. That made me sick o' schools and I wouldn't never go to one again, though my ol' man beat me up and the truant officers threatened to have me hung.

Well, while Speed was learnin' what was the principal products o' New Hampshire and Texas I was workin' round the freight-house and drivin' a dray.

We'd both been playin' ball all our lives; and when the town organized a semi-pro club we got jobs with it. We was to draw two bucks apiece for each game and they played every Sunday. We played four games before we got our first pay. They was a hole in my pants pocket as big as the home plate, but I forgot about it and put the dough in there. It wasn't there when I got home. Speed didn't have no hole in his pocket—you can bet on that! Afterward the club hired a good outfielder and I was canned. They was huntin' for another third baseman too; but, o' course, they didn't find none and Speed held his job.

The next year they started the Northern Peninsula League. We landed with the home team. The league opened in May and blowed up the third week in June. They paid off all the outsiders first and then had just money enough left to settle with one of us two Ishpeming guys. The night they done the payin' I was out to my uncle's farm, so they settled with Speed and told me I'd have to wait for mine. I'm still waitin'!

Gene Higgins, who was manager o' the Battle Creek Club, lived in Houghton, and that winter we goes over and strikes him for a job. He give it to us and we busted in together two years ago last spring.

I had a good year down there. I hit over .300 and stole all the bases in sight. Speed got along good too, and they was several big-league scouts lookin' us over. The Chicago Cubs bought Speed outright and four clubs put in a draft for me. Three of 'em—Cleveland and the New York Giants and the Boston Nationals—needed outfielders bad, and it would of been a pipe for me to of made good with any of 'em. But who do you think got me? The same Chicago Cubs; and the only outfielders they had at that time was Schulte and Leach and Good and Williams and Stewart, and one or two others.

Well, I didn't figure I was any worse off than Speed. The Cubs had Zimmerman at third base and it didn't look like they was any danger of a busher beatin' him out; but Zimmerman goes and breaks his leg the second day o' the season—that's a year ago last April—and Speed jumps right in as a regular. Do you think anything like that could happen to Schulte or Leach, or any o' them outfielders? No, sir! I wore out my uniform slidin' up and down the bench and wonderin' whether they'd ship me to Fort Worth or Siberia.

Now I want to tell you about the miserable luck Speed had right off the reel. We was playin' at St. Louis. They had a one-run lead in the eighth, when their pitcher walked Speed with one out. Saier hits a high fly to centre and Parker starts with the crack o' the bat. Both coachers was yellin' at him to go back, but he thought they was two out and he was clear round to third base when the ball come down. And Oakes muffs it! O' course he scored and the game was tied up.

Parker come in to the bench like he'd did something wonderful.

"Did you think they was two out?" ast Hank.

"No," says Speed, blushin'.

"Then what did you run for?" says Hank.

"I had a hunch he was goin' to drop the ball," says Speed; and Hank pretty near falls off the bench.

The next day he come up with one out and the sacks full, and the score tied in the sixth. He smashes one on the ground straight at Hauser and it looked like a cinch double play; but just as Hauser was goin' to grab it the ball hit a rough spot and hopped a mile over his head. It got between Oakes and Magee and went clear to the fence. Three guys scored and Speed pulled up at third. The papers come out and said the game was won by a three-bagger from the bat o' Parker, the Cubs' sensational kid third baseman. Gosh!

We go home to Chi and are havin' a hot battle with Pittsburgh. This time Speed's turn come when they was two on and two out, and Pittsburgh a run to the good—I think it was the eighth innin'. Cooper gives him a fast one and he hits it straight up in the air. O' course the runners started goin', but it looked hopeless because they wasn't no wind or high sky to bother anybody. Mowrey and Gibson both goes after the ball; and just as Mowrey was set for the catch Gibson bumps into him and they both fall down. Two runs scored and Speed got to second. Then what does he do but try to steal third—with two out too! And Gibson's peg pretty near hits the left field seats on the fly.

When Speed comes to the bench Hank says:

"If I was you I'd quit playin' ball and go to Monte Carlo."

"What for?" says Speed.

"You're so dam' lucky!" says Hank.

"So is Ty Cobb," says Speed. That's how he hated himself!

First trip to Cincy we run into a couple of old Ishpeming boys. They took us out one night, and about twelve o'clock I said we'd have to go back to the hotel or we'd get fined. Speed said I had cold feet and he stuck with the boys. I went back alone and Hank caught me comin' in and put a fifty-dollar plaster on me. Speed stayed out all night long and Hank never knowed it. I says to myself: "Wait till he gets out there and tries to play ball without no sleep!" But the game that day was called off on account o' rain. Can you beat it?

I remember what he got away with the next afternoon the same as though it happened yesterday. In the second innin' they walked him with nobody down, and he took a big lead off first base like he always does. Benton threwed over there three or four times to scare him back, and the last time he threwed, Hobby hid the ball. The coacher seen it and told Speed to hold the bag; but he didn't pay no attention. He started leadin' right off again and Hobby tried to tag him, but the ball slipped out of his hand and rolled about a yard away. Parker had plenty o' time to get back; but, instead o' that, he starts for second. Hobby picked up the ball and shot it down to Groh—and Groh made a square muff.

Parker slides into the bag safe and then gets up and throws out his chest like he'd made the greatest play ever. When the ball's throwed back to Benton, Speed leads off about thirty foot and stands there in a trance. Clarke signs for a pitch-out and pegs down to second to nip him. He was caught flatfooted—that is, he would of been with a decent throw; but Clarke's peg went pretty near to Latonia. Speed scored and strutted over to receive our hearty congratulations. Some o' the boys was laughin' and he thought they was laughin' with him instead of at him.

It was in the ninth, though, that he got by with one o' the worst I ever seen. The Reds was a run behind and Marsans was on third base with two out. Hobby, I think it was, hit one on the ground right at Speed and he picked it up clean. The crowd all got up and started for the exits. Marsans run toward the plate in the faint hope that the peg to first would be wild. All of a sudden the boys on the Cincy bench begun yellin' at him to slide, and he done so. He was way past the plate when Speed's throw got to Archer. The bonehead had shot the ball home instead o' to first base, thinkin' they was only one down. We was all crazy, believin' his nut play had let 'em tie it up; but he comes tearin' in, tellin' Archer to tag Marsans. So Jim walks over and tags the Cuban, who was brushin' off his uniform.

"You're out!" says Klem. "You never touched the plate."

I guess Marsans knowed the umps was right because he didn't make much of a holler. But Speed sure got a pannin' in the clubhouse.

"I suppose you knowed he was goin' to miss the plate!" says Hank sarcastic as he could.

Everybody on the club roasted him, but it didn't do no good.

Well, you know what happened to me. I only got into one game with the Cubs—one afternoon when Leach was sick. We was playin' the Boston bunch and Tyler was workin' against us. I always had trouble with lefthanders and this was one of his good days. I couldn't see what he throwed up there. I got one foul durin' the afternoon's entertainment; and the wind was blowin' a hundred-mile gale, so that the best outfielder in the world couldn't judge a fly ball. That Boston bunch must of hit fifty of 'em and they all come to my field.

If I caught any I've forgot about it. Couple o' days after that I got notice o' my release to Indianapolis.

Parker kept right on all season doin' the blamedest things you ever heard of and gettin' by with 'em. One o' the boys told me about it later. If they was playin' a double-header in St. Louis, with the thermometer at 130 degrees, he'd get put out by the umps in the first innin' o' the first game. If he started to steal the catcher'd drop the pitch or somebody'd muff the throw. If he hit a pop fly the sun'd get in somebody's eyes. If he took a swell third strike with the bases full the umps would call it a ball. If he cut first base by twenty feet the umps would be readin' the mornin' paper.

Zimmerman's leg mended, so that he was all right by June; and then Saier got sick and they tried Speed at first base. He'd never saw the bag before; but things kept on breakin' for him and he played it like a house afire. The Cubs copped the pennant and Speed got in on the big dough, besides playin' a whale of a game through the whole serious.

Speed and me both went back to Ishpeming to spend the winter—though the Lord knows it ain't no winter resort. Our homes was there; and besides, in my case, they was a certain girl livin' in the old burg.

Parker, o' course, was the hero and the swell guy when we got home. He'd been in the World's Serious and had plenty o' dough in his kick. I come home with nothin' but my suitcase and a hard-luck story, which I kept to myself. I hadn't even went good enough in Indianapolis to be sure of a job there again.

That fall—last fall—an uncle o' Speed's died over in the Soo and left him ten thousand bucks. I had an uncle down in the Lower Peninsula who was worth five times that much—but he had good health!

This girl I spoke about was the prettiest thing I ever seen. I'd went with her in the old days, and when I blew back I found she was still strong for me. They wasn't a great deal o' variety in Ishpeming for a girl to pick from. Her and I went to the dance every Saturday night and to church Sunday nights. I called on her Wednesday evenin's, besides takin' her to all the shows that come along—rotten as the most o' them was.

I never knowed Speed was makin' a play for this doll till along last Feb'uary. The minute I seen what was up I got busy. I took her out sleigh-ridin' and kept her out in the cold till she'd promised to marry me. We set the date for this fall—I figured I'd know better where I was at by that time.

Well, we didn't make no secret o' bein' engaged; down in the poolroom one night Speed come up and congratulated me. He says:

"You got a swell girl, Dick! I wouldn't mind bein' in your place. You're mighty lucky to cop her out—you old Horseshoes, you!"

"Horseshoes!" I says. "You got a fine license to call anybody Horseshoes! I suppose you ain't never had no luck?"

"Not like you," he says.

I was feelin' too good about grabbin' the girl to get sore at the time; but when I got to thinkin' about it a few minutes afterward it made me mad clear through. What right did that bird have to talk about me bein' lucky?

Speed was playin' freeze-out at a table near the door, and when I started home some o' the boys with him says:

"Good night, Dick."

I said good night and then Speed looked up.

"Good night. Horseshoes!" he says.

That got my nanny this time.

"Shut up, you lucky stiff!" I says. "If you wasn't so dam' lucky you'd be sweepin' the streets." Then I walks on out.

I was too busy with the girl to see much o' Speed after that. He left home about the middle o' the month to go to Tampa with the Cubs. I got notice from Indianapolis that I was sold to Baltimore. I didn't care much about goin' there and I wasn't anxious to leave home under the circumstances, so I didn't report till late.

When I read in the papers along in April that Speed had been traded to Boston for a couple o' pitchers I thought: "Gee! He must of lost his rabbit's foot!" Because, even if the Cubs didn't cop again, they'd have a city serious with the White Sox and get a bunch o' dough that way. And they wasn't no chance in the world for the Boston club to get nothin' but their salaries.

It wasn't another month, though, till Shafer, o' the Giants, quit baseball and McGraw was up against it for a third baseman. Next thing I knowed Speed was traded to New York and was with another winner—for they never was out o' first place all season.

I was gettin' along all right at Baltimore and Dunnie liked me; so I felt like I had somethin' more than just a one-year job—somethin' I could get married on. It was all framed that the weddin' was comin' off as soon as this season was over; so you can believe I was pullin' for October to hurry up and come.

One day in August, two months ago, Dunnie come in the clubhouse and handed me the news.

"Rube Oldring's busted his leg," he says, "and he's out for the rest o' the season. Connie's got a youngster named Joyce that he can stick in there, but he's got to have an extra outfielder. He's made me a good proposition for you and I'm goin' to let you go. It'll be pretty soft for you, because they got the pennant cinched and they'll cut you in on the big money."

"Yes," I says; "and when they're through with me they'll ship me Hellangone, and I'll be raggin' down about seventy-five bucks a month next year."

"Nothin' like that," says Dunnie. "If he don't want you next season he's go to ask for waivers; and if you get out o' the big league you come right back here. That's all framed."

So that's how I come to get with the Ath-a-letics. Connie give me a nice, comf'table seat in one corner o' the bench and I had the pleasure o' watchin' a real ball club perform once every afternoon and sometimes twice.

Connie told me that as soon as they had the flag cinched he was goin' to lay off some o' his regulars and I'd get a chance to play.

Well, they cinched it the fourth day o' September and our next engagement was with Washin'ton on Labor Day. We had two games and I was in both of 'em. And I broke in with my usual lovely luck, because the pitchers I was ast to face was Boehling, a nasty lefthander, and this guy Johnson.

The mornin' game was Boehling's and he wasn't no worse than some o' the rest of his kind. I only whiffed once and would of had a triple if Milan hadn't run from here to New Orleans and stole one off me.

I'm not boastin' about my first experience with Johnson though. They can't never tell me he throws them balls with his arm. He's got a gun concealed about his person and he shoots 'em up there. I was leadin' off in Murphy's place and the game was a little delayed in startin', because I'd watched the big guy warm up and wasn't in no hurry to get to that plate. Before I left the bench Connie says:

"Don't try to take no healthy swing. Just meet 'em and you'll get along better."

231

So I tried to just meet the first one he throwed; but when I stuck out my bat Henry was throwin' the pill back to Johnson. Then I thought: Maybe if I start swingin' now at the second one I'll hit the third one. So I let the second one come over and the umps guessed it was another strike, though I'll bet a thousand bucks he couldn't see it no more'n I could.

While Johnson was still windin' up to pitch again I started to swing— and the big cuss crosses me with a slow one. I lunged at it twice and missed it both times, and the force o' my wallop throwed me clean back to the bench. The Ath-a-letics was all laughin' at me and I laughed too, because I was glad that much of it was over.

McInnes gets a base hit off him in the second innin' and I ast him how he done it.

"He's a friend o' mine," says Jack, "and he lets up when he pitches to me."

I made up my mind right there that if I was goin' to be in the league next year I'd go out and visit Johnson this winter and get acquainted.

I wished before the day was over that I was hittin' in the catcher's place, because the fellers down near the tail-end of the battin' order only had to face him three times. He fanned me on three pitched balls again in the third, and when I come up in the sixth he scared me to death by pretty near beanin' me with the first one.

"Be careful!" says Henry. "He's gettin' pretty wild and he's liable to knock you away from your uniform."

"Don't he never curve one?" I ast.

"Sure!" says Henry. "Do you want to see his curve?"

"Yes," I says, knowin' the hook couldn't be no worse'n the fast one.

So he give me three hooks in succession and I missed 'em all; but I felt more comf'table than when I was duckin' his fast ball. In the ninth he hit my bat with a curve and the ball went on the ground to McBride. He booted it, but throwed me out easy—because I was so surprised at not havin' whiffed that I forgot to run!

Well, I went along like that for the rest o' the season, runnin' up against the best pitchers in the league and not exactly murderin' 'em.

Everything I tried went wrong, and I was smart enough to know that if anything had depended on the games I wouldn't of been in there for two minutes. Joyce and Strunk and Murphy wasn't jealous o' me a bit; but they was glad to take turns restin', and I didn't care much how I went so long as I was sure of a job next year.

I'd wrote to the girl a couple o' times askin' her to set the exact date for our weddin'; but she hadn't paid no attention. She said she was glad I was with the Ath-a-letics, but she thought the Giants was goin' to beat us. I might of suspected from that that somethin' was wrong, because not even a girl would pick the Giants to trim that bunch of ourn. Finally, the day before the serious started, I sent her a kind o' sassy letter sayin' I guessed it was up to me to name the day, and askin' whether October twentieth was all right. I told her to wire me yes or no.

I'd been readin' the dope about Speed all season, and I knowed he'd had a whale of a year and that his luck was right with him; but I never dreamed a man could have the Lord on his side as strong as Speed did in that World's Serious! I might as well tell you all the dope, so long as you wasn't there.

The first game was on our grounds and Connie give us a talkin' to in the clubhouse beforehand.

"The shorter this serious is," he says, "the better for us. If it's a long serious we're goin' to have trouble, because McGraw's got five pitchers he can work and we've got about three; so I want you boys to go at 'em for the jump and play 'em off their feet. Don't take things easy, because it ain't goin' to be no snap. Just because we've licked 'em before ain't no sign we'll do it this time."

Then he calls me to one side and ast me what I knowed about Parker.

"You was with the Cubs when he was, wasn't you?" he says.

"Yes," I says; "and he's the luckiest stiff you ever seen! If he got stewed and fell in the gutter he'd catch a fish."

"I don't like to hear a good ballplayer called lucky," says Connie. "He must have a lot of ability or McGraw wouldn't use him regular. And he's been hittin' about .340 and played a bang-up game at third base. That can't be all luck."

"Wait till you see him," I says; "and if you don't say he's the luckiest guy in the world you can sell me to the Boston Bloomer Girls. He's so lucky," I says, "that if they traded him to the St. Louis Browns they'd have the pennant cinched by the Fourth o' July."

And I'll bet Connie was willin' to agree with me before it was over.

Well, the Chief worked against the Big Rube in that game. We beat 'em, but they give us a battle and it was Parker that made it close. We'd gone along nothin' and nothin' till the seventh, and then Rube walks Collins and Baker lifts one over that little old wall. You'd think by this time them New York pitchers would know better than to give the guy anything he can hit.

In their part o' the ninth the Chief still had 'em shut out and two down, and the crowd was goin' home; but Doyle gets hit in the sleeve with a pitched ball and it's Speed's turn. He hits a foul pretty near straight up, but Schang misjudges it. Then he lifts another one and this time McInnes drops it. He'd ought to of been out twice. The Chief tries to make him hit at a bad one then, because he'd got him two strikes and nothin'. He hit at it all right—kissed it for three bases between Strunk and Joyce! And it was a wild pitch that he hit. Doyle scores, o' course, and the bugs suddenly decide not to go home just yet. I fully expected to see him steal home and get away with it, but Murray cut into the first ball and lined out to Barry.

Plank beat Matty two to one the next day in New York, and again Speed and his rabbit's foot give us an awful argument. Matty wasn't so good as usual and we really ought to of beat him bad. Two different times Strunk was on second waitin' for any kind o' wallop, and both times Barry cracked 'em down the third base line like a shot. Speed stopped the first one with his stomach and extricated the pill just in time to nail Barry at first base and retire the side. The next time he throwed his glove in front of his face in self-defense and the ball stuck in it.

In the sixth innin' Schang was on third base and Plank on first, and two down, and Murphy combed an awful one to Speed's left. He didn't have time to stoop over and he just stuck out his foot. The ball hit it and caromed in two hops right into Doyle's hands on second base before

Plank got there. Then in the seventh Speed bunts one and Baker trips and falls goin' after it or he'd of threw him out a mile. They was two gone; so Speed steals second, and, o' course, Schang has to make a bad peg right at that time and lets him go to third. Then Collins boots one on Murray and they've got a run. But it didn't do 'em no good, because Collins and Baker and McInnes come up in the ninth and walloped 'em where Parker couldn't reach 'em.

Comin' back to Philly on the train that night, I says to Connie:

"What do you think o' that Parker bird now?"

"He's lucky, all right," says Connie smilin'; "but we won't hold it against him if he don't beat us with it."

"It ain't too late," I says. "He ain't pulled his real stuff yet."

The whole bunch was talkin' about him and his luck, and sayin' it was about time for things to break against him. I warned 'em that they wasn't no chance—that it was permanent with him.

Bush and Tesreau hooked up next day and neither o'·them had much stuff. Everybody was hittin' and it looked like anybody's game right up to the ninth. Speed had got on every time he come up—the wind blowin' his fly balls away from the outfielders and the infielders bootin' when he hit 'em on the ground.

When the ninth started the score was seven apiece. Connie and Mc-Graw both had their whole pitchin' staffs warmin' up. The crowd was wild, because they'd been all kinds of action. They wasn't no danger of anybody's leavin' their seats before this game was over.

Well, Bescher is walked to start with and Connie's about ready to give Bush the hook; but Doyle pops out tryin' to bunt. Then Speed gets two strikes and two balls, and it looked to me like the next one was right over the heart; but Connolly calls it a ball and gives him another chance. He whales the groove ball to the fence in left center and gets round to third on it, while Bescher scores. Right then Bush comes out and the Chief goes in. He whiffs Murray and has two strikes on Merkle when Speed makes a break for home—and o' course, that was the one ball Schang dropped in the whole serious! 

They had a two-run lead on us then and it looked like a cinch for them

to hold it, because the minute Tesreau showed a sign o' weakenin' Mc-
Graw was sure to holler for Matty or the Rube. But you know how quick
that bunch of ourn can make a two-run lead look sick. Before McGraw
could get Jeff out o' there we had two on the bases.

Then Rube comes in and fills 'em up by walkin' Joyce. It was Eddie's
turn to wallop and if he didn't do nothin' we had Baker comin' up next.
This time Collins saved Baker the trouble and whanged one clear to the
woods. Everybody scored but him—and he could of, too, if it'd been necessary.

In the clubhouse the boys naturally felt pretty good. We'd copped
three in a row and it looked like we'd make it four straight, because we
had the Chief to send back at 'em the followin' day.

"Your friend Parker is lucky," the boys says to me, "but it don't look
like he could stop us now."

I felt the same way and was consultin' the time-tables to see whether
I could get a train out o' New York for the West next evenin'. But do
you think Speed's luck was ready to quit? Not yet! And it's a wonder we
didn't all go nuts durin' the next few days. If words could kill, Speed
would of died a thousand times. And I wish he had!

They wasn't no record-breakin' crowd out when we got to the Polo
Grounds. I guess the New York bugs was pretty well discouraged and the
bettin' was eight to five that we'd cop that battle and finish it. The Chief
was the only guy that warmed up for us and McGraw didn't have no
choice but to use Matty, with the whole thing dependin' on this game.

They went along like the two swell pitchers they was till Speed's innin', which in this battle was the eighth. Nobody scored, and it didn't
look like they was ever goin' to till Murphy starts off that round with a
perfect bunt and Joyce sacrifices him to second. All Matty had to do
then was to get rid o' Collins and Baker—and that's about as easy as
sellin' silk socks to an Eskimo.

He didn't give Eddie nothin' he wanted to hit, though; and finally he
slaps one on the ground to Doyle. Larry made the play to first base and
Murphy moved to third. We all figured Matty'd walk Baker then, and
he done it. Connie sends Baker down to second on the first pitch to

McInnes, but Meyers don't pay no attention to him—they was playin' for McInnes and wasn't takin' no chances o' throwin' the ball away.

Well, the count goes to three and two on McInnes and Matty comes with a curve—he's got some curve too; but Jack happened to meet it and—Blooie! Down the left foul line where he always hits! I never seen a ball hit so hard in my life. No infielder in the world could of stopped it. But I'll give you a thousand bucks if that ball didn't go kerplunk right into the third bag and stop as dead as George Washington! It was child's play for Speed to pick it up and heave it over to Merkle before Jack got there. If anybody else had been playin' third base the bag would of ducked out o' the way o' that wallop; but even the bases themselves was helpin' him out.

The two runs we ought to of had on Jack's smash would of been just enough to beat 'em, because they got the only run o' the game in their half—or, I should say, the Lord give it to 'em.

Doyle'd been throwed out and up come Parker, smilin'. The minute I seen him smile I felt like somethin' was comin' off and I made the remark on the bench.

Well, the Chief pitched one right at him and he tried to duck. The ball hit his bat and went on a line between Jack and Eddie. Speed didn't know he'd hit it till the guys on the bench wised him up. Then he just had time to get to first base. They tried the hit-and-run on the second ball and Murray lifts a high fly that Murphy didn't have to move for. Collins pulled the old bluff about the ball bein' on the ground and Barry yells, "Go on! Go on!" like he was the coacher. Speed fell for it and didn't know where the ball was no more'n a rabbit; he just run his fool head off and we was gettin' all ready to laugh when the ball come down and Murphy dropped it!

If Parker had stuck near first base, like he ought to of done, he couldn't of got no farther'n second; but with the start he got he was pretty near third when Murphy made the muff, and it was a cinch for him to score. The next two guys was easy outs; so they wouldn't of had a run except for Speed's boner. We couldn't do nothin' in the ninth and we was licked.

Well, that was a tough one to lose; but we figured that Matty was through and we'd wind it up the next day, as we had Plank ready to send back at 'em. We wasn't afraid o' the Rube, because he hadn't never bothered Collins and Baker much.

The two lefthanders come together just like everybody'd doped it and it was about even up to the eighth. Plank had been goin' great and, though the score was two and two, they'd got their two on boots and we'd hit ourn in. We went after Rube in our part o' the eighth and knocked him out. Demaree stopped us after we'd scored two more.

"It's all over but the shoutin'!" says Davis on the bench.

"Yes," I says, "unless that seventh son of a seventh son gets up there again."

He did, and he come up after they'd filled the bases with a boot, a base hit and a walk with two out. I says to Davis:

"If I was Plank I'd pass him and give 'em one run."

"That wouldn't be no baseball," says Davis—"not with Murray comin' up."

Well, it mayn't of been no baseball, but it couldn't of turned out worse if they'd did it that way. Speed took a healthy at the first ball; but it was a hook and he caught it on the handle, right up near his hands. It started outside the first-base line like a foul and then changed its mind and rolled in. Schang run away from the plate, because it looked like it was up to him to make the play. He picked the ball up and had to make the peg in a hurry.

His throw hit Speed right on top o' the head and bounded off like it had struck a cement sidewalk. It went clear over to the seats and before McInnes could get it three guys had scored and Speed was on third base. He was left there, but that didn't make no difference. We was licked again and for the first time the gang really begun to get scared.

We went over to New York Sunday afternoon and we didn't do no singin' on the way. Some o' the fellers tried to laugh, but it hurt 'em. Connie sent us to bed early, but I don't believe none o' the bunch got much sleep—I know I didn't; I was worryin' too much about the serious and also about the girl, who hadn't sent me no telegram like I'd ast her to. Monday mornin' I wired her askin' what was the matter and tellin' her I was gettin' tired of her foolishness. O' course I didn't make it so strong as that—but the telegram cost me a dollar and forty cents.

Connie had the choice o' two pitchers for the sixth game. He could use Bush, who'd been slammed round pretty hard last time out, or the Chief, who'd only had two days' rest. The rest of 'em—outside o' Plank—had a epidemic o' sore arms. Connie finally picked Bush, so's he could have the Chief in reserve in case we had to play a seventh game. Mc-Graw started Big Jeff and we went at it.

It wasn't like the last time these two guys had hooked up. This time they both had somethin', and for eight innin's runs was as scarce as Chinese policemen. They'd been chances to score on both sides, but the big guy and Bush was both tight in the pinches. The crowd was plumb nuts and yelled like Indians every time a fly ball was caught or a strike called. They'd of got their money's worth if they hadn't been no ninth; but, believe me, that was some round!

They was one out when Barry hit one through the box for a base. Schang walked, and it was Bush's turn. Connie told him to bunt, but he whiffed in the attempt. Then Murphy comes up and walks—and the bases are choked. Young Joyce had been pie for Tesreau all day or else McGraw might of changed pitchers right there. Anyway he left Big Jeff in and he beaned Joyce with a fast one. It sounded like a tire blowin' out. Joyce falls over in a heap and we chase out there, thinkin' he's dead; but he ain't, and pretty soon he gets up and walks down to first base. Tesreau had forced in a run and again we begun to count the winner's end. Matty comes in to prevent further damage and Collins flies the side out.

"Hold 'em now! Work hard!" we says to young Bush, and he walks out there just as cool as though he was goin' to hit fungoes.

McGraw sends up a pinch hitter for Matty and Bush whiffed him. Then Bescher flied out. I was prayin' that Doyle would end it, because Speed's turn come after his'n; so I pretty near fell dead when Larry hit safe.

Speed had his old smile and even more chest than usual when he come up there, swingin' five or six bats. He didn't wait for Doyle to try and steal, or nothin'. He lit into the first ball, though Bush was tryin' to waste it. I seen the ball go high in the air toward left field, and then I picked up my glove and got ready to beat it for the gate. But when I looked out to see if Joyce was set, what do you think I seen? He was lyin' flat on the ground! That blow on the head had got him just as Bush was pitchin' to Speed. He'd flopped over and didn't no more know what was goin' on than if he'd croaked.

Well, everybody else seen it at the same time; but it was too late. Strunk made a run for the ball, but they wasn't no chance for him to get near it. It hit the ground about ten feet back o' where Joyce was lyin' and bounded way over to the end o' the foul line. You don't have to be told that Doyle and Parker both scored and the serious was tied up.

We carried Joyce to the clubhouse and after a while he come to. He cried when he found out what had happened. We cheered him up all we could, but he was a pretty sick guy. The trainer said he'd be all right, though, for the final game.

They tossed up a coin to see where they'd play the seventh battle and our club won the toss; so we went back to Philly that night and cussed Parker clear across New Jersey. I was so sore I kicked the stuffin' out o' my seat.

You probably heard about the excitement in the burg yesterday mornin'. The demand for tickets was somethin' fierce and some of 'em sold for as high as twenty-five bucks apiece. Our club hadn't been lookin' for no seventh game and they was some tall hustlin' done round that old ballpark.

I started out to the grounds early and bought some New York papers to read on the car. They was a big story that Speed Parker, the Giants' hero, was goin' to be married a week after the end o' the serious. It didn't give the name o' the girl, sayin' Speed had refused to tell it. I figured she must be some dame he'd met round the circuit somewheres.

They was another story by one o' them smart baseball reporters sayin' that Parker, on his way up to the plate, had saw that Joyce was about ready to faint and had hit the fly ball to left field on purpose. Can you beat it?

I was goin' to show that to the boys in the clubhouse, but the minute I blowed in there I got some news that made me forget about everything else. Joyce was very sick and they'd took him to a hospital. It was up to me to play!

Connie come over and ast me whether I'd ever hit against Matty. I told him I hadn't, but I'd saw enough of him to know he wasn't no worse'n Johnson. He told me he was goin' to let me hit second—in Joyce's place—because he didn't want to bust up the rest of his combination. He also told me to take my orders from Strunk about where to play for the batters.

"Where shall I play for Parker?" I says, tryin' to joke and pretend I wasn't scared to death.

"I wisht I could tell you," says Connie. "I guess the only thing to do when he comes up is to get down on your knees and pray."

The rest o' the bunch slapped me on the back and give me all the encouragement they could. The place was jammed when we went out on the field. They may of been bigger crowds before, but they never was packed together so tight. I doubt whether they was even room enough left for Falkenberg to sit down.

The afternoon papers had printed the stuff about Joyce bein' out of it, so the bugs was wise that I was goin' to play. They watched me pretty close in battin' practice and give me a hand whenever I managed to hit one hard. When I was out catchin' fungoes the guys in the bleachers cheered me and told me they was with me; but I don't mind tellin' you that I was as nervous as a bride.

They wasn't no need for the announcers to tip the crowd off to the pitchers. Everybody in the United States and Cuba knowed that the Chief'd work for us and Matty for them. The Chief didn't have no trouble with 'em in the first innin'. Even from where I stood I could see that he had a lot o' stuff. Bescher and Doyle popped out and Speed whiffed.

Well, I started out makin' good, with reverse English, in our part. Fletcher booted Murphy's ground ball and I was sent up·to sacrifice. I done a complete job of it—sacrificin' not only myself but Murphy with a pop fly that Matty didn't have to move for. That spoiled whatever chance we had o' gettin' the jump on 'em; but the boys didn't bawl me for it.

"That's all right, old boy. You're all right!" they said on the bench—if they'd had a gun they'd of shot me.

I didn't drop no fly balls in the first six innin's—because none was hit out my way. The Chief was so good that they wasn't hittin' nothin' out o' the infield. And we wasn't doin' nothin' with Matty, either. I led off in the fourth and fouled the first one. I didn't molest the other two. But if Connie and the gang talked about me they done it internally. I come up again—with Murphy on third base and two gone in the sixth, and done my little whiffin' specialty. And still the only people that panned me was the thirty thousand that had paid for the privilege!

My first fieldin' chance come in the seventh. You'd of thought that I'd of had my nerve back by that time; but I was just as scared as though I'd never saw a crowd before. It was just as well that they was two out when Merkle hit one to me. I staggered under it and finally it hit me on the shoulder. Merkle got to second, but the Chief whiffed the next guy. I was gave some cross looks on the bench and I shouldn't of blamed the fellers if they'd cut loose with some language; but they didn't.

They's no use in me tellin' you about none o' the rest of it—except what happened just before the start o' the eleventh and durin' that in- nin', which was sure the big one o' yesterday's pastime—both for Speed and yours sincerely.

The scoreboard was still a row o' ciphers and Speed'd had only a fair amount o' luck. He'd made a scratch base hit and robbed our bunch of a couple o' real ones with impossible stops.

When Schang flied out and wound up our tenth I was leanin' against the end of our bench. I heard my name spoke, and I turned round and seen a boy at the door.

"Right here!" I says; and he give me a telegram.

"Better not open it till after the game," says Connie.

'Oh, no; it ain't no bad news," I said, for I figured it was an answer from the girl. So I opened it up and read it on the way to my position. It said:

"Forgive me, Dick—and forgive Speed too. Letter follows."

Well, sir, I ain't no baby, but for a minute I just wanted to sit down and bawl. And then, all of a sudden, I got so mad I couldn't see. I run right into Baker as he was pickin' up his glove. Then I give him a shove and called him some name, and him and Barry both looked at me like I was crazy—and I was. When I got out in left field I stepped on my own foot and spiked it. I just had to hurt somebody.

As I remember it the Chief fanned the first two of 'em. Then Doyle catches one just right and lams it up against the fence back o' Murphy. The ball caromed round some and Doyle got all the way to third base. Next thing I seen was Speed struttin' up to the plate. I run clear in from my position.

"Kill him!" I says to the Chief. "Hit him in the head and kill him, and I'll go to jail for it!"

"Are you off your nut?" says the Chief. "Go out there and play ball—and quit ravin'."

Barry and Baker led me away and give me a shove out toward left. Then I heard the crack o' the bat and I seen the ball comin' a mile a minute. It was headed between Strunk and I and looked like it would go out o' the park. I don't remember runnin' or nothin' about it till I run into the concrete wall head first. They told me afterward and all the papers said that it was the greatest catch ever seen. And I never knowed I'd caught the ball!

Some o' the managers have said my head was pretty hard, but it wasn't as hard as that concrete. I was pretty near out, but they tell me I walked to the bench like I wasn't hurt at all. They also tell me that the crowd was a bunch o' ravin' maniacs and was throwin' money at me. I guess the ground-keeper'll get it.

The boys on the bench was all talkin' at once and slappin' me on the back, but I didn't know what it was about. Somebody told me pretty soon that it was my turn to hit and I picked up the first bat I come to and starts for the plate. McInnes come runnin' after em and ast me whether I didn't want my own bat. I cussed him and told him to mind his own business.

I didn't know it at the time, but I found out afterward that they was two out. The bases was empty. I'll tell you just what I had in my mind: I wasn't thinkin' about the ball game; I was determined that I was goin' to get to third base and give that guy my spikes. If I didn't hit one worth three bases, or if I didn't hit one at all, I was goin' to run till I got round to where Speed was, and then slide into him and cut him to pieces!

Right now I can't tell you whether I hit a fast ball, or a slow ball, or a hook, or a fader—but I hit somethin'. It went over Bescher's head like a shot and then took a crazy bound. It must of struck a rock or a pop bottle, because it hopped clear over the fence and landed in the bleachers.

Mind you, I learned this afterward. At the time I just knowed I'd hit one somewheres and I starts round the bases. I speeded up when I got near third and took a runnin' jump at a guy I thought was Parker. I missed him and sprawled all over the bag. Then, all of a sudden I come to my senses. All the Ath-a-letics was out there to run home with me and it was one o' them I'd tried to cut. Speed had left the field. The boys picked me up and seen to it that I went on and touched the plate. Then I was carried into the clubhouse by the crazy bugs.

Well, they had a celebration in there and it was a long time before I got a chance to change my clothes. The boys made a big fuss over me. They told me they'd intended to give me five hundred bucks for my divvy, but now I was goin' to get a full share.

"Parker ain't the only lucky guy!" says one of 'em. "But even if that ball hadn't of took that crazy hop you'd of had a triple."

A triple! That's just what I'd wanted; and he called me lucky for not gettin' it!

The Giants was dressin' in the other part o' the clubhouse; and when I finally come out there was Speed, standin' waitin' for some o' the others. He seen me comin' and he smiled. "Hello, Horseshoes!" he says.

He won't smile no more for a while—it'll hurt too much. And if any girl wants him when she sees him now—with his nose over shakin' hands with his ear, and his jaw a couple o' feet foul—she's welcome to him. They won't be no contest!

Grimes leaned over to ring for the waiter.

"Well," he said, "what about it?"

"You won't have to pay my fare," I told him.

"I'll buy a drink anyway," said he. "You've been a good listener—and I had to get it off my chest."

"Maybe they'll have to postpone the wedding," I said.

"No," said Grimes. "The weddin' will take place the day after tomorrow—and I'll bat for Mr. Parker. Did you think I was goin' to let him get away with it?"

"What about next year?" I asked.

"I'm goin' back to the Ath-a-letics," he said. "And I'm goin' to hire somebody to call me 'Horseshoes!' before every game—because I can sure play that old baseball when I'm mad."

*Edward L. McKenna's story "Fielder's Choice" originally appeared in* Esquire *magazine. A period piece (35 cents for a magazine, a baseball game for a buck), it features a player's heroism in a dangerous situation. The baseball fiction writers of the 1940s and 1950s, of whom McKenna is typical, reveled in characters who had courage, grace, and personal modesty along with their talent. This is also a reflection of the actual ballplayers of that era, more of whom seem to have been authentic heroes. "Where have you gone, Joe DiMaggio?"*

## *Edward L. McKenna*

# FIELDER'S CHOICE (1946)

IT WAS SELDOM ENOUGH THAT Charles J. Horton went to see a ball game. He worked for the Third National, and from the beginning he had taught himself to remember that although a bank closes at three o'clock it doesn't pay to rush right off as soon as your books for the day are finished. No; you stay right on, making yourself useful and noticeable to your superiors. You're painfully careful about everything, and you never make an error. You take the extension courses at the University, even though you already have a Phi Beta Kappa key from the little school upstate. You attend the lectures given by the Institute of Banking. You carry the *Wall Street Journal,* or the *Commercial and Financial Chronicle,* and you read magazines that cost at least thirty-five cents. You pay some attention to your appearance, shaving each morning after your cold shower and your setting-up exercises, and your habit is costly as your purse can buy. You economize on beggars and waiters, and live at your college club, where the food is so bad it reminds you of the old fraternity house. Still, you get the stationery for nothing, and it gives you a certain cachet, or so you imagine. Your favorite book is your own bankbook, and you put by a little every month. You don't get married, and you're otherwise thrifty, neither drinking nor smoking nor going on parties, because if you really feel the need of recreation, can't you go to the movies or a theatre or a good restaurant all by yourself? You're really much better than most other people, and you've determined to get on, and so, perhaps, you will.

The program was working well enough for Charlie Horton. At twenty-eight, he was out of a teller's cage, and back of a desk and on the slow road to fortune. He had subordinates to whom he could be distant and severe, and two thousand dollars in his savings account, and a few good bonds, though he carried no life insurance whatsoever.

So, on this bright Saturday afternoon he was sitting behind first base, among people he rather disliked, and watching the acrobatics of eighteen athletes for whom, as individuals, he felt a faint contempt. One of them he knew, though he hadn't spoken to him for years. They'd gone to school together. Joe Marchand had been a popular hero, and Charlie Horton had been almost nobody.

Joe Marchand was more or less a popular hero still, though most experts agreed that he was slipping a little. He played right field for the Eagles, and had batted .342 last season. His arm was still all right, but he wasn't so fast in the field or on the bases. That was to be expected. He was almost thirty.

Joe had never finished high-school. When he was seventeen, he was picking up a few dollars playing semi-professional ball, and then he played two seasons for Scranton and one in the Southern League. Somebody saw him down there, and picked up his contract, and ever since then he'd been in the big money. There'd been seasons when he'd made eight and ten thousand. It was generally understood that he wasn't getting anything like that any more, but Joe never said so. Whatever it was, he never saved a cent more than enough to take him and his wife and his three kids through the winter.

Outside of his family, the things Joe liked best were baseball, close harmony, and twenty-five-cent-limit draw. He had always been crazy about playing ball, crazy about every sort of sport, every sort of game. Boxing, horse-racing, ice-hockey, hunting, fishing, cards, dice, billiards, and even golf fascinated him always. He wasn't a drinking man, and he didn't chase around, but he did like to gamble, and to watch games, and to play them.

He weighed a hundred and ninety pounds, and his face and neck and hands looked as if they'd been dipped in some brown stain. After a game they'd won, or on the Pullman, or back at the hotel, he and Art Herman and Petey Grant would start harmonizing. Joe had a barytone voice, not nearly so good as he imagined, but he knew a thousand songs all full of barber-shop and pleasing sentiment, and he never forgot a new wow, a new combination of confluent chords. Songs in which there were two separate and distinct first-tenor parts were his delight.

The only people he disliked in all the world were fresh fans and fresh bushers, and even the bushers soon got used to Joe, and the fans didn't ride him, as a rule. Anyhow, he played in right field. Nobody took him too seriously, except left-handers; he could murder them. His one great weakness was this: he was a bad waiter. When the count was two and two, unless he had a signal, he'd be apt to take a crack at the next one, whatever it was, for to be called out on strikes without swinging just ruined his afternoon. Also, it did not give him much pleasure to knock one into the infield, even though he scratched a hit out of it. Joe liked to sock them. From his first days in the league it was his great delight to watch the fielders playing deep for him, dropping back toward the fence and the bleachers when he walked out toward the plate. He wasn't a scientific hitter, but he certainly could lean on them.

He'd helped to win two pennants; this year, the Eagles weren't even in the first division. That didn't worry him or any of them. They were playing away, in a big town they liked, against the leaders of the league, and the Eagles didn't think so much of them, outside of their pitchers. It was a doubleheader, and the games made a difference in the league's standing, though not to them. Everybody felt pretty good. Contenders who amount to anything always like a crack at the champion, whether they beat him or not. Forty thousand people were out there to watch them, to jeer them in a pleasant enough sort of way, with the good-natured contempt of victors, even vicarious ones. It was August, the sun was nice, and not too bright, and the dry, scorched grass was good to feel beneath their feet. Some of them were kids, with years before them, some of them were on their way out, like Joe. Anyhow, they had this fine long summer afternoon.

The thing happened, in the beginning of the fourth.

Joe was coaching a runner on first, so he was nearest to it. He heard all the noise, the screaming, and turned around, and peered up at the stands behind him.

Just back of first base, the crowds were giving way to right and left, pushing and leaping. A sea of people was surging in each direction, and seats were breaking beneath them as they went, but there was almost nowhere for them to go. Out into the aisles they came, and fell upon those seated in the next section, and that in turn went rolling onward till the next aisle was reached. There was the crashing and creaking of rotted timber, the snap of arms of broken chairs, the thin sharp yelp of men in fear.

The first-base stand was collapsing.

"Hi!" shouted Joe. "Hi! Come on, you guys." With that, he went into the falling stand.

He didn't know quite what he was going to do. All he knew was that he was going where the trouble was, to do his best. There weren't many followed him. A few policemen charged into that stand, too. Cops haven't much sense either.

There was a pretty bad fifteen minutes or so in there. Maybe it was only ten, maybe it was only five. It didn't turn out to be so serious. Only a little part of the stands had actually fallen. Twenty-two people were killed, and about a hundred injured, not counting scratches, and black eyes, and torn clothing, and nervous systems somewhat impaired, or strengthened. Some five thousand men had looked suddenly upon the face of death. It leered at them, and as quickly turned away, and it only cost them a dollar apiece, and a bruise or two.

Joe came out of it all right, except that his right arm felt sort of funny. He hunched his shoulder up and around; it still felt funny. "Wonder how I got that?" he said to himself. He wouldn't have known. He'd made three or four trips into the middle of it, yelling and cursing, and pushing and pulling, and trying to do whatever he could. He remembered getting one man out from underfoot; the *Record* said he got three.

The shoulder was dislocated, he found that out at the clubhouse. "Tough luck, Joe" they said. "Ah, a coupla weeks," he said, to them, but to himself he said, "That's curtains. That's curtains."

It wasn't curtains. He played ball again, plenty of it. What was more, the owner of the club came to the hotel, the next day, with a copy of the *Record* in his hand.

"This true?" he said.

"No. It's my press-agent," said Joe.

"My daughter was in that stand," said the owner.

Joe looked at him.

"You go in there, you have no call to go in. You cripple yourself, for the sake of other people. All right. You got a job with this club, as long as I'm in baseball. Bum wing, or no bum wing. You hear me?"

"Yeah," said Joe. "Your—your daughter OK?"

"Yes. She's OK," said the owner. His name was, and is, Ben Siegal, and he is known to all the world as a soft-hearted, hot-headed sentimental slob who'd rather lose money in baseball than make it brewing beer.

There's a line in that *Record* story that Joe has never noticed. Under "Dead" there is this: Horton, Charles J. 28. Bank clerk, employed by Third National Bank.

*"Brooklyns Lose" was written by William Heuman for* Sports Illustrated *in 1954, the first year of that magazine's existence and a few short years before the Dodgers headed west. The sting of a loss to the Reds is revealed in the soul of a diehard Bums fan who, with his son, is plodding home after a long day at the ballpark. And who should be at the house to greet them but Uncle Nathan, a gloating Giants fan? This scenario is richly served up by Heuman in dialectal "Brooklynese," a literary treat.*

*William Heuman*

# BROOKLYNS LOSE
# (1954)

**I**T'S ONE OF THOSE LONG, drawn-out games at Ebbets Field, and it's not over till nearly six o'clock. We come out hot and tired, and with a little headache—you know how it is after a game—and the kid says he wants a hot dog.

"I like the long ones, Pop," he says.

You know the kind they sell outside the park at those little hot-dog stands, long and skinny and rubbery.

"Never mind," I tell him.

We're hurrying for the trolley car, and the big crowd is pouring out of the exit gates. It's almost six o'clock and Madge has the supper on the table, and I can see her fuming, and the kid's talking about hot dogs.

"Forget it," I tell him.

Who thinks about food when the Dodgers lose? You sit there for nearly three and a half hours and you try to root them home. You're with them every minute, every play, and you have it in the bag, and then it's gone over the wall.

"That was some home run," the kid says.

"Shut up," I tell him. "Keep quiet."

"Well, it was good, Pop. Way out toward center field."

A home run in the last inning which wins the ball game and sends the Brooklyns down to defeat is never a *good* home run. What the kid means is that it was well hit. I admit that. I'm a Brooklyn fan, but I admit that. The ball travels maybe four hundred feet before it clears the fence in right center, so it's a good hit. All right, but don't rub it in. Three and a half hours I sit there in the bleachers on a hot day and we lose anyway. So what's good about it?

A guy on the trolley says to me, "They shoulda passed him, that Kluszewski."

"Alston didn't wanna put the winning run on base," I tell him. "That's baseball. You play the averages."

"He didn't put Kluszewski on, neither," this guy says, grinning. "Klu hit it an' kept goin'."

This guy jokes, yet. This is a time for jokes when you have a ball game sewed up eight-to-seven in the ninth, and you lose it with a home-run ball.

I look out the window, and the guy says, "So tomorrow's another day."

I don't even look at him. That kind of guy I don't look at.

You don't mind losing a ball game now and then, but when you lose to Cincinnati it hurts, especially when you got it sewed up, and especially in September and you're way out of first place and that old lost column can murder you.

The kid's getting wise here. He's eleven now, and I've had him down to a lot of ball games, and he argues baseball with the other kids on the block.

He says now, "They shoulda took Oiskin out."

"Never mind," I tell him. "Forget about it."

Why can't they let it drop? It's over and we lose it, so it goes down in the records, and you never change the records, not even if the Russians come over and take this country. It's down in the books.

So maybe Alston should have taken Erskine out, and maybe put in Johnny Podres, and Podres walks three-four guys and it's over anyway, and Alston's a dope again. He should have left Erskine in.

I don't like to second-guess the manager. The guy is out there with his job to do, and he knows more about it than anybody else. Just like me in the shop. In the shop I know my job and I do it. I don't like a guy coming around and telling me it might work out better some other way.

I'm just saying, though, that if it was me in Alston's shoes I'd have had Shuba pinch-hit for Erskine the end of the eighth, and maybe bring us in another run or two, so when this big clown belts one over the wall in the ninth we still got the lead. With Erskine out for a pinch hitter I'd have stuck Roe in there for one inning with that slow stuff. It might have been a different ball game.

Like I say, though, you can't second-guess, and it's silly to work yourself up into a stew because we dropped one. Just forget about it; let it drop.

I hear a guy in the seat behind me say, "They shoulda pulled a squeeze in the seventh with Reese on third. When Dressen was runnin' this club we worked a lot of squeeze plays. We'd of had that extra run, and when Kluszewski hits that homer it's only tied up, an'—"

You see how they try to dope it out? It's dead; it's in the record books. So who's up when Reese is on third and one away? Gil Hodges is up, and Gil is a long-ball hitter. Since when do you ask your long-ball hitter to bunt? That guy behind me is crazy. Any kind of fly ball would have brought Reese in. So Hodges struck out; so Alston knew he was gonna strike out?

If it was me I'd have had Reese try to steal home when it was two out.

This Cincinnati guy was taking a long windup. I'm not telling Alston how to run his ball club, but you can see how it goes around and around inside your head. I've heard of guys going off their trolley arguing points like this.

Madge says when we come into the house at about six-thirty:

"What were you doing—standing outside the field asking for their autographs?"

She has that look on her face. The pots are still on the stove, all covered up, and they've been there for some time, I can see.

"It was a long game," I tell her.

"It's always a long game down there," she says, and the way she says "there" you'd think she was talking of some gin mill somewhere.

She should be married to a heavy drinker or a guy who plays the horses like some of them in the shop. I don't have any bad habits; I have a glass of beer now and then; I go to Ebbets Field. That's wrong?

"Sit down and eat your supper," Madge says.

"Pop wouldn't buy me a hot dog," the kid tells her.

"I'm not surprised," Madge says. "He probably didn't even know you were with him."

"I bought him two in the park," I snap. "He wants another one on the way home. What am I—Rockefeller?"

"He'd have had a better time at Brighton Beach," Madge says as she's banging the pots around on the stove.

"My vacation," I tell her. "Monday we go to the beach. Wednesday we go to the beach. What am I—a seal?"

"Sit down," she says.

I notice that there are four plates set out and I know who the other plate is for. He comes in from the parlor, snapping at his suspenders—the last guy I want to see tonight.

Uncle Nathan is my brother-in-law, a bachelor, and he lives in a rooming house around the corner from us. Every once in a while—and even once is too often—Madge invites him around for supper. I'm practically supporting this guy, and I think that, secretly, he likes the Giants.

"Lost again," Uncle Nathan grins as he sits down opposite me. "Heard it on the radio."

"Again," I tell him acidly. "Don't I know it's again?"

"The Reds," Uncle Nathan says. "The Cincinnati Reds from Cincinnati."

He's a guy who never goes to a ball game, but he can make remarks like that. He don't know first base from second.

"Kluszewski hit a home run and won the game in the ninth inning," the kid says, and I have to hear that over again.

"They should have a man like Kluszewski on first base for Brooklyn," Uncle Nathan says.

"What's wrong with Hodges?" I ask him. "What's wrong with a guy who hits over three hundred and drives in all them runs?"

"Eat your supper," Madge says.

Who feels like eating, especially with Uncle Nathan sitting across from you, smirking? Uncle Nathan is a small, pot-bellied guy with a circle of fuzzy hair around his bald head. All his life he's lived in Brooklyn, twenty minutes from the field, and never saw a game. That's a citizen!

"Who was it beat them this afternoon?" Uncle Nathan says. "I never heard of the guy."

"How many guys you ever heard of in baseball?" I ask him.

"Eat your supper, Joe," Madge says. "You'd all be a lot better off if you spent your time on something more educational."

I could make some remarks about that, too, but I don't. I got arguments up to the neck, already. Education. What's education but knowing something, and what's better to know than Brooklyn wins?

"Hear the Giants won this afternoon," Uncle Nathan says, without looking up from his plate. "Three-to-one over the Cardinals. They got it made."

"They'll fade in the stretch," I say. "They'll drop a few, and we'll catch them in the last week. We got a three-game series here, remember."

Imagine a guy talking about the Giants down here in Flatbush. A guy like that is crazy. He should be arrested.

I don't eat much tonight because I'm not hungry, and I guess I don't say much, either, because Madge says, as she's bringing out the dessert:

"All afternoon you yell your head off at the game. When you come home, you shut up like a clam."

"What's to say?" I ask her. "I gotta talk every minute?"

"He'd be talkin' plenty," Uncle Nathan says, "if the Dodgers had won."

I don't even bother to answer.

The kid, sitting next to me at the table, says, "That Kluszewski sure can hit."

We have pork chops for supper, but they don't taste good; the peas don't taste good either. Imagine a guy with a name you can't even pronounce licking the Dodgers? Down at the field I hear this Kluszewski's name pronounced about nine different ways. Any way you say it, though, it goes down in the books as a Brooklyn loss.

My wife says, "I spend the afternoon making a supper and he eats it like he was a bird."

"So I have to stuff myself every meal?" I say. "That's smart?"

I'm glad when I can get outside. I go down to the basement and get out the plastic hose. We live in a nice section in Flatbush here—two-family houses, with a little plat of ground out front. It's not much as far as ground goes, maybe six feet from the house to the sidewalk. Most everybody has a little shrubbery.

I get out the hose and I water the shrubbery because we haven't had any rain in a week. Next to me lives Saul Ruskin, who is my neighbor. Saul is sitting in one of those aluminum-and-plastic chairs that folds up, and you wonder how it holds his weight.

The plat out in front of Saul's house he's filled in with cement, so he has sidewalk from the house all the way to the curb, and no shrubbery, no grass or weeds to worry about.

"I should be a farmer?" Saul says. "I wanna raise crops, I move out to the suburbs."

Saul watches me as I hook up the hose. He has a stub of cigar in his mouth, and he says around the cigar, "A tough one to lose, Joe. Them Reds allus get hot against us."

"They have to win once in awhile," I tell him.

Saul is a dyed-in-the-wool Brooklyn rooter. I see he don't feel too good about this one, either, and it makes me feel a little better.

"These clubs come in here loaded," Saul says. "They save their best pitchers for Brooklyn. They do all their hittin' at Ebbets Field. It ain't right."

"That's baseball," I tell him as I start to squirt the shrubbery.

"Couple of Sundays back I see Pittsburgh," Saul says. "They score eighteen runs in two games. They don't score eighteen runs in a whole season. That's the way it goes."

"I know," I tell him sympathetically.

"That home run Klusoositz hits," Saul says. "It was a fluke, Joe?"

"He tagged it, Saul," I tell him. "He hits that long ball."

"Allus against us," Saul scowls. He pauses and then adds, "Alston maybe shoulda passed him, a guy hits like that."

"Man on second an' one out," I tell him. "Kluszewski ain't made a hit all day."

"Then he was due," Saul says. "You can't shut out a guy like that four-five times in one game. He was due."

"They took a chance. Erskine got him before."

The guy lives upstairs from me is just coming back from Sam Klein's candy store, where he has bought some cigarets, and he stops to talk. He says: "A good game, Joe?"

"Brooklyns lose, Lennie," Saul says. "That's a good game?"

"You know what I mean," Lennie says. "That lucky Klookitz."

"Kluszewski," I tell him.

"How the hell you say it," Lennie says, "It's still a home run. That right, Joe?"

We stand there for a while, chewing the rag while I squirt the shrubbery. Saul puffs on the cigar and sits there with his arms folded across his chest. Lennie Brannick sits on the stoop and lights up a cigaret.

"You give Dressen a club hitting like this," Lennie says, "an' he'd never lose a ball game. You know what I mean? Allus liked Dressen—a noisy guy, but a great manager."

"Alston's all right," I tell him.

"That club we got this year," Saul puts in, "a two-headed zebra could manage. They oughtta win for anybody; they oughtta even win for your brother-in-law Nathan, Joe."

"Leave us not get on that subject," I tell him.

My wife calls through the screen door, "If you're going down to Klein's, stop at the delicatessen and pick up a few bottles of beer, Joe. The empties are on the back step."

I turn off the water because them shrubs have enough now. I say to Saul Ruskin under my breath, "I have to feed him beer now. It's not enough he eats my food. Luxuries he gets."

"That's relatives for you," Saul nods. "I got a cousin like that."

I get the empty bottles from the back doorstep and I head down the street toward Klein's. This is my neighborhood; this is where I was born, not on this block, but a few blocks away. This is a nice block, nice people, all good Brooklyn rooters. You feel bad, and everybody feels bad with you. That's neighbors.

Outside Klein's is the usual bunch of kids, seventeen and eighteen years old, and it's all baseball with them, too. It's arguments about baseball, and what these kids don't know about the game you can stick in your hat and forget about.

One kid who knows me says, "Hello, Mr. Armbruster."

"How's it," I say.

"You up the game?" he asks. "You see that Klusookitz?"

"He kills that ball," I tell him.

"I see Roe strike that bum out three times," another boy says. "You give him that fast ball an' he moiders."

Inside, I talk to Sam Klein about the game.

"A hard one to lose," Sam says, "but you can't win 'em all, Joe."

"I know," I say.

"If he'd passed this Klusowsky," Sam says, "somebody else would have homered. That's fate, Joe."

"Maybe we can still afford to lose one," I tell him.

"Sure," Sam says. "Look how it used to be years ago. You win two out of five an' you think you done somethin'."

"It's still a great club," I tell him. "The best ever."

I come out of Klein's and stop by the delicatessen for some beer. I'm feeling pretty good now, the best since Kluszewski hit that home run and robbed us of a game. You know how it is when you have good neighbors? Everybody's on your side; everybody's rooting for you and with you. You can even stand a guy like Uncle Nathan. Where do you find neighbors like this?

I come down the walk toward my house, and Saul Ruskin hasn't moved from his chair on the sidewalk. I go past Saul, and he lifts two fingers in the V-for-victory sign.

"Tomorrow," says Saul.

How can you beat neighbors like that? How can you beat Brooklyn?

Uncle Nathan is standing by the screen door when I come in, and he says, "You gonna slit your throat tonight, Joe, because the Dodgers lost?"

"Jump in the lake," I tell him. "Take a long run an' jump in the lake."

Tomorrow we'll get 'em.

*It is said that baseball has its origins in the British game of rounders. How fitting, therefore, that one of baseball's best stories is from the pen of one of Britain's most celebrated writers, Pelham Grenville Wodehouse (1881–1975). A master of English style, imagery, and wit, P.G. Wodehouse is one of the most prolific writers of all time. Besides 92 books, he wrote stories, plays, and lyrics for Broadway musicals. Called the "funniest writer in the world," Wodehouse was educated at Dulwich College, honored by the D.Litt. from Oxford, and knighted by the Queen. In 1956 he became American as well as British when he obtained dual citizenship. Among his books are* My Man Jeeves *(1919),* Ukridge *(1924),* The Butler Did It *(1957), and* The Golf Omnibus *(1973). Written in 1910, "The Pitcher and the Plutocrat" is the oldest story in this collection.*

## *P. G. Wodehouse*

# THE PITCHER AND THE PLUTOCRAT (1910)

**T**HE MAIN DIFFICULTY IN WRITING a story is to convey to the reader clearly yet tersely the natures and dispositions of one's leading characters. Brevity, brevity—that is the cry. Perhaps, after all, the play-bill style is the best. In this drama of love, baseball, frenzied finance, and tainted millions, then, the principals are as follows, in their order of entry:

Isabel Rackstraw (a peach)
Clarence Van Puyster (a Greek god)
Old Man Van Puyster (a proud old aristocrat)
Old Man Rackstraw (a tainted millionaire)

More about Clarence later. For the moment let him go as a Greek god. There were other sides, too, to Old Man Rackstraw's character; but for the moment let him go as a Tainted Millionaire. Not that it is satisfactory. It is too mild. He was *the* Tainted Millionaire. The Tainted Millions of other Tainted Millionaires were as attar of roses compared with the Tainted Millions of Tainted Millionaire Rackstraw. He preferred his millions tainted. His attitude toward an untainted million was that of the sportsman toward the sitting bird. These things are purely a matter of taste. Some people like Limburger cheese.

It was at a charity bazaar that Isabel and Clarence first met. Isabel was presiding over the Billiken, Teddy Bear, and Fancy Goods stall. There she stood, that slim, radiant girl, buncoing the Younger Set out of its father's hard-earned with a smile that alone was nearly worth the money, when she observed, approaching, the handsomest man she had ever seen. It was—this is not one of those mystery stories—it was Clarence Van Puyster. Over the heads of the bevy of gilded youths who clustered round the stall their eyes met. A thrill ran through Isabel. She dropped her eyes. The next moment Clarence had bucked center; the Younger Set had shredded away like a mist; and he was leaning toward her, opening negotiations for the purchase of a yellow Teddy Bear at sixteen times its face value.

He returned at intervals during the afternoon. Over the second Teddy Bear they became friendly; over the third, intimate. He proposed as she was wrapping up the fourth Golliwog, and she gave him her heart and the parcel simultaneously. At six o'clock, carrying four Teddy Bears, seven photograph frames, five Golliwogs, and a Billiken, Clarence went home to tell the news to his father.

Clarence, when not at college, lived with his only surviving parent in an old red-brick house at the north end of Washington Square. The original Van Puyster had come over in Governor Stuyvesant's time in one of the then fashionable ninety-four-day boats. Those were the stirring days when they were giving away chunks of Manhattan Island in exchange for trading-stamps; for the bright brain which conceived the idea that the city might possibly at some remote date extend above Liberty

Street had not come into existence. The orginal Van Puyster had acquired a square mile or so in the heart of things for ten dollars cash and a quarter interest in a pedler's outfit. "The Columbus Echo and Vespucci Intelligencer" gave him a column and a half under the heading: "Reckless Speculator. Prominent Citizen's Gamble in Land." On the proceeds of that deal his descendants had led quiet, peaceful lives ever since. If any of them ever did a day's work, the family records are silent on the point. Blood was their long suit, not Energy. They were plain, homely folk, with a refined distaste for wealth and vulgar hustle. They lived simply, without envy of their richer fellow citizens, on their three hundred thousand dollars a year. They asked no more. It enabled them to entertain on a modest scale; the boys could go to college, the girls buy an occasional new frock. They were satisfied.

Having dressed for dinner, Clarence proceeded to the library, where he found his father slowly pacing the room. Silver-haired old Vansuyther Van Puyster seemed wrapped in thought. And this was unusual, for he was not given to thinking. To be absolutely frank, the old man had just about enough brain to make a jay-bird fly crooked, and no more.

"Ah, my boy," he said, looking up as Clarence entered. "Let us go in to dinner. I have been awaiting you for some little time now. I was about to inquire as to your whereabouts. Let us be going."

Mr. Van Puyster always spoke like that. This was due to Blood.

Until the servants had left them to their coffee and cigarettes, the conversation was desultory and commonplace. But when the door had closed, Mr. Van Puyster leaned forward.

"My boy," he said quietly, "we are ruined."

Clarence looked at him inquiringly.

"Ruined much?" he asked.

"Paupers," said his father. "I doubt if when all is over, I shall have much more than a bare fifty or sixty thousand dollars a year."

A lesser man would have betrayed agitation, but Clarence was a Van Puyster. He lit a cigarette.

"Ah," he said calmly. "How's that?"

Mr. Van Puyster toyed with his coffee-spoon.

"I was induced to speculate—rashly, I fear—on the advice of a man I chanced to meet at a public dinner, in the shares of a certain mine. I did not thoroughly understand the matter, but my acquaintance appeared to be well versed in such operations, so I allowed him to—and, well, in fact, to cut a long story short, I am ruined."

"Who was the fellow?"

"A man of the name of Rackstraw. Daniel Rackstraw."

"Daniel Rackstraw!"

Not even Clarence's training and traditions could prevent a slight start as he heard the name.

"Daniel Rackstraw," repeated his father. "A man, I fear, not entirely honest. In fact, it seems that he has made a very large fortune by similar transactions. Friends of mine, acquainted with these matters, tell me his behavior toward me amounted practically to theft. However, for myself I care little. We can rough it, we of the old Van Puyster stock. If there is but fifty thousand a year left, well—I must make it serve. It is for your sake that I am troubled, my poor boy. I shall be compelled to stop your allowance. I fear you will be obliged to adopt some profession." He hesitated for a moment. "In fact. work," he added.

Clarence drew at his cigarette.

"Work?" he echoed thoughtfully. "Well, of course, mind you, fellows *do* work. I met a man at the club only yesterday who knew a fellow who had met a man whose cousin worked."

He reflected for a while.

"I shall pitch," he said suddenly.

"Pitch, my boy?"

"Sign on as a professional ballplayer."

His father's fine old eyebrows rose a little.

"But, my boy, er—the—ah—family name. Our—shall I say *noblesse oblige?* Can a Van Puyster pitch and not be defiled?"

"I shall take a new name," said Clarence. "I will call myself Brown." He lit another cigarette. "I can get signed on in a minute. McGraw will jump at me."

This was no idle boast. Clarence had had a good college education, and was now an exceedingly fine pitcher. It was a pleasing sight to see him, poised on one foot in the attitude of a Salome dancer, with one eye on the batter, the other gazing coldly at the man who was trying to steal third, uncurl abruptly like the main spring of a watch and sneak over a swift one. Under Clarence's guidance a ball could do practically everything except talk. It could fly like a shot from a gun, hesitate, take the first turning to the left, go up two blocks, take the second to the right, bound in mid-air like a jack-rabbit, and end by dropping as the gentle dew from heaven upon the plate beneath. Briefly, there was class to Clarence. He was the goods.

Scarcely had he uttered these momentous words when the butler entered with the announcement that he was wanted by a lady at the telephone.

It was Isabel.

Isabel was disturbed.

"Oh, Clarence," she cried, "my precious angel wonder-child, I don't know how to begin."

"Begin just like that," said Clarence approvingly. "It's fine. You can't beat it."

"Clarence, a terrible thing has happened. I told papa of our engagement, and he wouldn't hear of it. He was furious. He c-called you a b-b-b—"

"A p-p-p—"

"That's a new one on me," said Clarence, wondering.

"A b-beggarly p-pauper. I knew you weren't well off, but I thought you had two or three millions. I told him so. But he said no, your father had lost all his money."

"It is too true, dearest," said Clarence. "I am a pauper. But I'm going to work. Something tells me I shall be rather good at work. I am going to work with all the accumulated energy of generations of ancestors who have never done a hand's turn. And some day when I—"

"Good-by," said Isabel hastily, "I hear papa coming."

The season during which Clarence Van Puyster pitched for the Giants is destined to live long in the memory of followers of baseball. Probably never in the history of the game has there been such persistent and widespread mortality among the more distant relatives of office-boys and junior clerks. Statisticians have estimated that if all the grandmothers alone who perished between the months of April and October that year could have been placed end to end they would have reached considerably further than Minneapolis. And it was Clarence who was responsible for this holocaust. Previous to the opening of the season skeptics had shaken their heads over the Giants' chances for the pennant. It had been assumed that as little new blood would be forthcoming as in other years, and that the fate of Our City would rest, as usual, on the shoulders of the white-haired veterans who were boys with Lafayette.

And then, like a meteor, Clarence Van Puyster had flashed upon the world of fans, bugs, chewing-gum, and nuts (pea and human). In the opening game he had done horrid things to nine men from Boston; and from then onward, except for an occasional check, the Giants had never looked back.

Among the spectators who thronged the bleachers to watch Clarence perform there appeared week after week a little, gray, dried-up man, insignificant except for a certain happy choice of language in moments of emotion and an enthusiasm far surpassing that of the ordinary spectator. To the trained eye there is a subtle but well-marked difference between the fan, the bug, and—the last phase—the nut of the baseball world. This man was an undoubted nut. It was writ clear across his brow.

Fate had made Daniel Rackstraw—for it was he—a tainted millionaire, but at heart he was a baseball spectator. He never missed a game. His library of baseball literature was the finest in the country. His baseball museum had but one equal, that of Mr. Jacob Dodson of Detroit. Between them the two had cornered, at enormous expense, the curio market of the game. It was Rackstraw who had secured the glove worn by Neal Ball, the Cleveland shortstop, when he made the only unassisted triple play in the history of the game; but it was Dodson who possessed the bat which Hans Wagner used as a boy. The two men were friends, as far as rival connoisseurs can be friends; and Mr. Dodson, when at leisure, would frequently pay a visit to Mr. Rackstraw's country home, where he would spend hours gazing wistfully at the Neal Ball glove buoyed up only by the thought of the Wagner bat at home.

Isabel saw little of Clarence during the summer months, except from a distance. She contented herself with clipping photographs of him from the evening papers. Each was a little more unlike him than the last, and this lent variety to the collection. Her father marked her new-born enthusiasm for the national game with approval. It had been secretly a great grief to the old buccaneer that his only child did not know the difference between a bunt and a swat, and, more, did not seem to care to know. He felt himself drawn closer to her. An understanding, as pleasant as it was new and strange, began to spring up between parent and child.

As for Clarence, how easy it would be to cut loose to practically an unlimited extent on the subject of his emotions at this time. One can figure him, after the game is over and the gay throng has dispersed, creeping moodily–but what's the use? Brevity. That is the cry. Brevity. Let us on.

The months sped by. August came and went, and September; and soon it was plain to even the casual follower of the game that, unless something untoward should happen, the Giants must secure the National League pennant. Those were delirious days for Daniel Rackstraw. Long before the beginning of October his voice had dwindled to a husky whisper. Deep lines appeared on his forehead; for it is an awful thing for a baseball nut to be compelled to root, in the very crisis of the season, purely by means of facial expression. In this time of affliction he found Isabel an ever-increasing comfort to him. Side by side they would sit at the Polo Grounds, and the old man's face would lose its drawn look, and light up, as her clear young soprano pealed out above the din, urging this player to slide for second, that to knock the stitching off the ball; or describing the umpire in no uncertain voice as a reincarnation of the late Mr. Jesse James.

Meanwhile, in the American League, Detroit had been heading the list with equal pertinacity; and in far-off Michigan Mr. Jacob Dodson's enthusiasm had been every whit as great as Mr. Rackstraw's in New York. It was universally admitted that when the championship series came to be played, there would certainly be something doing.

But, alas! How truly does Epictetus observe: "We know not what awaiteth us around the corner, and the hand that counteth its chickens ere they be hatched ofttimes graspeth but a lemon." The prophets who anticipated a struggle closer than any on record were destined to be proved false.

It was not that their judgment of form was at fault. By every law of averages the Giants and the Tigers should have been the two most evenly matched nines in the history of the game. In fielding there was nothing to choose between them. At hitting the Tigers held a slight superiority; but this was balanced by the inspired pitching of Clarence Van Puyster. Even the keenest supporters of either side were not confident. They argued at length, figuring out the odds with the aid of stubs of pencils and the backs of envelopes, but they were not confident. Out of all those frenzied millions two men alone had no doubts. Mr. Daniel Rackstraw said that he did not desire to be unfair to Detroit. He wished it to be clearly understood that in their own class the Tigers might quite possibly show to considerable advantage. In some rural league down South, for instance, he did not deny that they might sweep all before them. But when it came to competing with the Giants—Here words failed Mr. Rackstraw, and he had to rush to Wall Street and collect several tainted millions before he could recover his composure.

Mr. Jacob Dodson, interviewed by the Detroit "Weekly Rooter," stated that his decision, arrived at after a close and careful study of the work of both teams, was that the Giants had rather less chance in the forthcoming tourney than a lone gumdrop at an Eskimo tea party. It was his carefully considered opinion that in a contest with the Avenue B Juniors the Giants might, with an effort, scrape home. But when it was a question of meeting a live team like Detroit—Here Mr. Dodson, shrugging his shoulders despairingly, sank back in his chair, and watchful secretaries brought him round with oxygen.

Throughout the whole country nothing but the approaching series was discussed. Wherever civilization reigned, and in Jersey City, one question alone was on every lip: Who would win? Octogenarians mumbled it. Infants lisped it. Tired business men, trampled under foot in the rush for the West Farms express, asked it of the ambulance attendants who carried them to hospital.

And then, one bright, clear morning, when all Nature seemed to smile, Clarence Van Puyster developed mumps.

New York was in a ferment. I could have wished to go into details to describe in crisp, burning sentences the panic that swept like a tornado through a million homes. A little encouragement, the slightest softening of the editorial austerity, and the thing would have been done. But no. Brevity. That was the cry. Brevity. Let us on.

The Tigers met the Giants at the Polo Grounds, and for five days the sweat of agony trickled unceasingly down the corrugated foreheads of the patriots who sat on the bleachers. The men from Detroit, freed from the fear of Clarence, smiled grim smiles and proceeded to knock holes through the fence. It was in vain that the home fielders skimmed like swallows around the diamond. They could not keep the score down. From start to finish the Giants were a beaten side.

Broadway during that black week was a desert. Gloom gripped Lobster Square. In distant Harlem red-eyed wives faced silently scowling husbands at the evening meal, and the children were sent early to bed. Newsboys called the extras in a whisper.

Few took the tragedy more nearly to heart than Daniel Rackstraw. Each afternoon found him more deeply plunged in sorrow. On the last day, leaving the ground with the air of a father mourning over some prodigal son, he encountered Mr. Jacob Dodson of Detroit.

Now, Mr. Dodson was perhaps the slightest bit shy on the finer feelings. He should have respected the grief of a fallen foe. He should have abstained from exulting. But he was in too exhilarated a condition to be magnanimous. Sighting Mr. Rackstraw, he addressed himself joyously to the task of rubbing the thing in. Mr. Rackstraw listened in silent anguish.

"If we had had Brown—" he said at length.

"That's what they all say," whooped Mr. Dodson. "Brown! Who's Brown?"

"If we had had Brown, we should have—" He paused. An idea had flashed upon his overwrought mind. "Dodson," he said, "listen here. Wait till Brown is well again, and let us play this thing off again for anything you like a side in my private park."

Mr. Dodson reflected.

"You're on," he said. "What side bet? A million? Two million? Three?"

Mr. Rackstraw shook his head scornfully.

"A million? Who wants a million? I'll put on my Neal Ball glove against your Hans Wagner bat. The best of three games. Does that go?"

"I should say it did," said Mr. Dodson joyfully. "I've been wanting that glove for years. It's like finding it in one's Christmas stocking."

"Very well," said Mr. Rackstraw. "Then let's get it fixed up."

Honestly, it is but a dog's life, that of the short-story writer. I particularly wished at this point to introduce a description of Mr. Rackstraw's country home and estate, featuring the private ballpark with its fringe of noble trees. It would have served a double purpose, not only charming the lover of nature, but acting as a fine stimulus to the youth of the country, showing them the sort of home they would be able to buy some day if they worked hard and saved their money. But no. You shall have three guesses as to what was the cry. You give it up? It was "Brevity! Brevity!" Let us on.

The two teams arrived at the Rackstraw house in time for lunch. Clarence, his features once more reduced to their customary finely chiseled proportions, alighted from the automobile with a swelling heart. He could see nothing of Isabel, but that did not disturb him. Letters had passed between the two. Clarence had warned her not to embrace him in public, as McGraw would not like it; and Isabel accordingly had arranged a tryst among the noble trees which fringed the ballpark.

I will pass lightly over the meeting of the two lovers. I will not describe the dewy softness of their eyes, the catching of their breath, their murmered endearments. I could, mind you. It is at just such descriptions that I am particularly happy. But I have grown discouraged. My spirit is broken. It is enough to say that Clarence had reached a level of emotional eloquence rarely met with among pitchers of the National League, when Isabel broke from him with a startled exclamation, and vanished behind a tree; and, looking over his shoulder, Clarence observed Mr. Daniel Rackstraw moving toward him.

It was evident from the millionaire's demeanor that he had seen nothing. The look on his face was anxious, but not wrathful. He sighted Clarence, and hurried up to him.

"Say, Brown," he said, "I've been looking for you. I want a word with you."

"A thousand, if you wish it," said Clarence courteously.

"Now, see here," said Mr. Rackstraw. "I want to explain to you just what this ball game means to me. Don't run away with the idea I've had you fellows down to play an exhibition game just to keep me merry and bright. If the Giants win today, it means that I shall be able to hold up my head again and look my fellow man in the face, instead of crawling around on my stomach and feeling like thirty cents. Do you get that?"

"I am hep," replied Clarence with simple dignity.

"And not only that," went on the millionaire. "There's more to it. I have put up my Neal Ball glove against Mr. Dodson's Wagner bat as a side bet. You understand what that means? It means that either you win or my life is soured for keeps. See?"

"I have got you," said Clarence.

"Good. Then what I wanted to say was this. Today is your day for pitching as you've never pitched before. Everything depends on whether you make good or not. With you pitching like mother used to make it, the Giants are some nine. Otherwise they are Nature's citrons. It's one thing or the other. It's all up to you. Win, and there's twenty thousand dollars waiting for you above what you share with the others."

Clarence waved his hand deprecatingly.

"Mr. Rackstraw," he said, "keep your dough. I care nothing for money."

"You don't?" cried the millionaire. "Then you ought to exhibit yourself in a dime museum."

"All I ask of you," proceeded Clarence, "is your consent to my engagement to your daughter."

Mr. Rackstraw looked sharply at him.

"Repeat that," he said. "I don't think I quite got it."

"All I ask is your consent to my engagement to your daughter."

"Young man," said Mr. Rackstraw, not without a touch of admiration, "you have gall."

"My friends have sometimes said so," said Clarence.

"And I admire gall. But there is a limit. That limit you have passed so far that you'd need to look for it with a telescope."

"You refuse your consent."

"I never said you weren't a clever guesser."

"Why?"

Mr. Rackstraw laughed. One of those nasty, sharp, metallic laughs that hit you like a bullet.

"How would you support my daughter?"

"I was thinking that you would help to some extent."

"You were, were you?"

"I was."

"Oh?"

Mr. Rackstraw emitted another of those laughs.

"Well," he said, "it's off. You can take that as coming from an authoritative source. No wedding-bells for you."

Clarence drew himself up, fire flashing from his eyes and a bitter smile curving his expressive lips.

"And no Wagner bat for you!" he cried.

Mr. Rackstraw started as if some strong hand had plunged an auger into him.

"What!" he shouted.

Clarence shrugged his superbly modeled shoulders in silence.

"Say," said Mr. Rackstraw, "you wouldn't let a little private difference like that influence you any in a really important thing like this ball game, would you?"

"I would."

"You would hold up the father of the girl you love?"

"Every time."

"Her white-haired old father?"

"The color of his hair would not affect me."

"Nothing would move you?"

"Nothing."

"Then, by George, you're just the son-in-law I want. You shall marry Isabel; and I'll take you into partnership this very day. I've been looking for a good, husky bandit like you for years. You make Dick Turpin look like a preliminary three-round bout. My boy, we'll be the greatest team, you and I, that ever hit Wall Street."

"Papa!" cried Isabel, bounding happily from behind her tree.

Mr. Rackstraw joined their hands, deeply moved, and spoke in low, vibrant tones:

"Play ball!"

Little remains to be said, but I am going to say it, if it snows. I am at my best in these tender scenes of idyllic domesticity.

Four years have passed. Once more we are in the Rackstraw home. A lady is coming down the stairs, leading by the hand her little son. It is Isabel. The years have dealt lightly with her. She is still the same stately, beautiful creature whom I would have described in detail long ago if I had been given half a chance. At the foot of the stairs the child stops and points at a small, wooden object in a glass case.

"Wah?" he says.

"That?" says Isabel. "That is the bat Mr. Wagner used to use when he was a little boy."

She looks at a door on the left of the hall, and puts a finger to her lip.

"Hush!" she says. "We must be quiet. Daddy and grandpa are busy in there cornering wheat."

And softly mother and child go out into the sunlit garden.

*Chet Williamson's short fiction has appeared in many popular magazines, in-cluding the* New Yorker, Playboy, *and* Esquire. *He is also a well-known nov-elist, with seven books to his credit. His most recent book is* Second Chance *(1995). "Ghandi at the Bat" is a truly original baseball yarn about the Indian statesman. It originally appeared in the* New Yorker.

*Chet Williamson*

# GANDHI AT THE BAT (1983)

**H**ISTORY BOOKS AND AVAILABLE NEWSPAPER files hold no record of the visit to America in 1933 made by Mohandas K. Gandhi. For rea-sons of a sensitive political nature that have not yet come to light, all contemporary accounts of the visit were suppressed at the request of President Roosevelt. Although Gandhi repeatedly appeared in public during his three-month stay, the cloak of journalistic silence was seam-less, and all that remains of the great man's celebrated tour is this long-secreted glimpse of one of the Mahatma's unexpected nonpolitical ap-pearances, written by an anonymous press-box denizen of the day.

Yankee Stadium is used to roaring crowds. But never did a crowd roar louder than on yesterday afternoon, when a little brown man in a loin-cloth and wire-rimmed specs put some wood on a Lefty Grove fastball and completely bamboozled Connie Mack's A's.

It all started when Mayor John J. O'Brien invited M. K. ("Mahatma") Gandhi to see the Yanks play Philadelphia up at "The House That Ruth Built." Gandhi, whose ballplaying experience was limited to a few wallops with a cricket bat, jumped at the chance, and 12 noon saw the Mayor's party in the Yankee locker room, where the Mahatma met the Bronx Bombers. A zippy exchange occurred when the Mayor introduced the Lord of the Loincloth to the Bambino. "Mr. Gandhi," Hizzoner said, "I want you to meet Babe Ruth, the Sultan of Swat."

Gandhi's eyes sparkled behind his Moxie-bottle lenses, and he chuckled. "Swat," quoth he, "is a sultanate of which I am not aware. Is it by any chance near Maharashtra?"

"Say," laughed the Babe, laying a meaty hand on the frail brown shoulder, "you're all right, kiddo. I'll hit one out of the park for you today."

"No hitting, please," the Mahatma quipped.

In the Mayor's front-row private box, the little Indian turned down the offer of a hot dog and requested a box of Cracker Jack instead. The prize inside was a tin whistle, which he blew gleefully whenever the Bambino waddled up to bat.

The grinning guru enjoyed the game immensely—far more than the A's, who were down 3–1 by the fifth. Ruth, as promised, did smash a homer in the seventh, to Gandhi's delight. "Hey, Gunga Din!" Ruth cried jovially on his way to the Yankee dugout. "Know why my battin' reminds folks of India? 'Cause I can really Bangalore!"

"That is a very good one, Mr. Ruth!" cried the economy-size Asian.

By the top of the ninth, the Yanks had scored two more runs. After Mickey Cochrane whiffed on a Red Ruffing fastball, Gandhi remarked how difficult it must be to hit such a swiftly thrown missile and said, "I should like to try it very much."

"Are you serious?" Mayor O'Brien asked.

"If it would not be too much trouble. Perhaps after the exhibition is over," his visitor suggested.

There was no time to lose. O'Brien, displaying a panache that would have done credit to his predecessor, Jimmy Walker, leaped up and shouted to the umpire, who called a time-out. Managers McCarthy and Mack were beckoned to the Mayor's side, along with Bill Dinneen, the home-plate umpire, and soon all of Yankee stadium heard an unprecedented announcement:

"Ladies and gentlemen, regardless of the score, the Yankees will come to bat to finish the ninth inning."

The excited crowd soon learned that the reason for such a breach of tradition was a little brown pinch hitter shorter than his bat. When the pin-striped Bronx Bombers returned to their dugout after the last Philadelphia batter had been retired in the ninth, the Nabob of Nonviolence received a hasty batting lesson from Babe Ruth under the stands.

Lazzeri led off the bottom of the stanza, hitting a short chop to Bishop, who rifled to Foxx for the out. Then, after Crosetti fouled out to Cochrane, the stadium became hushed as the announcer intoned, "Pinch-hitting for Ruffing, Mohandas K. Gandhi."

The crowd erupted as the white-robed holy man, a fungo bat propped jauntily on his shoulder, strode to the plate, where he remarked to the crouching Mickey Cochrane, "It is a very big field, and a very small ball."

"C'mon, Moe!" Ruth called loudly to the dead-game bantam batter. "Show 'em the old pepper!"

"I will try, Mr. Baby!" Gandhi called back, and went into a batting stance unique in the annals of the great game—his sheet-draped posterior facing the catcher, and his bat held high over his head, as if to clobber the ball into submission. While Joe McCarthy called time, the Babe trotted out and politely corrected the little Indian's position in the box.

The time-out over, Grove threw a screaming fastball right over the plate. The bat stayed on Gandhi's shoulder. "Oh, my," he said as he turned and observed the ball firmly ensconced in Cochrane's glove. "That *was* speedy."

The second pitch was another dead-center fastball. The Mahatma swung, but found that the ball had been in the Mick's glove for a good three seconds before his swipe was completed. "Stee-rike two!" Dinneen barked.

The next pitch was high and outside, and the ump called it a ball before the petite pundit made a tentative swing at it. "Must I sit down now?" He asked.

"Nah, it's a ball," Dinneen replied. "I called it before you took your cut."

"Yes. I *know* that is a ball, and I did swing at it and did miss."

"No, no, a ball. Like a free pitch."

"Oh, I see."

"Wasn't in the strike zone."

"Yes, I see."

"So you get another swing."

"Yes."

"And if you miss you sit down."

"I just *did* miss."

"Play ball, Mister."

The next pitch was in the dirt. Gandhi did not swing. "Ball," Dinneen called.

"Yes, it is," the Mahatma agreed.

"Two and two."

"That is four."

"Two balls, two strikes."

"Is there not but one ball?"

"Two balls."

"Yes, I see."

"And two strikes."

"And if I miss I sit down."

Ruth's voice came booming from the Yankee dugout: "Swing early, Gandy baby!"

"When is early?"

"When I tell ya! I'll shout '*Now!*' "

Grove started his windup. Just as his leg kicked up, the Bambino's cry of "*Now!*" filled the park.

The timing was perfect. Gandhi's molasses-in-January swing met the Grove fastball right over the plate. The ball shot downward, hit the turf, and arced gracefully into the air toward Grove. "*Run,* Peewee, *run!*" yelled Ruth, as the crowd went wild.

"Yes, yes!" cried Gandhi, who started down the first-base line in what can only be described as a dancing skip, using his bat as a walking stick. An astonished Grove booted the high bouncer, then scooped up the ball and flung it to Jimmie Foxx at first.

But Foxx, mesmerized by the sight of a sixty-three-year-old Indian in white robes advancing merrily before him and blowing mightily on a tin whistle, failed to descry the stitched orb, which struck the bill of his cap, knocking it off his head, and, slowed by its deed of dishabille, rolled to a stop by the fence.

Gandhi paused only long enough to touch first and to pick up Jimmie's cap and return it to him. By the time the still gawking Foxx had perched it once more on his head, the vital vegetarian was halfway to second.

Right fielder Coleman retrieved Foxx's missed ball and now relayed it to Max Bishop at second, but too late. The instant Bishop tossed the ball back to the embarrassed Grove, Gandhi was off again. Grove, panicking, overthrew third base, and by the time left fielder Bob Johnson picked up the ball, deep in foul territory, the Tiny Terror of Tealand had rounded the hot corner and was scooting for home. Johnson hurled the ball on a true course to a stunned Cochrane. The ball hit the pocket of Cochrane's mitt and popped out like a muffin from a toaster.

Gandhi jumped on home plate with both sandalled feet, and the crowd exploded as Joe McCarthy, the entire Yankee squad, and even a beaming Connie Mack surged onto the field.

"I ran home," giggled Gandhi. "Does that mean that I hit a run home?"

"A home run, Gandy," said Ruth. "Ya sure did."

"Well, technically," said Umpire Dinneen, "it was a single and an over-throw and then—"

"*Shaddup*," growled a dozen voices at once.

"Looked like a homer to me, too," the ump corrected, but few heard him, for by that time the crowd was on the field, lifting to their shoulders a joyous Gandhi, whose tin whistle provided a thrilling trilling over the mob's acclaim.

Inside the locker room, Manager McCarthy offered Gandhi a permanent position on the team, but the Mahatma graciously refused, stating that he could only consider a diamond career with a different junior-circuit club.

"Which club would that be, kid?" said the puzzled Bambino.

"The Cleveland Indians, of course," twinkled the Mahatma.

An offer from the Cleveland front office arrived the next day, but India's top pinch-hitter was already on a train headed for points west—and the history books.

*James Farl Powers was born in 1917 in Jacksonville, Illinois. He is widely re-*
*spected as a brilliant satirist and meticulous craftsman. Much of his fiction is*
*deeply rooted in Catholic values and religious themes. Powers's best-known*
*book is* Morte D'Urban *(1962), which won the National Book Award and is*
*now included in the Modern Library collection of great books of the world. His*
*other books include* The Presence of Grace *(1956),* Look How the Fish Live
*(1975), and* Wheat That Springeth Green *(1968). "Jamesie" is based on*
*Powers's own childhood in Illinois, where he played baseball, basketball, and*
*football. The story originally appeared in a collection of his stories called* Prince
of Darkness and Other Stories *(1947).*

## *J. F. Powers*

# JAMESIE (1947)

**T**HERE IT WAS, ALL ABOUT Lefty, in Ding Bell's Dope Box.

We don't want to add coals to the fire, but it's common knowledge
that the Local Pitcher Most Likely To Succeed is fed up with the home
town. Well, well, the boy's good, which nobody can deny, and the
scouts are on his trail, but it doesn't say a lot for his team spirit, not to
mention his civic spirit, this high-hat attitude of his. And that fine
record of his—has it been all a case of him and him alone? How about
the team? The boys have backed him up, they've given him the runs,
and that's what wins ball games. They don't pay off on strike-outs.

There's one kind of player every scribe knows—and wishes he didn't—the lad who gets four for four with the willow, and yet, somehow, his team goes down to defeat—but does that worry this gent? Not a bit of it. He's too busy celebrating his own personal success, figuring his batting average, or, if he's a pitcher, his earned run average and strike-outs. The percentage player. We hope we aren't talking about Lefty. If we are, it's too bad, it is, and no matter where he goes from here, especially if it's up to the majors, it won't remain a secret very long, nor will he . . . See you at the game Sunday. Ding Bell.

"Here's a new one, Jamesie," his father said across the porch, holding up the rotogravure section.

With his father on Sunday it could be one of three things—a visit to the office, fixing up his mother's grave in Calvary, or just sitting on the porch with all the Chicago papers, as today.

Jamesie put down the *Courier* and went over to his father without curiosity. It was always Lindy or the *Spirit of St. Louis,* and now without understanding how this could so suddenly be, he was tired of them. His father, who seemed to feel that a growing boy could take an endless interest in these things, appeared to know the truth at last. He gave a page to the floor—that way he knew what he'd read and how far he had to go—and pulled the newspaper around his ears again. Before he went to dinner he would put the paper in order and wish out loud that other people would have the decency to do the same.

Jamesie, back in his chair, granted himself one more chapter of *Baseball Bill in the World Series.* The chapters were running out again, as they had so many times before, and he knew, with the despair of a narcotic, that his need had no end.

*Baseball Bill,* at fifty cents a volume and unavailable at the library, kept him nearly broke, and Francis Murgatroyd, his best friend . . . too stingy to go halves, confident he'd get to read them all as Jamesie bought them, and each time offering to exchange the old *Tom Swifts* and *Don Sturdys* he had got for Christmas—as though that were the same thing!

Jamesie owned all the *Baseball Bills* to be had for love or money in the world, and there was nothing in the back of this one about new titles being in preparation. Had the author died, as some of them did, and left his readers in the lurch? Or had the series been discontinued–for where, after *Fighting for the Pennant* and *In the World Series,* could Baseball Bill go? *Baseball Bill, Manager,* perhaps. But then what?

"A plot to *fix* the World Series! So that was it! Bill began to see it all. . . . The mysterious call in the night! The diamond necklace in the dressing room! The scribbled note under the door! With slow fury Bill realized that the peculiar odor on the note paper was the odor in his room now! It was the odor of strong drink and cigar smoke! And it came from his midnight visitor! The same! Did he represent the powerful gambling syndicate? Was *he* Blackie Humphrey himself? Bill held his towering rage in check and smiled at his visitor in his friendly, boyish fashion. His visitor must get no inkling of his true thoughts. Bill must play the game–play the very fool they took him for! Soon enough they would discover for themselves, but to their everlasting sorrow, the courage and daring of Baseball Bill. . . ."

Jamesie put the book aside, consulted the batting averages in the *Courier,* and reread Ding Bell. Then, not waiting for dinner and certain to hear about it at supper, he ate a peanut butter sandwich with catsup on it, and left by the back door. He went down the alley calling for Francis Murgatroyd. He got up on the Murgatroyd gate and swung–the death-defying trapeze act at the circus–until Francis came down the walk.

"Hello, Blackie Humphrey," Jamesie said tantalizingly.

"Who's Blackie Humphrey?"

"You know who Blackie Humphrey is all right."

"Aw, Jamesie, cut it out."

"And you want me to throw the World Series!"

"Baseball Bill!"

"In the World Series. It came yesterday."

"Can I read it?"

Jamesie spoke in a hushed voice. "So you're Blackie Humphrey?"

"All right. But I get to read it next."

"So you want me to throw the World Series, Blackie. Is that it? Say you do."

"Yes, I do."

"Ask me again, Call me Bill."

"Bill, I want you to throw the World Series. Will you, Bill?"

"I might." But that was just to fool Blackie. Bill tried to keep his towering rage in check while feigning an interest in the nefarious plot. "Why do you want me to throw it, Blackie?"

"I don't know."

"Sure you know. You're a dirty crook and you've got a lot of dough bet on the other team."

"Uh, huh."

"Go ahead. Tell me that."

While Blackie unfolded the criminal plan Bill smiled at him in his friendly, boyish fashion.

"And who's behind this, Blackie?"

"I don't know."

"Say it's the powerful gambling syndicate."

"It's them."

"Ah, ha! Knock the ash off your cigar."

"Have I got one?"

"Yes, and you've got strong drink on your breath, too."

"Whew!"

Blackie should have fixed him with his small, piglike eyes.

"Fix me with your small, piglike eyes."

"Wait a minute, Jamesie!"

"Bill. Go ahead. Fix me."

"OK But you don't get to be Bill all the time."

"Now blow your foul breath in my face."

"There!"

"Now ask me to have a cigar. Go ahead."

Blackie was offering Bill a cigar, but Bill knew it was to get him to break training and refused it.

"I see through you, Blackie." No, that was wrong. He had to conceal his true thoughts and let Blackie play him for a fool. Soon enough his time would come and . . . "Thanks for the cigar, Blackie," he said. "I thought it was a cheap one. Thanks, I'll smoke it later."

"I paid a quarter for it."

"Hey, that's too much, Francis!"

"Well, if I'm the head of the powerful—"

Mr. Murgatroyd came to the back door and told Francis to get ready.

"I can't go to the game, Jamesie," Francis said. "I have to caddy for him."

Jamesie got a ride with the calliope when it had to stop at the corner for the light. The calliope was not playing now, but yesterday it had roamed the streets, all red and gold and glittering like a hussy among the pious, black Fords parked on the Square, blaring and showing off, with a sign, Jayville vs. Beardstown.

The ballpark fence was painted a swampy green except for an occasional new board. Over the single ticket window cut in the fence hung a sign done in the severe black and white railroad manner. "Home of the Jayville Independents," but everybody called them the "Indees."

Jamesie bought a bottle of Green River out of his savings and made the most of it, swallowing it in sips, calling upon his will power under the sun. He returned the bottle and stood for a while by the ticket window making designs in the dust with the corrugated soles of his new tennis shoes. Ding Bell, with a pretty lady on his arm and carrying the black official scorebook, passed inside without paying, and joked about it.

The Beardstown players arrived from sixty miles away with threatening cheers. Their chartered bus stood steaming and dusty from the trip. The players wore gray suits with "Barons" written across their chests and had the names of sponsors on their backs—Palms Café, Rusty's Wrecking, Coca-Cola.

Jamesie recognized some of the Barons but put down a desire to speak to them.

The last man to leave the bus, Jamesie thought, must be Guez, the new pitcher imported from East St. Louis for the game. Ding Bell had it in the Dope Box that "Saliva Joe" was one of the few spitters left in the business, had been up in the Three Eye a few years, was a full-blooded Cuban, and ate a bottle of aspirins a game, just like candy.

The dark pitcher's fame was too much for Jamesie. He walked along-side Guez. He smelled the salt and pepper of the gray uniform, saw the scarred plate on the right toe, saw the tears in the striped stockings—the marks of bravery or moths—heard the distant chomp of tobacco being chewed, felt—almost—the iron drape of the flannel, and was reduced to friendliness with the pitcher, the enemy.

"Are you a real Cuban?"

Guez looked down, rebuking Jamesie with a brief stare, and growled. "Go away."

Jamesie gazed after the pitcher. He told himself that he hated Guez—that's what he did, hated him! But it didn't do much good. He looked around to see if anybody had been watching, but nobody had, and he wanted somebody his size to vanquish—somebody who might think Guez was as good as Lefty. He wanted to bet a million dollars on Lefty against Guez, but there was nobody to take him up on it.

The Indees began to arrive in ones and twos, already in uniform but carrying their spikes in their hands. Jamesie spoke to all of them except J. G. Nickerson, the manager. J. G. always glared at kids. He thought they were stealing his baseballs and laughing about it behind his back. He was a great one for signaling with a scorecard from the bench, like Connie Mack, and Ding Bell had ventured to say that managers didn't come any brainier than Jayville's own J. G. Nickerson, even in the big time. But if there should be a foul ball, no matter how tight the game or crucial the situation, J. G. would leap up, straining like a bird dog, and try to place it, waving the bat boy on without taking his eyes off the spot where it disappeared over the fence or in the weeds. That was why they called him the Foul Ball.

The Petersons—the old man at the wheel, a red handkerchief tied tight enough around his neck to keep his head on, and the sons, all players, Big Pete, Little Pete, Middle Pete, and Extra Pete—roared up with their legs hanging out of the doorless Model T and the brass radiator boiling over.

The old man ran the Model T around in circles, damning it for a run-away horse, and finally got it parked by the gate.

"Hold'er, Knute!" he cackled.

The boys dug him in the ribs, tickling him, and were like puppies that had been born bigger than their father, jollying him through the gate, calling him Barney Oldfield.

Lefty came.

"Hi, Lefty," Jamesie said.

"Hi, kid," Lefty said. He put his arm around Jamesie and took him past the ticket taker.

"It's all right, Mac," he said.

"Today's the day, Lefty," Mac said. "You can do it, Lefty."

Jamesie and Lefty passed behind the grandstand. Jamesie saw Lefty's father, a skinny, brown-faced man in a yellow straw katy.

"There's your dad, Lefty."

Lefty said, "Where?" but looked the wrong way and walked a little faster.

At the end of the grandstand Lefty stopped Jamesie. "My old man is out of town, kid. Got that?"

Jamesie did not see how this could be. He knew Lefty's father. Lefty's father had a brown face and orange gums. But Lefty ought to know his own father. "I guess it just looked like him, Lefty," Jamesie said.

Lefty took his hand off Jamesie's arm and smiled. "Yeah, that's right, kid. It just looked like him on account of he's out of town—in Peoria."

Jamesie could still feel the pressure of Lefty's fingers on his arm. They came out on the diamond at the Indees bench near first base. The talk quieted down when Lefty appeared. Everybody thought he had a big head, but nobody could say a thing against his pitching record, it was that good. The scout for the New York Yankees had invited him only last Sunday to train with them next spring. The idea haunted the others. J. G. had shut up about the beauties of teamwork.

J. G. was counting the balls when Jamesie went to the suitcase to get one for Lefty. J. G. snapped the lid down.

"It's for Lefty!"

"Huh!"

"He wants it for warm up."

"Did you tell this kid to get you a ball, Left?"

"Should I bring my own?" Lefty said.

J. G. dug into the suitcase for a ball, grunting, "I only asked him." He looked to Jamesie for sympathy. He considered the collection of balls and finally picked out a fairly new one.

"Lefty, he likes 'em brand new," Jamesie said. "Who's running this club?" J. G. bawled. But he threw the ball back and broke a brand new one out of its box and tissue paper. He ignored Jamesie's ready hand and yelled to Lefty going out to the bull pen, "Coming at you, Left," and threw it wild.

Lefty let the ball bounce through his legs, not trying for it. "Nice throw," he said.

Jamesie retrieved the ball for Lefty. They tossed it back and forth, limbering up, and Jamesie aped Lefty's professional indolence.

When Bugs Bidwell, Lefty's battery mate, appeared with his big mitt, Jamesie stood aside and buttoned his glove back on his belt. Lefty shed his red blanket coat with the leather sleeves and gave it to Jamesie for safekeeping. Jamesie folded it gently over his arm, with the white chenille "J" showing out. He took his stand behind Bugs to get a good look at Lefty's stuff.

Lefty had all his usual stuff—the fast one with the two little hops in it, no bigger than a pea; his slow knuckler that looked like a basketball, all the stitches standing still and staring you in the face; his sinker that started out high like a wild pitch, then dipped a good eight inches and straightened out for a called strike. But something was wrong—Lefty with nothing to say, no jokes, no sudden whoops, was not himself. Only once did he smile at a girl in the bleachers and say she was plenty . . . and sent a fast one smacking into Bugs's mitt for what he meant.

That, for a moment, was the Lefty that Jamesie's older cousins knew about. They said a nice kid like Jamesie ought to be kept away from him, even at the ballpark. Jamesie was always afraid it would get back to Lefty that the cousins thought he was poor white trash, or that he would know it in some other way, as when the cousins passed him on the street and looked the other way. He was worried, too, about what Lefty might think of his Sunday clothes, the snow-white blouse, the floppy sailor tie, the soft linen pants, the sissy clothes. His tennis shoes—sneakers, he ought to say—were all right, but not the golf stockings that left his knees bare, like a rich kid's. The tough guys, because they were tough or poor—he didn't know which—wore socks, not stockings, and they wore them rolled down slick to their ankles.

Bugs stuck his mitt with the ball in it under his arm and got out his Beechnut. He winked at Jamesie and said, "Chew?"

Jamesie giggled. He liked Bugs. Bugs, on loan from the crack State Hospital team, was all right—nothing crazy about him; he just liked it at the asylum, he said, the big grounds and lots of cool shade, and he was not required to work or take walks like the regular patients. He was the only Indee on speaking terms with Lefty.

Turning to Lefty, Bugs said, "Ever seen this Cuban work?"

"Naw."

"I guess he's got it when he's right."

"That so?" Lefty caught the ball with his bare hand and spun it back to Bugs. "Well, all I can promise you is a no-hit game. It's up to you clowns to get the runs."

"And me hitting a lousy .211."

"All you got to do is hold me. Anyhow what's the Foul Ball want for his five bucks—Mickey Cochrane?"

"Yea, Left."

"I ought to quit him."

"Ain't you getting your regular fifteen?"

"Yeah, but I ought to quit. The Yankees want me. Is my curve breaking too soon?"

"It's right in there, Left."

It was a pitcher's battle until the seventh inning. Then the Indees pushed a run across.

The Barons got to Lefty for their first hit in the seventh, and when the next man bunted, Lefty tried to field it instead of letting Middle Pete at third have it, which put two on with none out. Little Pete threw the next man out at first, the only play possible, and the runners advanced to second and third. The next hitter hammered a line drive to Big Pete at first, and Big Pete tried to make it two by throwing to second, where the runner was off, but it was too late and the runner on third scored on the play. J. G. from the bench condemned Big Pete for a dumb Swede. The next man popped to short center.

Jamesie ran out with Lefty's jacket. "Don't let your arm get cold, Lefty."

"Some support I got," Lefty said.

"Whyn't you leave me have that bunt, Lefty?" Middle Pete said, and everybody knew he was right.

"Two of them pitches was hit solid," Big Pete said. "Good anywhere."

"Now, boys," J. G. said.

"Aw dry up," Lefty said, grabbing a blade of chew. "I ought to quit you bums."

Pid Kirby struck out for the Indees, but Little Pete walked, and Middle Pete advanced him to second on a long fly to left. Then Big Pete tripled to the weed patch in center, clear up against the Chevrolet sign, driving in Little Pete. Guez whiffed Kelly Larkin, retiring the side, and the Indees were leading the Barons 2 to 1.

The first Baron to bat in the eighth had J. G. frantic with fouls. The umpire was down to his last ball and calling for more. With trembling fingers J. G. unwrapped new balls. He had the bat boy and the bat boy's assistant hunting for them behind the grandstand. When one fell among the automobiles parked near first, he started to go and look for himself, but thought of Jamesie and sent him instead. "If anybody tries to hold out on you, come and tell me."

After Jamesie found the ball he crept up behind a familiar blue Hupmobile, dropping to his knees when he was right under Uncle Pat's elbow, and then popping up to scare him.

"Look who's here," his cousin said. It had not been Uncle Pat's elbow at all, but Gabriel's. Uncle Pat, who had never learned to drive, sat on the other side to be two feet closer to the game.

Jamesie stepped up on the running board, and Gabriel offered him some popcorn.

"So you're at the game, Jamesie," Uncle Pat said, grinning as though it were funny. "Gabriel said he thought that was you out there."

"Where'd you get the cap, Jamesie?" Gabriel said.

"Lefty. The whole team got new ones. And if they win today J. G. says they're getting whole new uniforms."

"Not from me," Uncle Pat said, looking out on the field. "Who the thunder's wearing my suit today?"

"Lee Coles, see?" Gabriel said, pointing to the player. Lee's back—Mallon's Grocery—was to them.

Uncle Pat, satisfied, slipped a bottle of near beer up from the floor to his lips and tipped it up straight, which explained to Jamesie the foam on his mustache.

"You went and missed me again this week," Uncle Pat said broodingly. "You know what I'm going to do, Jamesie?"

"What?"

"I'm going to stop taking your old *Liberty* magazine if you don't bring me one first thing tomorrow morning."

"I will." He would have to bring Uncle Pat his own free copy and erase the crossword puzzle. He never should have sold out on the street. That was how you lost your regular customers.

Uncle Pat said, "This makes the second time I started in to read a serial and had this happen to me."

"Is it all right if the one I bring you tomorrow has got 'Sample Copy' stamped on it?"

"That's all right with me, Jamesie, but I ought to get it for nothing." Uncle Pat swirled the last inch of beer in the bottle until it was all suds.

"I like the *Post*," Gabriel said. "Why don't you handle the *Post?*"

"They don't need anybody now."

"What he ought to handle," Uncle Pat said, "is the *Country Gentleman.*"

"How's the Rosebud coming, Jamesie?" Gabriel asked. "But I don't want to buy any."

Uncle Pat and Gabriel laughed at him.

Why was that funny? He'd had to return eighteen boxes and tell them he guessed he was all through being the local representative. But why was that so funny?

"Did you sell enough to get the bicycle, Jamesie?"

"No." He had sold all the Rosebud salve he could, but not nearly enough to get the Ranger bicycle. He had to be satisfied with the Eveready flashlight.

"Well, I got enough of that Rosebud salve now to grease the Hup," Gabriel said. "Or to smear all over me the next time I swim the English Channel—with Gertrude Ederle. It ought to keep the fishes away."

"It smells nice," Uncle Pat said. "But I got plenty."

Jamesie felt that they were protecting themselves against him.

"I sent it all back anyway," he said, but that was not true; there were six boxes at home in his room that he had to keep in order to get the flashlight. Why was that the way it always worked out? Same way with the flower seeds. Why was it that whenever he got a new suit at Meyer Brothers they weren't giving out ball bats or compasses? Why was it he only won a half pound of bacon at the carnival, never a Kewpie doll or an electric fan? Why did he always get tin whistles and crickets in the Cracker Jack, never a puzzle, a ring, or a badge? And one time he had got nothing! Why was it that the five-dollar bill he found on south Diamond Street belonged to Mrs. Hutchinson? But he *had* found a quarter in the dust at the circus that nobody claimed.

"Get your aunt Kate to take that cap up in the back," Uncle Pat said, smiling.

Vaguely embarrassed, Jamesie said, "Well, I got to get back."

"If that's Lefty's cap," Gabriel called after him, "you'd better send it to the cleaners."

When he got back to the bench and handed the ball over, J. G. seemed to forget all about the bases being crowded.

"Thank God," he said. "I thought you went home with it."

The Barons were all on Lefty now. Shorty Parker, their manager, coaching at third, chanted, "Take him out . . . Take him out . . . Take him out."

The Barons had started off the ninth with two clean blows. Then Bugs took a foul ball off the chicken wire in front of the grandstand for one out, and Big Pete speared a drive on the rise for another. Two down and runners on first and third. Lefty wound up–bad baseball–and the man on first started for second, the batter stepping into the pitch, not to hit it but to spoil the peg to second. The runner was safe; the man on third, threatening to come home after a false start, slid yelling back into the sack. It was close and J. G. flew off the bench to protest a little.

After getting two strikes on the next batter, Lefty threw four balls, so wide it looked like a deliberate pitchout, and that loaded the bases.

J. G. called time. He went out to the mound to talk it over with Lefty, but Lefty waved him away. So J. G. consulted Bugs behind the plate. Jamesie, lying on the grass a few feet away, could hear them.

"That's the first windup I ever seen a pitcher take with a runner on first."

"It was pretty bad," Bugs said.

"And then walking that last one. He don't look wild to me, neither."

"He ain't wild, J. G.; I'll tell you that."

"I want your honest opinion, Bugs."

"I don't know what to say, J. G."

"Think I better jerk him?"

Bugs was silent, chewing it over.

"Guess I better leave him in, huh?"

"You're the boss, J. G. I don't know nothing for sure."

"I only got Extra Pete to put in. They'd murder him. I guess I got to leave Lefty in and take a chance."

"I guess so."

When J. G. had gone Bugs walked halfway out to the mound and spoke to Lefty. "You all right?"

"I had a little twinge before."

"A little what?"

Lefty touched his left shoulder.

"You mean your arm's gone sore?"

"Naw. I guess it's nothing."

Bugs took his place behind the plate again. He crouched, and

Jamesie, from where he was lying, saw two fingers appear below the mitt—the signal. Lefty nodded, wound up, and tried to slip a medium-fast one down the middle. Guez, the batter, poled a long ball into left—foul by a few feet. Bugs shook his head in the mask, took a new ball from the umpire, and slammed it hard at Lefty.

Jamesie saw two fingers below the mitt again. What was Bugs doing? It wasn't smart baseball to give Guez another like the last one!

Guez swung and the ball fell against the left field fence—fair. Lee Coles, the left fielder, was having trouble locating it in the weeds. Kelly Larkin came over from center to help him hunt. When they found the ball, Guez had completed the circuit and the score was 5 to 2 in favor of the Barons.

Big Pete came running over to Lefty from first base, Little Pete from second, Pid Kirby from short, Middle Pete from third. J. G., calling time again, walked out to them.

"C'mere, Bugs," he said.

Bugs came slowly.

"What'd you call for on that last pitch?"

"Curve ball."

"And the one before that?"

"Same."

"And what's Lefty give you?"

"It wasn't no curve. It wasn't much of anything."

"No," J. G. said. "It sure wasn't no curve ball. It was right in there, not too fast, not too slow, just right—for batting practice."

"It slipped," Lefty said. "Slipped, huh!" Big Pete said. "How about the other one?"

"They both slipped. Ain't that never happened before?"

"Well, it ain't never going to happen again—not to me, it ain't," J. G. said. "I'm taking you out!"

He shouted to Extra Pete on the bench, "Warm up! You're going in!" He turned to Lefty.

"And I'm firing you. I just found out your old man was making bets under the grandstand—and they wasn't on us! I can put you in jail for this!"

"Try it," Lefty said, starting to walk away.

"If you knew it, J. G.," Big Pete said, "whyn't you let us know?"

"I just now found it out, is why."

"Then I'm going to make up for lost time," Big Pete said, following Lefty, "and punch this guy's nose."

Old man Peterson appeared among them—somebody must have told him what it was all about. "Give it to him, son!" he cackled.

Jamesie missed the fight. He was not tall enough to see over all the heads, and Gabriel, sent by Uncle Pat, was dragging him away from it all.

"I always knew that Lefty was a bad one," Gabriel said on the way home. "I knew it from the time he used to hunch in marbles."

"It reminds me of the Black Sox scandal of 1919," Uncle Pat said. "I wonder if they'll hold the old man, too."

Jamesie, in tears, said, "Lefty hurt his arm and you don't like him just because he don't work, and his father owes you at the store! Let me out! I'd rather walk by myself than ride in the Hupmobile—with you!"

He stayed up in his room, feigning a combination stomachache and headache, and would not come down for supper. Uncle Pat and Gabriel were down there eating. His room was over the dining room, and the windows were open upstairs and down, but he could not quite hear what they said. Uncle Pat was laughing a lot—that was all for sure—but then he always did that. Pretty soon he heard no more from the dining room and he knew they had gone to sit on the front porch.

Somebody was coming up the stairs. Aunt Kate. He knew the wavering step at the top of the stairs to be hers, and the long pause she used to catch her breath—something wrong with her lungs? Now, as she began to move, he heard ice tinkling in a glass. Lemonade. She was bringing him some supper. She knocked. He lay heavier on the bed and with his head at a painful angle to make her think he was suffering. She knocked again. If he pinched his forehead it would look red and feverish. He did. Now.

"Come in," he said weakly.

She came in, gliding across the room in the twilight, tall and white as a sail in her organdy, serene before her patient. Not quite opening his eyes, he saw her through the lashes. She thought he was sick all right, but even if she didn't, she would never take advantage of him to make a joke, like Uncle Pat, prescribing, "A good dose of salts! That's the ticket!" Or Gabriel, who was even meaner, "An enema!"

He had Aunt Kate fooled completely. He could fool her every time. On Halloween she was the kind of person who went to the door every time the bell rang. She was the only grownup he knew with whom it was not always the teeter-totter game. She did not raise herself by lowering him. She did not say back to him the things he said, slightly changed, accented with a grin, so that they were funny. Uncle Pat did. Gabriel did. Sometimes, if there was company, his father did.

"Don't you want the shades up, Jamesie?"

She raised the shades, catching the last of that day's sun, bringing the ballplayers on the wall out of the shadows and into action. She put the tray on the table by his bed.

Jamesie sat up and began to eat. Aunt Kate was the best one. Even if she noticed it, she would say nothing about his sudden turn for the better.

She sat across from him in the rocker, the little red one he had been given three years ago, when he was just a kid in the first grade, but she did not look too big for it. She ran her hand over the front of his books, frowning at Baseball Bill, Don Sturdy, Tom Swift, Horatio Alger, Jr., and the *Sporting News*. They had come between him and her.

"Where are the books we used to read, Jamesie?"

"On the bottom shelf."

She bent to see them. There they were, his old friends and hers—hers still. Perseus. Theseus. All those old Greeks. Sir Lancelot. Merlin. Sir Tristram. King Arthur. Oliver Twist. Pinocchio. Gulliver. He wondered how he could have liked them, and why Aunt Kate still did. Perhaps he still did, a little. But they turned out wrong, most of them, with all the good guys dying or turning into fairies and the bad guys becoming dwarfs. The books he read now turned out right, if not until the very last page, and the bad guys died or got what was coming to them.

"Were they talking about the game, Aunt Kate?"

"Your uncle was, and Gabriel."

Jamesie waited a moment. "Did they say anything about Lefty?"

"I don't know. Is he the one who lost the game on purpose?"

"That's a lie, Aunt Kate! That's just what Uncle Pat and Gabriel say!"

"Well, I'm sure I don't know—"

"You *are* on their side!"

Aunt Kate reached for his hand, but he drew it back. "Jamesie, I'm sure I'm not on anyone's side. How can I be? I don't know about baseball—and I don't care about it!"

"Well, I do! And I'm not one bit sick—and you thought I was!"

Jamesie rolled out of bed, ran to the door, turned, and said, "Why don't you get out of my room and go and be with them! You're on their side! And Uncle Pat drinks *near beer!*"

He could not be sure, but he thought he had her crying, and if he did it served her right. He went softly down the stairs, past the living room, out the back door, and crept along the house until he reached the front porch. He huddled under the spiraea bushes and listened to them talk. But it was not about the game. It was about President Coolidge. His father was for him. Uncle Pat was against him.

Jamesie crept back along the house until it was safe to stand up and walk. He went down the alley. He called for Francis.

But Francis was not home—still with his father, Mrs. Murgatroyd said.

Jamesie went downtown, taking his own special way, through alleys, across lots, so that he arrived on the Square without using a single street or walking on a single sidewalk. He weighed himself on the scales in front of Kresge's. He weighed eighty-four pounds, and the card said, "Cultivate your good tastes and make the most of your business connections."

He bought a ball of gum from the machine in front of the Owl Drugstore. It looked like it was time for a black one to come out, and black was his favorite flavor, but it was a green one. Anyway he was glad it had not been white.

He coveted the Louisville Sluggers in the window of the D. & M. Hardware. He knew how much they cost. They were autographed by

Paul Waner, Ty Cobb, Rogers Hornsby, all the big-league stars, and if Lefty ever cracked his, a Paul Waner, he was going to give it to Jamesie, he said.

When Lefty was up with the Yankees—though they had not talked about it yet—he would send for Jamesie. He would make Jamesie the bat boy for the Yankees. He would say to Jake Ruppert, the owner of the Yankees, "Either you hire my friend, Jamesie, as bat boy or I quit." Jake Ruppert would want his own nephew or somebody to have the job, but what could he do? Jamesie would have a uniform like the regular players, and get to travel around the country with them, living in hotels, eating in restaurants, taking taxicabs, and would be known to everybody as Lefty's best friend, and they would both be Babe Ruth's best friends, the three of them going everywhere together. He would get all the Yankees to write their names on an Official American League ball and then send it home to Francis Murgatroyd, who would still be going to school back in Jayville—poor old Francis; and he would write to him on hotel stationery with his own fourteen-dollar fountain pen.

And then he was standing across the street from the jail. He wondered if they had Lefty locked up over there, if Uncle Pat and Gabriel had been right—not about Lefty throwing a game—that was a lie!—but about him being locked up. A policeman came out of the jail. Jamesie waited for him to cross the street. He was Officer Burkey. He was Phil Burkey's father, and Phil had shown Jamesie his father's gun and holster one time when he was sleeping. Around the house Mr. Burkey looked like everybody else, not a policeman.

"Mr. Burkey, is Lefty in there?"

Mr. Burkey, through for the day, did not stop to talk, only saying, "Ah, that he is, boy, and there's where he deserves to be."

Jamesie said "Oh yeah!" to himself and went around to the back side of the jail. It was a brick building, painted gray, and the windows were open, but not so you could see inside, and they had bars over them.

Jamesie decided he could do nothing if Mr. Burkey was off duty. The street lights came on; it was night. He began to wonder, too, if his father would miss him. Aunt Kate would not tell. But he would have to come in the back way and sneak up to his room. If it rained tomorrow he would stay in and make up with Aunt Kate. He hurried home, and did not remember that he had meant to stay out all night, maybe even run away forever.

The next morning Jamesie came to the jail early. Mr. Burkey, on duty, said he might see Lefty for three minutes, but it was a mystery to him why anyone, especially a nice boy like Jamesie, should want to see the bum. "And don't tell your father you was here."

Jamesie found Lefty lying on a narrow iron bed that was all springs and no covers or pillow.

"Lefty," he said, "I came to see you."

Lefty sat up. He blinked at Jamesie and had trouble getting his eyes to see.

Jamesie went closer. Lefty stood up. They faced each other. Jamesie could have put his hand through the bars and touched Lefty.

"Glad to see you, kid."

"Lefty," Jamesie said, "I brought you some reading." He handed Lefty Uncle Pat's copy of *Liberty* magazine.

"Thanks, kid."

He got the box of Rosebud salve out of his pocket for Lefty.

"Well, thanks, kid. But what do I do with it?"

"For your arm, Lefty. It says 'recommended for aches and pains.' "

"I'll try it."

"Do you like oranges, Lefty?"

"I can eat 'em."

He gave Lefty his breakfast orange.

A funny, sweet smell came off Lefty's breath, like perfume, only sour. Burnt matches and cigar butts lay on the cell floor. Did Lefty smoke? Did he? Didn't he realize what it would do to him?

"Lefty, how do you throw your sinker?"

Lefty held the orange and showed Jamesie how he gripped the ball along the seams, how he snapped his wrist before he let it fly.

"But be sure you don't telegraph it, kid. Throw 'em all the same—your fast one, your floater, your curve. Then they don't know where they're at."

Lefty tossed the orange through the bars to Jamesie.

"Try it."

Jamesie tried it, but he had it wrong at first, and Lefty had to reach through the bars and show him again. After that they were silent, and Jamesie thought Lefty did not seem very glad to see him after all, and remembered the last gift.

"And I brought you this, Lefty."

It was *Baseball Bill in the World Series.*

"Yeah?" Lefty said, momentarily angry, as though he thought Jamesie was trying to kid him. He accepted the book reluctantly.

"He's a pitcher, Lefty," Jamesie said, "Like you, only he's a right-hander."

The sour perfume on Lefty's breath came through the bars again, a little stronger on a sigh.

Wasn't that the odor of strong drink and cigar smoke–the odor of Blackie Humphrey? Jamesie talked fast to keep himself from thinking. "This book's all about Baseball Bill and the World Series," he gulped, "and Blackie Humphrey and some dirty crooks that try to get Bill to throw it, but . . ." He gave up; he knew now. And Lefty had turned his back.

After a moment, during which nothing happened inside him to explain what he knew now, Jamesie got his legs to take him away, out of the jail, around the corner, down the street–away. He did not go through alleys, across lots, between buildings, over fences. No. He used the streets and sidewalks, like anyone else, to get where he was going–away– and was not quite himself.

*Kimball McIlroy's story "Joe, The Great McWhiff" originally appeared in Esquire. It's a whacky spoof about a gorilla named Joe who is purchased from the zoo to pitch in the majors. Many real baseball players have been nicknamed after God's creatures. There was Pepper Martin, the "Wild Horse of the Osage" and also "Ducky" Joe Medwick. Tris Speaker was the "Gray Eagle," and Lou Gehrig became the "Iron Horse" for his durability as a player. Who can forget Mark "The Bird" Fidrych, Bill "Mad Dog" Madlock, or Ron "The Penguin" Cey? There was a Goose Goslin and Goose Gossage and Catfish Hunter. But Joe is a real animal, and boy can he pitch.*

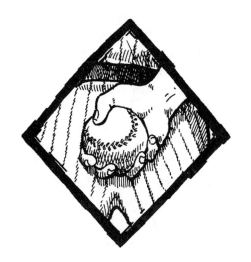

*Kimball McIlroy*

# JOE, THE GREAT McWHIFF (1946)

"I GOT A GREAT PITCHER for you, Tom," Shorty Cohn said, breaking into my office at the ballpark. "Greatest pitcher I ever saw. Come look him over and we'll sign him up."

In these times you're interested in a player just so he's got two arms and a low classification, so I asked, "Where's he at?"

"The zoo," Shorty said. "He lives there. Quit asking questions and get started. First thing you know the Yanks will have him signed."

"OK," I said, "if he can throw, just throw." Shorty called a cab to take us to the zoo and when we got there he dragged me to the monkey house. Nobody was there but monkeys, millions of them, making a racket. Shorty didn't say a word. He took me over to a cage marked GO-RILLA. Inside the cage was the biggest monkey I ever saw.

"That's him," Shorty said.

I said, "I ought to fire you right now."

Shorty said, "You just watch."

There was a pile of coconuts on the floor of the monkey's cage. Shorty got a banana and poked it through the bars. When the monkey saw the banana he picked up a coconut and let fly.

I blinked. That coconut traveled so fast I hadn't even seen it.

"He don't like bananas," Shorty explained, working the trick a couple of times more so I could watch.

"Come on, Shorty," I said. "I got work to do."

"You mean you ain't going to sign him up? Did you ever see an arm like that?"

"He's got a real arm," I admitted, watching the monkey. Those coconuts went like rifle bullets and they never missed.

"How many guys would hit one of those coconuts?" says Shorty. "Sign him up. He's even OK in the draft. You can pitch him against the Sox tomorrow."

"What would the rules say about him?" I asked, beginning to waver.

Shorty sneered. "Is there anything in the rules says you can't have an ape pitching for you?"

It wasn't until we were in the cab with the monkey sitting between us that I realized what I had done.

"We bought him," Shorty said. "First we got to sign him to a contract. We'll witness it very legal as his guardians. Then we got to get him a uniform. Then we got to give him a name. For the program." Shorty scratched his head. "We'll give him a good business name–Joe McWhiff."

Well, the monkey was ours now, and he *could* pitch.

The minute we started to explain things to the rest of the team the big problem was who was going to room with him, but Shorty stopped the argument by pointing out that it didn't matter because we had a two-week home stand first.

Shorty had it all figured out that we'd stake Joe down on the mound and give Al Bates, our catcher, a banana. There was nothing in the rules against staking a pitcher down. Al would hold the banana where he wanted Joe to throw the ball.

I agreed to pitch Joe against the Sox the next afternoon. We had some trouble getting Joe into his uniform for the game. When Shorty led him out the Sox raised a loud squawk. "It ain't legal," they said. "There ain't nothing in our contract says we got to play against an ape."

"Is there anything in your contract says you *don't* have to?" Shorty asked.

That stopped them. They finally agreed to play the game, but under protest.

Shorty staked Joe down near the rubber and Al went to the plate. The umpire called, sort of doubtfully, "Play ball!" Al took a banana out of his pocket and held it where he wanted the pitch. Joe wound up and let go. Al yanked the banana away and stuck out his mitt.

Nobody saw the ball but everybody heard it land in the mitt. The umpire yelled, "Strike one!" The batter looked dazed. He kept right on looking dazed while Joe burned two more right through the center of the plate.

Joe had a wind-up that would have baffled Houdini. Sometimes he let the ball go from one place and sometimes from another. It didn't matter much where he let it go from because the batters couldn't see it anyway.

When the inning was over Shorty turned to me.

"What do you think of him, Tom?" he asked. "Did I get you a pitcher or didn't I?"

The Sox got only three hits off him, all three by just holding their bats straight out in front of them and then by letting the ball bounce straight into center field.

Shorty had it all figured out how he'd get around Joe batting. He'd decided Joe'd never be a hitter anyway and that the thing to do was to have him put out as soon as possible. It worked all right the first time. The Sox pitcher was evidently planning to get rid of Joe with a beanball. Only Joe caught it and tossed it back at him.

Naturally, the umpire said, "You're out!"

After that the Sox got smart, and when Joe came to bat next they purposely walked him. But all Shorty did was lead Joe off the base-line and make him automatically out that way.

The first time they called a balk on Joe was in the third inning. He was waiting on the mound and all of a sudden he seemed to go into his wind-up.

"That was a balk!" the Sox manager shouted.

Shorty was out of the dugout like a rabbit. "That was no balk," he yelled. "He's scratching."

There was quite an argument about it until the umpire said to Shorty, "You show me the difference between that and his wind-up, and I'll reverse my decision."

Shorty tried, but he couldn't convince them. When he came back to the dugout he said, "We'll have to get him some flea powder."

Aside from his balks and the three hits Joe was never in any trouble and we won the game going away. When it was over the Sox manager came around to see us. He was mad—fighting mad.

"We're going to protest to the president of the League," he said. "Maybe there's nothing in the rules says you can't pitch a monkey but you can't tell me it's according to the spirit of the game."

"You got beat by a better man," Shorty said. "You should take your beating and quit squawking."

After he'd gone Shorty said to me, "We signed Joe up legal. There's nothing wrong with his contract. Pitching that game didn't tire Joe a bit. Why don't we pitch him in every game from here on? He could win them all for us."

So we pitched him the next day and he won that game, too. On the Sunday he won a doubleheader. We were turning the fans away by the gross at the box office, so many of them wanted to see Joe. After the Sunday games the Sox manager dropped around again.

"We heard from the front office," he said. "They won't make a decision until they send somebody to look this monkey over for himself. You'll see, though. They'll make you replay all them games."

Shorty laughed at him. The Monday papers from all over the country were full of stories about Joe, and it didn't look like we could miss. We were starting a series with the Yanks. The top baseball writers from all the big papers were there to watch Joe do his stuff.

Someone told us that Joe McCarthy, the Yanks' pilot, had been talking to the Sox manager, but that didn't worry Shorty.

"If you can't see 'em, you can't hit 'em," he pointed out.

Rizzuto was the first man up. He held his bat out and singled into left. Rolfe followed him and singled into right the same way. I looked at Shorty. Selkirk singled into center, scoring Rizzuto.

Joe didn't seem to have lost any of his speed and Al was calling for the ball in the right places. DiMaggio swung his bat a little and hit a double, scoring Rolfe and Selkirk. Someone yelled, "Take him out!" It was the first time they'd ever done that with Joe.

I watched closely when Keller came to bat and finally I saw what was happening. Knowing that Joe could hit the banana every time, the New York batters were sneaking a look at it and holding their bats where the ball was going to come.

In the third inning we had to take Joe out. Shorty was broken-hearted. "What'll we do?" he asked me.

It didn't help any when the Boss, who'd been doing nothing but patting us on the back during Joe's winning streak, came around and said: "You guys should know better than to try and make a pitcher out of a monkey and a monkey out of me. One more trick like that and I'll fire the both of you."

We tried Joe on Tuesday and Wednesday and both times the Yanks knocked him out of the box within the space of three innings. The papers were beginning to make sarcastic cracks about "the great McWhiff" and about the two wise guys who thought they had the baseball racket beat, meaning Shorty and me.

"Even Joe's worrying," Shorty told me on Wednesday night. "He's starting to brood. He just sits and stares at them there Yank pitchers."

Then, to make matters worse if possible, who should show up there before the game on Thursday but Mr. Herbert Gilbert Norbert from the

League front office. He was the secretary in charge of Public Decorum and Good Order. He called Shorty and me before him as if we had been schoolboys. "I am here to observe this monkey," he said. "Complaint has been made and I must be satisfied that he is qualified in personality to support the dignity of the game."

"Now look, Mr. Secretary," Shorty said right away, "Joe's all right. He's a gentleman both on the field and off."

Mr. Norbert acted very doubtful. "I hear the monkey hasn't been doing so well recently. Lost his last three starts. Now if he's no good I'm sure you won't mind releasing him if I ask you to."

"He'll get back into form," Shorty said. "He's just having a bad week."

"Now, I want to be fair," Mr. Norbert said. "Suppose you put him in there today. If he looks good, you can keep him. If he doesn't, you release him. That's fair, isn't it?"

It was fair enough, but that didn't help. The Yanks had Joe all figured out. We hadn't been planning to pitch him. He didn't look so hot against the Yanks.

Shorty worked over him like a mother before the game. When Shorty came in, after staking Joe down, he said, "It's a funny thing but Joe don't seem to be brooding any more. I think he figures he can take this game."

Rizzuto walked out to the plate full of confidence. Al took out the banana and Joe let fly with the ball. Rizzuto held out his bat.

The ball went *smack* into Al's mitt and the umpire yelled, "Strike one!"

Rizzuto looked at his bat and then got ready for the next pitch. It went *smack* into Al's mitt, too. So did the third one.

I couldn't understand it, and I didn't understand it any better when the same thing happened to Rolfe and Selkirk. Joe retired the side on nine straight pitches.

But when Al Bates came into the dugout the sweat was rolling down his face and he shook.

"Tom," he said in a voice that came up from his heels, "now he's throwing curves."

And Joe was. I guess he'd been watching the way the Yankee pitchers flicked their wrists when they tossed curve balls.

"What a brain!" Shorty said proudly. "He's got everything, even brains."

Joe pitched a no-hitter and the fans went crazy. Shorty was jumping up and down like a little boy. After the game Mr. Norbert came down to the dugout.

"Your monkey pitched a good game," he said. "A fine game. And I'll stick to my bargain. But first I'd like to meet him. You don't see many monkeys playing baseball. It's out of the ordinary."

That's a matter of opinion, but all Shorty said was, "Sure, Mr. Norbert. Joe'd like to meet you too. Come on out to the mound."

A good half of the customers had stayed in the stands to look at Joe who still was chained at the pitcher's box. Norbert swelled his chest and shot his cuffs as he walked out before the public.

My mind was going around in circles with thoughts of winning the pennant by thirty games and taking the World Series in four straight no-hitters.

"Joe's a fine fellow, Mr. Norbert," Shorty said as we came up to the mound. "He's the best behaved pitcher I ever met. Shake hands with Mr. Norbert, Joe."

Joe and Norbert shook hands. All the stands gave a cheer and Mr. Norbert took off his hat and bowed to them. Shorty unchained Joe, and we walked toward the plate together. One of the umpires was taking spare balls from the underground box.

"I can't see any reason why he shouldn't pitch for you," Norbert was saying. "He seems very decent and dependable."

Shorty beamed. "Joe's no trouble at all."

Norbert reached into his pocket while he was talking and pulled out a banana. "Here's a little present for Joe," he said, holding it out.

Before Shorty or I could move Joe had snatched a ball from the umpire and let fly. Norbert dodged and started to run. Joe jerked his chain out of Shorty's hand, helped himself to an armful of the balls and ran after Norbert.

"Drop the banana, Mr. Norbert," I yelled.

He didn't hear me. He was heading out toward center field and behind him came Joe, firing a baseball every few steps. They all hit Norbert straight as an arrow just below the hip pockets and at every shot Norbert gave a yell and a leap and the crowd gave a cheer. Norbert disappeared through the center field gates just as Joe's last baseball landed on him.

"Well," Shorty said, "we've lost our pitcher."

"His career is ended." Shorty was almost crying. "Norbert will have to stand up to write the report on him, but Joe is through." Then Shorty gave a howl. "Where did Norbert get that banana?"

The umpire had an idea. "I wouldn't want to say for sure," he said, "but Joe McCarthy looked like he was holding a banana behind him after the game."

"And I wasn't watching him." This was the last straw that broke Shorty's heart. "That's what happens when you don't watch everybody. What's baseball coming to if there's guys in it who would do a thing like that?"

*Arthur "Bugs" Baer's story "The Crambury Tiger" was originally published in* Collier's. *The story is partially based on some actual events in the life of the legendary Ty Cobb. It really happened in May 1912 that Cobb responded to a heckler during a game by jumping into the stands and beating him up with flying fists. The fan was handicapped, and when Cobb was given a ten-day suspension without pay by American League President Ban Johnson, Cobb's Detroit Tigers teammates refused to play in a game against the Philadelphia Athletics. This one-day "strike" is believed to be the first in the history of major-league baseball. (Alas, if it were only the last.) But the game was played anyway, as the Tigers' owner rounded up a team of semi-pro players to take the field. The real outcome of the game is told in Baer's story, albeit with colorful exaggeration. Parts of the story were depicted by Hollywood in the 1994 movie* Cobb.

*Arthur (Bugs) Baer*

# THE CRAMBURY TIGER (1942)

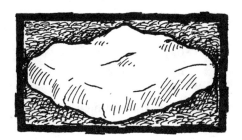

**S**URE, THE TROUBLE WAS OVER a girl. What isn't?

Tink was too good-looking for his own good before there were movies. He had the tickets to make the big leagues but he was as lazy as a fed cat. Tink could pitch at times.

Nippers had the general appearance of an accident looking for a lawyer and he had a profile you could saw lumber with. He couldn't field good enough to stop a water wheel in a dry spell. But he sure shook that pepper-box around the infield.

Playing semipro baseball in the summer was a softer touch than face powder. We got around like ringworms and if we weren't bums we would certainly do until bums came along.

I called myself a semipro although it might have been closer to three-eighths. Too much beer in Bustleton is what stopped me in addition to other habits that would have tightened the hide on a bloodhound's jowls. John McGraw once sent a scout to look me over but he decided I was too much of a grandstand player when I wasn't throwing them into the bleachers.

At the bat I couldn't hit all the leather in the world if I owned all the lumber. But both Tink and Nippers could throw their weight around at the plate. I was so round-shouldered I had to have my coats made twice as long in the back as in the front. I guess I played in more places than sunbeams in a forest. I wound up as the only left-handed shortstop in semipro baseball, but I finished better than Tink.

Fast as Nippers got a girl in the small towns Tink would take her away from him. But once he gave Nippers a girl, and it was just too bad.

It was all the fault of Ty Cobb. And a bit over like a baker's dozen.

Now, I know that Ty never heard of us cow-pasture punks who used a fence post for a bat and slid into a lot of things that weren't second base. But when he came up from Georgia to the Detroits he was gamer than a dentist pulling his own teeth and could take it like a carpet on the line. But he was as touchy as fingerprint powder and would climb a mountain to take a punch at an echo.

Ty fought everybody on the Detroits until the other Tigers realize that all he wants to do is win baseball games. Then they get in back of him as solid as wet sand and Detroit cops the berries in 1907, '08 and '09—and almost repeats in '10 and '11. But they go very bad in the spring of '12 and Cobb is sorer than ingrown hairs on a porcupine.

There's no living with Ty when he's in that mood, so when a grandstand manager in New York named Lucas or Lookis or something like that gives him the Bronx roll call from the dollar seats, Ty climbs into the stands and hands him a dry shave with his knuckles. The other Yankee fans choose up sides and Cobb is elected Queen of the May on the sixteenth of that month as I remember. The Yanks fans were sure going to town on Ty's transportation system when the entire Detroits barge into the stands and rescue him with their baseball bats. When the cops pull everybody loose from their pet holds it turns out that the fellow Cobb popped has no fingers on his right hand.

Well, Ty didn't know that and Lucas or Lookis has certainly used some pretty rough talk. That doesn't stop Ban Johnson from giving Cobb the indefinite works with the option of making it permanent.

The entire Detroits club their mad money in a lump and send Ban a testimonial telegram:

> Feeling that Mr. Cobb is being done an injustice by your action in suspending him, we the undersigned refuse to play in another game until such action is adjusted to our satisfaction. We want him reinstated or there will be no game. If players cannot have protection we must protect ourselves." (Signed) Sam Crawford, Jim Delahanty, Davey Jones, Oscar Stanage, Oscar Vitt, George Moriarity, Jack Onslow, Ed Willett, Bill Burns, Covington, Paddy Bauman, Louden, George Mullen and all the others.

That makes it serious for the Detroit owners if they don't put a team in the field on Saturday, May 18, 1912, in Philly where their next game is. Owner Navin can lose his franchise and can be plastered with a five-grand fine.

Manager Hughey Jennings comes to Philly at the Aldine Hotel and gives out word that he is in the market for a brand-new Detroit team and no reasonable offer will be refused. Any ballplayer who can stop a grapefruit from rolling uphill or hit a bull in the pants with a bass fiddle has got a chance of going direct from the semipros to the Detroits and no questions asked.

Tink, Nippers and me are booked to play for Millville in southern Jersey the next day but we light out for the Aldine Hotel in time to run into a parade of seven hundred semipros all anxious to fill Ty Cobb's shoes. A baseball writer named Isaminger on the *North American* said that seven hundred was about the right number. The seven hundred of us semipros walk single-file past Jennings and he taps the ones he wants on the shoulder with a pool cue like we were buttons on a wire over a billiard table. He runs us fifty or no count and that's his team for tomorrow.

Out of that fifty he will pick nine players who will get fifty smackers each. Then he will pick a couple more for emergency who will get twenty-five just for sitting on the bench. That was almost a full season's salary for a semipro in Philly. Tink and me are among the fifty but Nippers can't score with the pool cue even though he has a piece of chalk in his vest pocket.

That all gets into the papers and the Georgia folks get behind Cobb. A congressman named William Schley Howard made a speech about it in Washington and sent Ty a wire as follows:

> As Georgians we commend your action in resenting uncalled-for insult in New York. We hope for your complete exoneration and reinstatement in clean sport of baseball. Congratulations to you as a leader and fighter of your profession.

Howard signed the telegram and it was seconded by a famous senator from Georgia named Hoke Smith. Howard also tagged Senator Bacon's name to it. One more signature and Gordon McKay of the Inquirer said it would have been an amendment to the Constitution. Cobb got thousands of wires and letters and the Wall Street brokers got up a petition for him that I guess they could use themselves now.

Cobb spent that Friday night in conference with his fellow Detroits and they sent a telegram or two. The White Sox were playing the Red Sox in Boston, so Ty wired Harry Lord of the Chicagos and Smokey Joe Wood of the Bostons asking if they would join a protective association of players with short tempers. That was thirty years ago and Lord and Wood are still giving the matter their serious consideration. Us ballplayers stick together like a wishbone in a pulling contest.

Philly is giving the strike of the Detroits a lot of publicity because their Athletics look like sure pennant winners even though the Red Sox finally cop and Washington winds up second. So, even if Nippers doesn't make the grade he decides to cut Millville and watch us play for the Detroits. When you're a semipro, your schedule is as loose as a skeleton on roller skates. The three of us light out for the A's park Saturday morning at eight o'clock. We swiped a bottle of milk and a loaf of bread off a porch and ate it under a bridge.

At ten, Jennings drives up with his trunks and bats. He has picked fifty ballplayers on suspicion and he wants to see if we are guilty or not. He also has two faithful Detroits with him named Sugden and McGuire and I'll tell you about them. They are so old they can sleep in a swamp without mosquito netting. At the present time Jennings was using them for coaches and scouts but he announces McGuire will catch anything that comes near him, and Sugden will play first base for everything except fast grounders and overthrows. Jennings elects himself captain, manager, coach and utility. I know my baseball and I remember Sugden was with Baltimore in 1889 and here it is 1912. He was a fatigued old gent who should have spent his summers pointing out sea shells for his grandkids to pick up.

There was a McGuire with Washington in 1892 when Washington was in the National League. I think he bobbed around a lot and finally tried umpiring, but he has spots before his eyes and gives a batter his base on four of them.

That leaves seven positions for Jennings to fill and Tink and me are out. But we make the bench for twenty-five smackers and that suits us. He picks a semipro named Travers to pitch and a good lightweight fighter Billy McHarg for third. There are also a couple of old-timers from Georgetown University and a few more sand lotters who can field all right but can't hit their weight on a diet.

The fellow who got the toughest break was the semipro picked to play Ty Cobb's spot in center. His monicker was too wide for the printers and it came out in the Sunday papers this way, "L'n'h's'r." Today nobody knows whether his name was Loopenhouser or Lagenhassinger and I bet his wife still calls him a liar when he says he once played on the Detroits.

Anyway, the fans didn't ask for their money back when they saw a lot of bums in Tigers' clothing. Here's the way the game came out in the box scores:

| DETROIT | A | BH | O | A | E |
|---|---|---|---|---|---|
| McGarr, 2b | 4 | 0 | 3 | 0 | 1 |
| McHarg, 3b | 1 | 0 | 2 | 0 | 0 |
| Irwin, 3b, c | 3 | 2 | 1 | 2 | 1 |
| Travers, p | 3 | 0 | 7 | 0 | 1 |
| McGarvey, lf | 3 | 0 | 1 | 0 | 3 |
| L'n'h's'r, cf | 4 | 0 | 1 | 0 | 0 |
| Sugden, 1b | 3 | 1 | 2 | 1 | 1 |
| McGuire, c | 2 | 1 | 3 | 1 | 2 |
| Smith, 3b | 1 | 0 | 1 | 0 | 0 |
| Meaney, ss | 2 | 0 | 3 | 0 | 1 |
| Ward, rf | 2 | 0 | 0 | 0 | 0 |
| x Jennings | 1 | 0 | 0 | 0 | 0 |
| Totals | 29 | 4 | 24 | 4 | 9 |

x Batted for exercise

| ATHLETICS | A | BH | O | A | E |
|---|---|---|---|---|---|
| Maggert, lf | 4 | 3 | 0 | 0 | 0 |
| Strunk, cf | 6 | 4 | 0 | 0 | 0 |
| Collins, 2b | 6 | 5 | 0 | 1 | 0 |
| Baker, 3b | 5 | 2 | 0 | 0 | 0 |
| Murphy, rf | 3 | 2 | 1 | 0 | 0 |
| McInnis, 1b | 6 | 3 | 7 | 0 | 0 |
| Barry, ss | 4 | 2 | 3 | 1 | 1 |
| Lapp, c | 4 | 1 | 16 | 1 | 0 |
| Coombs, p | 1 | 0 | 0 | 1 | 0 |
| Brown, p | 3 | 2 | 0 | 2 | 0 |
| Pennock, p | 1 | 1 | 0 | 1 | 0 |
| Totals | 43 | 25 | 27 | 7 | 1 |

| | | Runs | Hits | Errors |
|---|---|---|---|---|
| DETROIT | 0 0 0 0 2 0 0 0 0 | 2 | 4 | 9 |
| ATHLETICS | 3 0 3 0 8 4 4 2 x | 24 | 25 | 1 |

**SUMMARY OF THE GAME**

**RUNS**, Sugden, McGuire, Maggert 2, Strunk 2, Collins 4, Baker 3, Murphy 4, McInnis 2, Barry 2, Lapp, Brown 2, Pennock.
**TWO-BASE HITS,** Maggert, Strunk, Barry, Pennock.
**THREE-BASE HITS,** Strunk, Baker, Murphy, Irwin 2, Brown, Maggert.
**SACRIFICE HIT,** Lapp.
**SACRIFICE FLY,** Barry.
**STOLEN BASES,** Collins 4, Baker, Murphy, McInnis 2, McGarvey.
**STRUCK OUT,** By Coombs 3, by Brown 5, by Pennock 7, by Travers 1.
**DOUBLE PLAY,** McGarvey and Smith.
**LEFT ON BASES,** Detroit 4, Athletics 4.
**FIRST BASE ON ERRORS,** Athletics 2
**BASES ON BALLS,** Coombs 1, Pennock 1, Travers 7.
**TIME OF GAME,** One hour and forty minutes.
**UMPIRES,** Dineen and Perrine.

Outside of shooing Sugden and McGuire around the bases for old times' sake the A's bore down all the way like guards putting a strait jacket on the star pupil in a laughing academy. Eddie Collins did more yelling than Solomon's thousand wives catching him out with another dame. Eddie hustled all the way like a long-haired rabbit in a prairie fire. This was a regular baseball contest and it held the Detroit franchise. I still feel sorry for L'n'h's'r, who blew his big chance like a pyromaniac sneezing on his last match. It was just as well that I never got into the game because I raised a pompadour of goose pimples on the bench.

Jennings saved the bacon for Navin but when Ban Johnson got the result of the game between the A's and the Pick-ups and heard that four apostrophes were playing center field for Cobb he called himself out on that one strike.

For the first time in his life Ban copped a plea and let Cobb off with a ten-day suspension. The regular Detroits played again and got their uniforms back from the semipros. All except the one shirt that Tink wore home under his coat. It belonged to Ty.

Tink wore the Detroit shirt next Monday morning out on the sand lots in the park and word went around that he was one of the striking Detroits who refused to go back. There's a Glassboro scout there and when he hears that, he gets hotter than a one-cycle engine. He offers Tink fifteen dollars a game but Tink is stringing a couple of towns along and finally nails twenty bobbins for himself for Crambury on Decoration Day. I went with the deal and got eight dollars for playing shortstop.

Tink won for Crambury by his pitching and batting and actually lived up the Detroit "D" on his shirt. The visiting team couldn't holler about it because they were padded like an idiot's cell themselves. The Crambury fans and the local girls thought he was the top berries and there was one pretty little girl who went for him big.

Going home on the train that night Tink told me her name was Jennie and her father was a motorman. Well, that's society for Tink. He pitches four Saturdays straight for Crambury and wins against Big Timber, Tacony, Southwark and Upper Darby. But for some reason he switches to Pennsylvania towns in August even though Crambury is offering him up to thirty-five dollars a game. I'm still playing short for short dough and I see Jennie each Saturday afternoon looking for Tink. She asked me about him and I said he had sprained his arm and gone back home to Philly. She doesn't even know his last name.

Well, the biggest day in semipro baseball in Jersey and Pennsylvania is Labor Day. Crambury is going to play its big rival North Chester for the weedbending championship and it wants Tink. But Tink is going to Bound Brook for less money and I know why. I tell the Crambury manager I can get a pretty good man named Nippers but he says the local folks want a big leaguer and I tell him that maybe I can get one. He says he will pay forty for a leaguer and raise me from eight to ten. I tell Nippers about it and he tells Tink he will split the forty with him if he will lend Nippers his Cobb shirt for Labor Day.

That's twenty more in the bag for Tink and he grabs it. When I tell the Crambury manager that I have another Detroit pitcher who walked out with Cobb and didn't go back he snaps it up.

Nippers touched up the big D on his chest with black ink until it stood out like a frog's eyes. On Labor Day he looked like a leaguer and pitched all the way like one coming down to the ninth. North Chester is leading one to nothing mostly because they have a ringer from the Tri-State who can pitch and bat. He smacks a homer in the first half of the ninth and is a little winded, so he hits a Crambury in the ribs, passes one, and they move up on an infield out. The next bird is a soft touch and it brings Nippers up with two on, two out and a single needed to cop.

It gets down to three and two on Nippers and it's closer than beds in a charity ward. Nippers is waving his bat at the big Tri-Stater, who winds up and is about to let it go when he sees he is pitching to two men at the plate. The other fellow is a middle-aged gent and he is packing a shotgun, which is aimed at Nippers. The Crambury manager claims a balk but the umpire disallows because nobody can out-pitch a shotgun. The fellow with the gun then explains himself.

"I've lived in this town for sixty years," he said, "and the population has been exactly six hundred and thirty-two from 1852 to 1912. The reason for that is every time somebody is born somebody leaves town."

Well, Nippers wants to know what that has to do with him. The old boy said, "My daughter told me to look for a fellow with a Detroit D on his shirt," so I know now it's the motorman speaking, "and you're going to marry her."

Well, we plead with the old man to let the game go on and settle the matter in a legal way. But he swings the gun around to the umpire and says, "Pridemore, you're the Justice of the Peace and you're going to marry my daughter with this Detroit fellow." He calls out, "Jennie," and Jennie walks out of the crowd with her head down and a handkerchief stuffed in her mouth to hold her sobs back. She never once looks up during the ceremony, not even when the Crambury runner on third tries to steal home when Pridemore is asking, "Do you take this man for your lawful wedded husband?"

He goes back when the shotgun swings his way for Jennie's daddy knows his baseball. Then the ceremony is over and Jennie looks up and sees it isn't Tink and she faints. She's married to Ty Cobb's shirt all because Lucas or Lookis or something had to shoot his face off. Pridemore makes a wave of his hand that declares the couple married and starts the game again.

The fans go back to their places, everybody on the field gets set, the runners take a big lead and the Tri-Stater winds up and lets her go.

Nippers takes a toehold on some loose dust and swings. Well, the happy bridegroom misses it farther than a dunce getting Constantinople in a spelling bee.

Nippers is now in a fine spot. He is struck-out and married on a wide outshoot.

Jennie's daddy has brought her around OK and he also collects Nippers and they go down the road looking like Daniel Boone moving his family farther west. I get myself invited to the wedding supper and the motorman isn't a bad sort of apple-knocker if you let him have his way. I tell Nippers that I will take the Detroit shirt back to Tink, but I advise him to keep the whole forty buttons for himself for he has earned it. Nippers keeps the shirt.

Let me tell you something about Ty's shirt. It must be magic because the bird who wears it acts like a leaguer. It is better for nailing a job in a small town than an average of 99.9 in a civil service quiz for letter carriers. Nippers has a couple more pitching jobs that fall and wins both. He gets sixty-five dollars for the last game of the season. Along about February at the end of winter I hear the population of Crambury has finally hopped to six-hundred and thirty-three. Also that Nippers is offered a trial with a Hoss and Buggy League in Carolina.

Down there he meets Tink, fights him for the shirt and hammers him to a blister. They meet a second time that season and Nippers breaks the blister. The man wearing Cobb's shirt gets to think he is Ty and when the war busts loose in 1917 Nippers enlists and wins a whole flock of decorations.

He goes over the top in his Detroit shirt and eighty-seven Germans surrender to him because they think a new nation has declared war on the Kaiser.

When he got home to Crambury, Jennie and number six hundred and thirty-three are waiting for him. He starts in pitching again and he gets offers from the Three-Eye, the International and the South Atlantic leagues. But he refuses to play in any town that doesn't fit his shirt.

And, Believe It or the Marching Chinese, before the 1919 season is half over, the population of Crambury is one less than its average for sixty years, for Jennie and six hundred and thirty-three have packed up and gone west with Nippers, who is a fine husband and loving father, but once he gets out there on that baseball field, is meaner than the man who invented uphill.

And he gives Ty Cobb his shirt back. For Nippers now has a Detroit shirt of his own.

*Lloyd Biggle, Jr. was born in Waterloo, Iowa, and has a Ph.D. from the University of Michigan. He is the author of more than 20 books, mostly in the areas of science fiction and mystery novels. Two of his science fiction novels,* The World Menders *(1971) and* Monument *(1976), are especially well-known. Biggle's "Who's on First?" is from his collection titled* A Galaxy of Strangers *(1976). It was written in 1960 and the events are set in 1998. Back in 1960, 1998 was a long way off. Now it's just around the corner.*

*Lloyd Biggle, Jr.*

# WHO'S ON FIRST?
# (1960)

*Priority Rating: Routine*
*From: Jard Killil, Minister of Juvenile Affairs*
*To: All Planetary Police Organizations*
    *All Interplanetary Patrol Units*
*Subject: Juvenile detention escapee Muko Zilo*
*Enclosures: Character analysis, film strips, retinal patterns*
    *All law enforcement agencies are hereby informed of the escape of Muko Zilo from the Juvenile Rehabilitation Center on Philoy, Raff III, Sector 1311. Escapee is presumed to have fled the planet in a stolen space yacht, Stellar Class II, range unlimited. His probable destination is unknown.*

LLOYD BIGGLE, JR.

*Escapee is not considered dangerous. He possesses low-grade intelligence and has no psi ability higher than Class F.*

*Kindly notify Philoy JRC immediately upon detention.*

The major-league baseball season of 1998 was only two weeks old, and Manager Pops Poppinger wished it was over and done with. Since opening day his Pirates had managed to lose fourteen games while winning none, and Pops had only the Baseball Managers' Tenure act of 1993 to thank for the fact that he was still gainfully employed. He'd had that same act to thank for his regular paychecks during the 1996 and 1997 seasons.

"But it can't last," he muttered. "Congress will repeal the thing and cite me as the reason."

He strode through the locker room without a glance at his lounging ballplayers, entered his private office, and slammed the door. He did not want to talk to anyone, especially if that anyone happened to be wearing a Pirate's uniform. He dropped an armful of newspapers onto his desk, tilted back in his chair until he could plant his size thirteen feet in a comfortable position, and opened the top paper to the sports pages. The headline made him wince. "WHEN IS A PIRATE?" it demanded. Pops stuck a cigar in his mouth as he read and forgot to light it.

"In the venerable days of yore," the article said,

> when professional athletic organizations found it necessary to attach themselves to some unfortunate city in the mistaken belief that civic loyalty would induce the population to attend games in person and pay for the privilege, the fair city of Pittsburgh spawned two notable gangs of thieves, the baseball Pirates and the football Steelers. Both organizations had their days of glory. Within the memories of men now living, if you care to believe it, the Pirates won five consecutive world championships and the Steelers four.

> "Those days of myth and fable are far behind us. If the Steelers stole anything worth mentioning during the football season just concluded, it escaped this writer's attention. The 1998 Pirates are so far removed from thievery that they will not take a game as a gift. They emphati-

324

cally demonstrated their moral uprightness yesterday, when their opposition was stricken with that most tragic of baseball diseases, paralytic generosity. The Dodgers committed six errors and presented the Pirates with nine unearned runs. The Dodgers won the game, 27 to 9.

Pops crumpled the paper and tossed it over his shoulder. "Bah! Let 'em rave. It's for sure I ain't got any ballplayers but I got lots of tenure."

The telephone rang, and he picked it up and growled a response.

"Who's pitching today, Pops?" a cheerful voice asked.

"I dunno," Pops said. "If you reporters find some guy in the press box that ain't got a sore arm, send him down."

He slammed down the phone and reached for another paper. "PIRATES STILL IN REVERSE," the headline said. Pops tossed that one aside without reading it.

A knock rattled the door. Pops ignored it. The knock sounded again, and the door opened wide enough to admit the large, grinning face of Dipsey Marlow, the Pirates' third-base coach.

"Scram!" Pops snapped

"Some kid here to see you, Pops."

"Tell him I got a bat boy. I got a whole team of bat boys."

"He's older than that—I think. He says he's got a letter for you."

Pops straightened up and grinned. "From Congress?"

"He says it's from Pete Holloway."

"Send him in."

The kid shuffled in awkwardly. His dimensions looked to be about five feet five inches—in both directions. Oddly enough, he was not fat. There was an unhealthy thinness about his freckled face, and his overly large ears gave his features a whimsical grotesqueness, but he was shaped like a box and he moved like one. He dragged to a stop in front of Pops's desk, fumbled through four pockets, and came up with a letter.

"Mr. Poppinger?"

The high, squeaky voice made Pops's ears ring. "I'm ashamed to admit it." Pops said, "but that's my name."

"Mr. Holloway told me to give this to you."

"The last I heard of Pete Holloway, he was lost in the woods up in Maine."

"He still is, sir. I mean, he's still in Maine."

"You came clear out here to California just to give me this?"

"Yes, sir."

Pops took the envelope and ripped it open.

"Dear Pops," he read. "This here kid Zilo is the most gawdawful ballplayer I ever see on two legs. He is also the luckiest man south of the North Pole. Put him in center with a rocking chair and a bottle of beer and every ball hit to the outfield will drop in his lap. He'll even catch some of them. Sign him and you'll win the pennant. Yours, Pete. P.S. He also is lucky with the bat."

Pops scratched his head and squinted disbelievingly at Zilo. "What d'ya play?"

"Outfield," Zilo said. He quickly corrected himself. "Outfield, sir."

"Where in the outfield?"

"Anywhere, sir. Just so it's the outfield, sir."

Pops wasn't certain whether he should throw him out or go along with the gag. "I got three outfielders that get by. How about second or short? Between first and third I got nothing but grass."

"Oh, no, sir. Mr. Holloway had me play short, and I made nine errors in one inning. Then he moved me to the outfield."

"I'm surprised he didn't kill you." Pops said. He continued to eye Zilo disbelievingly. "You actually played baseball for Pete?"

"Yes, sir. Last summer, sir. I went to see him a week ago to find out when I could start playing again, and he said he thought you could use me because your season started before his does."

"What'd you bat?"

"Six forty, sir."

Pops winced. "What'd you field?"

"A thousand, sir. In the outfield. In the infield it was zero."

Pops got up slowly. "Son, Pete Holloway is an old friend of mine, and he never gave me a bad tip yet. I'll give you a tryout."

"That's very kind of you, sir."

"The name is Pops. And it ain't kind of me after what happened yesterday."

Pops was standing in the corner of the dugout with Ed Schwartz, the club secretary, when the new Pirate walked out onto the field. Pops took one look, clapped his hand to his forehead, and gasped, "My God!"

"I told you I'd find him a uniform," Ed said. "I didn't guarantee to find him one that fit. He just isn't made the way our uniforms are made, and if I were you I'd make sure I wanted to keep him before I called the tailor. Otherwise, if you release him we'll have a set of uniforms on our hands that won't fit anyone or anything except maybe that oversized water cooler in the league offices."

Pops walked over to the third-base coaching box, where Dipsey Marlow was standing to watch batting practice. The Dodger dugout had just got its first incredulous look at Zilo, and Pops waited until the uproar subsided somewhat before he spoke.

"Think Pete is pulling my leg?" He asked.

"It wouldn't be like Pete, but it's possible."

"The way things is going, he ought to know better. I'll look him up when the season is over and shoot him."

Dipsey grinned happily. He was rather pleased with himself in spite of yesterday's loss. As third-base coach he'd been the loneliest man in the Western Hemisphere for seven straight days while the Pirates were being shut out without a man reaching third. Even if his team was losing, he liked to have some traffic to direct.

"You got nothing to lose but ball games," he said.

Zilo had taken his place in the batter's box. He cut on the first pitch, and the ball dribbled weakly out toward the pitcher's mound.

"He's a fly swatter," Dipsey said disgustedly.

Zilo poked two more lazy ground balls and lifted a pop fly to the third baseman. Apparently satisfied, he borrowed a glove and wandered out to left field. He dropped a couple of balls that were hit right at him and stumbled over his own feet when he tried to go a few steps to his left.

"It's a joke," Pops said. "Pete must have seen him catch one. That's what he meant by him being lucky."

Dipsey walked out to left field to talk with Zilo. He came back looking foolish. "The kid says it's all right—he's just testing the atmosphere. It'll be different when the game starts."

"He says he hit six forty," Pops said dreamily.

"You going to use him?"

"Sure I'll use him. If I'm gonna shoot Pete, I gotta have a reason that'll stand up in court. As soon as we get ten runs behind, in he goes."

Pops headed back toward the dugout, and some tourists in box seats raised a lusty chorus of boos as he passed. Pops scowled and quickened his pace. The dratted tourists were ruining the game. There had been a time when a manager could concentrate on what he was doing, but now he had to operate with a mob of howling spectators literally hanging over his shoulder and shouting advice and criticism into his ears. It got on the players' nerves, too. There was the Giants' Red Cowan, who'd been a good pitcher until they opened the games to tourists. The noise so rattled him that he had to retire.

"Why can't they stay home and see it on TV, like everybody else?" Pops growled.

"Because they pay money, that's why," Ed Schwartz said. "There's a novelty or something in seeing a ball game in the flesh, and it's getting so some of these tourists are planning their vacations so they can take in a few games. Bill Willard—the *L.A. Times* man—was saying that the National League now is California's number one tourist attraction. The American League is doing the same thing for Arizona."

The boos sounded again, and Pops ducked into the dugout out of sight. "I don't mind their watching," he said, "if only they'd keep their mouths shut. When I started managing there wasn't anyone around during a game except the TV men, and they were too busy to be giving me advice. Even the sportswriters watched on TV. Now they camp here the whole season, and you can't go out after the morning paper without finding one waiting for an interview."

"The tourists are here to stay, so you might as well get used to them,

Ed said. There's even some talk about putting up hotels for them, so they won't have to commute from Fresno to see the games."

Pops sat down and borrowed Ed's pen to make out his lineup. Ed looked over his shoulder and asked, "How come you're not using that new guy?"

"I'm saving him until we get far enough behind."

"You mean until the second inning?" Ed said, and ducked as Pops fired a catcher's mask.

"That's the trouble with those tenure laws," Pops said. "They had to go and include the club secretaries."

The game started off in a way sadly familiar to Pops. The Dodgers scored three runs in the first inning and threatened to blast the Pirates right out of the league. Then, with the bases loaded and one out, the Pirate's third baseman managed to hang onto a sizzling line drive and turn it into a double play. Pops's breathing spell lasted only until the next inning. Lefty Effinger, the Pirates' pitcher, spent a long afternoon falling out of one hole and into another. In nine innings he gave up a total of seventeen hits, but a miraculous succession of picked-off runners, overrun bases, and double plays kept the Dodgers shut out after those first three runs.

In the meantime, Dodger pitcher Rip Ruster was having one of his great days. He gave up a scratch single in the second and a walk in the fourth, and by the ninth inning he had fanned twelve, to the gratification of the hooting, jeering tourists.

The last of the ninth opened with Ruster striking out the first two Pirates on six pitches, and the Pirates in the dugout started sneaking off to the dressing room. Then first baseman Sam Lyle ducked away from an inside pitch that hit his bat and blooped over the infield for a single. Pops called for the hit and run, and the next batter bounced the ball at the Dodger shortstop. The shortstop threw it into right field, and the runners reached second and third. Ruster, pacing angrily about the mound, walked the next batter on four pitches.

Pops jumped from the dugout and called time. "Hit six forty, did he?" Pops muttered and yelled, "Zilo!"

The beaming Zilo jumped up from the far end of the bench. "Yes, sir?"

"Get out there and hit!"

"Yes Sir!"

He shuffled toward the plate, and the uproar sent up by the tourists rocked the grandstand. Dipsey Marlow called time again and hurried over to the dugout.

"You off you rocker? We got a chance to win this one. Get that thing out of there and use a left-hander."

"Look," Pops said, "You know derned well the way Ruster is pitching we're lucky to get a loud foul off of him. That hit was luck, and the error was luck, and the base on balls happened only because Ruster got mad. Now he'll cool off, and the only thing that keeps this going is more luck. Pete says the kid's lucky, and I want some of it."

Marlow turned on his heel and stalked back to the coaching box.

Ruster coiled up and shot a bullet at home plate. Zilo swatted at it awkwardly—and popped it up.

The second baseman backed up three steps, waved the rest of the infield away, and got ready to end the game. The base runners, running furiously with two out, came down the stretch from third in a mournful procession. Zilo loped along the base path watching the Dodger second baseman and the ball.

The ball reached the top of its arc and suddenly seemed to carry. The second baseman backed confidently into position, changed his mind, and backed up again. The ball continued to float toward the outfield. The second baseman turned and raced toward center field with his eyes on the misbehaving ball. The center fielder had been jogging toward the infield. Now he broke into a run. The second baseman leaped for the ball. The center fielder dove for it. Neither man touched it, and they went down in a heap as the ball bounced and frolicked away.

The lumbering Zilo crossed home plate before the startled right fielder could retrieve the ball. The Pirates had won, 4 to 3, and they hoisted Zilo to their shoulders and bore him off to the dressing room. The Dodgers quitted the field to an enthusiastic chorus of boos.

Pops went out to the third-base coaching box, where Dipsey Marlow still stood gazing vacantly toward the outfield.

"Luck," Pops said and gently led him away.

Rodney Wilks, the Pirates' brisk little president, flew over from L.A. that evening and threw a victory celebration in the ultramodern building that housed the National League offices. All of the players were there, and those who had families brought them. Women and children congregated in one room and the men in another. Champagne and milk shakes flowed freely in both rooms.

National League President Edgar Rysdale looked in on the party briefly but approvingly. A team in a slump was bad for all the teams—bad for the league. When the race was a good one, fans frequently paid a double TV fee, watching two games at once or, if they had only one set, switching back and forth. If one team was floundering, National League fans would watch only one game. They might even patronize the American League. So the victory pleased the league president and also the other owners, who stopped by to sample the champagne and talk shop with Wilks.

Fred Carter, the Dodger manager, also looked in on the party. Zilo's freak pop fly had ruined a nine-game winning streak for him, but he seemed more puzzled than mournful. He backed Pops into a corner and said with a grin, "I been watching pop flies for thirty-five years, and I never saw one act like that. Did the kid magnetize his bat, or something?"

Pops shrugged. "I been watching baseball forty-five years, and I see something new seven times a week."

"Just the same, the next time that kid comes up I'm passing out the butterfly nets. He don't look like much of a hitter. Where'd you get him?"

"Pete Holloway sent him out."

Carter arched his eyebrows. "He must have something, then."

"Pete says he ain't got a thing except luck."

"Isn't that enough? I'm going over to watch the Reds and Giants. Want to come?"

"Nope. Now that I finally won one, I'm gonna get some sleep tonight."

Pops saw Ed Schwartz talking with Zilo, and he went over to see what line the club secretary might be handing out. Ed was talking about the old days, and Zilo was listening intently, his dark eyes sparkling.

"Each team had its own city," Ed said, "and its own ballpark. Think of the waste involved. Eventually there were twenty-four teams in each league, which meant forty-eight ballparks, and even during the playing season they were in use only half the time, when the teams were playing at home. And the season only lasted six months. And there was all that traveling. We froze one day in Montreal and baked the next in New Orleans. Our hotel bill for the season used to look like the national debt, not to mention the plane fares. It was rough on the players in other ways. They only saw their families when they were playing at home, and just as they got settled somewhere they'd be traded and maybe have to move clear across the country—only to be traded again the next season or even the next week. Putting the entire league in one place solved everything. The climate is wonderful, and we almost never have a game postponed because of bad weather. We're down to eight teams in a league, which anyway is as many as the fans can keep track of. We have two fields, and they're used twice a day, for two afternoon and two night games. Each team has its own little community. Baseball, Cal is growing, boy, and lots of players are settling here permanently and buying their own homes. You'll want to, too. It's a wonderful place."

"It's a soft place for club secretaries," Pops growled. "Ed used to have to worry about baggage, plane schedules, hotel reservations, and a million and one other things. Now all he has to do is get the equipment moved a couple of hundred yards from one park to the other, now and then, and he gripes about it. Has he stopped talking long enough to get you settled?"

"Oh, yes, sir," Zilo said. "I'm rooming with Jerry Fargo."

"All right. Come out early tomorrow. You gotta learn to catch a fly ball without getting hit on the head."

Dipsey Marlow nudged Pops's arm and pulled him aside. "Going to play him tomorrow?"

"Might. We could use a little luck every day."

"I been listening to the big boys. Know what they're going to do? Put up a flock of temporary stands at World Series time. They think they might get fifteen thousand people out here for every game."

"That's their business," Pops said.

"Just tell me why anyone wants to take a trip and pay a stiff price to see a ball game when he can sit at home and see it for fifty cents?"

"People are funny," Pops said. "Sometimes they're almost as funny as ballplayers."

President Wilks came over and placed a full glass in Pops's hand. Pops sipped the champagne and grimaced. "It's all right, I guess, but it'll never take the place of beer."

"Finish in first division," Wilks said, "and I'll buy you enough beer to take you through the off season."

Pops grinned. "How about putting that in my contract?"

"I will," Wilks promised. "Do you want it in bottles or kegs?"

"Both."

"I'll take care of it first thing in the morning." He grinned and prodded Pops in the ribs, but behind the grin his expression was anxious. "Do you think we have a chance?"

"Too early to say. Sure, we only won one out of fifteen, but we're only ten games out of first. We been looking like a bunch of schoolkids, and if we keep that up we finish last. If we snap out of it—well, the season's got a long way to go."

"I hope you snap out of it," Wilks said. "Managers have tenure, but club presidents haven't."

Pops found a bottle of beer to kill the taste of the champagne, and he made a quiet exit after instructing Marlow to get the players home to bed at a reasonable hour. The National League's two playing fields were a blaze of light, and the shouts of the two crowds intermingled. There seemed to be a lot of tourists in attendance—and tourists at night games made even less sense than tourists at afternoon games. It'd be midnight before some of them got back to their hotels. Pops walked slowly back to Pirateville, grumbling to himself. The large mansion intended for the manager Pops had turned over to Dipsey Marlow, who needed the room for his eight kids. Pops lived in a small house a short distance down the street. His middle-aged daughter Marge kept house for him, and she was already in bed. She didn't like baseball.

*Priority Rating: Routine*
*From: Jard Killil, Minister of Juvenile Affairs*
*To: All Planetary Police Organizations. Sectors 1247; 2162; 889; 1719*
  *All Interplanetary Patrol Units, Sectors 1247; 2162; 889; 1719*
*Subject: Juvenile Detention Escapee Muko Zilo*
*Reference: Previous memorandum of 13B927D8 and enclosures*
  *Information from several sources indicates that an unidentified ship, possibly that of Escapee Zilo, traveled on a course roughly parallel to Trade Route 79B, which would take it into or through your sectors. Because of the time elapsed since his escape, it is assumed that Zilo has found an effective planetary hiding place. Immediate investigation requested. Escapee is not—repeat—not dangerous.*
  *Kindly notify Philoy JRC immediately upon detention.*

Pops opened a three-game series against the Cubs with Zilo in left field. He figured the youngster would do the least damage there, since he was pitching Simp Simpson, his best right-hander, and the Cubs had seven left-handed batters in their lineup. At least that much of his strategy worked. In the first six innings only two balls were hit to left. One was a line drive single that Zilo bobbled for an error as the runner reached second. The other was a foul fly on which Zilo seemed about to make a miraculous catch until his feet got tangled and spilled him. At the plate he waved his bat futilely and struck out twice while the Cubs were taking a five-run lead.

In the last of the sixth the Pirates got men on first and second. It was Zilo's turn to bat. Dipsey Marlow called time, and as the tourists hooted impatiently he strode to the dugout. "Take him out," he said.

"Why?" Pops asked. "He's still batting .333. That's better than the rest of these dopes."

"You gotta understand this luck thing. Yesterday it was luck to put him in. Today it's luck to take him out. I found a spider in my locker today, and that means—"

"Hit and run on the first pitch," Pops said.

Zilo fanned the air lustily and dribbled a grounder toward the first baseman. Suddenly it took an unaccountable eight-foot bounce over his head and rolled into the outfield, picking up speed. Zilo pulled up at first, breathing heavily, and the two runners scored.

Sam Lyle followed with a lazy fly ball to right. Zilo moved off first base and halted to watch the progress of the ball. The right fielder seemed to be having difficulties. He wandered about shading his eyes, backed up, and finally lost the ball in the sun. The center fielder had come over fast, and he shouted the right fielder away, backed up slowly, and finally turned in disgust to watch the ball drop over the fence. Lyle trailed the floundering Zilo around the bases, and the Pirates trailed by a run, 5 to 4.

Three fast outs later, Dipsey Marlow returned to the dugout and squeezed in beside Pops. "I take it all back," he said. "I won't argue with you again the rest of the season. But this spider of mine—"

Pops cupped his hands and shouted. "Let's HOLD 'em now. Let's WIN this one!"

"—this spider of mine was in my sweat shirt, and my old mother always used to say spider in your clothes means money. Will the players get a cut of what those fifteen thousand tourists pay to watch a Series game?"

"The World Series is still a couple of hundred games away," Pops said. "Let's worry about it later. Get to work and pick us off a sign or two."

In the eighth inning, Zilo got a rally started with a pop fly that three infielders chased futilely. He moved to second on a ground ball that took a bad hop and he scored on a soft line drive that curved sharply and landed between the outfielders. The Pirates pushed over two more runs on hits that were equally implausible and took a two-run lead into the ninth.

The Cubs came back with a vengeance. The first two batters lashed out sizzling singles. Pops prodded his bullpen into action and went out to talk with Simpson. They stood looking down at the next Cub batter, the burly catcher Bugs Rice.

"Don't let him pull one," Pops said.

"He won't pull one," Simp said derterminedly through clenched teeth.

Rice did not pull one. He didn't have to. He unloaded on the first pitch and drove it far, far away into left field, the opposite field. Pops sat down with the crack of the bat and covered his face with his hands.

"Now we gotta come from behind again," he moaned. "And we won't. I know we ain't *that* lucky."

Suddenly the men on the bench broke into excited cheers, and a scattering of applause came from the tourists. Pops looked up, saw runners on second and third, saw the scoreboard registering one out.

"What happened?" he yelped.

"Zilo caught it," Dipsey Marlow said. "Didn't think he had it in him, but he backed up to the fence and made a clean catch. Took so much time getting the ball back to the infield that the runners had time to touch up and advance, but he caught it."

"He didn't. I heard it hit the bat, and I saw it go. It should have cleared the fence by twenty feet."

"Your eyes and ears aren't as young as they used to be. Zilo caught it against the fence."

Pops shook his head. He huddled down in a corner of the dugout while Simpson fanned one batter and got another on a tap to the infield, and the Pirates had won two in a row.

That was the beginning. The Pirates pushed their winning streak to twelve, lost one, won eight more. They were twenty and fifteen and in fourth place. Zilo became a national sensation. Lucky Zilo Fan Clubs sprang up across the country, and he kept his batting average around the .450 mark and even got another home run when a solid fly ball to the outfield took crazy bounces in nineteen directions while Zilo lumbered around the bases. The rest of the team took courage and started playing baseball.

But not even a lucky Zilo could lift the Pirates above fourth place. Pops's pitching staff was a haphazard assortment of aching, overage veterans and unpredictable, inexperienced youths. One day they would be unhittable; the next day they'd be massacred, and Pops found to his sorrow that luck was no answer to a nineteen-run deficit. Still, the season drifted along with the Pirates holding desperately to fourth, and Pops began to think they might even stay there.

Then Zilo sprained his ankle. The trainer outfitted him with crutches and applied every known remedy and a few unknown ones that Zilo suggested, but the ankle failed to respond.

"It beats me," the trainer said to Pops. "Things that should make it better seem to make it worse."

"How long will he be out?" Pops asked gloomily.

"I won't even guess. The way it's reacting, it could last him a lifetime."

Pops breathed a profane farewell to first division.

Zilo hobbled to every game on his crutches and watched with silent concentration from a box behind the dugout. Oddly enough, for a time the team's luck continued. Ground balls took freakish bounces, fly balls responded to unlikely air currents, and on some days opposition pitchers suffered such a loss of control that they would occasionally wander in and stare at home plate, as though to assure themselves that it was still there. Ollie Richards, the Reds' ace and one of the best control pitchers in either league, walked seventeen batters in three innings and left the game on the short end of a 6 to 3 score without having given up a hit.

Zilo's good-natured, freckled face took on an unhealthy pallor. Wrinkles furrowed his brow and his eyes held a tense, haunted look. As the team's luck began to fade, he grew increasingly irritable and despondent. On the day they slipped to fifth place, he met Pops after the game and asked, "Could I speak with you, sir?"

"Sure," Pops said. "Come along."

Pops held the door as Zilo swung through on his crutches. He got the youngster seated and then he settled back with his own feet propped up on his desk. "Ankle any better?"

"I'm afraid not, sir."

"Takes time, sometimes."

"Sir," Zilo said, "I know I'm not a good ballplayer. Like they say, I'm just lucky. Maybe this will be the last season I'll play."

"I wouldn't say that," Pops said. "You're young, and luck has took a lot of men a long way in baseball."

"Anyway, sir, I like to play, even if I'm not good. And I'd like to have us win the pennant and play in the World Series."

"Wouldn't mind having another winner myself before I retire."

"What I'd like to do, sir, is go home for a while. I think I could get my ankle fixed up there, and I'd like to bring back some friends who could help us."

Pops was amused. "Ballplayers?"

"I think they'd be better than I am, sir. Or luckier, maybe. Do you—would you give them a trial?"

"I'd give anybody a tryout," Pops said seriously. "Especially shortstops and second basemen and pitchers, but I'd have a look at anybody."

Zilo pushed himself erect on his crutches. "I'll get back as soon as I can."

"All right. But leave a little of that luck here, will you?"

Zilo turned and looked at Pops strangely. "I wish I could, sir. I really wish I could."

Ed Schwartz took Zilo to L.A. and put him on a plane for the East. For Maine. And at Baseball, Cal, the Pirates won two more games and went into a cataclysmic slump. They lost ten straight and slipped to sixth place. Pops put through a phone call to the Maine address Zilo had given him and was informed that there was no such place. Then he called Pete Holloway.

"I wondered what was happening to you," Pete said. "I haven't seen the kid. He dropped out of nowhere last summer and played a little sand-lot ball for me. He never told me where he came from, but I don't think it was Maine. If he shows up again, I'll get in touch with you."

"Thanks," Pops said. He hung up slowly.

Ed Schwartz said thoughtfully, "I suppose I better get a detective on it."

"Detectives," Pops said and wearily headed for the field and another shellacking.

Two more weeks went by. The detectives traced Zilo to Maine, where he seemed to have vanished from the ken of mortal man. The Pirates were tottering on the brink of last place.

Then Pops received an airmail letter from Zilo—from Brazil.

"I got lost," he wrote plaintively. "We crashed in the jungle and they won't let us leave the country."

Pops called President Wilks into conference, and Wilks got on the phone to Washington. He knew enough of the right people to make the necessary arrangements and keep the matter out of the papers. Zilo was flown back on a chartered plane, and he brought four friends with him.

Ed Schwartz met them in L.A. and rushed them out to Baseball, Cal, in President Wilks's own plane. They arrived during the fourth inning of another Pirate beating.

"How's the ankle?" Pops demanded.

Zilo beamed. "Just fine, sir."

"Get in there, then."

Zilo got his friends seated in the president's box and then he went out to loft a long fly ball over the fence for a home run. The Pirates came to life. Everyone hit, and a 10 to 0 drubbing was transformed like magic into a 25 to 12 victory.

After the game Zilo introduced his friends. They were John Smith, Sam Jones, Robert White, and William Anderson. Smith and Jones, Zilo said, were infielders. White and Anderson were pitchers.

Ed Schwartz took in their proportions with a groan and went to work on the uniform problem. They were built like Zilo but on a much more lavish scale. They towered over Pops, answered his questions politely, and showed a childlike interest in all that went on about them.

Pops called one of his catchers over and introduced him to White and Anderson. "See what they got," he said. The catcher led them away, and Pops took Smith and Jones out for infield practice. He watched goggle-eyed as they covered ground like jet-propelled gazelles and made breathtaking leaps to pull down line drives.

The catcher returned, drew Pops aside, and said awesomely, "They got curves that break three feet. They got sliders that do a little loop-the-loop and cross the plate twice. They got fastballs that I'm scared to catch.

LLOYD BIGGLE, JR.

They got pitches that change speed four times between the mound and the plate. If you're figuring on pitching those guys, you can get yourself another catcher."

Pops turned the ceremony of signing them over to Ed Schwartz, handed releases to four players who weren't worth the space they were taking up on the bench, and went home to his first good night's sleep in more than a month.

*Priority Rating: Urgent*
*From: Jard Killil, Minister of Juvenile Affairs*
*To: All Planetary Police Organizations*
    *All Interplanetary Patrol Units*
*Subject: Juvenile detention escapees*
*Enclosures: Character analyses, film strips, retinal patterns*
   *All law enforcement agencies are hereby informed of the escape of four inmates of the Juvenile Rehabilitation Center on Philoy, Raff III, Sector 1311. Escapees have high psi ratings and may use them dangerously. Kindly give this matter top priority attention and notify Philoy JRC immediately upon detention.*

The next day Pops started Anderson against the Braves. The Pirates bounced forty hits over and through and around the infield and scored thirty-five runs. Anderson pitched a no-hit game and struck out twenty-seven. White duplicated the performance the following day. Thereafter Pops pitched them in his regular rotation. He wasn't sure whether they hypnotized everyone in the park or just the ball, but as Dipsey Marlow put it, they made the ball do everything but stop and back up.

Pops's other pitchers suddenly looked like champions with Smith and Jones playing behind them. In spite of their boxlike builds, they ranged about the infield with the agility of jack rabbits. No one ever measured exactly how high they went up after line drives, but one sportswriter claimed they were a hazard to air traffic and should be licensed as aircraft. They sped far into the outfield after fly balls. Jones made more catches in right field than the right fielder, and it was not an unusual sight to see Jones and Smith far out in center contesting the right to a descending ball while the center fielder beat a hasty retreat. And both men swung murderous bats.

The Pirates had won fifty-seven games in a row and rewritten the record book when Zilo timidly knocked on the door of Pops's office. He was carrying a newspaper, and he looked disturbed.

"Sir," he said anxiously, "it says here that we're ruining baseball."

Pops chuckled. "They always say that when one team starts to pull away."

"But—is it true?"

"Well, now. If we kept on winning the way we are now, that won't do the game any good. People like to see a close race, and if one team wins too much, or loses too much, a lot of people stop watching the games. But don't let it worry you. We'll do our best to go on winning, but we'll drop a few, one of these days, and things will be back to normal. Your friends been playing over their heads and we've been luckier than usual."

"I see," Zilo said thoughtfully.

That evening Pops ruefully wished he'd kept his big mouth shut. Talk about jinxing a winning streak!

Anderson got knocked out in the first inning and lost his first game. White failed the next day, and the Pirates dropped five straight. Then they got off on another winning streak, but the talk about their ruining the game had quieted down. Pops never bothered to remind Zilo about how right he'd been. He wasn't going to jinx the team again.

"Those baseball players of yours," his daughter said to him one evening. "You know—the funny-looking ones."

"Sure, I know," Pops dead-panned. "What about 'em?"

"They're supposed to be pretty good, aren't they?"

Pops grinned wickedly. "Pretty fair." It would have been a waste of time referring Marge to what was left of the record book.

"I was over at the bowling alley with Ruth Wavel, and they were there bowling. They had everybody excited."

"How'd they do?"

"I guess they must be pretty good at that, too. They knocked all the pins over."

Pops grinned again. Marge's idea of a sport was crossword puzzles, and she could go through an entire season without seeing a single game. "Nothing unusual about that," he said. "Happens all the time."

She seemed surprised. "Does it? The people there thought it was something special."

"Someone was pulling your leg. How many strikes did they get?"

"How many what?"

"How many times did they knock all the pins down?"

"They knocked all of them down every time. All evening. It was the first time they'd ever bowled, too."

"Natural athletic ability," Pops muttered. They'd never played baseball before, either, except that Zilo had coached them a little. The more he thought about it, the odder it seemed, but he wasn't one to argue with no-hit games and home runs and sensational fielding plays.

"What'd you say?" Marge asked.

"Never look a gift ballplayer in the mouth," Pops said and went to bed.

*To all ships of the space navy sectors 2161, 2162, 2163. General Alert. Five escapees Juvenile Rehabilitation Center Philoy Raff III piloting stolen space yacht Stellar Class II range unlimited have been traced through Sector 2162. Destination unsurveyed quadrant C97. Contact base headquarters Sector 2162 for patrol assignments. Acknowledge. Zan First Admiral.*

The pennant race leveled into a five-team contest for first place. The Pirates stayed in first or second, playing sometimes with unbelievable brilliance and sometimes with incredible ineptitude. Pops took the race stoically and tried to ignore the tourist hysteria that enveloped Baseball, Cal. He was doing so much better than anyone expected—so much better than he had thought possible even in his wildest moments of pre-season optimism—that it really didn't matter where he finished. He was a cinch to be Manager of the Year. He might add a pennant and a World Series, or he might not. It didn't matter.

Another season might see him in last place again, and a smart manager went out as a winner—especially a smart manager who was well along in his sixties. Pops called a news conference and announced his retirement at the end of the season.

"Before or after the World Series?" a reporter asked.

"No comment," Pops said.

The club owners erected their World Series stands early, and the tourists jammed them—fifteen thousand for every game. Pops wondered where they came from. National League President Rysdale wandered about smiling fondly over the daily television receipts, and President Wilks sent Pops a load of beer that filled his basement.

Over in Baseball, Arizona, the American League officials were glum. The Yankees, who were mainly distinguished for having finished last more frequently than any other team in major-league history, had suddenly and inexplicably opened up a twenty-game lead, and nobody cared any longer what happened in the American League.

"Three weeks to go," Pops told his team. "What d'ya say we wrap this thing up?"

"Right!" Zilo said happily.

"Right!" Smith, Jones, Anderson, and White chorused.

The Pirates started another winning streak.

*To all ships of the Space Navy patroling unsurveyed quadrant C97. Prepare landing parties for planetary search. This message your authorization to investigate any planet with civilization at level 10 or below. Contact with civilizations higher than level 10 forbidden. Space intelligence agents will be furnished each ship to handle high-civilization planets. Acknowledge. Zan First Admiral.*

The last week of the season opened with the Pirates in first place, two games ahead of the Dodgers. A provident schedule put the Dodgers and Pirates in a three-game series. The league hastily erected more stands, and with twenty-two thousand howling tourists in attendance and half of Earth's population watching on TV, White and Anderson put together no-hit games and the Pirate batters demolished the Dodger pitching staff. The Pirates took all three games.

Pops felt enormously tired and relieved that it was finished. He had won his pennant and he didn't see how he could lose the World Series. But he had never felt so old.

President Wilks threw another champagne party, and the sportswriters backed Pops into a corner and fired questions.

"How about that retirement, Pops? Still going through with it?"

"I've gone through with it."

"Is it true that Dipsey Marlow will take your place?"

"That's up to the front office. They ain't asked my opinion."

"What if they did ask your opinion?"

"I'd faint."

"Who'll start the series? Anderson or White?"

"I'll flip a coin," Pops said. "It don't matter. Either of them could pitch all thirteen games and not feel it."

"Does that mean you'll go all the way with just Anderson and White?"

"I'll use four starters, like I have most of the season."

"Going to give the Yankees a sporting chance, eh?"

"No comment," Pops said.

President Wilks and League President Rysdale rescued him from the reporters and took him to Rysdale's private office.

"We have a proposal from the American League," Rysdale said. "We'd like to know what you think of it and what you think the players would think of it. They want to split up the Series and play part of the games here and part of them in Arizona. They think it would stir up more local interest."

"I wouldn't like it," Pops said. "What's wrong with the way it is now? Here one year, there the next year, it's fair to both sides. What do they want to do—travel back and forth between games?"

"We'd start out with four games here, and then play five in Arizona and the last four back here. Next year we'd start out with four in Arizona. It used to be done that way years ago."

"One ballpark is just like another," Pops said. "Why travel back and forth?"

"They think we would draw more tourists that way. As far as we're concerned, we're drawing capacity crowds now. It might make a difference in Arizona, because there are fewer population centers there."

"They suggested it because it's in Califorina this year," Pops said. "Next year they'd want to change back."

"That's a thought," Rysdale said. "I'll tell them it's too late to make the change this year, but we might consider it for next year. That'll give us time to figure all the angles."

"For all I care, you can play in Brazil next year," Pops told him.

In the hallway, Pops encountered half a dozen of his players crowding around infielder Jones. "What's up?" he asked Dipsey Marlow.

"Just some horsing around. They were practicing high jumps, and Jones cleared three meters."

"So?"

"That's a world record by almost half a meter. I looked it up."

*To Jard Killil, Minister of Juvenile Affairs. Spaceship presumed that of JRC escapees found in jungle unsurveyed. Quadrant C97 planet has type 17D civilization. Intelligence agents call situation critical. Am taking no action pending receipt further instructions. Requesting Ministry take charge and assume responsibility. Zan First Admiral.*

Pops retired early the night before the Series opened. He ordered his players to do the same. Marge was out somewhere. Pops hadn't gone to sleep, but he was relaxing comfortably when she came in an hour later.

She marched straight through the house and into his bedroom. "Those ballplayers of yours—the funny-looking ones—they were at the bowling alley."

Pops took a deep breath. "They were?"

"They'd been drinking!"

Pops sat up and reached for his shoes. "You don't say."

"And they were bowling, only—they weren't bowling. They'd pretend to throw the ball but they wouldn't throw it, and the pins would fall down anyway. The manager was mad."

"No doubt," Pops said, pulling on his trousers.

LLOYD BIGGLE, JR.

"They wouldn't tell anyone how they did it, but every time they waved the ball all the pins would fall down. They'd been drinking."

"Maybe that's how they did it," Pops said, slipping into his shirt.

"How?"

"By drinking."

He headed for the bowling alley at a dead run. The place was crowded with players from other teams, American and National League, and quite a few sportswriters were around. The writers headed for Pops, and he shoved them aside and found the manager. "Who was it?" he demanded.

"Those four squares of yours. Jones, Smith, Anderson, White."

"Zilo?"

"No. Zilo wasn't here."

"Did they make trouble?"

"Not the way you mean. They didn't get rough, though I had a time getting them away from the alleys. They left maybe ten minutes ago."

"Thanks," Pops said.

"When you find them, ask them how they pulled that gag with the pins. They were too drunk to tell me."

"I got some other things to ask them," Pops said.

He pushed his way through the crowd to a phone booth and called Ed Schwartz.

"I'll take care of it," Ed said. "Don't you worry about a thing."

"Sure. I won't worry about a thing."

"They may be back at their rooms by now, but we won't take any chances. I'll handle it."

"I'll meet you there," Pops said.

He slipped out a side door and headed for Bachelor's Paradise, the house where the unmarried Pirates lived with a couple of solicitous houseboys to look after them. All the players were in bed—except Smith, Jones, Anderson, White, and Zilo. The others knew nothing about them except that Zilo had been concerned about his friends and gone looking for them.

"You go home," Ed said. "I'll find them."

346

Pops paced grimly back and forth, taking an occasional kick at the furniture. "You find them," he said, "and I'll fine them."

He went home to bed, but he did not sleep. Twice during the night he called Ed Schwartz, and Ed was out. Pops finally reached him at breakfast-time, and Ed said, trying to be cheerful, "No news is supposed to be good news, and that's what I have. No news. I couldn't find a trace of them."

The reporters had picked up the story, and their headlines mocked Pops over his coffee. "PIRATE STARS MISSING!"

Ed Schwartz had notified both President Wilks and President Rysdale, and the league president had called in the FBI. By ten o'clock, police in every city in the country and a number of cities in other countries were looking for the missing Pirates, but they remained missing.

When Pops reached the field for a late-morning workout, there still was no word. He banned newsmen from the field and dressing room, told Lefty Effinger he might have to start, and went around trying to cheer up his players. The players remembered only too vividly their fourteen-game losing streak at the beginning of the season and the collapse that followed Zilo's departure. Gloom hung so thickly in the dugout that Pops wished he could think of a market for it. He could have bottled and sold it.

An hour before game time, Pops was called to the telephone. It was Ed Schwartz, calling from L.A. "I found them," he said. "They're on their way back. They'll be there in plenty of time."

"Good," Pops said.

"Bad. They're still pretty high—all except Zilo. I don't know if you can use them, but that's your problem."

Pops slammed down the phone.

"Did they find 'em?" Dipsey Marlow asked.

"Found 'em dead drunk."

Marlow rubbed his hands together. "Just let me at 'em. Ten minutes, that's all I ask. I'll have 'em dead sober."

"I dunno," Pops said. "These guys may not react the way you'd expect."

The delinquent players were delivered with time to spare, and Marlow went to work enthusiastically. He started by shoving them into a cold shower, fully dressed. Zilo stood looking on anxiously.

"I'm sorry," he said to Pops. "I'd have stopped them, but they went off without me. And they never had any of that alcohol before and they didn't know what it would do to them."

"That's all right," Pops said. "It wasn't your fault."

Zilo had tears in his eyes. "Do you think they can play?"

"Leave 'em to me," Marlow said. "I'm just getting started." But when he emerged later, he looked both confused and frustrated. "I just don't know," he said. "They tell me they're all right, and they look all right, but I think they're still drunk."

"Can they play?" Pops demanded.

"They can walk a straight line. I won't say how long a straight line. I suppose you got nothing to lose by playing them."

"There ain't much else I can do," Pops said. "I could start Effinger, but what would I use for infielders?"

Even Pops, who had seen every World Series for forty-five years as player, manager, or spectator, had to admit that the winter classic had its own unique flavor of excitement. He felt a thrill and a clutching emptiness in his stomach as he moved to the top step of the dugout and looked out across the sunlit field. Along both foul lines, the temporary stands were jammed with tourists. Beyond them, areas were roped off for standees, and the last tickets for standing room had been sold hours before. There was no space left of any kind.

Ed Schwartz stood at Pops's elbow looking at the crowd. "What is it that's different about a submarine sandwich when you buy it at the ballpark?" he asked.

"Ptomaine," Pops growled.

Clutching his lineup card, he strode toward home plate to meet the umpires and Yankee manager Bert Basom.

Basom grinned maliciously. "Your men well rested? I hear they keep late hours."

"They're rested well enough," Pops said.

A few minutes later, with the national anthem played and the flag raised, Pops watched critically as Anderson took his last warmup pitches. He threw lazily, as he always did, and if he was feeling any after effects it wasn't evident to Pops.

But Anderson got off to a shaky start. The Yankees' leadoff man clouted a tremendous drive to left, but Zilo made one of his sensational, lumbering catches. The second batter drove one through the box. Jones started after it, got his feet tangled, and fell headlong. Smith flashed over with unbelievable speed, gloved the ball, and threw to first—too late. Anderson settled down, then, and struck out the next two batters.

Zilo opened the Pirates' half of the first with one of his lucky hits, and Smith followed him with a lazy fly ball that cleared the fence. The Pirates led, 2 to 0.

The first pitch to Jones was a called strike. Jones whirled on the umpire, his large face livid with rage. His voice carried over the noise of the crowd. "You wouldn't know a strike zone if I measured it out for you!"

Pops started for home plate, and Jones saw him coming and meekly took his place in the box. Pops called time and went over to talk to Dipsey Marlow.

"Darned if I don't think he's still tight. Maybe I should lift him."

"Let him bat," Dipsey said. "Maybe he'll connect."

The pitcher wasted one and followed it with a curve that cut the outside corner. "Strike two!" the umpire called.

Jones's outraged bellow rattled the center-field fence. "What?" he shrieked. He stepped around the catcher and stood towering over the umpire. "Where's the strike zone? Where was the pitch?"

The umpire gestured impatiently to show where the ball had crossed the plate. Pops started out of the dugout again. The umpire said brusquely, "Play ball!"

Still fuming, Jones moved back to the batter's box. His high pitched voice carried clearly. "You don't even know where the strike zone is!"

The pitcher wound up again, and as the ball sped plateward Jones suddenly leaped into the air—and stayed there. He hovered six feet above the ground. The ball crossed the plate far below his dangling legs, was missed completely by the startled catcher, and bounced to the screen.

The umpire did not call the pitch. He took two steps forward and stood looking up at Jones. The crowd came to its feet, and players from both teams edged from their dugouts. A sudden, paralyzed hush gripped the field.

"Come down here!" the umpire called angrily.

"What'd you call that pitch? Strike, I suppose. Over the plate between my knees and armpits, I suppose."

"Come down here!"

"You can't make me."

"Come down here!"

"You show me where it says in the rules that I have to bat with both feet on the ground!"

The umpire moved down the third-base line and summoned his colleagues for a conference. Pops walked out to home plate, and Zilo followed him.

"Jones," Zilo said pleadingly.

"Go to hell," Jones snarled. "I know I'm right. I'm still in the batter's box."

"Please," Zilo pleaded. "You'll spoil everything. You've already spoiled everything."

"So what? It's time we showed them how this game should be played."

"I'm taking you out, Jones," Pops said. "I'm putting in a pinch hitter. Get back to the dugout."

Jones shot up another four feet. "You can't make me."

The umpire returned. "I'm putting you out of the game," he said. "Leave the field immediately."

"I've already left the field."

Pops, Zilo, and the umpire stood glaring up at Jones, who glared down at them. Into that impasse came Smith, who walked slowly to home plate, soared over the heads of those on the ground, and clouted Jones on the jaw. Jones descended heavily. Smith landed nearby, calmly drying his hands on his trousers.

Effective as his performance was, nobody noticed it. All eyes were on the sky, where a glistening tower of metal was dropping slowly toward the outfield. It came ponderously to rest on the outfield grass while the outfielders fled in panic. The crowd remained silent.

A port opened in the tower's side, and a landing ramp came down. The solitary figure that emerged did not use it. He stepped out into midair and drifted slowly toward the congregation at home plate. There he landed, a tremendous figure, square like Zilo and his friends but a startling nine feet tall and trimly uniformed in a lustrous brown with ribbons and braid in abundance.

Zilo, Jones, and Smith stood with downcast eyes while the others stared. Anderson and White moved from the dugout and walked forward haltingly. The stranger spoke one crisp sentence that no one understood—except Zilo, Jones, Smith, Anderson, and White.

Smith and Jones lifted slowly and floated out to the ship, where they disappeared through the port. Anderson and White turned obediently and trudged to the outfield to mount the ramp. Only Zilo lingered.

A few policemen moved nervously from the stands and surrounded the ship. The hush continued as the tourists stared and half of Earth's population watched on TV.

Zilo turned to face Pops. Tears streaked his face. "I'm sorry, Pops," he said. "I hoped we could finish it off for you. I really wanted to win this World Series. But I'm afraid we've got to go."

"Go where?" Pops asked.

"Where we came from. It's another world."

"I see. Then—then that's how come you guys played so well."

Zilo blubbered miserably, trying to wipe his eyes. His good-natured, freckled face looked tormented. "The others did," he sobbed. "I'm only a Class F telekinetic myself, and that isn't much where I come from. I did the best I could, but it was a terrible strain keeping the balls I hit away from the fielders and stopping balls from going over the fence and holding balls up until I could catch them. When I hurt my ankle I tried to help out from the bench, and it worked for a while. Sometimes I could even control the ball enough to spoil a pitcher's control, but usually when the ball was thrown fast or hit hard I couldn't do anything with it unless I was in the outfield and it had a long way to go. So I went home where I could get my ankle fixed, and when I came back I brought the others. They're really good—all of them Class A. Anderson and White—those are just names I had them use—they could control the ball so well they made it look like they were pitching. And no matter how hard the ball was hit, they could control it, even when they were sitting on the bench."

Pops scratched his head and said dazedly, "Made it look like they were pitching?"

"They just pretended to throw, and then they controlled the ball—well, with their minds. Any good telekinetic could do it. They could have pitched just as well sitting on the bench as they did on the pitcher's mound, and they could help out when one of our other pitchers was pitching. And Smith and Jones are levitators. They could cover the ground real fast and go up as high as they wanted to. I had a terrible time keeping them from going too high and spoiling everything. I was going to bring a telepath, too, to steal signs and things, but those four were the only ones who'd come. But we did pretty good anyway. When we hit the ball, Anderson and White could make it go anywhere they wanted, and they could control the balls the other team hit, and nothing could get past Smith and Jones unless we wanted it to. We could have won every game, but the papers said we were spoiling baseball, so we talked it over and decided to lose part of the time. We did the best we could. We won the pennant, and I hoped we could win this World Series, but they had to go and drink some of that alcohol, and I guess Jones would have spoiled everything even if we hadn't been caught."

The stranger spoke another crisp sentence, and Zilo wiped the tears from his face and shook Pops's hand. "Good-bye, Pops," he said. "Thanks for everything. It was lots of fun. I really like this baseball."

He walked slowly out to the ship, passing the police without a glance, and climbed the ramp.

Reporters were edging out onto the field, and the stranger waved them back and spoke English in a booming voice. "You shall have a complete explanation at the proper time. It is now my most unpleasant duty to call upon your nation's President to deliver the apologies of my government. Muko Zilo says he did the best he could. He did entirely too much."

He floated back to the ship. The ramp lifted, and the police scattered as the ship swished upward. The umpire-in-chief shrugged his shoulders and gestured with his mask. "Play ball!"

Pops beckoned to a pinch hitter, got a pitcher warming up to replace Anderson, and strode back to the dugout. "They been calling me a genius," he muttered to himself. "Manager of the Year, they been calling me. And how could I lose?"

A sportswriter leaned down from the stands. "How about a statement, Pops?"

Pops spoke firmly. "You can say that the best decision I made this year was to resign."

An official statement was handed out in Washington before the game was over. That the Yankees won the game, 23 to 2, was irrelevant. By that time, even the players had lost interest.

*Priority Rating: Routine*
*From: Jard Killil, Minister of Juvenile Affairs*
*To: Milz Woon, Minister of Justice*
*Subject: Escapees from the Juvenile Rehabilitation Center, Philoy, Raff III, Sector 1311.*

*A full report on the activity of these escapees no doubt has reached your desk. The consequences of their offense are so serious they have not yet been fully evaluated. Not only have these escapees forced us into premature contact with a Type 17D civilization for which neither we nor they were prepared, but our best estimate is that the escapees have destroyed a notable cultural institution of that civilization. I believe that their ages should not be used to mitigate their punishment. They are juveniles, but they nevertheless are old enough to know right from wrong, and their only motive seems to be that they were enjoying themselves. I favor a maximum penalty.*

Baseball, as students of the game never tired of pointing out, was essentially a game of records and statistics. The records were there for all to see—incredible records, with Jones and Smith tied with 272 home runs and batting above .500, with Anderson and White each hurling two dozen no-hit games, and with the strikeouts, and the extra-base hits, and the double plays, and the games won, and the total bases, and the runs batted in, and the multitudinous individual and team records that the Pirates had marked up during the season. The record book was permanently maimed.

Who had done this? Four kids, four rather naughty kids, who—according to the strange man from outer space—were not especially bright. And these four kids had entered into a game requiring the ultimate in skill and intelligence and training and practice, entered into it without ever playing it before, and made the best adult ballplayers the planet Earth could produce look like a bunch of inept Little Leaguers.

The records could be thrown out, but they could not be forgotten. And it could not be forgotten that the four kids had made those records when they weren't half trying—because they didn't want to make Earth's ballplayers look too bad. No one cared to consider what would have happened had the people from outer space sent a team made up of intelligent adults.

The Yankees took the World Series in seven straight games, and few people cared. The stands were empty, and so sparse was the TV audience that the Series ended as a financial catastrophe. A committee met to decide what to do about the aliens' records and reached no decision. Again, no one cared.

The baseball establishment, fussing futilely with long-range plans to correct the damage, suddenly realized that the awards for the Most Valuable Players and Managers of the Year and the various individual championships had not been made. The oversight was not protested. People had other things on their minds.

And when a dozen TV comedy teams simultaneously resurrected an ancient, half-legendary, half-forgotten comedy sketch, they got no laughs whatsoever. The sketch was called "Who's on First?"

*Stuart Dybeck grew up in Chicago and teaches at Western Michigan University. He is the author of a book of poetry,* Brass Knuckles *(1979) and a novel,* Childhood and Other Neighborhoods *(1980). "Death of a Right Fielder" was published in* Harper's *magazine and is included in a book of Dybeck's short stories called* The Coast of Chicago. *His story is reminiscent of A. E. Houseman's poem "To an Athlete Dying Young."*

*Stuart Dybeck*

# DEATH OF A RIGHT FIELDER (1990)

**A**FTER TOO MANY BALLS WENT out and never came back, we went out to check. It was a long walk—he always played deep. Finally we saw him; from a distance he resembled the towel we sometimes threw down for second base.

It was hard to tell how long he'd been lying there, sprawled on his face. Had he been playing infield, his presence, or lack of it, would of course have been noticed immediately. The infield demands communication—the constant, reassuring chatter of team play. But he was remote, clearly an outfielder. The infield is for wisecrackers, pepper pots, gum-poppers; the outfield is for loners, onlookers, brooders who would rather study clover and swat gnats than holler. People could pretty much be divided between infielders and outfielders. Not that one always has a choice. He didn't necessarily choose right field so much as accept it.

There were several theories as to what killed him. From the start, the most popular was that he'd been shot. Perhaps from a passing car, possibly by that gang calling themselves the Jokers, who played sixteen-inch softball in the center of the housing project on the concrete diamond with painted bases, or by the Latin Lords, who didn't play sports, period. Or maybe some pervert with a telescopic sight, shooting from a bedroom window, or a mad sniper from a water tower, or a terrorist with a silencer from the expressway overpass, or maybe it was an accident, a stray slug from a robbery, or shoot-out, or assassination attempt miles away.

No matter who pulled the trigger, it seemed more plausible to ascribe his death to a bullet than to natural causes like, say, a heart attack. Young deaths are never natural; they're all violent. Not that kids don't die of heart attacks. But he never seemed the type. Sure, he was quiet, but not the quiet of someone always listening for the heart murmur his parents repeatedly warned him about since he was old enough to play. Nor could it have been leukemia. He wasn't a talented enough athlete to die of that. He'd have been playing center, not right, if leukemia was going to get him.

The shooting theory was better, even though there wasn't a mark on him. Couldn't it have been, as some argued, a high-powered bullet traveling with such velocity that its hole fused behind it? Still, not everyone was satisfied. Other theories were formulated, rumors became legends over the years: He'd had an allergic reaction to a bee sting; been struck by a single bolt of lightning from a freak, instantaneous electrical storm; ingested too strong a dose of insecticide from the grass blades he chewed; or sonic waves, radiation, pollution, etc. And a few of us like to think it was simply that, chasing a sinking liner, diving to make a shoestring catch, he broke his neck.

There was a ball in the webbing of his mitt when we turned him over.

His mitt had been pinned under his body and was coated with an almost luminescent gray film. The same gray was on his black high-top gym shoes, as if he'd been running through lime, and it was on the bill of his baseball cap—the blue felt one with the red C that he always denied stood for the Chicago Cubs. He may have been a loner, but he didn't want to be identified with a loser. He lacked the sense of humor for that, lacked the perverse pride that sticking with a loser season after season breeds, and the love. He was just an ordinary guy, .250 at the plate, and we stood above him not knowing what to do next. By then the guys from the other outfield positions had trotted over. Someone, the shortstop probably, suggested team prayer. So we all just stood there, silently bowing our heads, pretending to pray while the shadows moved darkly across the outfield grass. After a while the entire diamond was swallowed and the field lights came on.

In the bluish squint of those lights, he didn't look like someone we'd once known—nothing looked quite right—and we hurriedly scratched a shallow grave, covered him over, and stamped it down as much as possible so that the next right fielder, whoever he'd be, wouldn't trip. It could be just such a seemingly trivial stumble that would ruin a great career before it had begun, or hamper it years later the way Mantle's was hampered by bum knees. One can never be sure the kid beside you isn't another Roberto Clemente; and who can ever know how many potential Great Ones have gone down in the obscurity of their neighborhoods? And so, in the catcher's phrase, we "buried the grave" rather than contribute to any further tragedy. In all likelihood, the next right fielder, whoever he'd be, would be clumsy too, and if there was a mound to trip over he'd find it and break his neck, and soon right field would get the reputation as haunted, a kind of sandlot Bermuda Triangle, inhabited by phantoms calling for ghostly fly balls, where no one but the most desperate outcasts, already on the verge of suicide, would be willing to play.

Still, despite our efforts, we couldn't totally disguise it. A fresh grave is stubborn. Its outline remained visible—a scuffed bald spot that might have been mistaken for an aberrant pitcher's mound except for the bat jammed in the earth with the mitt and blue cap hooked over the handle. Perhaps we didn't want to make it disappear completely–a part of us was resting there. Perhaps we wanted the new right fielder, whoever he'd be, to notice and wonder about who played there before him, realizing he was not the only link between past and future that mattered.

As for us, we walked back, but by then it was too late—getting on to supper, getting on to the end of summer vacation, time for other things, college, careers, settling down and raising a family. Past thirty-five the talk starts about being over the hill, about a graying Phil Niekro in his forties still fanning them with the knuckler as if it's some kind of miracle, beating the odds. And maybe the talk is right. One remembers Willie Mays, forty-two years old and a Met, dropping that can-of-corn fly in the '73 Series, all that grace stripped away and with it the conviction, leaving a man confused and apologetic about the boy in him. It's sad to admit it ends so soon, but everyone knows those are the lucky ones. Most guys are washed up by seventeen.

*Arnold Hano's "The Umpire Was a Rookie" comes from the* Saturday Evening
Post. *Besides his short stories, Hano is well-known for his sports biographies,
including* Roberto Clemente: Batting King *(1973),* Kareem: A Basketball
Great *(1975), and* Muhammad Ali: The Champion *(1977). This story is
about an umpire's first game in the big leagues, and what a hectic day it is.*

*Arnold Hano*

# THE UMPIRE WAS
# A ROOKIE (1956)

**H**IS NAME WAS BILL NEEDY, a man of up-and-down lines and high
shoulders, not broad and tapering like the ballplayers who had trudged
up the same iron stairway. So the fans clustered below did not ask him
for autographs, even though he carried the same sort of black bag in his
right hand.

He heard a hoarse voice say, "Must be a new trainer or somethin',"
and then he was out of the chilly mid-April sunshine, moving quickly
through the white-tile corridor to the door marked UMPIRE'S DRESS-
ING ROOM.

The three other men were already in their dark uniforms, and their eyes swung to him as he threw his bag onto a long wooden bench and began swiftly to undress.

The biggest of the three, a red-faced, white-haired man with a jaw that unhinged like a swinging lantern, put down the ball-and-strike indicator he was playing with, and walked over.

Needy knew him, of course. He was McQuinn, the senior umpire in the league. McQuinn, whom he had watched on his living-room screen during last year's World Series, a man with a bellowing voice and a quietly domineering manner.

"You Needy?" McQuinn said, and Needy was amused at how soft-spoken McQuinn really was, off the diamond.

Needy stood up. He was shirtless now, white-skinned compared with the others, thin and bony-chested. He sensed the difference between himself and them, and he hoped that it went no further than the tans they had acquired during spring training down South.

"Yes," he said, "I'm Needy." He was annoyed at the squeak in his voice. "You're Mr. McQuinn."

McQuinn laughed, and Needy heard the bellow. "You hear that? Mr. McQuinn. I hope you two bums learn something from that."

The tallest one, a turkey-necked, red-headed man, walked over, and even in those three steps, Needy saw the boy from the plow who had become one of the finest pitchers the league had seen in the last quarter century. He drawled, "I'm Carlson," and Needy wanted to say, "Yes, I've seen you pitch." Carlson had been with the Cubs for fourteen years until his fastball deserted him. Five years ago he had returned to the major leagues as an umpire.

But Needy couldn't say that, because he had never seen Carlson pitch. He had never, in fact, been inside a major-league park before this day.

He nodded and took the tall man's hand and felt all the pressure that was at the same time warm and crushing.

The third man, short and thick through the waist, bowlegged and bald, waddled over to Needy. "If you mister me," he said, "I'll fall down dead. All I ever hear is insults. I'm Jankowicz."

"Needy," he said again, clearing his throat, and he stood there, wondering whether he would ever match up to them or even come close.

They eyed him with frank curiosity. He was the new man in the league, called up just yesterday to replace Jake Mandell, the umpire who had broken his leg getting off a plane at Idlewild, flying in from an exhibition in Cleveland. The doctors said Mandell would be staring up at the ceiling for nearly two months.

Wiley, the league president, had wired the three top minor-league heads for their recommendations. They all had different choices, but Needy's league president had called the commissioner of all baseball on his private phone and talked for a half hour. The commissioner spoke to Wiley. Wiley picked Needy.

So the three other umpires stood a few yards off and watched Needy. And Needy felt the perspiration trickle down his ribs.

McQuinn broke the silence finally. He said, "I suppose you've boned up on the ground rules?"

Needy nodded. "Your league has pretty much the same rules we had back in the Association. That makes it easier."

McQuinn nodded his great head. "It does," he said, "but this is a tough park."

Needy frowned. He had shown his new league badge to the park attendant earlier that day and walked all over Robin Field, studying the angles and the shadows, the high fence in right field where balls sometimes stuck in the chicken wire, the sharp corner in left where the play got out of sight unless the third-base umpire was swift in getting back. Needy was not to umpire at third, and he guessed that was why. He was to be at second base, where the plays were often tough and dusty and bruising, but where they fell into a pattern: double play, hit-and-run, steal, force-out, pick-off.

In a way, Needy was glad he was going to be at second. It might force a quick showdown. Tad Roush was the Robin manager. He also was the Robin shortstop. Needy knew Roush firsthand. The two had tangled in the Association five years ago.

Then Carlson broke in. "Not the playing field, son," he said, and

Needy smiled thinly. They must have been within five years of the same age. "He means the park. The fans."

And Needy understood. The fans were different here, so Needy had heard, men and women who had become a legend, just as their borough on the wrong side of the muddy river had become a legend. They were fans who came early and started howling long before the first pitch—and Needy could hear them even now through the thick white-tile walls—fifty-two thousand of them, the most vociferous, partisan fans in the world.

Jankowicz said, "They're tough out here, all right." He shook his head and grinned. "I've had my share of beer in my day, but I hate to have it thrown at me."

"With soft tomatoes as a side dish," McQuinn added.

"I've been through it," Needy said quietly.

"Good," McQuinn said. "When you've been through it, you either go one way or the other. You must have gone the right way, boy, or you wouldn't be here today. They don't take chickens or lilies in this league. Now, the other league—" He snorted in contempt.

The other two laughed. Needy knew how each big league thought it was the only league. But Needy wasn't laughing. McQuinn didn't know the real trouble. Needy had seen fans litter the field with vile epithets and pulpy fruit. It had never bothered him much. The real trouble was himself and Roush. McQuinn didn't know about that. Needy doubted that anybody knew about it or remembered. Maybe Roush hadn't remembered. After all, it was an unimportant game, five years back, and Roush had gone a long way since then.

A bell rang softly in the dressing room and the three other men seemed to stiffen a bit, their smiles fading. "Come on," McQuinn said, taking Needy's arm; "let's go meet them." And the four umpires moved swiftly through the door and onto the gravel path, through the exit door next to the Robins' dugout.

They stepped to the plate while the fans called down their stereotyped insults, and Needy grinned. They weren't so tough. And then a raucous voice from the stands yelled, "All right, McQuinn, don't call 'em like you did when the Phils were in last time, you blind bum!" And a snicker filtered from the stands.

Needy stiffened. Lord, he thought, they remembered from one season to the next. They were riding McQuinn for a call he'd made no more recently than last September, at least seven months ago.

Needy stood at the plate, watching the opposing pitchers wheel in their last practice throws, while the ground crew motored its rollers over the moist, sweet-smelling infield dirt, and from the stands came a rising murmur as the new season rushed up.

And Roush came out of the Robin dugout, a prancing man with toed-in steps, head down, a sheet of paper in his hand. The fans saw him and began to roar, and Roush waved his free hand without looking up. From the Titan dugout came Chub Fowler, the lineup in his hand, too, and Needy heard Roush shoot a word at Fowler. The Titan manager's face flushed hot and angry. Roush, Needy knew then, hadn't changed.

Needy moved away from the cluster at the plate so that Roush would have to see him. He wanted that part over quickly. But Roush, head down, pushed by as though he knew he had the center of the stage. He was a showboat, Needy knew, and then, in his grudging heart, he added, *but a hell of a ballplayer.*

Roush stopped and nodded curtly to McQuinn and Carlson and Jankowicz. "Good afternoon, you blind bats," he said softly. Then he turned to Needy. He put his hands on his hips and said, "Hello, choke-up."

Needy felt his throat tighten and he knew the flush was rising to his temples.

McQuinn pushed past Jankowicz, coming chest to chest with Roush. "Cut it," he said quietly, but there was a bristling quality to his voice. "Cut it, I say. I won't stand for your language."

Roush didn't budge a half inch. His voice was as low as McQuinn's, but rasping and hard. "Listen," he said, "when you bums yell play ball, I'll watch my tongue. But right now you're just guests in this house, and my boss owns this house. Until that first pitch comes in, this game is in the hands of the club owners. Not you." He whirled on Needy again, and the venom lay in his throat. "Choke-up Needy, the yellowest umpire ever to call 'em wrong. Too chicken to call 'em as he sees 'em." Then he spun away and stalked off.

McQuinn roared this time. "Roush! Come here." And Roush turned, wide-eyed. "The ground rules," McQuinn said.

Roush waved his hands. "Whatever you say, Mac. We won't need any rules today." And he minced to the dugout.

McQuinn turned to Chub Fowler. He said, "I'm sorry, Chub. The smiling little skipper is off to his usual start."

Fowler growled and handed McQuinn his line-up. "Maybe we'll run some of it off," he said, and he ambled to the visiting dugout.

Needy watched Fowler, and then he looked at McQuinn, and he froze. The big umpire was staring at him with icy blue eyes. "You're a major-league umpire, Needy," he said. "Act like one."

Needy nodded and tried to say something, but his voice failed him, and then McQuinn waved the three of them to their bases before he bent to the plate, whisk broom in his gnarled hand.

The field was empty except for the four umpires, and then the Robins poured from the dugout, Roush leading them, and the fifty-two thousand fans got up and roared. They stayed standing as the PA system crackled and the announcer said, "Ladies and gentlemen our national anthem."

But Needy barely heard it. He turned to center field to watch the flag go up into the blue sky, and he remembered. . . .

It hadn't been an important game, though Needy knew now how important it really was. And, more than that, how important they all are, the 10–2 games between a first-place team and a cellar team, and a 2–1 affair between two clubs battling for the lead. To an umpire, they're all the same. Needy knew it now.

It was the end of September, and Roush's club had already clinched the Association flag. They were playing at home, three days before the season would end, most of the regulars resting, but Roush still in there. Roush's team was losing 6–1, though Roush had started one double play and pivoted like a flying ghost on two others, and now, in the bottom of the ninth, with two out, he had hit the ball to the center-field wall for a triple.

It was a hot day, Needy remembered, fearfully hot, and it had been a hot month, a hot summer. Needy was behind the plate, weighted down with mask and protector. Somebody had once said an umpire takes hell, but that the hours couldn't be beat. That was before night ball, Needy thought, and hot days like this.

So he leaned in behind the catcher, the ball-and-strike indicator telling him it was two out, one out away from the dressing room and a quick beer, and the pitcher missed twice with curve balls, as Roush pranced down the line from third base.

Nobody was watching very closely, most of the fans having gone home in the seventh inning when Roush's pitcher was hammered for four runs. Not that there had been many to begin with. Maybe twelve hundred, Needy thought. No more than five hundred still remained.

So, when Roush started down the line and seemed to stumble, Needy hoped he'd come in all the way, for he'd surely be out, and the game would be over. The pitcher hadn't started his motion, but Roush had had a bad start. Then the batter suddenly put his hand to his eyes and stepped out of the box. Four or five times that day, swirling spirals of dust had attacked home plate, and Needy had been forced to call "Time," each time a batter stepped out.

But somehow, as his hand went up and he started to say "Time," he saw Roush continue down the line, and he saw the pitcher quickly throw to the plate. The catcher took the toss, blocked off Roush and put the tag on the runner.

There was a feeble cheer from the stands, and five hundred people slowly began to walk across the field to the exit gates. Roush got up and looked at Needy. He jabbed the edge of his hand against his own throat. "You choke-up rat," he said, "why didn't you call time?"

Needy hadn't said anything, but he knew Roush was right. He had quit on his assignment. It wasn't important whether Roush stole home or not; it was only important that Needy call it as he saw it. And he had seen the batter step out before the pitcher went into action toward the plate. He knew it and Roush knew it, and maybe the batter knew it, but he hadn't seemed to care.

Roush cared. It was baseball, and baseball was life and blood to him. Needy knew he, too, should have cared. He should have called time even then, with the five hundred fans scattered all over the diamond, paper falling to the grass, the bags being ripped up by the ground-keepers. He should have waved his hands and roared until he had controlled them, and then resumed play.

But he hadn't. He had just walked past Roush, trying to reason that it hadn't mattered, that the ball game wouldn't have changed, that the team standings wouldn't have changed. He tried to forget. . . .

And standing here at second base in Robin Field, the flag flapping against the blue sky, he knew he had never forgotten it.

Nor had Roush. The ball came spinning out from behind the plate, and Roush had it, tossing it to his second baseman, and then turning to Needy.

"Choke-up," he whispered to the umpire. "Chicken minor-leaguer."

Needy knew he didn't have to take it. The game was still not in the umpires' hands, but he was a human being being abused. There wasn't much he could do. But he could answer Roush, fire a hot word at the shortstop to let him know he was alive and fighting back.

Instead he moved behind the bag and slightly to the left of second base, as the first Titan moved in and McQuinn bellowed, "Play ball!" And just as quickly, Roush seemed to forget all about Needy, close to the bag. He bent slightly, his body swaying, his arms hanging, knees slightly hinged, and Needy watched his mouth move and a flow of words waft to the pitcher's mound. The game began.

Needy had heard it said that a major-league baseball game is unlike any minor-league game, no matter the quality of play. Now he believed it. A cloak hung over the field, a shimmering wave of electricity that coursed through the action, crackled in the air with every pitch, rose and fell with hits and outs. And behind the cloak was the booming that whooshed from the stands, like a heavy hand or the ocean rolling in. It was lightning and thunder, Needy thought, the sizzling atmosphere on the diamond and the roaring from the stands.

The Titans scored first. In the fourth inning, the Titan batter, a man named Jewell who batted left-handed and choked up on his stick three inches, pulled a line drive down the first-base line past Rogers, the Robin first baseman, and into the corner where the Robin bull-pen crew sat beneath a sun canopy.

The Robin right fielder raced to the line and into foul territory, took the rolling ball with his gloved hand, whirled and threw into second base. It was a fine throw, but Jewell hooked to the center of the diamond and grabbed off the inside edge of the bag. Needy bent to the play, head through the low cloud of dust, and he spread-eagled his hands.

Instantly Roush was at him, feet stamping, voice raised in indignant clamor, but Needy stood firm and when Roush wouldn't quit, he turned his back and walked away. It was not a serious beef, Needy knew, because Roush knew as well as he that Jewell had beaten the throw. So Roush growled and kicked dirt and went back to his position, and Needy grinned. Roush had played it four-square, fighting a close call against his team, but watching his tongue. Maybe, Needy thought, the Robin manager was going to let bygones be bygones.

The next hitter was Thomas, another left-hander, and though the Robin pitcher threw on the outside, Thomas still dragged his bunt down the first-base line, moving Jewell to third.

And Mayo, the Titans' No. 4 hitter, the league's home-run king and stolen-base leader, hit to the edge of the center-field wall, where Earl Rider had just enough room to make the catch. Jewel sauntered home and the Titans led 1–0.

It stayed that way into the seventh, a 1–0 game that was taking longer to play than any 1–0 game Needy had ever seen. The pitchers violated the twenty-second rule on nearly every pitch, and Needy knew how foolish the rule was.

When Mayo came up, there was always a short conference, and even after it ended, the Robin pitcher would lean in for a full thirty seconds, his eyes boring a path to the plate, trying to find the groove past Mayo's lunging bat. And Earl Rider had the Titan pitcher in the same grip, the long look, the signals shaken off again and again, catcher Festrun calling time and insisting on a pitch while the fans muttered and buzzed and called down their timeless hue.

In the seventh, Roush came up with one out. He slashed two bats at the grass, talking as he minced forward, and then he threw one behind him, and dug himself in.

The Titan pitcher threw, a quick white blur, and Roush was flat on his back. The mutter from the stands grew thick and ugly. But Roush was up, wiping himself off, snarling an obscenity that McQuinn behind the plate pretended he didn't hear. And Roush drilled the next pitch past the Titan pitcher's left ear and into center field.

At first base, Roush pointed his finger at the pitcher, and the Titan came down from the mound two steps to hurl a word at the Robin manager. McQuinn then hustled forward, waving his arms. And time dragged, while the sun faded, dipping to the lip of the stands over first base, lengthening the shadows.

Roush led off from first and taunted the pitcher with three quick steps down the line, drew a throw, and then started his lead again. On the second pitch, he went.

Festrun came out of his crouch with the ball in his clenched fist and he threw, true and swiftly, to the second baseman covering the bag. Needy drifted over, eyes searching, and Roush came in, one leg high. The tag was made and Needy started to go up with his right hand, but then the ball came squirting out of the glove, rolling toward the shortstop. Needy broke off his call and dropped his hands down low, yelling, "Safe, safe!"

The second baseman rolled to his feet and called "Time!" and held up his dripping red wrist.

The Titan doctor came out and cleaned the dirt from the spike wound, and then started to lead the infielder away. But the Titan insisted he could play, and the doctor shrugged, slapped on a piece of plaster and walked away, shaking his head.

Then the second baseman turned to Needy and said, "He kicked me you know."

Needy nodded. "I guess he did, son. Nothing I can do about it. Kick him back next time," and Roush laughed out loud.

It was part of the game Needy didn't like, but there was nothing anybody ever did to remedy it. It was the way the game was played. There were rules about interference and roughness, but the line could seldom be drawn. So the umpire ignored the contact and watched the bases.

Now Roush led away, and the Titan pitcher threw four times to big Rogers, wasting one, and Rogers swung and missed three times.

The Titan pitcher then took off his glove and wiped his hand with a towel that he directed from the dugout, when Earl Rider took his bent-over stance, waving a big brown bat. And on the first pitch, Needy heard the pitcher groan with the delivery. It was what Casey Stengel liked to call a dead fish, a fastball, down the pipe, waist high, thrown to Rider's strength.

The ball disappeared over the right-field wall, clearing it by about forty feet, and the Robins led, 2–1.

They stayed that way through the eighth, and Needy looked at his watch and saw that two and a half hours had gone by as they came into the ninth. The public-address announcer made his usual statement about fans not being allowed on the playing field until all players had reached the dugouts, and the fans made a derisive sound.

It was then Needy realized that the game was nearly over, that Roush was not riding him any more than he was the other umpires. Needy felt suddenly that the problem had somehow resolved itself. He gave a short little laugh, and Roush, twelve feet away, looked at him cold-eyed, his mouth mocking and twisted. Needy felt the afternoon chill, and he knew he was wrong. It wasn't resolved. It wouldn't be until he and Roush had tangled again.

The first man in the ninth was a pinch hitter for the Titan pitcher, a red-faced man with a plug of tobacco in his cheek and the grinning self-confidence of a man who believed no pitcher on earth could get him out. He was Joads, who couldn't catch fly balls and couldn't throw, so he didn't play regularly, but who hit close to .350 in his two hundred at bats each season.

The Robin pitcher tried to curve Joads, but the ball hung on the inside corner, and Joads stroked it off the wall, where the right fielder made a swift recovery, and Joads lumbered into first, the grin still splitting his wide red face. Then he lumbered off again, for a pinch runner, and Roush spoke sharply with his pitcher.

Finally Roush called his catcher, a man named Camps, to the hill and they talked until McQuinn pushed his way to the mound.

Needy heard the big umpire say, "What's it to be, Roush? You sticking with him or you calling in the reliefer?"

Roush said, "I dunno. That's a real tough one."

McQuinn flushed and towered over Roush. "Don't con me," he said. "Make up your mind. I won't stand for any stalling."

Roush said, "Who's stalling?" I'm trying to think. Get your beef off me, and I'll be able to figure it out."

McQuinn said quietly, "I'll give you fifteen seconds, Roush."

Roush stared at the sky and squinted, and Needy could see the Robin's manager's lips moving. Needy tried to hide his grin. Roush was actually counting off the seconds.

Then he stopped and said, "I got it. It's the reliefer." He waved to the bull pen with his right hand, and the right-handed knuckleball thrower strolled in, carrying his jacket, and began to warm up.

Needy watched from behind second, marveling that Camps could catch such a thing as the reliefer threw. Every one was a knuckler, writhing in mid-air like a drunken butterfly. Then McQuinn held up his hand for the game to pick up where it had stopped, a Titan on first, nobody out, the ninth inning, and the Robins leading, 2–1.

The knuckler got Lark, the Titan lead-off hitter, to go for a chest-high floater, and the Titan hit it straight up in the air. The ball disappeared in Camps's mitt, and there was one out.

But Jewell, who hadn't been stopped all afternoon, singled to right field and the Titan runner fled past Needy into third.

The thunder was two-edged now, the Titan fans who had braved the river and crossed into enemy territory, and the Robins, upset and grumbling as the lead teetered.

Roush raised his hand and yelled "Time!" and turned to the bull pen. He wanted a left-hander to pitch to Thomas.

The sun fell over the edge of the stands, and the field lay in shadow, but lightning still hovered over the players' heads. Needy felt himself waiting with the fans now, impartial as ever concerning the game's outcome, yet intensely interested.

He watched the left-hander, a stocky hurky-jerky man named Lombardo, pitch curveballs to Thomas, but they were breaking too much and too soon, and on six pitches the bases were loaded.

Again Roush stopped the game, and a third time he signaled to the bull pen. The hitter was Mayo, the big, fleet Titan who could do everything so well. And when time was in again, Needy saw that Roush had his team playing halfway. Roush wanted to cut off the tying run at the plate, but he wasn't all the way in. The double play could still be made, though Needy knew that Mayo was as fast a man getting down the line as anybody in baseball.

The new pitcher eyed the bases, Thomas coming off first. The other Titan runners drifted away, and Roush kept darting toward second, feinting Jewell back to the bag. Roush's mouth was still moving, the words flowing to the mound, and Needy felt them hang like drones in the air.

"Come on, boy," Roush was saying. "Come on boy; nobody hits." Then the reliefer took a deep breath and threw hard to Mayo.

It was a fastball, Needy thought, on the inside, and Mayo started to lunge. The pitch broke. It had not been a fastball at all, but a curve, thrown hard and loose, fooling the big Titan.

But Mayo somehow got a piece of it, hitting it on a high bounce past the mound, headed for the hole between second base and Roush. Needy moved in toward the bag from behind, seeing Thomas hurtling down the line, Mayo bulleting his way toward first and Roush gliding over, surefooted, a swift ghost on the brown dirt.

The thought crossed Needy's mind that Thomas would be an easy force, once Roush came up with the ball, but the winging Mayo would be a different story. Then Needy banished the thought; his problem lay at second, not first.

Roush reached to his left with his gloved hand while on the dead run eight feet from second base, and then he plucked the ball out with his right hand, leveled his arm back and threw like a rifle to first, a split second before his foot hit second base, kicking dust high into the air.

It was then that Needy's ankle buckled under him and he fell, sprawling heavily while the picture of Roush making his throw before he touched second became frozen-fixed in his mind. Needy never knew that big Rogers, at first, stretched into the diamond while Mayo leaped for the bag. Nor did Needy hear the ball spank into the first baseman's glove, umpire Carlson booming, "He's out!" All Needy heard was the thunder pounding out from the stands as he rolled to his feet to make his call.

But nobody was watching him, the players fleeing to the dugouts, and fifty-two thousand people starting to pour onto the field. Even Roush was gone. Only Thomas was near, sitting on second base, staring up at Needy, openmouthed.

For Needy stood stock-still, arms spread-eagled, yelling, "Safe, safe, safe!" He knew why Thomas couldn't believe the call. Roush had him beaten by five full steps. But Roush had taken the chance that Needy wouldn't have the guts to make the insane call he was now making. Roush had thrown the ball before his foot touched second, and the force play had never been made.

Needy knew it, and he knew why it had happened. He'd have bet his life on it. Roush had seen what he had seen. The shortstop knew that Mayo, moving like a whippet down the first-base line, would beat the throw unless he got rid of the ball right away. The tying run was thundering homeward.

It was McQuinn who finally noticed Needy, still standing at second, arms held out and low, the time-honored sign of a man being called safe.

The big ump charged to second base and said, "What's the matter, man? Are you crazy?"

Needy looked at his chief. The park cops were in a tight cordon at the foul lines, keeping the fans from trampling the young infield grass, but they couldn't keep them from roaming all over the outfield. It was a swirling, still roaring throng, most of them happy, all of them knowing they had seen a fine game, and glad to be on their way home.

"I'm sorry, Mac, but the man is safe."

McQuinn looked at him peculiarly and said, "Roush touched the bag. I saw the dust rise up."

Needy shook his head stubbornly. He thought, *What am I getting into?* The field was strewn with debris. It was like that day five years ago, except a thousand times worse. He said, "He touched the bag after he got rid of the ball. Thomas is safe."

McQuinn started to rub his jaw and then he began to grin, and finally he started to laugh out loud, a bellowing laugh that brought tears to his eyes. "I swear," he said, "if you weren't standing here, I wouldn't believe it. Now what do we do?"

Needy said, "We get the game going again."

McQuinn turned and yelled, "Carl, Janko, come here! This crazy pup's starting a rhubarb and we'll have to back him up!" The two umpires raced to second and scratched their heads as McQuinn filled them in.

Thomas suddenly got up from his perch on second base and said, "Excuse me, but if I'm safe, is time still in?" He was ready to keep running.

McQuinn roared. "Hell no! I call time right now!"

Thomas began to yell to the near-empty Titan dugout. "Hey, I'm safe, I'm safe!"

Needy said, "And your club is leading three-two."

McQuinn howled, "Now, what the devil does that mean?"

Carlson grinned. "I get him, chief. He means the men on second and third. They both scored. As a matter of fact," he said, winking at McQuinn, "I noticed Jewell touch home plate in case you didn't. The lad's right. The Titans are ahead, three-two."

"And probably piling out of their uniforms this minute," Jankowicz said. "What happens now?"

Needy said, "You boys wouldn't want me to change my decision, would you? Because," he said, "I won't, you know."

A handful of Titans began to drift onto the field. The word began to spread through the filing throng and Needy heard the first ominous mutter.

Somebody said. "Whaddya mean, the game's not over? Sure it is."

"No," somebody else said, fifteen feet from second. "That new jerk of an umpire says Thomas ain't out. They ought to mobilize the bum."

McQuinn turned to Needy. "All right, bum, take it from here."

Needy said, "It's very simple. The rules don't cover it, but you're in charge. Make an announcement over the PA that the game isn't over, that you'll give everybody—fans and players—a half hour to get back in their seats and to their positions, and that the game will continue."

Carlson said, "We could have 'em play it off some other time."

Jankowicz grinned. "No," he said. "That's too easy. I like the lad's idea. . . . Go on, Mac, make the announcement."

"Not me," McQuinn said. "Don't pass the buck to me. Let the lad do it."

Jankowicz said, "Go to it, boy. I must say you've got guts. Are they going to love you here!"

Needy shook his head. He knew it didn't matter. Love him or hate him, it didn't matter. Respect him. That was all. He started to walk to the Robin dugout to ask where the PA mike was. It would have been very easy to make the out call, he knew. But he had never even thought of it.

And thirty minutes later, before a crowd gone blood-mad as it heaped abuse on Needy, Tad Roush led his ball club back onto the field.

The shortstop took his post, raised two fingers in the air and called, "Two out, men, two out! We'll get it back!"

Then Roush turned, before his pitcher threw, and said to Needy, "Welcome to the big league, you blind bat." He was grinning. Needy ignored him, to watch the ball game.

*T. Coraghessan Boyle was born in 1948 in New York's Hudson Valley and now resides outside Santa Barbara, California. He is the founder and director of the Creative Writing Program in the English Department at the University of Southern California. Boyle's fiction has appeared in the* New Yorker, Harper's, *the* Atlantic Monthly, *and* Playboy. *He has written five novels, most recently* The Road to Welville *(1993). "The Hector Quesadilla Story" appears in his book* Greasy Lake and Other Stories *(1986).*

## *T. Coraghessan Boyle*

# THE HECTOR QUESADILLA STORY (1986)

**H**E WAS NO JOLTIN' JOE, no Sultan of Swat, no Iron Man. For one thing, his feet hurt. And God knows no legendary immortal ever suffered so prosaic a complaint. He had shinsplints too, and corns and ingrown toenails and hemorrhoids. Demons drove burning spikes into his tailbone each time he bent to loosen his shoelaces, his limbs were skewed so awkwardly his elbows and knees might have been transposed, and the once-proud knot of his frijole-fed belly had fallen like an avalanche. Worse: he was old. Old, old, old, the graybeard hobbling down the rough-hewn steps of the Senate building, the ancient Mariner chewing on his whiskers and stumbling in his socks. Though they listed his birth date as 1942 in the program, there were those who knew better: it was way back in '54, during his rookie year for San Buitre, that he had taken Asunción to the altar, and even in those distant days, even in Mexico, twelve-year-olds didn't marry.

When he was younger—really young, nineteen, twenty, tearing up the Mexican League like a saint of the stick—his ears were so sensitive he could hear the soft rasping friction of the pitcher's fingers as he massaged the ball and dug in for a slider, fastball, or change-up. Now he could barely hear the umpire bawling the count in his ear. And his legs. How they ached, how they groaned and creaked and chattered, how they'd gone to fat! He ate too much, that was the problem. Ate prodigiously, ate mightily, ate as if there were a hidden thing inside him, a creature all of jaws with an infinite trailing ribbon of gut. Hueves con chorizo with beans, tortillas, camarones in red sauce, and a twelve-ounce steak for breakfast, the chicken in mole to steady him before afternoon games, a sea of beer to wash away the tension of the game and prepare his digestive machinery for the flaming machaca and pepper salad Asunción prepared for him in the blessed evenings of the home stand.

Five foot seven, one hundred eighty-nine and three-quarters pounds. Hector Hernán Jesus y María Quesadilla. Little Cheese, they called him. Cheese, Cheese, Cheesus, went up the cry as he stepped in to pinch-hit in some late inning crisis, Cheese, Cheese, Cheesus, building to a roar until Chavez Ravine resounded as if with the holy name of the Savior Himself when he stroked one of the clean line-drive singles that were his signature or laid down a bunt that stuck like a finger in jelly. When he fanned, when the bat went loose in the fat brown hands and he went down on one knee for support, they hissed and called him *Viejo*.

One more season, he tells himself, though he hasn't played regularly for nearly ten years and can barely trot to first after drawing a walk, One more. He tells Ascunción too: One more, One more, as they sit in the gleaming kitchen of their house in Boyle Heights, he with his Carta Blanca, she with her mortar and pestle for grinding the golden petrified kernels of maize into flour for the tortillas he eats like peanuts. Una más, she mocks. What do you want, the Hall of Fame? Hang up your spikes Hector.

He stares off into space, his mother's Indian features flattening his own as if the legend were true, as if she really had taken a spatula to him in the cradle, and then, dropping his thick lids as he takes a long slow swallow from the neck of the bottle, he says: Just the other day driving home from the park I saw a car on the freeway, a Mercedes with only two seats, a girl in it, her hair out back like a cloud, and you know what the license plate said? His eyes are open now, black as pitted olives. Do you? She doesn't. Cheese, he says. It said Cheese.

Then she reminds him that Hector Jr. will be twenty-nine next month and that Reina has four children of her own and another on the way. You're a grandfather, Hector! A moment slides by, filled with the light of the sad waning sun and the harsh Yucatano dialect of the radio announcer. *Hombres* on first and third, one down. *Abuelo,* she hisses, grinding stone against stone until it makes his teeth ache. Hang up your spikes, *abuelo.*

But he doesn't. He can't. He won't. He's no grandpa with hair the color of cigarette stains and a blanket over his knees, he's no toothless old gasser sunning himself in the park—he's a big leaguer, proud wearer of the Dodger blue, wielder of stick and glove. How can he get old? The grass is always green, the lights always shining, no clocks or periods or halves or quarters, no punch-in and punch-out. This is the game that never ends. When the heavy hitters have fanned and the pitchers' arms gone sore, when there's no joy in Mudville, taxes are killing everybody, and the Russians are raising hell in Guatemala, when the manager paces the dugout like an attack dog, mind racing, searching high and low for the canny veteran to go in and do single combat, there he'll be—always, always, eternal as a monument—Hector Quesadilla, utility infielder, with the .296 lifetime batting average and service with the Reds, Phils, Cubs, Royals, and L.A. Dodgers.

So he waits. Hangs on. Trots his aching legs round the outfield grass before the game, touches his toes ten agonizing times each morning, takes extra batting practice with the rookies and slumping millionaires. Sits. Watches. Massages his feet. Waits through the scourging road trips in the Midwest and along the East Coast, down to muggy Atlanta, across to stormy Wrigley and up to frigid Candlestick, his gut clenched round an indigestible cud of meatloaf and instant potatoes and wax beans, through the terrible nightgames with the alien lights in his eyes, waits at the end of the bench for a word from the manager, for a pat on the ass, a roar, a hiss, a chorus of cheers and catcalls, the marimba pulse of bat striking and the sweet looping arc of the clean base hit.

And then comes a day, late in the season, the homeboys battling for the pennant with the big-stick Braves and the sneaking Jints, when he wakes from honeyed dreams in his own bed that's like an old friend with the sheets that smell of starch and soap and flowers, and feels the pain stripped from his body as if at the touch of a healer's fingertips. Usually he dreams nothing, the night a blank, an erasure, and opens his eyes on the agonies of the martyr strapped to a bed of nails. Then he limps to the toilet, makes a poor discolored water, rinses the dead taste from his mouth, and staggers to the kitchen table where food, only food, can revive in him the interest in drawing another breath. He butters tortillas and folds them into his mouth, spoons up egg and melted jack cheese and frijoles refritos with the green salsa, lashes into his steak as if it were cut from the thigh of Kerensky, the Atlanta relief ace who'd twice that season caught him looking at a full-count fastball with men in scoring position. But not today. Today is different, a sainted day, a day on which sunshine sits in the windows like a gift of the Magi and the chatter of the starlings in the crapped-over palms across the street is a thing that approaches the divine music of the spheres. What can it be?

In the kitchen it hits him: pozole in a pot on the stove, carnitas in the saucepan, the table spread with sweetcakes, buñuelos, and the little marzipan *dulces* he could kill for. *Feliz cumpleaños*, Asunción pipes as he steps through the doorway. Her face is lit with the smile of her mother, her mother's mother, the line of gift-givers descendant to the happy conquistadors and joyous Aztecs. A kiss, a *dulce*, and then a knock at the door and Reina, fat with life, throwing her arms around him while her children gobble up the table, the room, their grandfather, with eyes that swallow their faces. Happy birthday, Daddy, Reina says, and Franklin, her youngest, is handing him the gift.

And Hector Jr.?

But he doesn't have to fret about Hector Jr., his firstborn, the boy with these same great sad eyes who'd sat in the dugout in his Reds uniform when they lived in Cincy and worshipped the pudgy icon of his father until the parish priest had to straighten him out on his hagiography, Hector Jr. who studies English at USC and day and night writes his thesis on a poet his father has never heard of, because here he is, walking in the front door with his mother's smile and a store-wrapped gift—a book, of course. Then Reina's children line up to kiss the *abuelo*—they'll be sitting in the box seats this afternoon—and suddenly he knows so much: He will play today, he will hit, oh yes, can there be a doubt? He sees it already. Kerensky, the son of a whore. Extra innings. Koerner or Manfredonia or Brooksie on third. The ball like an orange, a mango, a muskmelon, the clean swipe of the bat, the delirium of the crowd, and the gimpy *abuelo,* a big leaguer still, doffing his cap and taking a tour of the bases in a stately trot, Sultan for a day.

Could things ever be so simple?

In the bottom of the ninth, with the score tied at five and Reina's kids full of Coke, hotdogs, peanuts, and ice cream and getting restless, with Asunción clutching her rosary as if she were drowning and Hector Jr.'s nose stuck in some book, Dupuy taps him to hit for the pitcher with two down and Fast Freddie Phelan on second. The eighth man in the lineup, Spider Martinez from Muchas Vacas, D.R., has just whiffed on three straight pitches and Corcoran, the Braves' left-handed relief man, is all of a sudden pouring it on. Throughout the stadium a hush has fallen over the crowd, the torpor of suppertime, the game poised at apogee. Shadows are lengthening in the outfield, swallows flitting across the face of the scoreboard, here a fan drops into his beer, there a big mama gathers up her purse, her knitting, her shopping bags and parasol and thinks of dinner. Hector sees it all. This is the moment of catharsis, the moment to take it out.

As Martinez slumps toward the dugout, Dupuy, a laconic, embittered man who keeps his suffering inside and drinks Gelusil like water, takes hold of Hector's arm. His eyes are red-rimmed and paunchy, doleful as a basset hound's. Bring the runner in, Champ, he rasps. First pitch fake a bunt, then hit away. Watch Booger at third. Uh-huh, Hector mumbles, snapping his gum. Then he slides his bat from the rack—white ash, tape-wrapped grip, personally blessed by the Archbishop of Guadalajara and his twenty-seven acolytes—and starts for the dugout steps, knowing the course of the next three minutes as surely as his blood knows the course of his veins. The familiar cry will go up—Cheese, Cheese, Cheesus—and he'll amble up to the batter's box, knocking imaginary dirt from his spikes, adjusting the straps of his golf gloves, tugging at his underwear and fiddling with his batting helmet. His face will be impenetrable. Corcoran will work the ball in his glove, maybe tip back his cap for a little hair grease and then give him a look of psychopathic hatred. Hector has seen it before. Me against you. My record, my career, my house, my family, my life, my mutual funds and beer distributorship against yours. He's been hit in the elbow, the knee, the groin, the head. Nothing fazes him. Nothing. Murmuring a prayer to Santa Griselda, patroness of the sun-blasted Sonoran village where he was born like a heat blister on his mother's womb, Hector Hernán Jesus y María Quesadilla will step into the batter's box, ready for anything.

But it's a game of infinite surprises.

Before Hector can set foot on the playing field, Corcoran suddenly doubles up in pain, Phelan goes slack at second, and the catcher and shortstop are hustling out to the mound, tailed an instant later by trainer and pitching coach. First thing Hector thinks is a groin pull, then appendicitis, and finally, as Corcoran goes down on one knee, poison. He'd once seen a man shot in the gut at Obregon City, but the report had been loud as a thunderclap and he hears nothing now but the enveloping hum of the crowd. Corcoran is rising shakily, the trainer and pitching coach supporting him while the catcher kicks meditatively in the dirt, and now Mueller, the Atlanta *cabeza*, is striding big-bellied out of the dugout, head down as if to be sure his feet are following orders.

Halfway to the mound, Mueller flicks his right hand across his ear quick as a horse flicking its tail, and it's all she wrote for Corcoran.

Poised on the dugout steps like a bird dog, Hector waits, his eyes riveted on the bullpen. Please, he whispers, praying for the intercession of the Niño and pledging a hundred votary candles—at least, at least. Can it be? Yes, milk of my Mother, yes—Kerensky himself strutting out onto the field like a fighting cock. Kerensky!

Come to the birthday boy, Kerensky, he murmurs, so certain he's going to put it in the stands he could point like the immeasurable Bambino. His tired old legs shuffle with impatience as Kerensky stalks across the field, and then he's turning to pick Asunción out of the crowd. She's on her feet now, Reina too, the kids come alive beside her. And Hector Jr., the book forgotten, his face transfigured with the look of rapture he used to get when he was a boy sitting on the steps of the dugout. Hector can't help himself: He grins and gives them the thumbs-up sign.

Then as Kerensky fires his warm-up smoke, the loudspeaker crackles and Hector emerges from the shadow of the dugout into the tapering golden shafts of the late-afternoon sun. That pitch, I want that one, he mutters, carrying his bat like a javelin and shooting a glare at Kerensky, but something's wrong here, the announcer's got it screwed up: BATTING FOR RARITAN, NUMBER THIRTY-NINE, DAVE TOOL. What the—? And now somebody's tugging at his sleeve and he's turning to gape with incomprehension at the freckle-faced batboy, Dave Tool striding out of the dugout with his big forty-two-ounce stick, Dupuy's face locked up like a vault, and the crowd, on its feet, chanting Tool, Tool, Tool! For a moment he just stands there, frozen with disbelief. Then Tool is brushing by him and the idiot of a batboy is leading him toward the dugout as if he were an old blind fisherman poised on the edge of the dock.

He feels as if his legs have been cut from under him. Tool! Dupuy is yanking him for Tool? For what? So he can play the lefty-righty percentages like some chess head or something? Tool, of all people. Tool, with his thirty-five home runs a season and lifetime B.A. of .234, Tool who's worn so many uniforms they had to expand the league to make room for him, what's he going to do? Raging, Hector flings down his bat and comes at Dupuy like a cat tossed in a bag. You crazy, you jerk, he sputters. I woulda hit him, I woulda won the game. I dreamed it. And then, his voice breaking: It's my birthday for Christ's sake!

But Dupuy can't answer him, because on the first pitch Tool slams a real worm burner to short and the game is going into extra innings.

By seven o'clock, half the fans have given up and gone home. In the top of the fourteenth, when the visitors came up with a pair of runs on a two-out pinch-hit home run, there was a real exodus, but then the Dodgers struck back for two to knot it up again. Then it was three up and three down, regular as clockwork. Now, at the end of the nineteenth, with the score deadlocked at seven all and the players dragging themselves around the field like gutshot horses, Hector is beginning to think he may get a second chance after all. Especially the way Dupuy's been using up players like some crazy general on the western front, yanking pitchers, juggling his defense, throwing in pinch runners and pinch hitters until he's just about gone through the entire roster. Asunción is still there among the faithful, the foolish, and the self-deluded, fumbling with her rosary and mouthing prayers for Jesus Christ Our Lord, the Madonna, Hector, the home team, and her departed mother, in that order. Reina too, looking like the survivor of some disaster, Franklin and Alfredo asleep in their seats, the niñitas gone off somewhere–for Coke and dogs, maybe. And Hector Jr. looks like he's going to stick it out too, though he should be back in his closet writing about the mystical so-and-so and the way he illustrates his poems with gods and men and serpents. Watching him, Hector can feel his heart turn over.

In the bottom of the twentieth, with one down and Gilley on first–he's a starting pitcher but Dupuy sent him in to run for Manfredonia after Manfredonia jammed his ankle like a turkey and had to be helped off the field–Hector pushes himself up from the bench and ambles down to where Dupuy sits in the corner, contemplatively spitting a gout of tobacco juice and saliva into the drain at his feet. Let me hit, Bernard, come on, Hector says, easing down beside him.

Can't, comes the reply, and Dupuy never even raises his head. Can't risk it, Champ. Look around you—and here the manager's voice quavers with uncertainty, with fear and despair and the dull edge of hopelessness—I got nobody left. I hit you, I got to play you.

No, No, you don't understand—I'm going to win it, I swear.

And then the two of them, like old bankrupts on a bench in Miami Beach, look up to watch Phelan hit into a double play.

A buzz runs through the crowd when the Dodgers take the field for the top of the twenty-second. Though Phelan is limping, Thorkelsson's asleep on his feet, and Dorfman, fresh on the mound, is the only pitcher left on the roster, the moment is electric. One more inning and they tie the record set by the Mets and Giants back in '64, and then they're making history. Drunk, sober, and then drunk again, saturated with fats and nitrates and sugar, the crowd begins to come to life. Go Dodgers! Eat shit! Yo Mama! Phelan's a bum!

Hector can feel it too. The rage and frustration that had consumed him back in the ninth are gone, replaced by a dawning sense of wonder—he could have won it then, yes, and against his nemesis Kerensky too—but the Niño and Santa Griselda have been saving him for something greater. He sees it now, knows it in his bones: He's going to be the hero of the longest game in history.

As if to bear him out, Dorfman, the kid from Albuquerque, puts in a good inning, cutting the bushed Braves down in order. In the dugout, Doc Pusser, the team physician, is handing out the little green pills that keep your eyes open and Dupuy is blowing into a cup of coffee and staring morosely out at the playing field. Hector watches as Tool, who'd stayed in the game at first base, fans on three straight pitches, then he shoves in beside Dorfman and tells the kid he's looking good out there. With his big cornhusker's ears and nose like a tweezer, Dorfman could be a caricature of the green rookie. He says nothing. Hey, don't let it get to you, kid—I'm going to win this one for you. Next inning or maybe the inning after. Then he tells him how he saw it in a vision and how it's his birthday and the kid's going to get the victory, one of the biggest of all time. Twenty-four, twenty-five innings maybe.

Hector had heard of a game once in the Mexican League that took three days to play and went seventy-three innings, did Dorfman know that? It was down in *Culiacán*. Chito Martí, the converted bullfighter, had finally ended it by dropping down dead of exhaustion in center field, allowing Sexto Silvestro, who'd broken his leg rounding third, to crawl home with the winning run. But Hector doesn't think this game will go that long. Dorfman sighs and extracts a bit of wax from his ear as Pantaleo, the third-string catcher, hits back to the pitcher to end the inning. I hope not, he says, uncoiling himself from the bench, my arm'd fall off.

Ten o'clock comes and goes. Dorfman's still in there, throwing breaking stuff and a little smoke at the Braves, who look as if they just stepped out of *Night of the Living Dead*. The home team isn't doing much better. Dupuy's run through the whole team but for Hector, and three or four of the guys have been in there since two in the afternoon; the rest are a bunch of ginks and gimps who can barely stand up. Out in the stands, the fans look grim. The vendors ran out of beer an hour back, and they haven't had dogs or kraut or Coke or anything since eight-thirty.

In the bottom of the twenty-seventh Phelan goes berserk in the dugout and Dupuy has to pin him to the floor while Doc Pusser shoves something up his nose to calm him. Next inning the balls-and-strikes ump passes out cold and Dorfman, who's beginning to look a little fagged, walks the first two batters but manages to weasel his way out of the inning without giving up the go-ahead run. Meanwhile, Thorkelsson has been dropping ice cubes down his trousers to keep awake, Martinez is smoking something suspicious in the can, and Ferenc Fornoi, the third baseman, has begun talking to himself in a tortured Slovene dialect. For his part, Hector feels stronger and more alert as the game goes on. Though he hasn't had a bite since breakfast he feels impervious to the pangs of hunger, as if he were preparing himself, mortifying his flesh like a saint in the desert.

And then, in the top of the thirty-first, with half the fans asleep and the other half staring into nothingness like the inmates of the asylum of Our Lady of Guadeloupe where Hector had once visited his half-wit uncle when he was a boy, Pluto Morales cracks one down the first-base line and Tool flubs it. Right away it looks like trouble, because Chester Bubo is running around right field looking up at the sky like a bird-watcher while the ball snakes through the grass, caroms off his left foot, and coasts like silk to the edge of the warning track. Morales meanwhile is rounding second and coming on for third, running in slow motion, flat-footed and hump-backed, his face drained of color, arms flapping like the undersized wings of some big flightless bird. It's not even close. By the time Bubo can locate the ball, Morales is ten feet from the plate, pitching into a face-first slide that's at least three parts collapse and that's it, the Braves are up by one. It looks black for the home team. But Dorf-man, though his arm has begun to swell like a sausage, shows some grit, bears down and retires the side to end the historic top of the unprece-dented thirty-first inning.

Now, at long last, the hour has come. It'll be Bubo, Dorfman, and Tool for the Dodgers in their half of the inning, which means that Hec-tor will hit for Dorfman. I been saving you, Champ, Dupuy rasps, the empty Gelusil bottle clenched in his fist like a hand grenade. Go on in there, he murmurs and his voice fades away to nothing as Bubo pops the first pitch up in back of the plate. Go on in there and do your stuff.

Sucking in his gut, Hector strides out onto the brightly lit field like a nineteen-year-old, the familiar cry in his ears, the haggard fans on their feet, a sickle moon sketched in overhead as if in some cartoon strip fea-turing drunken husbands and the milkman. Asunción looks as if she's been nailed to the cross, Reina wakes with a start and shakes the little ones into consciousness, and Hector Jr. staggers to his feet like a battered middleweight coming out for the fifteenth round. They're all watching him. The fans whose lives are like empty sacks, the wife who wants him home in front of the TV, his divorced daughter with the four kids and another on the way, his son, pride of his life, who reads for the doctor of philosophy while his crazy *padrecito* puts on a pair of long stockings and chases around after a little white ball like a case of arrested devel-opment. He'll show them. He'll show them some *cojones*, some true grit and desire: The game's not over yet.

On the mound for the Braves is Bo Brannnerman, a big mustachioed machine of a man, normally a starter but pressed into desperate relief service tonight. A fine pitcher—Hector would be the first to admit it—but he just pitched two nights ago and he's worn thin as wire. Hector steps up to the plate, feeling legendary. He glances over at Tool in the on-deck circle, and then down at Booger, the third-base coach. All systems go. He cuts at the air twice and then watches Brannerman rear back and release the ball: Strike one. Hector smiles. Why rush things? Give them a thrill. He watches a low outside slider that just about bounces to even the count, and then stands there like a statue as Brannerman slices the corner of the plate for strike two. From the stands, a chant of *Viejo, Viejo,* and Asunción's piercing soprano, Hit him, Hector!

Hector has no worries, the moment eternal, replayed through games uncountable, with pitchers who were over the hill when he was a rookie with San Buitre, with pups like Brannerman, with big leaguers and Hall of Famers. Here it comes, Hector, ninety-two m.p.h., the big *gringo* trying to throw it by you, the matchless wrists, the flawless swing, one terrific moment of suspended animation—and all of a sudden you're starring in your own movie.

How does it go? The ball cutting through the night sky like a comet, arching high over the center fielder's hapless scrambling form to slam off the wall while your legs churn up the base paths, rounding first in a gallop, taking second, and heading for third . . . but wait, you spill hot coffee on your hand and you can't feel it, the demons apply the live wire to your tailbone, the legs give out and they cut you down at third while the stadium erupts in howls of execration and abuse and the niñitos break down, faces flooded with tears of humiliation, Hector Jr. turning his back in disgust, and Asunción raging like a harpie, *Abuelo! Abuelo! Abuelo!*

Stunned, shrunken, humiliated, you stagger back to the dugout in a maelstrom of abuse, paper cups, flying spittle, your life a waste, the game a cheat, and then, crowning irony, that bum Tool, worthless all the way back to his washerwoman grandmother and the drunken muttering whey-faced tribe that gave him suck, stands tall like a giant and sends the first pitch out of the park to tie it. Oh, the pain. Flat feet, fire in you legs, your poor tired old heart skipping a beat in mortification. And now

Dupuy, red in the face, shouting: The game could be over but for you, you crazy gimpy old beaner washout! You want to hide in your locker, bury yourself under the shower room floor, but you have to watch as the next two men reach base and you pray with fervor that they'll score and put an end to your debasement. But no, Thorkelsson whiffs and the new inning dawns as inevitable as the new minute, the new hour, the new day, endless, implacable, world without end.

But wait, wait: Who's going to pitch? Dorfman's out, there's nobody left, the astonishing thirty-second inning is marching across the scoreboard like an invading army and suddenly Dupuy is standing over you—no, no, he's down on one knee, begging. Hector, he's saying, didn't you use to pitch down in Mexico when you were a kid, didn't I hear that someplace? Yes, you're saying, yes, but that was—

And then you're out on the mound, in command once again, elevated like some half-mad old king in a play, and throwing smoke. The first two batters go down on strikes and the fans are rabid with excitement, Asunción will raise a shrine, Hector Jr. worships you more than all the poets that ever lived, but can it be? You walk the next three and then give up the grand slam to little Tommy Oshimisi! Mother of God, will it never cease? But wait, wait, wait: Here comes the bottom of the thirty-second and Brannerman's wild. He walks a couple, gets a couple out, somebody reaches on an infield single, and the bases are loaded for you, Hector Quesadilla, stepping up to the plate now like the Iron Man himself. The wind up, the delivery, the ball hanging there like a piñata, like a birthday gift, and then the stick flashes in your hands like an archangel's sword, and the game goes on forever.

# PERMISSIONS ACKNOWLEDGMENTS

Grateful acknowledgment is extended to the following authors and publications.

Frank Deford, "Casey at the Bat," from *Sports Illustrated*, July 18, 1988, pp. 52–75. Reprinted by permission of the publisher.

Ernest L. Thayer, "Casey at the Bat," originally published in the *San Francisco Examiner*, June 3, 1888.

Zane Grey, "The Rube's Waterloo," from *The Redheaded Outfield and Other Stories*, (New York: Grosset and Dunlap Publishers, 1920). © 1921 by Zane Grey, renewed 1949 by Lina Elise Grey.

Ring Lardner, "Alibi Ike," originally published in the *Saturday Evening Post*, 1915.

"Three New Twins Join Club in Spring," © 1988 by Garrison Keillor. First published in the *New Yorker*, from *We Are Still Married: Stories and Letters* by Garrison Keillor. Used by permission of Viking Penguin, a division of Penguin Books USA Inc.

"Goodwood Comes Back," from *The Circus In The Attic And Other Stories*, © 1941, renewed 1969 by Robert Penn Warren, reprinted by permission of Harcourt Brace & Company.

Eliot Asinof, "The Rookie," courtesy of Eliot Asinof.

Gerald Beaumont, "The Crab," originally published in *Hearts of Diamond*, (New York: Dodd, Mead and Company, 1920).

James Thurber, "You Could Look It Up," © 1942 James Thurber. © 1970 Helen Thurber and Rosemary A. Thurber. From *My World—And Welcome To It*, published by Harcourt Brace and Company.

"Smoke," from *A Model World and Other Stories*, by Michael Chabon. © 1991 by Michael Chabon. By permission of William Morrow & Company, Inc.

W. C. Heinz, "One Throw," reprinted by permission of the William Morris Agency, Inc. on behalf of the Author. © 1950 by W. C. Heinz, renewed 1978 by W. C. Heinz.

Ring Lardner, "My Roomy," originally published in the *Saturday Evening Post*, 1914.

Ashley Buck, "A Pitcher Grows Tired," courtesy of *Esquire* magazine.

Damon Runyon, "Baseball Hattie," courtesy of *American Play Company, Inc.*

Herbert Warren Wind, "The Master's Touch," originally published in *Crowell-Collier*, 1951.

"What Did We Do Wrong?," © 1985 by Garrison Keillor. First published in the *New Yorker*. From *We Are Still Married: Stories and Letters* by Garrison Keillor. Used by permission of Viking Penguin, a division of Penguin Books USA Inc.

Ring Lardner, "Horseshoes," originally published in the *Saturday Evening Post*, 1914.

Edward L. McKenna, "Fielder's Choice," courtesy of *Esquire* magazine.

William Heuman, "Brooklyn's Lose," originally published in *Sports Illustrated*, 1954.

P. G. Wodehouse, "The Pitcher and the Plutocrat," originally published in *Collier's*, 1910.

Chet Williamson, "Gandhi at the Bat," from the *New Yorker*, June 20, 1983. Courtesy of Chet Williamson.

J. F. Powers, "Jamesie," originally published in *Prince of Darkness and Other Stories*. Courtesy of J. F. Powers.

Kimball McIlroy, "Joe, The Great McWhiff," courtesy of *Esquire* magazine.

Arthur (Bugs) Baer, "The Crambury Tiger," originally published in *Collier's*, 1942.

Lloyd Biggle, Jr., "Who's on First?," from *A Galaxy Of Strangers.* © renewed by the author, 1986. Courtesy of Lloyd Biggle, Jr.

"Death of a Right Fielder," from The *Coast Of Chicago* by Stuart Dybek. © 1990 by Stuart Dybeck. Reprinted by permission of Alfred A. Knopf Inc.

Arnold Hano, "The Umpire Was a Rookie," originally published in the *Saturday Evening Post*, 1956.

"The Hector Quesadilla Story," from *Greasy Lake and Other Stories* by T. Coraghessan Boyle. © 1979, 1981, 1982, 1983, 1984, 1985 by T. Coraghessan Boyle. Used by permission of Viking Penguin, a division of Penguin Books USA Inc.